STUDIES IN THE HISTORY OF MUSIC   4

Lewis Lockwood and Christoph Wolff, General Editors

MARK EVAN BONDS

Wordless Rhetoric

Musical Form and the Metaphor of the Oration

Harvard University Press
Cambridge, Massachusetts, and London, England   1991

Library of Congress Cataloging-in-Publication Data

Bonds, Mark Evan.
   Wordless rhetoric : musical form and the metaphor of the oration /
Mark Evan Bonds.
      p.   cm.—(Studies in the history of music ; 4)
   Includes bibliographical references and index.
   ISBN 0-674-95602-8
   1. Music—Philosophy and aesthetics.   2. Musical form.   I. Title.
II. Series: Studies in the history of music (Cambridge, Mass.) ; 4.
ML3845.B6   1991
781.8—dc20   90-26494
                                                                    CIP
                                                                    MN

To Dorothea

Acknowledgments

This book has benefited greatly from my discussions with a number of people, most notably Lewis Lockwood, Reinhold Brinkmann, Christoph Wolff, Katherine Bergeron, John Daverio, and Elaine Sisman. In addition to making helpful comments on an earlier draft, James Webster was kind enough to provide me with the manuscript of his own forthcoming monograph on Haydn's "Farewell" Symphony. Vincent Panetta reviewed a number of the French translations included here.

I am also grateful to the staff of the Eda Kuhn Loeb Music Library at Harvard University, particularly John Howard and Nym Cooke, who supplied many of the sources cited in this book. Holly Mockovak and Dick Seymour of the Boston University Music Library were similarly helpful in procuring needed items. My thanks, too, to J. Samuel Hammond of Duke University for providing copies of several extraordinarily obscure sources.

Special thanks go to Massimo Ossi, who not only reviewed the translations from Italian treatises included here but also prepared nearly all of the musical examples. I owe him many cups of coffee.

Finally, I cannot adequately acknowledge the help of Jeremy Yudkin, my colleague at Boston University, whose careful reading of an earlier draft of this book improved both its content and its form immeasurably, from the level of the phrase to the structure of the whole.

Contents

WORDLESS RHETORIC

Abbreviations

AfMw	*Archiv für Musikwissenschaft*
AMZ	*Allgemeine musikalische Zeitung* (Leipzig)
BAMZ	*Berliner Allgemeine musikalische Zeitung*
DVjs	*Deutsche Vierteljahrsschrift für Literaturwissenschaft und Geistesgeschichte*
JAMS	*Journal of the American Musicological Society*
JMT	*Journal of Music Theory*
MQ	*Musical Quarterly*
New Grove	*The New Grove Dictionary of Music and Musicians.* 20 vols. Ed. Stanley Sadie. London: Macmillan, 1980.

Musical Form and Metaphor

"Form" is one of the most widely used terms in aesthetics. It is also one of the most ambiguous. Two of its most common meanings are in fact diametrically opposed. "Form" is commonly used to denote those features a given work shares with a large number of others, yet it is also often understood as the unique structure of a particular work.

These differences cannot be easily reconciled, for they reflect two fundamentally different attitudes toward the relationship between form and content. The idea of form as a structural pattern shared by a large number of unrelated works rests on the premise that a work's form can be distinguished from its content. The idea of form as the unique shape of an individual work, on the other hand, precludes any such distinction.

Both of these attitudes are legitimate, and both play an important role in analysis. In practice, most critics deal with the semantic paradox of "form" by making some kind of terminological distinction between "outer" and "inner" form, or between "forms" and "form," or "form" and "structure." Yet such distinctions, while useful, do not address the underlying paradox by which the same root term—not only in English, but in German, French, and other languages as well—can apply to such widely divergent ideas.

The semantic paradox of "form" is a linguistic vestige of a conceptual unity that no longer exists. In the theory and aesthetics of music, the distinction between "inner" and "outer" form is a relatively recent phenomenon, one that began to emerge only toward the end of the eighteenth century and in the early decades of the nineteenth. It coincided with—and as I shall argue in later chapters, it is directly related to—three important developments in musical thought. The first of these was the emergence of form itself as an abstract concept. Throughout the eighteenth century, accounts of what we now think of as conventional movement-length forms (sonata form, rondo, and so on) were almost invariably presented within broader discussions of such issues as melody, harmony, rhythm, or genre, or within accounts of such aesthetic concepts as unity, variety, or coherence. "Form" became an established rubric in manuals of compositional pedagogy only later; the term itself, significantly enough, appears only sporadically in eighteenth-century writings on music and did not become a widely accepted category in its own right until the second third of the nineteenth century.

The second development, closely related to the first, was the increasingly detailed description of those common structural conventions that had already been in use for a generation or more. Sonata form, for example, had played a prominent role in instrumental music since at least the 1760s; and yet while one can find scattered attempts throughout subsequent decades to describe this structural convention, it was not until the 1790s that such accounts began to go into any appreciable degree of detail.

The third of these changes, which also occurred toward the end of the eighteenth century, was the growing conviction that the unique, "inner" form of a work was aesthetically superior to its conventional, "outer" form. As specific forms came to be described in more detail, the aesthetic importance of these conventional structures was consistently deemed inferior to the unique nature of the work at hand.

Nowhere are these changes more concisely illustrated than in the writings of the theorist and composer Heinrich Christoph Koch (1749–1816). With the exception of one important passage, which I shall consider in detail in Chapter 2, Koch's treatment of form as an independent category is still quite tentative throughout his *Versuch einer Anleitung zur Composition* (1782–1793), the most extensive and detailed compositional treatise of the Classical era.[1] Koch uses the term "Form" repeatedly and even provides an entry for it in the work's index, but at no point does he venture any clear or concise definition. His subsequent *Musikalisches Lexikon* of 1802 similarly fails to provide a separate entry or definition for the term, in spite of its repeated use there. Yet only five years later, Koch supplies precisely such an account in the abridged edition of the same musical dictionary.[2]

In the second and third volumes of his *Versuch,* Koch provides the earliest detailed accounts of what we now call sonata form, the most important movement-length structural convention of the Classical era. Yet it is typical

1. Koch, *Versuch einer Anleitung zur Composition,* 3 vols. (Leipzig: A. F. Böhme, 1782–1793; rpt. Hildesheim: Olms, 1969). Throughout this book, the term "Classical era" is used as a convenient shorthand to designate a period extending from approximately 1770 through 1820.

2. Koch, *Musikalisches Lexikon,* 2 vols. (Frankfurt/Main: A. Hermann d.j., 1802; rpt. Hildesheim: Olms, 1964); idem, *Kurzgefasstes Handwörterbuch der Musik* (Leipzig: J. F. Hartknoch, 1807; rpt. Hildesheim: Olms, 1981).

of his time that these two accounts appeared not within discussions of musical form per se, but rather within extended discourses on melody. The first account is presented under the more specific rubric of modulation, the second within a description of various genres (symphony, concerto, and so on). In the final volume of the *Versuch,* Koch also makes one of the earliest categorical distinctions between "inner" and "outer" form in music, but he stops short of making any explicit differentiation between their aesthetic value or importance.

Over the course of the nineteenth century, more and more theorists wrote with increasing specificity about both the nature of large-scale formal conventions and the more abstract concept of form in general. Almost without exception, however, these same writers consistently deprecated the very structures they described in such detail, attributing "true" form to the unique characteristics of a work rather than to those features it shares with many others. The two concepts of form were thus imbued with increasingly disparate aesthetic values. This outlook, epitomized in Adolf Bernhard Marx's epochal *Die Lehre von der musikalischen Komposition* (1837–1847), is the basis of most modern-day attitudes toward form. Today, the existence of specific formal stereotypes is generally acknowledged—if at times only grudgingly and with considerable qualification—but the artistic merit of a given work is seen to reside in its "inner" qualities, those unique features that set it apart from all other manifestations of whatever stereotypical form it happens to represent.

Both of these concepts of form, as I shall argue in Chapter 1, are necessary for analysis, yet neither is sufficient. The challenge, then, is to reconcile these disparate perspectives. This is not to say that there is something inherently wrong with paradoxes; indeed, in this particular instance, the tension between these two very different ideas of form serves as a useful reminder that form is too broad and subtle a concept to be explained by any one approach. Yet there is a danger in accepting this paradox of form too readily, particularly in analyzing a repertoire that antedates the conceptual dichotomy between "inner" and "outer" form.

The emergence of this dichotomy was due not so much to changes in the conventional forms as to changes in fundamental attitudes toward the nature of form itself. There was of course no single, monolithic view of musical form in either the eighteenth or the nineteenth century, any more than there is today; the term is so broadly encompassing that nearly every writer who has ever commented on a specific work of music may be said to have addressed the issue of form. But there were certain basic premises of form that changed between the late eighteenth and the mid-nineteenth centuries. We can best understand these changing premises by tracing the shift in the metaphors used to describe form.

To the rather limited extent that eighteenth-century authors commented on large-scale, movement-length form at all, they generally tended to rely upon the imagery and vocabulary of rhetoric. While parallels between music and rhetoric had long been recognized, it was not until the eighteenth century that music came to be described as a language in its own right, independent of any verbal text. And within this conceptual metaphor of music as a language, a broad range of eighteenth-century theorists and aestheticians considered an individual work of instrumental music to be a kind of wordless oration whose purpose was to move the listener. The rationale behind the structure of this oration, in turn, was held to manifest certain basic parallels to the rationale behind the formal conventions of traditional, verbal rhetoric.

After 1800, writers gradually abandoned the metaphor of the oration, preferring instead to describe the musical work as an organism and its form as an organic relationship of individual parts to the whole. The musical work was now imbued with the force of life itself. Whereas the eighteenth century's metaphor had emphasized the temporal nature of the work in performance and viewed form primarily from the perspective of a listening audience, the preferred metaphor of the nineteenth and twentieth centuries has been more spatial in perspective, in that it considers the work and its constituent units as a simultaneously integrated whole. Organic imagery emphasizes the autonomy of both the artwork and its creator; the listener, in effect, becomes an interested third party.

This shift in metaphors reflects fundamental changes in the concept of both music in general and musical form in particular. While today we tend to think of the form of any given work from the perspective of the work itself (and thus indirectly from the perspective of the composer), theorists and aestheticians of the eighteenth century consistently approached the issue of form from the perspective of the listener. In its orientation toward the audience, its vocabulary, and its categories of thought, this earlier idea of form was essentially rhetorical. Koch, the most penetrating theorist of his generation, all but equates movement-length form with rhetoric in his *Musikalisches Lexikon* of 1802, explicitly confirming a tendency already present in his earlier *Versuch*. His rhetorical concept of musical form, as I shall argue in Chapters 2 and 3, was neither arbitrary nor isolated. On the contrary, it was part of a long tradition that extended across the continent. It included such major figures as Johann Mattheson, Jakob Adlung, Johann Philipp Kirnberger, Carl Ludwig Junker, Johann Nikolaus Forkel, and Georg Joseph Vogler in Germany; Jérome-Joseph de Momigny, Alexandre Etienne Choron, and Anton Reicha in France; and Francesco Galeazzi in Italy.

In spite of the chronological and geographical breadth of this tradition,

Koch was correct to observe that while "a great deal about rhetoric may be found scattered here and there in writings on music," it had "not yet been the fortune of the human spirit to bring these writings together in a systematic order."[3] A good part of the problem, it would seem, lies in the nature of rhetoric, which in its own way encompasses an even broader range of ideas than "form" itself.

The term "rhetoric" has been used so widely in recent years—often indiscriminately—that it is best to state at the outset what a rhetorical concept of musical form does *not* entail. It is not to be equated directly to Mattheson's well-known but widely misunderstood attempt to draw parallels between the form of a musical movement and the structure of an oration (exordium, narratio, propositio, and so on). This attempt will be discussed in some detail in Chapter 2; suffice it to say for the moment that Mattheson's outline represents only one manifestation of a rhetorical conception of form. Nor does the rhetorical concept of form refer to the use of "figures" which, when arrayed in a sequential order, could create a large-scale whole.

Instead, "rhetoric" is to be understood here in the much broader sense as defined by Aristotle: "the faculty of discovering the possible means of persuasion in reference to any subject whatever."[4] Rhetoric, by this definition, is not a specfic body of rules or devices, but rather "the rationale," as one modern writer has described it, "of the informative and suasory in discourse."[5] In this sense, form is the manner in which a work's content is made intelligible to its audience. Conventional patterns, by providing listeners with points of reference and predictability, facilitate the presentation of a content that necessarily varies from work to work.

When viewed in this broad light, the metaphor of the musical work as an oration, as I argue in Chapter 2, provides a means by which internal, generative forces may be reconciled with external conventions. It offers a conceptual framework that, in the case of specific schemas like sonata form, offers an alternative to the dichotomy between the large-scale thematic events and the harmonic outline of a movement. It offers, moreover, a conceptual basis applicable to all forms prevalent throughout the period under discussion here, including even such problematic "non-forms" as the fantasia and the capriccio. And as I argue in Chapter 4, it also provides an important antecedent for the Romantic view of instrumental music as an autonomous art.

3. Koch, *Musikalisches Lexikon,* "Rhetorik."
4. Aristotle, *The "Art" of Rhetoric,* I.II.2., trans. John Henry Freese (Cambridge, Mass.: Harvard University Press, 1947).
5. Donald C. Bryant, *Rhetorical Dimensions in Criticism* (Baton Rouge: Louisiana State University Press, 1973), p. 14.

Many of the parallels between musical form and rhetoric have been recognized in recent years; but all too often scholars have dismissed such analogies as instances of "mere" metaphor, as "unmusical" explanations of musical phenomena.[6] But to dismiss the rhetorical metaphor of musical form on these grounds is to misconstrue the nature of metaphor itself. Metaphors are necessarily limited, for a total congruence of characteristics between terms or objects would amount to nothing less than identity. There is no reason, moreover, to consider imagery drawn from rhetoric as being somehow less valid than more "musical" terminology. Since classical antiquity, writers on music have in fact resorted to metaphor repeatedly in an attempt to expand their vocabulary, and an understanding of the metaphorical origins of these terms can only help our efforts to make sense of passages whose meanings might otherwise remain obscure.[7] And the literary arts—grammar and rhetoric in particular—have long been an important source of musical terminology. It is easy to forget how many "musical" terms, like "theme," "period," "phrase," and even "composition," are derived from grammar and rhetoric. Nor were these terms "dead" metaphors for writers of the eighteenth century: theorists repeatedly commented on the analogous functions of literary and musical themes, phrases, and periods.

To insist on a distinction between "musical" and "unmusical" explanations is thus neither reasonable nor helpful. Metaphors are more than a mere substitution of one term for another: they reflect broader processes of thought that often associate extended networks of images and functions beyond the individual terms in question. The language we use to describe any concept inevitably shapes the manner in which we understand it, and metaphors represent one of the most important means by which to extend and alter the meaning of existing terms. Certain metaphors, in fact, are so deeply ingrained in our patterns of perception that they function as cogni-

6. See, for example, Fred Ritzel, *Die Entwicklung der "Sonatenform" im musiktheoretischen Schrifttum des 18. und 19. Jahrhunderts* (Wiesbaden: Breitkopf & Härtel, 1968), and John Neubauer, *The Emancipation of Music from Language: Departure from Mimesis in Eighteenth-Century Aesthetics* (New Haven: Yale University Press, 1986). Ritzel calls Forkel's analogy to language the "vulnerable point" of his argument about form, his outlook an "exception" (pp. 127, 106); rhetoric itself is a "standard foreign to music" (p. 20), and Mattheson's "dry rhetorical theories" had little influence on the remainder of the century (p. 47). According to Neubauer, Forkel "clung" to the "outdated language of musical rhetoric in accounting for the developmental sections" of sonata-form movements (p. 34). And while Neubauer concedes that musical rhetoric is a "code" for "some important music" of the seventeenth and eighteenth centuries, we should "judge the thrust of the theoretical effort from our vantage point as mistaken" (p. 40).

7. See, for example, Jeremy Yudkin's illuminating commentary on musical terms drawn from grammar and rhetoric in contemporary accounts of early medieval polyphony: "The *Copula* According to Johannes de Garlandia," *Musica disciplina*, 34 (1980), 67–84; and "The Anonymous of St. Emmeram and Anonymous IV on the *Copula*," *MQ*, 70 (1984), 1–22.

tive instruments, actively shaping our apprehension of the broader network of ideas related to the original metaphor.[8] As George Lakoff and Mark Johnson point out, some metaphors are so pervasive as to fashion our view of the world, often in ways of which we are largely unconscious. Using as an example the conceptual metaphor of "argument" as a "war," Lakoff and Johnson cite an entire family of related images attached to this metaphor, all of which combine to shape the manner in which we conceive of and conduct arguments: we develop a *strategy* by which to *attack* an opponent's *position* while *defending* our own in the hopes of *winning* a *dispute*. A culture in which "an argument is viewed as a dance, the participants are seen as performers, and the goal is to perform in a balanced and aesthetically pleasing way" would "view arguments differently, experience them differently, carry them out differently, and talk about them differently."[9]

⌈In their respective eras of predominance, both the rhetorical and organic metaphors of musical form have been sufficiently widespread and powerful to act as cognitive instruments. It is thus all the more important that we recognize this shift in perspective, lest the organic (spatial) metaphor that has prevailed since the mid-nineteenth century exercise a disproportionate influence over our historical interpretations of the rhetorical (temporal) metaphor that predominated in eighteenth- and early nineteenth-century accounts of form.⌋

Approaching a work of music theory or aesthetics with the question of how appropriate certain rhetorical metaphors may or may not be within that particular text is therefore a precarious procedure at best.[10] Such an approach views metaphor as "something to be eliminated as quickly as possible," in order "to get down to the literal meaning that the metaphor covers up."[11] Rather than limit ourselves to examining what "literal" meanings metaphors express, we should broaden our inquiry to include what concep-

8. Max Black, "More on Metaphor," in *Metaphor and Thought,* ed. Andrew Ortony (Cambridge: Cambridge University Press, 1979), p. 39. See also George Lakoff and Mark Johnson, *Metaphors We Live By* (Chicago: University of Chicago Press, 1980); Earl R. MacCormac, *A Cognitive Theory of Metaphor* (Cambridge, Mass: M.I.T. Press, 1985); and Eva Feder Kittay, *Metaphor: Its Cognitive Force and Linguistic Structure* (Oxford: Clarendon Press, 1987).

9. Lakoff and Johnson, *Metaphors We Live By,* p. 5.

10. As, for example, in Nancy K. Baker, "Heinrich Koch and the Theory of Melody," *JMT,* 20 (1976), 3; and Günther Wagner, "Anmerkungen zur Formtheorie Heinrich Christoph Kochs," *AfMw,* 41 (1984), 86–112. One notable exception to this tendency is found in Nicole Schwindt-Gross, *Drama und Diskurs: Zur Beziehung zwischen Satztechnik und motivischem Prozess am Beispiel der durchbrochenen Arbeit in den Streichquartetten Mozarts und Haydns* (Laaber: Laaber-Verlag, 1989), a study that came to my attention too late for adequate incorporation into this book.

11. Jerry L. Morgan, "Observations on the Pragmatics of Metaphor," in *Metaphor and Thought,* ed. Ortony, p. 147.

tions a metaphor implies.[12] [Metaphors prompt insight, and the metaphor of the musical work as an oration in eighteenth- and early nineteenth-century accounts of movement-length form is something more than a linguistic *faute de mieux*. The fact that there was a need for new terms is in itself revealing, and the centrality of the rhetorical terms that were so widely accepted reflects some of the basic premises behind contemporary attitudes toward the issue of form. Rhetoric was by no means the only metaphor applied to musical form prior to 1800, but for more than a century it was clearly the predominant one.]

Another common objection to interpreting Classical form through the imagery of rhetoric is the notion that this approach represents an outmoded vestige of Baroque thought. In point of fact, the application of this image specifically to the idea of large-scale, movement-length form did not gain widespread acceptance until the second half of the eighteenth century. What little attention has been given to musical rhetoric in the Classical era has tended to focus on one rather specific element of the field, the device of musico-rhetorical figures.[13] And while there can be no question that the use of figures and "topics" survived well into the Classical era, it is clear that this practice, important as it may be, constitutes only one facet of the broader idea of music as a rhetorical art.

With its emphasis on the role of the listener, the Classical era's rhetorical concept of form seems strikingly contemporary for us today in many respects, for it entails an analytical method analogous to recent reader-oriented theories of literary criticism. These similarities, outlined in Chapter 5, provide a historical foundation to more recent theories of form that assign a central role to the listener and his expectations of structural events in the analysis of movement-length form. Scholars in other fields, most notably in literary criticism, have long recognized the analytical value of a rhetorical approach to large-scale formal conventions. Recent reinterpretations of genre theory, in particular, have opened new perspectives on the analysis of structural stereotypes. Genre is now seen more as a convention than a category, as a "pigeon" rather than as a "pigeonhole."[14] This distinc-

12. See Samuel R. Levin, *Metaphoric Worlds: Conceptions of a Romantic Nature* (New Haven: Yale University Press, 1988), p. ix; and Mark Turner, *Death Is the Mother of Beauty: Mind, Metaphor, Criticism* (Chicago: University of Chicago Press, 1987), pp. 16–21.

13. See, for example, Leonard Ratner, *Classic Music: Expression, Form, and Style* (New York: Schirmer, 1980); Gernot Gruber, "Musikalische Rhetorik und barocke Bildlichkeit in Kompositionen des jungen Haydn," in *Der junge Haydn*, ed. Vera Schwarz (Graz: Akademische Druck- und Verlagsanstalt, 1972), pp. 168–191; Wye Jamison Allanbrook, *Rhythmic Gesture in Mozart* (Chicago: University of Chicago Press, 1983).

14. Alastair Fowler, *Kinds of Literature: An Introduction to the Theory of Genres and Modes* (Cambridge, Mass.: Harvard University Press, 1982), p. 37.

tion is crucial. The classification of genres and their related forms, as an end in itself, leads to little more than an inert model. But when viewed as a convention, genre establishes itself as "the basis of the conventions that make literary communication possible," and the "processes of generic recognition" become "fundamental to the reading process."[15] Genres are no longer viewed as "taxonomic classes," but as "groups of norms and expectations which help the reader to assign functions to various elements in the work . . . The 'real' genres are those sets of categories or norms required to account for the process of reading."[16]

This kind of thinking can be applied to musical forms as well. Specific conventions, too often viewed (and either denigrated or rejected) as categories, can be studied more profitably as the musical equivalent of plot archetypes. Each manifestation of a stereotypical form provides a framework in which the processes of formal recognition become essential to the act of listening.

The focus of this book, then, is the changing concept of musical form over a period extending from roughly 1730 until 1850, as reflected in the rise and fall of rhetoric as a central metaphor in accounts of form. In terms of the theorists themselves, this era extends from Johann Mattheson through Adolf Bernhard Marx—that is to say, from the earliest, somewhat tentative attempts to account for musical form in the early eighteenth century, down through the systematic "codification" of specific formal conventions in the middle of the nineteenth. The emphasis throughout is on the evolution of concepts that are specifically applicable to instrumental music. A vocal work's text offers a basic and obvious point of departure for the analysis of form; indeed, the perceived aesthetic superiority of vocal music over instrumental music until relatively late in the eighteenth century goes a long way toward explaining just why sustained theoretical accounts of form as an abstract category began to appear only near the end of the century. Earlier theorists, concerned primarily with vocal music, could reasonably assume that a work's structure would be determined to a considerable extent by its text, which in turn would ordinarily vary from piece to piece. But the growing stature of instrumental music throughout the eighteenth century produced new interest in the more abstract principles of form. By 1799, an anonymous reviewer of four symphonies by Mozart could go so far as to proclaim that a composer displays the greatest genius *only* in instrumental music, "for there he is limited solely to the language of sounds. His

15. Ibid., pp. 36, 259.
16. Jonathan Culler, *The Pursuit of Signs: Semiotics, Literature, Deconstruction* (Ithaca, N.Y.: Cornell University Press, 1981), p. 123.

thoughts have their own clarity in themselves, without being supported by poetry."[17] It is the contemporary effort to account for "pure" musical form that is my principal concern here. The demonstrable and important connections between vocal and instrumental forms deserve serious consideration, but the issues of text-setting raise a variety of problems that go well beyond the concept of form in its more abstract sense, independent of textual dictates and restraints. Dance music and program music similarly incorporate structural motivations that are extra-musical; accordingly, these genres also stand outside the scope of this study.

Any discussion of musical form runs the risk of being overly abstract if it is too general, but of only limited applicability if it is too specific. Throughout this book, I shall try to avoid these extremes by focusing principally on one large-scale stereotype—sonata form—and by attempting to integrate the analysis of specific sonata-form movements with a broader understanding of musical form in the late eighteenth and early nineteenth centuries. By using sonata form as a paradigm for the concept of musical form, I do not mean to suggest that other structural conventions, such as the rondo, minuet, theme and variations, or fugue, are somehow less worthy of consideration: indeed, one of the most serious shortcomings of recent theories of Classical sonata form is the lack of a conceptual basis of form that can be applied to these other structural stereotypes as well. But sonata form is clearly the most important of all instrumental forms of the period: it appears in the large majority of first movements in symphonies, sonatas, string quartets, and the like, as well as in many slow movements and finales. And in many respects, it is also the most subtle and complex of the various conventional structures from this period.

In reinterpreting theoretical concepts of the eighteenth and early nineteenth centuries, I have tried to draw on as wide a range of contemporary sources as possible, from the musical repertoire itself to didactic treatises to aesthetic systems of music and the arts in general. The original functions of these sources were obviously quite disparate. The musical repertoire includes its own nonverbal accounts of form as articulated by composers and provides both the criteria and *raison d'être* for evaluating verbally articulated theories of form. The didactic treatises I have cited range from simple tutors to the most sophisticated discussions of the more technical aspects of music. The distinction between the more demanding of these treatises and those devoted to aesthetics is not always easy to maintain. But the aesthetic treatises, on the whole, are directed more toward the general reader interested in the philosophy of music than toward the aspiring composer. In many instances, these works consider music within the broader context of aes-

17. *AMZ*, I (1799), col. 494.

thetics as a whole. What is important for our purposes, however, is that the rhetorical concept of form is to be found in all of these categories of writings, in sources aimed at a broad spectrum of readers.

In surveying such a variety of sources, I have not attempted to review the works of any single author or composer systematically. My purpose instead has been to identify broad lines of thought that transcend not only individual writers but also the generic categories of theory, pedagogy, and aesthetics. My discussion of Forkel's concept of musical rhetoric in Chapter 2, for example, focuses on those elements common to many other writers, intentionally leaving aside any detailed discussion of the many fascinating views that are peculiarly Forkel's own. And while concentrating on a single category of sources can be highly rewarding, as John Neubauer has shown in his recent survey of eighteenth-century aestheticians, such an approach also has its limitations, as Neubauer himself acknowledges.[18] An aesthetician, particularly if he is not a musician by training, tends to approach his subject from a perspective quite different from that of the composer or pedagogue, whose aims and methods are necessarily more concrete. There is a tendency among general aestheticians, moreover, to emphasize those elements common to all the arts. But this approach is not necessarily evident in the more technical literature of any given field. The much-debated issue of mimesis offers a good case in point. The imitation of nature, as Batteux argued in his influential *Les beaux-arts réduits à un même principe* (1746), is the one element common to all the arts, including music. Yet while this idea was taken up with great enthusiasm by aestheticians, it seldom found its way into the more technically oriented manuals of musical composition. Part of a broader attempt to unite music with the other arts, the concept of mimesis ultimately seems to have had little influence upon the more mechanical aspects of composition. Contemporary comparisons between music and painting or music and architecture, in similar fashion, are seldom if ever translated into the professional vocabulary of the craft of music. [Rhetoric, on the other hand, is an image used by aestheticians, theorists, and pedagogues alike in explaining the art of music in general and the concept of form in particular.]

At the same time, these verbal sources are not without their own limitations. In accounting for specific large-scale forms, theory lags behind practice, as is so often the case, and for the period under consideration here, it is especially difficult to weigh such factors as the relative influence exercised by any given work or writer. Geographical considerations are particularly difficult to evaluate. For all its many composers, the Austro-

18. Neubauer, *Emancipation,* pp. 4–5.

Bohemian realm produced remarkably little in the way of musical theory or aesthetics.[19] It does not necessarily follow, however, that the French and north-German sources cited here are therefore invalid as an aid to interpreting the music of Viennese Classicism. The scattered references to rhetoric that do exist in the relatively few south German, Austro-Bohemian, and Italian sources all suggest that there is no fundamental north-south division on this issue. From about 1790 onward, moreover, French, north German, and Italian writers alike consistently cite Haydn's music as a model of modern instrumental composition.

A handful of writers from the eighteenth and early nineteenth centuries prove themselves to be unusually articulate in exploring the concept of form. And while I emphasize the writings of these authors in particular— Johann Mattheson, Johann Nicolaus Forkel, and Heinrich Christoph Koch in the eighteenth century; Jérome Joseph de Momigny, Anton Reicha, and Adolf Bernhard Marx in the nineteenth—I also seek to show the extent to which their ideas are representative of their respective generations.

By the same token, I make no attempt to survey here the considerable and growing number of recent writings on either sonata form or form in general. Again, my purpose is to identify basic methodologies and fundamental approaches. And if in the first chapter of this book I focus on the work of two particular individuals, Leonard Ratner and Charles Rosen, it is because they have proven themselves to be among the most articulate and influential writers of our own day.

"Form" in music is an elusive subject in part because it can so easily be construed as an omnipresent force, touching in some way on virtually every element of music. It is inextricably linked to a variety of other, equally wide-ranging concepts such as style and genre, none of which can be adequately addressed here. Nor, I must emphasize once again, is form an issue susceptible of any one "solution." A variety of methodologies is both useful and necessary. In the process of illuminating one particular perspective over the course of one particular historical period, I am all too aware of the many valuable alternatives not addressed here. At the same time, the use of imagery drawn from the discipline of rhetoric is an issue that has remained largely outside recent critical debate on the concept of musical form in the Classical era. By reasserting its importance for the eighteenth and early nineteenth centuries, I hope to stimulate a renewed discussion of the significance of rhetoric in our own understanding of a repertoire that is deceptively familiar.

19. See Carl Dahlhaus, "Romantische Musikästhetik und Wiener Klassik," AfMw, 29 (1972), 167–181.

CHAPTER 1

The Paradox of Musical Form

Definitions of musical form almost inevitably call attention to the paradox by which a single term can be applied with equal justification to two fundamentally different concepts: form as an aggregate of features that many unrelated works have in common, and form as an element of that which makes an individual work unique. The tension inherent in this paradox is useful, for it reminds us that no single perspective of musical form is sufficient by itself.

At the same time, we should not be so quick to accept this paradox without first considering the impetus behind its relatively recent emergence in the late eighteenth and early nineteenth centuries. Nor should we forget that the process of defining any one formal stereotype, like sonata form, is itself fraught with paradox: in isolating and identifying those features common to all sonata-form movements, we run the risk of misunderstanding the very essence of that form, and indeed, the essence of form itself.

Generative and Conformational Approaches to Form

The concept of musical form encompasses two basic perspectives that differ radically from each other. On the one hand, "form" is often used to denote those various structural elements that a large number of works share in common. In terms of practical analysis, this approach to form looks for lowest common denominators and views individual works in comparison with such stereotypical patterns as sonata form, rondo, ABA, and the like. For the sake of convenience, this view of form may be called "conformational," as it is based on the comparison of a specific work against an abstract, ideal type.

The contrasting perspective sees form as the unique shape of a specific work. This view, unlike the first, is essentially generative, in that it considers how each individual work grows from within and how the various elements of a work coordinate to make a coherent whole. In its most extreme manifestations, the generative idea of form makes no essential distinction between the form and content of a given work.

The fact that a single term should apply to two such disparate views reflects the historically close relationship of the two. Yet this terminological paradox also helps to obscure the very real distinctions that need to be maintained between form as a pattern and form as the product of a generative process. Both approaches are valid, yet neither is sufficient for musical analysis. Looking for stereotypical patterns can help call attention to deviations from a recognized norm, but it cannot explain these deviations. At the same time, analyzing a work entirely "from within" cannot account for the striking structural similarities that exist among a large number of quite independent works.

⌈The problem with most recent discussions of musical form has not been one of extremism—most writers concede that there is at least some merit to both perspectives—so much as one of irreconcilability. The middle ground, to date, has been less a reconciliation of these two points of view than a tacit and largely unilluminating acceptance of their paradoxical co-existence.⌋

In recent years, the drive to reconcile these two perspectives has been undermined by the widespread suspicion that the conformational approach to form is of questionable value in the analysis of specific works. While the fundamental validity of generative analysis has never been called into serious question, conformational analysis has come under increasingly severe criticism over the last forty years. The very notion of comparing an individual work with a prototypical norm is widely regarded with disdain. The problem, as Carl Dahlhaus has noted, lies not so much in the legitimacy of deriving abstract formal types from a large body of works, as in the fact that the application of these formal schemes ultimately tends to call attention to moments of apparently secondary importance.[1]

As a result, the tendency over the last few decades has been to downplay or dismiss altogether the very existence of stereotypical norms. The structural convention known as "sonata form" provides a case in point. The term itself, after more than a century of heavy use, is now widely subjected to extreme qualification and equivocation when applied to the music of the eighteenth century. William S. Newman, in his three-volume "history of the sonata idea," consistently places the term "sonata form" within quota-

---

1. Dahlhaus, "Zur Theorie der musikalischen Form," *AfMw*, 34 (1977), 20.

tion marks, giving decided preference throughout to the generative idea of form.[2] "Sonata style" and "sonata principle," as Joseph Kerman correctly points out, have become "the preferred terms in recent years."[3]

The most recent monograph on the subject, Charles Rosen's *Sonata Forms*, deftly skirts the issue by using the plural.[4] Rosen offers no central definition of the form in the singular, preferring to deal instead with smaller categories such as "minuet sonata form," "aria sonata form," "slow-movement sonata form," and the like. According to Rosen, we have been falsely led to assume that "there was such a thing as 'sonata form' in the late eighteenth century, and that the composers knew what it was, whereas nothing we know about the situation would lead us to suppose anything of the kind. The feeling for any form, even the minuet, was much more fluid."[5]

Sonata form, in Rosen's view, "is not a definite form like a minuet, a da capo aria, or a French overture: it is, like the fugue, a way of writing, a feeling for proportion, direction, and texture rather than a pattern." Rosen's essentially generative outlook toward form leads him to conclude that sonata form is in fact "an immense melody, an expanded classical phrase."[6]

This disparagement of the conformational approach to analysis is as old as the systematic classification of specific forms. Since the mid-nineteenth century, theorists have been quick to point out that the identification of large-scale conventions in the analysis of a work (ABA, rondo, sonata form, and so on) is comparable to an anatomical exercise, a process that addresses the "external body" but not the "internal soul" of the work at hand.[7] In the early years of this century, Donald Francis Tovey persistently criticized what he called the "jelly-mould" theory of sonata form. And Heinrich Schenker, for altogether different reasons, derided traditional accounts of the form based on superficial norms.[8] This decided antipathy toward external conventions is now a standard element in most discussions

2. Newman, *The Sonata in the Classic Era*, 3rd ed. (New York: Norton, 1983), p. 115.

3. Kerman, review of *Sonata Forms* by Charles Rosen, *New York Review of Books*, 23 October 1980, p. 51.

4. Rosen, *Sonata Forms* (New York: Norton, 1980; rev. ed. 1988).

5. Rosen, *The Classical Style: Haydn, Mozart, Beethoven* (New York: Norton, 1971), p. 52.

6. Ibid., pp. 30, 87.

7. See Carl Dahlhaus, "Gefühlsästhetik und musikalische Formenlehre," *DVjs*, 41 (1967), 505–516.

8. See, for example, Schenker's "Vom Organischen der Sonatenform," *Das Meisterwerk in der Musik*, 2 (1926), 45–46; idem, *Der freie Satz*, 2 vols. (Vienna: Universal, 1935), I, 211–212; and Stephen Hinton, "'Natürliche Übergänge': Heinrich Schenkers Begriff von der Sonatenform," *Musiktheorie*, 5 (1990), 101–116. On Tovey, see Joseph Kerman, "Theories of Late Eighteenth-Century Music," in *Studies in Eighteenth-Century British Art and Aesthetics*, ed. Ralph Cohen (Berkeley and Los Angeles: University of California Press, 1985), pp. 217–244.

of large-scale form. In *The New Grove Dictionary of Music and Musicians,* for example, James Webster emphasizes at the very outset that "sonata form is . . . not a mould into which the composer has poured the contents; each movement grows bar by bar and phrase by phrase."[9] Eugene K. Wolf, in *The New Harvard Dictionary of Music,* similarly argues that "sonata form is best viewed not as a rigid, prescriptive mold, but rather as a flexible and imaginative intersection of modulation, the thematic process, and numerous other elements."[10]

It is easy to agree with such views. The "jelly-mould" idea of form is clearly inadequate for any analysis that hopes to get very far beneath the surface of a work. The generative approach to form, on the other hand, has proven its analytical value so consistently that it needs no defense, here or elsewhere.

At the same time, the *a priori* categorization of specific forms remains essential in the analysis of individual works. No matter how deprecated the idea of a stereotypical pattern may be, it must still be integrated into a broader theoretical concept of form if we are to understand any number of important works of music.

Some specific examples can help to illustrate this point. In the first movement of his String Quartet in F Major, Op. 59, No. 1, Beethoven eschews the standard repetition of the sonata-form exposition. While relatively unusual for its time (1806), this device is by no means unprecedented and in itself does not offer any genuine analytical insights. What makes this particular strategy meaningful is the manner in which the composer integrates this event—or non-event, as it might be called—into the movement's structure as a whole.

The beginning of the development section (mm. 103ff.) is the key passage. Beethoven begins with an exact repetition of the movement's opening measures, identical down to the smallest details of phrasing and dynamics. Only in m. 107, with the repeated eighth-note pairs and the arrival on G♭, do we realize that we are now in fact in the development section. Measures 103–106, in effect, constitute a false repeat of the beginning of the exposition.

The autograph score provides special insights for this particular passage.[11] Beethoven's original manuscript is full of extensive changes, but at no point is there any indication that the composer intended to repeat the first half (the exposition) of this movement. In fact, he specifically added at the top

9. Webster, "Sonata Form," *New Grove.*

10. Wolf, "Sonata Form," *The New Harvard Dictionary of Music* (Cambridge, Mass.: Harvard University Press, 1986).

11. The autograph score, in the Staatsbibliothek Preussischer Kulturbesitz, Berlin, is available in a facsimile edition, with an introduction by Alan Tyson (London: Scolar Press, 1980).

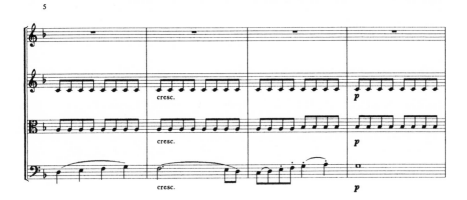

1.1a Beethoven, String Quartet Op. 59, No. 1, first movement, mm. 1–12

1.1b Beethoven, String Quartet Op. 59, No. 1, first movement, mm. 97–112

of the score "La prima parte solamente una volta," as if to say to the copyist: "The absence of a repeat sign for the exposition is not a mistake." And although the composer struggled with the question of whether or not to repeat much of the *second* half of the movement (corresponding essentially to the development and recapitulation sections, mm. 112–342 of the final version), there is no indication of any deleted repeat sign that would have affected the first half.

The false exposition repeat in mm. 103–106, then, appears to have been central to Beethoven's conception of the movement's overall dimensions. In a movement characterized by the qualities of forward momentum and thematic elision, the composer effectively avoids a conventional cadence on the dominant at the end of the exposition; yet he also manages to articulate the beginning of the development section by calling attention quite forcefully to what it is *not:* a repeat of the exposition. In other words, Beethoven manages to elide the juncture between exposition and development and at the same time call attention to the onset of the development with unusual clarity. (This same technique of simultaneous large-scale elision and articulation, significantly enough, is also to be found at the juncture between the development and recapitulation, mm. 242–245, where the cadential figure from mm. 19–22 is recapitulated in the tonic *before* the onset of the "true" recapitulation at m. 254, which corresponds to the movement's opening.)

What makes the device so effective here is the composer's manipulation of his listeners' expectations: Beethoven is relying on his listeners' knowledge of the conventions of sonata form. The sheer economy of this manipulation is striking, and once again, the autograph score allows us to consider Beethoven's changing thoughts on the precise manner of articulating this false exposition repeat. His original idea had been to repeat the first *six* measures of the movement, rather than only the first four as in the final version (mm. 103–106):

1.2   Beethoven, String Quartet Op. 59, No. 1, first movement, beginning of development section, from the autograph score

1.2   continued

It was only later that the composer realized he could create the illusion of an exposition repeat more economically by deleting the two measures corresponding to mm. 5–6. In addition to being more efficient, the end result is also more effective, for the final version gives added emphasis to the dissonant, "developmental" G♭ in m. 108. The thematic deviations of m. 107 notwithstanding, it is the arrival on this G♭ that announces unambiguously that the development has already begun. In the final version, Beethoven enhances this simultaneous sense of arrival and departure still further by emphasizing the registral isolation of this G♭. The (deleted) repetition of mm. 6–7 had already brought us to the G-natural above it, overshooting the subsequent G♭. By means of this deletion, Beethoven avoids a sense of registral redundancy and heightens, both literally and figuratively, the moment of departure.

In its finished state, this passage can of course be interpreted in many ways. But it is difficult to imagine a satisfactory analysis that does not in some way attempt to reconcile the events of mm. 106–108 with the concept of sonata form as an abstract, *a priori* pattern, one that includes a progression from an exposition to a developmental section. *really?*

An earlier but similar instance of a composer calling explicit attention to the conventions of large-scale form may be found in the technique of false recapitulation, which Haydn cultivated with special intensity during the late 1760s and early 1770s.[12] The first movement of the Symphony No. 41 in C Major (composed no later than 1770, probably ca. 1766–1769)[13] incorpo-

12. For a more detailed discussion of this technique, see my "Haydn's False Recapitulations and the Perception of Sonata Form in the Eighteenth Century" (Ph.D. diss., Harvard University, 1988).

13. The suggested date of ca. 1766–1769 is from James Webster's forthcoming monograph on Haydn's Symphony No. 45. The *terminus ante quem* of 1770 is from a dated man-

rates the standard elements of exposition (mm. 1–79), development (mm. 80–132), and recapitulation (mm. 133–202) within the traditional bipartite framework that was so common throughout the Classical era (mm. 1–79 :|: 80–202). The exposition moves from the tonic to the dominant, with a new and contrasting theme (mm. 58ff.) to help articulate the arrival on G major, the secondary area of harmonic stability. The development, in turn, loses no time in introducing a sense of extreme instability. It begins by outlining a fully diminished seventh chord (mm. 80–82) unrelated to anything heard before in the work. Haydn then manipulates fragments of a theme heard previously in the exposition (mm. 83–96). Together with the absence of any solid bass line, these procedures combine to give the passage in mm. 80–96 a decidedly unstable, developmental quality.

Haydn negates this instability with a single stroke by reintroducing the opening theme in the tonic at m. 97. The augmented orchestration at the moment of return corresponds to the fullest version of the theme heard up

1.3a   Haydn, Symphony No. 41, first movement, mm. 1–10

uscript copy of the work cited in Georg Feder's work-list for *The New Grove Haydn* (New York: Norton, 1983), p. 147.

1.3b Haydn, Symphony No. 41, first movement, mm. 80–110

to this point (mm. 19ff.) and adds another touch of authenticity to what will eventually prove to be a false recapitulation. As in the case of the Beethoven quartet, only a small quantity of material (in both instances as little as four measures) is needed to conjure up in the mind of the listener a sense of structural articulation. The impression that one major segment of the movement has ended and another has begun is achieved with a remarkable economy of material.

The fermata in m. 100 provides the first hint that the development may not yet be over. And while the resumption of the consequent phrase in m. 101 dispels such passing doubts temporarily, the diminished seventh chord in m. 104 signals the onset of a long sequential passage moving through a variety of keys. The development, quite clearly, is still under way. The tonic does not return again until m. 133, but this time its return is definitive. The articulation of this true recapitulation is emphasized by the simultaneous return of the opening theme in its original orchestration.

Neither of these interpretations—of the Beethoven quartet or of the Haydn symphony—is particularly radical. Yet each analysis rests on a concept of sonata form that is no longer fashionable, one that grants a central role to the use of standard patterns within the works in question. These analyses, in other words, are based on the assumption that a construct now known as sonata form did exist in the minds of at least some eighteenth-century composers and presumably in the minds of at least some listeners as well. Viewed from this perspective, these two movements offer a kind of wordless commentary on the two most critical junctures within a sonata-form movement: the articulation between exposition and development, in the Beethoven quartet, and the articulation between development and recapitulation, in the Haydn symphony. There can be no doubt that in these particular instances Beethoven and Haydn were both playing upon the expectations of their contemporary audiences, specifically as regards the structural conventions of large-scale first movements.

These analyses illustrate the need to reconsider the theoretical premises underlying the new orthodoxy of form. The generative approach, for the most part, seeks to explain the recurrence of stereotypical patterns as the product of internal forces. Rosen, for example, argues that "the abstract forms . . . do not make their effects by breaking 'rules,'" and that "the element of surprise . . . does not depend upon a deviation from some imagined musical norm outside the individual work." The "movement, the development, and the dramatic course of a work all can be found latent in the material," which can "be made to release its charged force so that the music . . . is literally impelled from within."[14]

14. Rosen, *The Classical Style*, pp. 296, 120.

Yet we cannot adequately address these specific passages from Beethoven and Haydn without reference to "a musical norm outside the individual work." Nor is it at all clear in what sense these events are "latent" in the opening material. An analytical approach based on the assumption that "it is the work itself . . . that provides its own expectations, disappoints and finally fulfills them,"[15] while useful up to a point, simply will not suffice by itself here or in any number of other similar instances.

At the same time, neither of these analyses could be expanded along their present lines to provide an even remotely satisfactory account of either movement as a whole. While the conformational approach may be essential in explaining these particular passages, this approach also cannot stand by itself. It must be integrated with an analytical methodology that is more generative in nature. In the case of Beethoven's Op. 59, No. 1, one would need to trace the manipulation and ultimate expansion of a relatively small number of thematic, harmonic, and rhythmic motives into a coherent whole, as well as the strategic exploitation of texture, register, and dynamics.

The first four measures of the opening theme, to cite only one case in point, revolve around the tonic, as might be expected, but in the second inversion rather than in root position. This initial sense of instability has important implications for the remainder of the movement, for it provides a central element in the forward drive that is so characteristic of the movement as a whole. It also offers a convincing motivation for the remarkable fact that the first root harmonization of the opening theme in the tonic does not occur until the beginning of the coda, in m. 348, well over four-fifths of the way through the entire movement. This delay further heightens the climactic nature of an event that occurs only after the recapitulation has spun its course. Similar generative devices can be traced throughout the Haydn symphony as well.

Generative analysts have argued along similar lines with great effect, maintaining that conventional structures are a broader manifestation of smaller-scale events. In the early years of this century, Hermann Kretzschmar derided the "cult of externalism" and reduced the understanding of large-scale form to the comprehension of a basic motive or theme. "The task of tracing the sense of four hundred measures," for Kretzschmar, was tantamount to reducing an entire movement to "four or eight measures," to "a theme or a period."[16] Ernst Kurth similarly advocated an analysis of "inner" form,[17] and many writers have followed this path in analyz-

15. Ibid., p. 296.
16. Kretzschmar, "Anregungen zur Förderung musikalischer Hermeneutik," *Jahrbuch der Musikbibliothek Peters für 1902*, p. 64.
17. See, for example, Kurth's *Bruckner*, 2 vols. (Berlin: Max Hesse, 1925), esp. vol. 1, part 2, "Die Formdynamik."

ing sonata form. William S. Newman, for example, advocates a shift of emphasis from questions of external conventions to "stylistic or generative traits."[18] In preparing his "history of the sonata idea," Newman found that "an effort to consider musical form as a generative process—that is, as the structural result of tendencies inherent in its primary ideas—seemed to yield a more fluid approach to form analysis."[19] More recently, Jan LaRue has maintained that "a plural, descriptive approach cannot be used to clarify our understanding" of the evolution of Classical forms; "we must rely on fundamental, generative principles, not taxonomic surveys."[20] And Leonard Ratner has provided historical justification for such an approach by identifying eighteenth-century treatises, most notably by Joseph Riepel and Heinrich Christoph Koch, that advocate the expansion of small-scale constructs into larger ones.[21]

To varying degrees, these generative views of form all rely on the conceptual metaphor of the musical work as an organism. Indeed, the modern history of organic form can be traced back to the very period under investigation here: Goethe, the early German Romantics, and Coleridge all played important roles in the idea's early development.[22] By the beginning of the twentieth century, even such disparate theorists as Schenker and Ebenezer Prout could share a common philosophical conviction that all works of art, as organisms, could ultimately be reduced to a germinal unit. In Prout's formulation, "all music is an *organic growth,* and . . . the binary and ternary forms are developed from the simplest motives by as natural a process of evolution as that by which an oak grows out of an acorn."[23] Schenker, too, saw music as a process of growth, albeit from the *Ursatz*

18. Newman, *The Sonata in the Classic Era,* p. 119. See also Newman's "Musical Form as a Generative Process," *Journal of Aesthetics and Art Criticism,* 12 (1954), 301–309.

19. Newman, *The Sonata in the Baroque Era,* 3rd ed. (New York: Norton, 1972), p. 5.

20. LaRue, review of *Sonata Forms* by Charles Rosen, *JAMS,* 34 (1981), 560.

21. Ratner, "Eighteenth-Century Theories of Musical Period Structure," *MQ,* 42 (1956), 439–454. Ratner's work has paved the way for many subsequent interpretations of periodicity in eighteenth-century theory. See Baker, "Koch and the Theory of Melody"; idem, "From *Teil* to *Tonstück:* The Significance of the *Versuch einer Anleitung zur Composition* by Heinrich Christoph Koch" (Ph.D. diss., Yale University, 1978); Elaine Sisman, "Small and Expanded Forms: Koch's Model and Haydn's Music," *MQ,* 68 (1982), 444–475; Wolfgang Budday, *Grundlagen musikalischer Formen der Wiener Klassik* (Kassel: Bärenreiter, 1983); and Hermann Forschner, *Instrumentalmusik Joseph Haydns aus der Sicht Heinrich Christoph Kochs* (Munich: Emil Katzbichler, 1984).

22. The historical origins of the organic concept of form will be dealt with at greater length in Chapter 3.

23. Prout, *Applied Forms: A Sequel to 'Musical Form,'* 2nd ed. (London: Augener, 1896), p. 1. Unless otherwise noted, all emphases cited are in the original source. On the predominance of organicism in twentieth-century analysis, see Joseph Kerman, "The State of Academic Music Criticism," in *On Criticizing Music: Five Philosophical Perspectives,* ed. Kingsley Price (Baltimore: Johns Hopkins University Press, 1981), pp. 38–54.

rather than the unit of the motive.[24] More recent writers, most notably Newman, LaRue, Ratner, Wolf, and Rosen, have since contributed immensely to our understanding of the process of musical growth and the critical role played by such generative elements as melody, phrase construction, harmonic rhythm, and texture. The "concinnity" of these elements (to use LaRue's favored term) contributes vitally to the construction of sonata form and, for that matter, all forms.

In practice, however, it is difficult to bridge the gap between small-scale units and large-scale forms in an entirely convincing manner. Most analysts of the generative persuasion have chosen to concentrate on these smaller-scale units, focusing primarily on events somewhere between a single four-measure phrase and a larger unit of sixteen or thirty-two measures.[25] Even Koch, the most eloquent and perceptive of eighteenth-century theorists in this field, had to rely on two quite different approaches in dealing with form at the level of the phrase and at the level of the complete movement. Koch's method of teaching composition, based on the expansion and combination of small phrases into increasingly larger units, is typical of his era. According to Koch's generative construct, a unit of the smallest level (the *Satz*) can ultimately become a part of any number of forms, such as sonata form, rondo, theme and variations.[26] Through the techniques of repetition, extension, and incision, a small, four-measure unit can be expanded into a variety of larger structures. In this respect, he equates the nature of a larger form with the techniques of expansion applied to an opening unit of thought.

Yet it is highly revealing that the minuet should be the largest formal stereotype that Koch and others describe in this fashion. The minuet, in practice, was a favorite didactic tool among eighteenth-century theorists, for it tended to be a relatively straightforward construct made up of fairly simple and regular metrical units; as such, it was ideally suited to explaining

24. As William A. Pastille points out, however, Schenker espoused a quite different view earlier in his career; see Pastille, "Heinrich Schenker, Anti-Organicist," *19th-Century Music,* 8 (1984), 29–36.

25. Anthony Newcomb is one of the few writers to have explicitly voiced misgivings about the current preoccupation of analysis with small-scale units: "Those Images That Yet Fresh Images Beget," *Journal of Musicology,* 2 (1983), 227–245. The essence of Newcomb's remarks, dealing with Wagner's music dramas, could also be applied to the issue of sonata form in the Classical era. Musicologists are apparently not alone in their preference for dealing with questions of small-scale form: Seymour Chatman, "On Defining 'Form'," *New Literary History,* 2 (1971), 225, points out that "our best formal and stylistic descriptions of individual authors . . . are predominantly based on units smaller than the sentence." Chatman goes on to call for a stylistics "that leads to terms for characterizing large-scale structures on their own . . . and, further, an integration of these [terms] with the more molecular aspects of an author's style" (p. 225).

26. This point is particularly clear from Elaine Sisman's diagram illustrating "Koch's Levels of Musical Structure" in her "Small and Expanded Forms," p. 445.

the rudiments of constructing a movement-length whole.[27] Koch provides extended commentary and numerous examples illustrating the links between smaller and larger units (between the *Satz* and the *Periode*), but his methodology changes markedly when he attempts to account for the connections between multiple *Perioden* in a movement larger and aesthetically more ambitious than a minuet. He presents these extended constructs in a far more cursory, descriptive manner, working very much along the lines of a conformationally oriented theory of form.

This change from a generative to a conformational methodology in moving from small- to large-scale structures is by no means peculiar to Koch.[28] It reflects an awareness on the part of both earlier and later theorists that the principle of growth alone cannot adequately account for the nature of large-scale structural conventions. Koch and others recognized, in effect, what Leonard B. Meyer has since dubbed the "fallacy of hierarchic uniformity," the "tacit and usually unconscious assumption that the same forces and processes which order and articulate one hierarchic level are operative, are equally effective, and function in the same fashion in the structuring of all levels." A sonata-form movement, like any complex musical structure, is a hierarchical system that coheres through various levels of organization. But it would be "a serious mistake," as Meyer points out, "to assume that the principles or 'laws' governing the organization of one hierarchic level are necessarily the same as those of some other level."[29] Thus even Wolf, who argues that a "hierarchical system implies relative autonomy of individual components as well as the integration of these components into a larger whole," follows Koch's lead in using one methodology to explain the successive concatenation of motives, subphrases, phrases, periods, and double periods in mid-eighteenth-century music, yet a quite different approach to describe the various kinds of standard movement-length patterns constructed out of these units.[30] Wolf's interpretation of mid-eighteenth-century phrase structure and form is among the best available, and the fact that he relies on the kind of conformationally oriented diagrams originally devised by Jan LaRue in no way weakens the force of his logic. Indeed, the very fact that LaRue's diagrams have proven so widely useful is itself a

27. See, for example, Johann Mattheson, *Der vollkommene Capellmeister* (Hamburg: Herold, 1739), pp. 224–225; Joseph Riepel, *Anfangsgründe zur musikalischen Setzkunst: De rhythmopoeïa, oder von der Tactordnung* (Augsburg: J. J. Lotter, 1752), p. 1; Koch, *Versuch*, III, 129–130. See also below, p. 50.

28. See below, pp. 79–80, 84–85, 119–120.

29. Meyer, *Music, the Arts, and Ideas: Patterns and Predictions in Twentieth-Century Culture* (Chicago: University of Chicago Press, 1967), pp. 96, 258.

30. Wolf, *The Symphonies of Johann Stamitz: A Study in the Formation of the Classic Style* (Utrecht: Bohn, Scheltema & Holkema, 1981), chs. 8 and 9.

testimony to the value of the conformational perspective. But it is important to recognize the essential distinction between the generative and conformational approaches to analysis. The former emphasizes the process of growth common to virtually all forms, while the latter emphasizes the broad structural differences among the various products of growth.

By itself, the generative approach ultimately begs the question of large-scale form. "Growth" is an essential concept to an understanding of form, but it tends to blur the distinction between a work's form and its content. At what point does a movement's basic idea end and its growth begin? Granted, there are undeniable differences in general character and structure among opening themes of rondos, minuets, sets of variations, and so on. Yet it would not be at all difficult to imagine the theme from the opening of the finale to Haydn's Symphony No. 90, a sonata-form movement, as the beginning of a rondo, or the opening theme of the first movement to the Symphony No. 41 (see Example 1.3a) as the basis for a minuet. Where, then, does growth end and form begin? If growth culminates only in a completed movement, then form and content cannot really be distinguished from each other. If, in other words, we choose to define form as "the shape of a musical composition as defined by *all* of its pitches, rhythms, dynamics, and timbres,"[31] then form becomes omnipresent and in effect disappears altogether.

Rosen's solution, to treat a range of diverse structures as varieties of sonata form, provides valuable insights into the similarities among a number of these stereotypical structures, but this approach, as Koch and others already recognized, also has its limitations. To use this one particular model as the underlying principle of so many different Classical forms, as Jan LaRue observes, is "like calling a tricycle an automobile, simply because both vehicles have wheels."[32] And while "form" is a word that Rosen prefers to avoid whenever possible, his own analyses consistently rely on the reader's (and the listener's) knowledge of what would seem to be an archetypal pattern of events within the course of an instrumental movement.[33] Still more troubling is the fact that Rosen's approach offers no theoretical basis applicable to other forms that lie outside the realm of the "sonata style," such as fantasia, theme and variations, or fugue.

In terms of practical analysis, a purely generative perspective of form remains especially hard-pressed to explain the remarkable phenomenon of composers' "discovering" sonata form over and over again with each new

31. *New Harvard Dictionary of Music,* "Form." Emphasis added. This is the first of two definitions, the other being "a loose group of general features shared in varying degrees by a relatively large number of works."
32. LaRue, review of *Sonata Forms,* p. 560.
33. Ibid., p. 559.

work, the form emerging afresh and unexpected, as it were, from a given work's germinal unit. The common presence of a repeat sign midway through the movement (and often enough once again at the end, especially before 1800) further weakens the persuasiveness of a strictly generative approach toward form.[34] And although probably no one would maintain that the thousands of manifestations of sonata form are somehow historically coincidental—that hundreds of composers arrived at the same solution independently of one another—few analyses openly acknowledge the extent to which composers worked within the context of formal conventions. There can be no doubt that style and content shape the structural manifestation of any well-written movement, and generative approaches to form are essential in establishing the relationships that do exist between small- and large-scale forms. But it would be ludicrous to argue that sonata form was not at least in part an *a priori* schema available to the composer. Hollace Schafer's recent sketch studies have confirmed that Haydn, for one, routinely worked within the established outlines of movement-length constructs, mapping out specific points of large-scale articulation (including the onset of the development and the moment of recapitulation) at a relatively early stage in the creative process.[35] Sonata form, for Haydn, was in fact a point of departure, a mold, albeit a flexible one.

The problem in recent analysis, it should be emphasized once again, is not one of extremism: most writers employ both generative and conformational techniques in varying proportions. But there is a disturbing absence of any theoretical basis of form that can reconcile the generative and conformational approaches in a convincing fashion. It is altogether symptomatic of this state of affairs that the term "form" itself is now becoming increasingly rare, and that "sonata style" and "sonata principle" have become "the preferred terms."

What is needed, then, is a general theory of form that can account for conventional patterns and at the same time do justice to the immense diversity that exists within the framework of these patterns. The issue, in effect, is how to reconcile the conventional with the individual, the stereotypical with the unique. A satisfactory theory of structural conventions like sonata form must be able to account for both intrinsic (unique) and extrinsic (conventional) procedures using a consistent set of parameters. How is it that so many works can follow the same general outline and yet be so entirely different in character and content? Why is it that so many composers

34. See Michael Broyles, "Organic Form and the Binary Repeat," *MQ*, 66 (1980), 339–360.

35. Schafer, "'A Wisely Ordered *Phantasie*': Joseph Haydn's Creative Process from the Sketches and Drafts for Instrumental Music," 2 vols. (Ph.D. diss., Brandeis University, 1987), esp. I, 145–162, 212–214.

from the eighteenth and nineteenth centuries relied so heavily on such a small number of stereotypical constructs? And precisely how do the concepts of "inner" and "outer" form relate to each other?

There are no simple answers to these questions, but there is much to be gained from considering the eighteenth century's own approach to these issues. As I shall argue in Chapter 2, it was the conceptual metaphor of rhetoric that mediated between these two approaches to form throughout the better part of the eighteenth century and the early years of the nineteenth.

But before considering the contemporary theoretical sources of this period, we must first reevaluate the extent to which our modern-day acceptance of the paradox of form has governed our reading of theoretical sources from the eighteenth and early nineteenth centuries—that is to say, sources from an era that antedates the dichotomy between "inner" and "outer" form. The continuity that links the Classical era with our own is deceptive. For while the music of Haydn, Mozart, and Beethoven is among the earliest to have enjoyed an unbroken tradition of performance in the concert hall down to our own day, we have only recently begun to learn just how much the nature of the instruments, performance techniques, standards of tempo, and locales of performance—in short, the very sound and perception of the music—have changed. The theoretical premises of musical form have undergone changes since that time that are every bit as important. Yet even the most widely accepted recent attempts to interpret eighteenth-century sources have been influenced, to a surprising degree, by nineteenth-century concepts of form. Only by reevaluating the basis for present-day attitudes toward Classical forms can we begin to recognize the discontinuity of theoretical thought that separates the age of Haydn, Mozart, and Beethoven from our own. Sonata form, the most important structural convention of the Classical era, provides a useful illustration of these changes.

Sonata Form and the Limits of Definition

Definitions, like metaphors, both reflect and shape our understanding of ideas. And with concepts as problematic as "form" and "sonata form," it is clear that our definitions of these terms play an important role in our understanding of the musical works that represent their many manifestations.

In the absence of any formal eighteenth-century definitions of sonata form, scholars have understandably directed a good deal of attention toward identifying the form's essential features—that is to say, those characteristics common to all its manifestations. Indeed, this search for form-defining elements reflects Aristotle's own definition of the very concept of "form" itself as "the essence of each thing."[36] By this line of reasoning, any variability in regard to a particular element automatically precludes that element from playing any role in the definition of the form. Thus the presence of contrasting themes within the exposition, a basic element in later nineteenth-century accounts, has rightly been rejected as an essential feature of Classical sonata form. A contrasting theme, while often present, is far from universal in eighteenth-century manifestations of the form and therefore cannot be considered a form-defining element.

What the many manifestations of Classical sonata form do share is a basic harmonic outline, moving from the tonic to a closely related secondary key (usually the dominant if the movement is in major, or the relative major if the movement is in minor), then to an area of harmonic instability, followed by a return to the tonic. Within this construct, the number, character, and placement of thematic ideas can vary widely. While this harmonic framework may be embedded within other forms (for example, the opening section of a minuet, or an individual variation within a set of variations), it is this particular outline as an independent whole that distinguishes Classical sonata form from other conventional structures.

Whatever their differences in interpretation, virtually all recent accounts of Classical sonata form agree that large-scale tonality plays the most important role in defining the structure of this form.[37] Leonard Ratner's schema of sonata form, which has won widespread acceptance, succinctly summarizes the nature of this structure:[38]

$$\| : \quad \text{I (or i)} \; \rightarrow \; \text{V(or III)} \quad : \| : \; X \; \rightarrow \; I : \|$$

Tonic Major	→	Dominant	Unstable →	Tonic
	or		(non-tonic)	
Tonic Minor	→	Relative Major		

But by isolating and giving prominence to essential characteristics, a definition can also misshape our understanding of an idea. In the case of sonata form, the search for form-defining elements has in fact inhibited an accurate

36. Aristotle, *Metaphysics,* trans. Hugh Tredennick (Cambridge, Mass.: Harvard University Press, 1933), 1032b1.

37. See, for example, Newman, *The Sonata in the Baroque Era; The Sonata in the Classic Era;* Jens Peter Larsen, "Sonatenform-Probleme," in *Festschrift Friedrich Blume zum 70. Geburtstag,* ed. Anna Amalie Abert and Wilhelm Pfannkuch (Kassel: Bärenreiter, 1963), pp. 221–230; Ritzel, *Die Entwicklung der "Sonatenform";* Rosen, *The Classical Style,* pp. 99–100; Webster, "Sonata Form," *New Grove;* and Wolf, "Sonata Form," *New Harvard Dictionary of Music.*

38. Ratner, *Classic Music,* p. 218. Ratner's schema will be discussed in greater detail below.

reconstruction of the eighteenth century's conception of the form. The need to define sonata form is clear enough; but in the process of working toward this goal, we must keep in mind that definitions, by their very nature, are limited in function. Identifying those elements common to all manifestations of sonata form does not provide an adequate framework for accommodating crucial features that happen not to be form-defining.

The dispute over whether sonata form is a harmonic or a thematic construct illustrates the limits of definition. Most scholars today would agree that the answer depends in large part upon whether one is referring to eighteenth- or nineteenth-century theories of the form. Throughout much of the nineteenth century and well into the twentieth, writers generally viewed sonata form as a thematic construct. In an account dating from around 1840, for example, Carl Czerny introduces the form in the following manner:

The first movement consists of two parts, the first of which is usually repeated. This first part must comprise:
1. The principal subject.
2. Its continuation or amplification, together with a modulation into the nearest related key.
3. The middle subject in this new key.
4. A new continuation of this middle subject.
5. A final melody, after which the first part thus closes in the new key, in order that the repetition of the same may follow unconstrainedly.

The second part of the first movement commences with a development of the principal subject, or of the middle subject, or even of a new idea, passing through several keys, and returning again to the original key. Then follows the principal subject and its amplification, but usually in an abridged shape, and so modulating, that the middle subject may likewise re-appear entire, though in the original key: after which, all that follows the middle subject in the first part, is here repeated in the original key, and thus the close is made.[39]

These "textbook" descriptions—so called because they proliferated in dozens of instructional manuals on musical composition—place particular emphasis on the principle of long-range melodic contrast between an opening "masculine" theme and a subsequent "feminine" theme. Czerny goes

39. Czerny, *School of Practical Composition*, trans. John Bishop, 3 vols. (London: Robert Cocks, ca. 1848), I, 33. On the tangled publishing history of this work, see William S. Newman, "About Carl Czerny's Op. 600 and the 'First' Description of 'Sonata Form'," *JAMS*, 20 (1967), 513–515. There is evidence that the work was either entirely or substantially completed as early as 1840, but no copy of the original German version appears to have survived. An earlier (ca. 1832) account of sonata form by Czerny appears in his "Translator's Appendix" to Anton Reicha's *Vollständiges Lehrbuch der musikalischen Composition*, 4 vols. (Vienna: Anton Diabelli), I, 316–330; see Peter Cahn, "Carl Czernys erste Beschreibung der Sonatenform (1832)," *Musiktheorie*, 1 (1986), 277–279.

on to discuss at greater length the contrast between the movement's opening thematic material and the "middle" or "second" theme of the exposition:

Now follows the middle subject, which must consist of a new idea. A good middle subject is much more difficult to invent, than the commencement; for *first:* it must possess a new and more beautiful and pleasing melody than all which precedes; and *secondly,* it must be very different from the foregoing, but yet, according to its character, so well suited thereto, that it may appear like the object or result of all the preceding ideas, modulations or passages . . .

When good and beautiful ideas have been conceived, the construction of the first part presents, as we perceive, no difficulty; because, we must always proceed in a settled form. For, if this order were evaded or arbitrarily changed, the composition would no longer be a regular Sonata.[40]

Czerny's description and the more subtle accounts by subsequent writers like Adolf Bernhard Marx (1845) and Johann Christian Lobe (1850) reflect contemporary compositional practice, in which the contrast of themes within a movement plays an important structural role. As the harmonic idiom became increasingly chromatic over the course of the nineteenth century, the traditional polarity of dominant and tonic began to lose its central role in the structure of sonata-form movements: composers began to modulate toward more and different keys in both the exposition and the recapitulation. Thus the nineteenth century's concept of sonata form placed special emphasis on the presence of a contrasting "second theme" in the exposition.

This view of sonata form, with its emphasis on thematic contrast, continued well into the twentieth century. There were occasional voices of dissent from writers like Tovey and Schenker, who, as noted earlier, were among the first to point out the inadequacy of descriptions based solely or even primarily on thematic content. Tovey, in particular, granted primary importance to the structural function of a movement's large-scale harmonic outline. But it was not until 1949 that Leonard Ratner, in a seminal essay, provided historical documentation to support Tovey's view.[41] Citing a number of composition treatises from the Classical era, Ratner was able to argue persuasively that eighteenth-century theorists, in contrast to their nineteenth-century counterparts, conceived of sonata form as a fundamentally harmonic design.

40. Czerny, *School of Practical Composition,* I, 35.
41. "Harmonic Aspects of Classic Form," *JAMS,* 2 (1949), 159–168. Ratner's Ph.D. dissertation of the same title (University of California, 1947) provides a more detailed examination of these issues.

To varying degrees, Riepel (1755), Portmann (1789), Koch (1787, 1793), Galeazzi (1796), Kollmann (1799), and Gervasoni (1800) do in fact discuss the structure in terms of contrasting areas of harmonic stability and instability.[42] Kollmann's "plan of modulation," found in "most sonatas, symphonies, and concertos," is often cited as a typical contemporary account of eighteenth-century sonata form:

Each *section,* may be divided into two *subsections;* which in the whole makes *four* subsections.

The *first* subsection must contain the setting out from the key towards its fifth in major, or third in minor; and it may end with the chord of the key note or its fifth, but the latter is better. The *second* subsection comprehends a first sort of elaboration, consisting of a more natural modulation than that of the third subsection; it may be confined to the fifth or third of the key only, or also touch on some related, or even non-related keys if only no formal digression is made to any key but the said fifth in major, or third in minor. The *third* subsection or beginning of the second section, comprehends a second sort of elaboration, consisting of digressions to all those keys and modes which shall be introduced besides that of the fifth (or third); and being the place for those abrupt modulations, or enharmonic changes, which the piece admits or requires. The *fourth* subsection contains the return to the key, with a third sort of elaboration, similar to that of the first subsection.[43]

On the basis of accounts like this, numerous scholars have followed Ratner's lead in viewing eighteenth-century sonata form as a harmonic outline whose thematic conventions are too diverse to be incorporated into any definition of the form. Ratner's schema of I - V :|: X - I also reflects eighteenth-century thought in that it treats sonata form as an essentially bipartite structure, divided by a repeat sign roughly midway through the movement. Beginning in the early decades of the nineteenth century, this repeat sign would become increasingly less common—Beethoven's piano sonatas, taken as a whole, are a good example of this shift in practice[44]—and within fifty years, most theorists were treating the form as an essentially tripartite structure, consisting of sections now known as exposition, development, and recapitulation. The double bar in the middle of the movement, if present at all, was considered a mere relic of earlier convention.

42. Joseph Riepel, *Anfangsgründe zur musikalischen Setzkunst: Grundregeln zur Tonordnung insgemein* (Ulm: C. U. Wagner, 1755); Johann Gottlieb Portmann, *Leichtes Lehrbuch der Harmonie, Composition und des Generalbasses* (Darmstadt: J. J. Will, 1789); Koch, *Versuch,* II and III (1787–1793); Francesco Galeazzi, *Elementi teorico-pratici di musica,* II (Rome: M. Puccinelli, 1796); August F. C. Kollmann, *An Essay on Practical Musical Composition* (London: Author, 1799); Carlo Gervasoni, *La scuola della musica,* 2 vols. (Piacenza: Nicolò Orcesi, 1800; rpt. Bologna: Forni, n.d.). These various accounts will be discussed in more detail below.

43. Kollmann, *Essay on Practical Musical Composition,* p. 5.

44. For a survey of this change, see Broyles, "Organic Form."

It is this thematic, tripartite view of Classical sonata form that has been so soundly rejected over the past forty years. The mid-nineteenth-century concept, with its strong emphasis on thematic contrast, is correctly recognized today as an anachronism when applied to the music of the Classical era.[45] Haydn's "monothematic" sonata-form constructs, in particular, defy analysis on the basis of thematic contrast: many of these movements repeat what is essentially the opening theme at the onset of the dominant portion of the exposition. In the first movement of the Symphony No. 104 in D Major, for example, the opening idea reappears in the exposition just at the moment when nineteenth-century listeners would have expected a substantially different, contrasting theme. Thematic contrasts do exist within a great number of eighteenth-century movements, and Galeazzi, for one, describes this technique in some detail.[46] But this kind of contrast is not accorded the central importance it would assume in later nineteenth-century accounts of sonata form.

Since around the middle of our own century, then, the "textbook" concept of sonata form for the Classical era has given way to a freer, more fluid concept defined primarily on the basis of harmonic structure. Recent discussions of sonata form in the eighteenth century, accordingly, have emphasized the diversity of procedures within this framework and the variety of choices open to composers. Thematic events, to use Ratner's metaphor, constitute a variable "superstructure" that interlocks into the elemental "basis" of the harmonic outline; it is the movement's harmonic shape and not its thematic elements that define the form.[47]

Brief and superficial as the above summary may be, it provides at least a broad outline of what is generally accepted to be the historical evolution of the theory of sonata form: an essentially bipartite harmonic construct in the eighteenth century, replaced by an essentially tripartite thematic construct in the nineteenth, replaced in turn in the mid-twentieth century by the rediscovery of the bipartite harmonic model for music of the Classical era.

In many respects, this view of the history of the theory of sonata form has much to recommend it, for nineteenth-century writers do indeed lay far greater stress upon the principle of thematic contrast than their

45. Jane R. Stevens, in "Georg Joseph Vogler and the 'Second Theme' in Sonata Form: Some 18th-Century Perceptions of Musical Contrast," *Journal of Musicology*, 2 (1983), 278–304, convincingly calls into question the traditional interpretation of one of the few passages in eighteenth-century theory reputedly describing a contrasting "second theme" as an element of form in eighteenth-century music.

46. Galeazzi, *Elementi*, II, 256. For other, less explicit references, see Charles Burney, *A General History of Music*, ed. Frank Mercer, 2 vols. (New York: Harcourt, Brace, n.d.; orig. pub. 1789), II, 866; and Johann Friedrich Daube, *Anleitung zur Erfindung der Melodie und ihrer Fortsetzung*, 2 vols. (Vienna: C. G. Täubel, 1797–1798), II, 38.

47. Ratner, *Classic Music*, p. 221.

eighteenth-century counterparts. But at a deeper level, this view overemphasizes the differences between eighteenth- and nineteenth-century theories of the form. In so doing, it poses a number of problems:

1. It implies a fundamental and relatively rapid change between eighteenth- and nineteenth-century accounts of sonata form that is not reflected in contemporary sources.

✳2. In its search for a lowest common denominator (large-scale harmony), it tends to suppress the significance of other elements that do in fact figure prominently in eighteenth-century accounts of sonata form.

3. It rests strongly upon evidence from pedagogical treatises, sources that cannot be interpreted adequately without taking into account their openly didactic function.

4. It fails to provide the basis for a broader concept of form applicable to constructs other than sonata form itself, such as the rondo, fugue, or theme and variations.

5. It imposes an aesthetic dichotomy between "inner" and "outer" form that is not reflected in contemporary eighteenth-century accounts.

Let us consider each of these points in turn.

1. *The implication of a fundamental and relatively rapid change between eighteenth- and nineteenth-century accounts of sonata form.* In spite of a gradually increasing emphasis on thematic contrast over the course of the nineteenth century, accounts of sonata form do not in fact alter in any fundamental sense between the 1790s (Koch, Galeazzi, Kollmann, Gervasoni) and the 1840s (Czerny and Marx). Theorists of both generations consistently describe a movement's thematic ideas in relation to its harmonic outline and vice versa. The later dialectical contrast between "first" and "second" themes supplements, but does not supersede, the traditional outline of tonal progressions. Czerny and Marx, just like Koch and Kollmann, describe sonata form as a harmonic pattern moving from the tonic to a related but contrasting secondary key (the exposition), and from there to a period of relative instability (development) before returning definitively to the tonic (recapitulation). For mid-nineteenth-century theorists, the presence of a contrasting "second" theme does not by itself signal a sonata-form movement. Even by "textbook" standards, the course of events after the exposition must follow an established harmonic outline if the movement at hand is to be considered representative of sonata form. Indeed, it is not until 1827 that any writer specifically equates the form of a movement with its har-

monic outline.[48] And when Marx calls one of Haydn's "monothematic" movements an "older type of sonata form," it is important to recognize that Marx considered this movement a manifestation of that form on the basis of its large-scale harmonic structure, in spite of the fact that it lacks a contrasting "second" theme.[49]

In this respect, the dichotomy between harmonic (eighteenth-century) and thematic (nineteenth-century) accounts of sonata form is a false one. It has been fostered, in large measure, by recent efforts to define Classical sonata form according to its lowest common denominator. In identifying the form-defining essentials of eighteenth-century repertoire, scholars have tended to exaggerate the differences between eighteenth- and nineteenth-century writers while neglecting deeper continuities of thought.

From a purely functional point of view, the most important break in critical thinking about sonata form has in fact taken place only in the last forty years. The basic shift occurred not between Koch and Marx, but rather between Koch, Czerny, and Marx, on the one hand, and Tovey, Ratner, and Newman on the other. [Critical accounts of sonata form have moved from a compositional, didactic context to one that is more analytical and historical in nature. These historically oriented accounts differ not merely in content but more importantly in kind from both the eighteenth- and the nineteenth-century views of the form. To limit the overtly derogatory designation of "textbook form" to writers from the mid-nineteenth century onward, beginning with Marx and Czerny, postulates a degree of discontinuity between Koch and Marx that is historically misleading, for it obscures the direct line of pedagogical descent from the eighteenth century into the nineteenth. The earliest discussions of sonata form, after all, appear in treatises directed at would-be composers. Riepel's treatise is in the form of a dialogue between pupil and scholar; Koch consistently addresses the "aspiring composer"; and Galeazzi and Kollmann both make frequent reference to the reader as a "student." From the standpoint of function, Koch's description of sonata form is every bit as much in the "textbook" tradition as Marx's.

Nor is it accurate to distinguish earlier theorists such as Koch and Kollmann from Marx and Lobe on the grounds that the later writers "prescribed" the form and gave it a specific name.[50] The charge of prescriptivism

hmm... prescriptivism.

48. Heinrich Birnbach, "Über die verschiedene Form grösserer Instrumentaltonstücke aller Art und deren Bearbeitung," *BAMZ,* 4 (1827), 269. See below, p. 147.

49. Adolf Bernhard Marx, *Die Lehre von der musikalischen Komposition,* 4 vols. (Leipzig: Breitkopf & Härtel, 1837–1847), III, 563–567.

50. A good deal of attention—perhaps too much—has been devoted to identifying the earliest use of the term "sonata form" to describe the structure of a single movement. The

could be leveled with some justification against Czerny, who did in fact take a rather rigid approach toward the teaching of form, but it would be historically inaccurate to extend guilt by chronological association to his contemporaries as well. Marx, in particular, goes to great lengths to emphasize that his description of sonata form represents nothing more than a heuristic norm, and that exceptions to this norm abound. Indeed, Marx's view of form is at times remarkably organicist: "There are as many forms as works of art . . . Content and form [are] inseparably one."[51] Marx is most commonly perceived to have been an encyclopedic codifier of musical forms, and his analyses of earlier repertoire do in fact suffer from a markedly teleological bias.[52] But his celebrated "codification" of sonata form is immediately followed by an even longer (yet frequently overlooked) discussion of the many exceptions to the norm he has just finished describing.[53] The opening of this neglected passage should be sufficient to dispel Marx's unjustified reputation as a rigid prescriptivist. Having outlined the "standard" version of sonata form, Marx steps back to take a more careful look at the broader issues:

table of contents to volume 5 (1828) of Marx's *Berliner Allgemeine musikalische Zeitung* has been cited as the first such use of the term, but Marx had in fact used it as early as 1824 in a retrospective essay in the first volume of the same journal (pp. 444–448). He notes that the historical period of Haydn and Mozart is characterized by "more extended musical ideas and a richer sequence of melodies: the sonata- and rondo-form became predominant [*die Sonaten- u. Rondoform wurde herrschend*] . . . By the first term [*Sonatenform*], we mean the joining of two sections of melodies (the first in the tonic, the second in the dominant—or the first in the tonic minor, the second in the relative major), usually repeated after an interpolation [*Zwischensatz,* i.e., development section], with the second section transposed . . . into the tonic, as in almost all movements of symphonies, quartets, and sonatas."

51. Marx, *Lehre,* II, 5, and III, 568. On organicism in Marx's theories, see Kurt-Erich Eicke, *Der Streit zwischen Adolph Bernhard Marx und Gottfried Wilhelm Fink um die Kompositionslehre* (Regensburg: Gustav Bosse, 1966), pp. 56–65; Lotte Thaler, *Organische Form in der Musiktheorie des 19. und beginnenden 20. Jahrhunderts* (Munich: Emil Katzbichler, 1984); and Gudrun Henneberg, *Idee und Begriff des musikalischen Kunstwerks im Spiegel des deutschsprachigen Schrifttums der ersten Hälfte des 19. Jahrhunderts* (Tutzing: Hans Schneider, 1983).

52. Ratner argues that Marx's approach is essentially retrospective in its inclusion of music from previous generations, most notably Haydn and Mozart: "Theories of Form: Some Changing Perspectives," in *Haydn Studies: Proceedings of the International Haydn Conference, Washington, D.C., 1975,* ed. Jens Peter Larsen, Howard Serwer, and James Webster (New York: Norton, 1981), p. 347. But while Marx did expand the range of repertoire upon which the pedagogy of form was based, his self-avowed standard was the music of Beethoven, and his fundamental goal remained the teaching of form rather than its historical elucidation.

53. Marx, *Lehre,* III, "Die Sonatenform," pp. 212–246; "Nähere Erörterung der Sonatenform," pp. 247–291.

A Closer Examination of Sonata Form

In the previous section, it was important to provide an introduction to the under-standing of this form in the most direct manner possible. The importance of this form will become increasingly clear the farther we progress. But at this rapid pace, it was impossible to achieve a fully satisfactory understanding; and it would have been contrary to the fundamental principle of a course of true artistic instruction had we been more interested in conveying exhaustive insight rather than in leading the student once again along the shortest path to the road of learning and creation. (It is in this respect that a course of artistic instruction is fundamentally different from a purely or predominantly scientific one.) For this reason, we adhered almost exclusively to a single model that could be applied in different ways.

We must now turn our attention to a closer examination of (and at the same time, the evidence available in) the works of the masters. In this manner, the preliminary fundamentals discussed earlier will be related to the works of others.[Understanding and capability will thus ripen simultaneously, without being separated from one another; the former will not become abstract knowledge, deathly as it is dead; while the latter will not degenerate into an act of merely empirical imitation (which con-stantly raises the threat of one-sidedness and mannerism).[54]]

In an appendix to the third volume of his *Lehre* (pp. 568–570), Marx once again emphasizes the didactic nature of sonata form's basic pattern (the *Grundform*). Here as elsewhere, Marx was keenly aware of the potential abuse of his pedagogically motivated codification, and he explicitly deni-grates the empty schematization of which he himself is so often accused.[55]

It could perhaps be argued that the greater quantity of detail in Marx's writings qualitatively alters the nature of his discussion. Marx's account is more thorough than those by any of his predecessors, to be sure, but his treatment represents a logical continuation and expansion of ideas that can be traced back through Birnbach and Reicha to Koch and to some extent even to Riepel. The schematization of sonata form was already well under way by the end of the eighteenth century, and it continued throughout the nineteenth. The repertoire considered paradigmatic for aspiring composers

54. Ibid., III, 247.

55. Marx's theoretical writings are in need of a thorough reevaluation more sympathetic than that available in Birgitte Moyer's "Concepts of Musical Form in the Nineteenth Century, with Special Reference to A. B. Marx and Sonata Form" (Ph.D. diss., Stanford, 1969). Partial reconsiderations are offered by Dahlhaus, "Gefühlsästhetik und musikalische Formenlehre"; idem, "Ästhetische Prämissen der 'Sonatenform' bei Adolf Bernhard Marx," *AfMw*, 41 (1984), 73–85; Ian Bent, *Analysis* (New York: Norton, 1987); idem, "An-alytical Thinking in the First Half of the Nineteenth Century," in *Modern Musical Scholar-ship*, ed. Edward Olleson (Stocksfield, Northumberland: Oriel Press, 1978), pp. 151–166; and Scott Burnham, "Aesthetics, Theory, and History in the Works of A. B. Marx" (Ph.D. diss., Brandeis University, 1988).

changed over the course of time, as might be expected, keeping pace with contemporary developments in style, but the function of these essentially didactic accounts did not.

The reputed dichotomy between eighteenth-century harmonic and nineteenth-century thematic views of sonata form has thus tended to distort the terms of recent debate surrounding Classical sonata form. Largely in reaction against demonstrably anachronistic models from the nineteenth century, recent scholarship has tended to emphasize what Classical sonata form is *not*. In effect, it is our twentieth-century reactions to nineteenth-century ideas that for the most part have dictated the focus of how we read eighteenth-century theory.

2. *The tendency to suppress the significance of elements other than harmony that do in fact figure prominently in eighteenth-century accounts of sonata form.* In the process of (rightly) debunking the myth of thematic contrast in Classical sonata form, Ratner and others have exaggerated the contrasts between eighteenth- and nineteenth-century theories of the form. Almost all recent accounts of Classical sonata form have focused the debate about the role of thematic materials primarily on the exposition. Even Bathia Churgin, who has argued eloquently that the "specialization of thematic functions" was "a cardinal feature of Classic sonata form," concentrates almost entirely on the exposition in her single most important essay on the form.[56] Here again, it is the focal point of nineteenth-century interests—the contrast first presented within the exposition—that has shaped the manner in which scholars have interpreted eighteenth-century repertoire and theory.

If we consider other elements of sonata form beyond the exposition, it becomes clear that eighteenth-century theorists themselves took a much broader view of the role of thematic material in the construction of movement-length form. The moment of recapitulation, for example, is almost always described in terms of both thematic material and tonality. According to Galeazzi,

however remote the Modulation is from the main key of the composition, it must draw closer little by little, until the Reprise, that is, the first Motive of Part One in the proper natural key in which it was originally written, falls in quite naturally and regularly. If the piece is a long one, the true Motive in the principal key is taken up once again, as it has been said, but if one does not want to make the composition too long, then it shall be enough to repeat instead the Characteristic Passage

56. Bathia Churgin, "Francesco Galeazzi's Description (1796) of Sonata Form," *JAMS*, 21 (1968), 182.

[Galeazzi's term for what would later come to be known as the "second theme"] transposed to the same fundamental key.[57]

In his *Scuola della musica* of 1800, Carlo Gervasoni seems to take the simultaneous return of the tonic and the opening theme for granted in the first movement of a sonata. He mentions the event twice in passing, and his tone strongly suggests that he assumes the reader's familiarity with this phenomenon.[58] Johann Gottlieb Portmann, who makes no particular mention of thematic ideas in what would eventually come to be designated as the exposition and the development sections of a sonata-form movement, similarly cites the simultaneous return of the opening theme and the tonic at the beginning of the recapitulation:

In the second half, I begin to modulate by making any number of deviations . . . This [major dominant] then brings me back to D major, the tonic, in which I repeat the opening theme [*Thema*], which I allow to be heard together with my other melodic ideas and turns previously presented in the secondary key. I stay [in the tonic] and close in it.[59]

It is clear from the context that "das Thema" here is not just any theme, but the movement's opening idea, its *Hauptsatz*.[60]

At various points in his *Versuch,* Koch also discusses this juncture in terms of both harmonic and thematic content. The "third period," that is, the recapitulation, "begins generally . . . with the opening theme once again, in the main key."[61] This "last period of our first allegro, which is devoted primarily to the main key, usually begins with the opening theme once again in this [tonic] key, but occasionally may also begin with another main

57. Galeazzi, *Elementi*, II, 258–259. Translation from Churgin, "Francesco Galeazzi's Description," pp. 195–196.

58. Gervasoni, *La scuola della musica*, I, 467–468.

59. Portmann, *Leichtes Lehrbuch*, p. 50.

60. See also the entry under "Hauptsatz" in Johann Georg Sulzer's *Allgemeine Theorie der schönen Künste*, 2nd ed., 4 vols. (Leipzig: Weidmann, 1792–1794; rpt. Hildesheim: Olms, 1967): "The *Hauptsatz* is generally called the theme"; Koch, *Musikalisches Lexikon*, "Hauptsatz"; and Johann Joachim Quantz, *Versuch einer Anweisung, die Flöte traversiere zu spielen* (Berlin: J. F. Voss, 1752), p. 115. There is a particularly striking confirmation of this interpretation of Portmann's account in the autograph score of Haydn's String Quartet Op. 54, No. 1, where at m. 126 of the first movement, over a diminished seventh chord in the three lower voices, the composer notes simply "T[h]ema" on the first violin's line. See Lewis Lockwood's remarks on this passage in *The String Quartets of Haydn, Mozart, and Beethoven: Studies of the Autograph Manuscripts,* ed. Christoph Wolff (Cambridge, Mass.: Harvard University Department of Music, 1980), p. 117. On the relationship between *Hauptsatz* and *Thema*, see also below, pp. 94–95, 99–100.

61. Koch, *Versuch*, II, 224.

melodic idea."[62] Koch also notes that the third period "begins in the main key, and usually with the opening theme. After the repetition of the theme, a few melodic sections from the first half of the first period are . . . presented in a different connection."[63]

Even Kollmann's "plan of modulation," quoted earlier, incorporates a considerable amount of material on the movement's thematic components. In the second edition (1812) of his *Essay on Practical Musical Composition* ("With Considerable Additions and Improvements"), Kollmann clarifies his earlier use of the term "elaboration" by juxtaposing it with a new concept, that of the "proposition." The "proposition" to be "elaborated" is the equivalent of what Koch would have called the *Hauptsatz*. It comprises the "first subsection of a piece," and its function is "to fix, and impress on the hearer, the key, mode, and character of the piece."

The *second* subsection begins, as it were, to enlarge upon the first proposition, in the *nearest* points of view; which is what I call the first sort of elaboration . . . The *third* subsection, or first part of the second section, enlarges upon the first proposition in all those more or less *distant* points of view, which the nature of the piece admits of, and the fancy of a judicious composer may suggest. It is therefore the place where real digressions to other related and foreign keys, are most at home; and comprehends what I call the second sort of elaboration . . . The *fourth* subsection once more resumes the first proposition, and still enlarges upon it in such *nearest* points of view, as are opposite to those of the second subsection; which is what I call the third sort of elaboration.[64]

The "resumption" of "the first proposition" is Kollmann's way of describing a return to the movement's opening theme at the moment of recapitulation. His concept of form, as Ian Bent points out, represents a mixture of both thematic and harmonic elements.[65]

By Ratner's definition, this tonic reiteration of the initial theme at the onset of the recapitulation is not an essential element of the form, and none of the theorists cited above in fact prescribes such a return. But Gervasoni, Portmann, and Kollmann offer no other alternative, and Koch and Galeazzi explicitly note the conventionality of this procedure. From the standpoint of defining the form, Ratner is absolutely correct in stating that "while a strong return to the tonic at the *beginning* of the recapitulation has dramatic force, it is not essential to the harmonic unity of the form . . . A play on the idea of return, both harmonically and melodically, can be made without

62. Ibid., III, 311.
63. Ibid., III, 420.
64. Kollmann, *An Essay on Practical Musical Composition,* 2nd ed. (London: Author, 1812), p. 3.
65. Bent, "Analytical Thinking," pp. 152–154.

prejudice to the overall plan."[66] From the standpoint of explaining the thematic conventions of this form, however, this approach conveys little or no sense of which techniques were typical and which were not.

Ratner's interpretation of these theoretical accounts is worth considering in some detail, for his treatment of Classical sonata form has exerted enormous influence on more than a generation of scholars, and rightly so. No one has played a greater role in overturning anachronistic nineteenth-century conceptions of eighteenth-century form. [But his readings of contemporary theorists are strongly colored by his broader efforts to define the form according to its essentials—that is to say, according to its large-scale tonal organization.]

There is an impressive body of evidence to support this predominantly harmonic view of form; yet there is compelling testimony from the period to suggest that this perspective by itself is too limited. Ratner has little to say about Galeazzi's detailed account of thematic events within a sonata-form movement, nor does he explain why this author's account of sonata form should appear under the rubric of "On Melody in Particular, and on its Parts, Sections, and Rules."[67] And while Ratner deals with the accounts of Portmann and Kollmann at some length, he does not specifically address their accounts of the thematic identity of the moment of recapitulation. Similarly, he attaches only limited importance to Koch's observations on what constitutes typical practice at the moment of recapitulation. Ratner ignores two of the three passages by Koch quoted above, and in his most recent discussion of the third mixes paraphrase with translation in such a way as to alter its meaning. Koch's original ("Der letzte Periode unsers ersten Allegro . . . fängt am gewöhnlichsten wieder mit dem Thema, zuweilen aber auch mit einem andern melodischen Haupttheile in dieser Tonart an") becomes "The recapitulation . . . 'begins with the opening theme or another important melodic figure' . . ."[68] In this rendering, the phrases "am gewöhnlichsten" ("usually") and "zuweilen aber auch" ("but on occasion also") are omitted. [What results is a choice between two types of melodic material at the moment of recapitulation: (1) the opening theme; or (2) any subsequent material deemed "important." In Ratner's version, the implicit likelihood of a composer's choosing one or the other is more or less equal. But "zuweilen aber auch" represents a fairly strong contradiction. The correct English equivalent is not "sometimes A, sometimes B"

---

66. Ratner, *Classic Music*, p. 229. Emphasis in the original.

67. Galeazzi, *Elementi*, II, pt. 5, sec. 2, article 3.

68. Ratner, *Classic Music*, p. 229. In his earlier "Harmonic Aspects of Classic Form" (1949), p. 162, Ratner quotes the first of these two passages only in the original German but omits the word *aber* in *zuweilen aber auch*.

but rather "most commonly A, but occasionally B."[69] In Ratner's account of this passage, the relative normality of beginning the recapitulation with the opening theme is suppressed.]

The importance of a correct rendering here goes beyond this single instance, for Ratner's interpretation is symptomatic of a wider tendency to identify harmonic essentials at the expense of thematic conventions. From the standpoint of defining the form, Ratner is certainly correct to point out that "this option indicates that the recapitulation was, for Koch, fundamentally a harmonic matter."[70] But in the passage just cited, Koch is in fact describing typical practice, not defining sonata form. The great majority of recapitulations from the last third of the century, particularly in first movements, do begin with a simultaneous reiteration of the opening theme and the tonic. And every major theorist of the time who addresses the issue of what we now call sonata form describes this important juncture in terms of both its tonality and its thematic content. Even Riepel calls attention to the return of the opening theme at the onset of what we now call the recapitulation, and he includes such a return within the extended musical example illustrating his discussion.[71]

Ratner does concede a degree of significance to thematic elements within large-scale constructs, and he attempts to integrate the thematic interpretation of sonata form into a harmonic framework. The tonal plan, to quote in full his metaphor cited earlier, "establishes a two-phase basis into which the three-phase thematic superstructure is interlocked."[72] But the value of viewing form from the perspective of thematic events is ultimately disparaged, for such an approach "does not account for the unique rhetorical elements of the classic style that enabled sonata form to attain its breadth and organic unity." Because of its flexibility, the harmonic, two-part interpretation of sonata form is considered "dynamic," while the thematic three-part view is implicitly deprecated as "static," for it is concerned with "identifying and placing themes."[73] Yet eighteenth-century writers are in fact concerned with the identity and placement of themes, even if the focus of their concerns is somewhat different from that of their nineteenth-century counterparts. If one disregards the chimera of long-range thematic con-

---

69. Newman's and Baker's translations both give more accurate renditions of this passage. Newman, in *Sonata in the Classic Era*, p. 34, is careful to specify that for Koch, "Thema" in this context denotes the opening theme of the movement. See also above, n. 60.

70. Ratner, "Harmonic Aspects" (1949), p. 162.

71. Riepel, *Anfangsgründe . . . Grundregeln zur Tonordnung*, pp. 72–74.

72. Ratner, *Classic Music*, p. 221. See also Wolf, "Sonata Form": "The basis for sonata form is the open modulatory plan of binary form."

73. Ratner, *Classic Music*, p. 220.

trast—and it is one of Ratner's many achievements to have disposed of this particular myth—one must somehow account for the fact that contemporary writers did indeed incorporate thematic elements into their discussions of form.

3. *A strong reliance upon evidence from pedagogical treatises.* The recent image of a harmonic framework and a thematic superstructure to explain eighteenth-century accounts of sonata form holds a certain attraction, for it accommodates both harmonic and thematic elements. But it is derived largely from accounts that are essentially didactic in function and thus necessarily restricted in scope. And while pedagogy and analysis have traditionally gone hand-in-hand, both before and after the eighteenth century, there is a fundamental difference between the goals and methods of these two functions. How one teaches a concept, as Marx had been at some pains to point out, is often quite different from how one actually views that concept. The analytical approach is essentially descriptive ("a circle is the locus of all points equidistant from a given point"), while the didactic approach is essentially prescriptive ("to construct a circle, rotate a compass with one arm fixed until the other arm has returned to its starting point").[74] This distinction has important implications for how we read eighteenth-century sources.

Early in the second volume of his *Versuch,* Koch explicitly notes the limitations of the pedagogical perspective and the consequent potential for misunderstanding:

I now want to . . . attempt to show the aspiring composer how a piece of music must arise within the mind of a creating composer, if the piece is to achieve the intention of art.

At the very beginning of the Introduction to Part One [in volume one], I promised to draw a line of distinction between harmony and melody, and to answer—in such a way that the decision could set one's mind at ease—the well-known controversy as to whether harmony or melody takes precedence, whether a piece of music can be reduced ultimately to melody or to harmony. I do not know how some of my readers . . . can have got it into their heads that I intended to give it as my opinion there that it must be harmony which first arises in the mind of the composer in the formation of a piece of music . . .

. . . Neither melody nor harmony can constitute the initial substance of a piece of music. Each carries characteristic features of something which must be presupposed to precede both of them, and this is the . . . key . . . This quantity of all the musical notes determined by one tonic note constitutes the true primary material of a work of music; that is, it constitutes that from which all the sections of the entire

74. See Herbert A. Simon, "The Architecture of Complexity," *Proceedings of the American Philosophical Society,* 106 (1962), 479.

work are formed. If this material, these notes, are made audible in succession, then the material has been used melodically; but if some of the notes that constitute this material are made audible simultaneously, then the material has been used harmonically.

Seen in this manner, the issue, it seems to me, can be pursued no further from the material point of view. For neither melody nor harmony can constitute the final level of reduction of a piece of music. The two derive precisely from one and the same substance; this substance is simply treated differently in melody than in harmony.

From this it is clear that it could not possibly have been my intention to have stated . . . that the composer in the act of creation should think primarily of harmony.[75]

Koch's remarks, as he himself notes, reflect the perennial eighteenth-century debate over the primacy of harmony or melody in music, and his response is one that had already been suggested by such earlier writers as Mattheson, Scheibe, and Mizler.[76] Less obviously, Koch's remarks are also a reflection of contemporary compositional pedagogy. Like so many other theorists of his time, Koch had begun his work with a discussion of harmony. In the five years between the publication of volumes one and two of his treatise, however, he sensed that there had been a mistaken perception of his earlier comments on the role of harmony in the compositional process. He realized, in retrospect, that it was necessary to distinguish between his own pedagogical approach—presenting the fundamentals of harmony first—and the act of composition itself. Koch's comments thus foreshadow those of Marx quoted earlier: the methodological constraints of pedagogy should not be confused with the act of artistic creation or, by extension, with analysis, which can be seen in large measure as an attempt to understand not only the products but also the process of artistic creation.

That at least some didactic treatises of the eighteenth century should structure their discussions of sonata form around a movement's harmonic plan does not necessarily mean that composers or listeners perceived form to be an essentially harmonic phenomenon, or that our present-day interpretations should view form primarily in these terms. From a pedagogical point of view, harmony had long been considered an essentially mechanical matter and therefore eminently teachable. Indeed, throughout the eighteenth century, a strong tradition linked the teaching of composition to the

75. Koch, *Versuch,* II, 47–50. Translation adapted in part from Ian Bent, "The 'Compositional Process' in Music Theory, 1713–1850," *Music Analysis,* 3 (1984), 29–30. Bent's essay includes further comments on portions of this passage.

76. See Mattheson, *Capellmeister,* pp. 133–134; Johann Adolph Scheibe, *Critischer Musikus,* 2nd ed. (Leipzig: B. C. Breitkopf, 1745), p. 204; Lorenz Mizler, *Neu eröffnete musikalische Bibliothek,* 2 (1743), pt. 1, pp. 64–65.

realization of figured bass. This practice is reflected in the titles of such important treatises as Heinichen's *Generalbass in der Composition* (Dresden, 1728), Sorge's *Vorgemach der musikalischen Komposition, oder . . . Anweisung zum General-Bass* (Lobenstein, 1745–1747), and Kirnberger's *Grundsätze des Generalbasses als erste Linien zur Composition* (Berlin, 1781).[77] Johann Sebastian Bach, according to his son Carl Philipp Emanuel, routinely began instruction in composition with the fundamentals of figured bass.[78]

Melody, by contrast, was not only more variable from piece to piece but also pedagogically more elusive. It was considered to be the product of creative genius, a phenomenon that could not be described so readily in words. Even while conceding that "melody has no less expressive force than harmony," Jean-Philippe Rameau, the most influential writer on harmony in the eighteenth century, insisted that "giving rules" for the writing of melody was "almost impossible, since good taste plays a greater part in this than anything else."[79] This helps explain both the scarcity of contemporary treatises on melody and the corresponding abundance of manuals on harmony.

As the lowest common denominator among sonata-form movements, large-scale harmonic structure is an entirely appropriate starting point for pedagogical discussions of movement-length forms. Riepel, Portmann, Kollmann, and Gervasoni all present modulatory schemes that can serve as points of departure for the aspiring composer's own works. Gervasoni, for example, urges students to study the compositions of established composers and to note the "disposition of the themes" as well as the "progression of the modulations," and to use these as norms for the "construction of a composer's first sonatas, weaving into them a new melody entirely of one's own devising."[80] The technique of preserving the large-scale harmony of an existing work and creating new themes to fit within this pattern is recommended by numerous pedagogues of the eighteenth and early nineteenth centuries.

The rise of a more specific pedagogy of abstract forms, *Formenlehre*, on the other hand, was closely associated with the rise of *Melodielehre*, as Carl Dahlhaus has pointed out.[81] The first important pedagogical treatise on mel-

77. On the close relationship between compositional pedagogy and figured bass, see Peter Benary, *Die deutsche Kompositionslehre des 18. Jahrhunderts* (Leipzig: Breitkopf & Härtel, 1961), pp. 49–54, 61–68.

78. See *Bach-Dokumente III: Dokumente zum Nachwirken Johann Sebastian Bachs, 1750–1800*, ed. Hans-Joachim Schulze (Kassel: Bärenreiter, 1972), p. 289.

79. Rameau, *Traité de l'harmonie* (Paris: Ballard, 1722), p. 142; translation from Philip Gossett's edition, *Treatise on Harmony* (New York: Dover, 1971), p. 155.

80. Gervasoni, *La scuola della musica*, I, 469–470.

81. See Dahlhaus, "Zur Theorie der musikalischen Form," 20–37.

ody, Mattheson's *Kern melodischer Wissenschaft* (1737) offers the earliest extended account of large-scale form.[82] Important changes in musical style were creating the need for a new *Satzlehre:* the shorter-phrased melodies of the mid-century style demanded novel approaches to the construction of individual melodies and their subsequent concatenation into movement-length forms.[83] In contrast to the more numerous treatises on harmony and thorough bass, it is primarily the *Melodielehren* of the eighteenth century that address the issue of movement-length form, albeit with varying degrees of detail and success.[84]

Koch's *Versuch,* written some fifty years after Mattheson's *Kern melodischer Wissenschaft,* incorporates the most detailed account of melody in the entire eighteenth century. By no small coincidence, it also provides one of the two most detailed contemporary accounts of Classical sonata form. The other extended description of the form, by Galeazzi, likewise appears within a discussion of melody.[85] Other accounts equating melody with formal structure will be considered in detail in Chapter 2; for the moment, it is important to note that while accounts of harmony are common, those dealing with melody are relatively rare. Galeazzi, for one, seems rather amazed that no one before him had addressed the role of melody in composition:

We have in fact a vast quantity of authors who have written with varying degrees of success on the subject of harmony, but there is not a single one, so far as I know, who has dealt with the principal element of modern music, that is, melody. I have made an attempt along this new path, and I must ask forgiveness of my readers if I have had to create new vocabulary, hitherto unused in music . . .[86]

Anton Reicha voices similar sentiments in his *Traité de mélodie* of 1814. Music rests on "two columns of equal grandeur and importance, melody and harmony; yet in spite of the many treatises on harmony published over the past several centuries, there is not a single one on melody."[87]

---

82. Mattheson's discussion of form in this treatise will be examined in detail in Chapter 2.

83. The emergence of *Formenlehre* as distinguished from *Satzlehre* is discussed by Arnold Feil, "Satztechnische Fragen in den Kompositionslehren von F. E. Niedt, J. Riepel und H. Chr. Koch" (Ph.D. diss., Heidelberg, 1955).

84. For a survey of these eighteenth-century treatises, see Guido Kähler, "Studien zur Entstehung der Formenlehre in der Musiktheorie des 18. und 19. Jahrhunderts (von W. C. Printz bis A. B. Marx)" (Ph.D. diss., Heidelberg, 1958). See also George J. Buelow, "The Concept of 'Melodielehre': A Key to Classic Style," *Mozart-Jahrbuch 1978/79,* pp. 182–195.

85. See above, p. 43.

86. Galeazzi, *Elementi,* II, xvii.

87. Reicha, *Traité de mélodie* (Paris: Author, 1814), p. i. It follows that in his discussion of sonata form, Reicha, too, takes note of the importance of thematic events, including the normality of a simultaneous return of the opening theme and the tonic at the moment of recapitulation (p. 48).

Neither Galeazzi nor Reicha was the first to address the issue of melody, of course, but their belief that they were the first to do so reflects a broader reality: that treatises on melody in the eighteenth and early nineteenth centuries lack the kind of pedagogical tradition found in comparable works devoted to harmony, thoroughbass, and counterpoint.[88] The small number of *Melodielehren* is also symptomatic of yet another contemporary attitude: that melody is the province of genius and not of pedagogy.

Throughout the Classical era, form was more closely associated with melody than with harmony; this is a point that will be considered in much greater detail in Chapter 2. Melody, with rare exceptions, was not an object of sustained pedagogical attention in the eighteenth century. In attempting to reconstruct eighteenth-century concepts of sonata form, we must remember that the teaching of form was necessarily based on that which could be taught. And against a pedagogical tradition strongly rooted in the theory of harmony and the "unteachability" of melody, the importance of such references to thematic events in pedagogical accounts of specific forms should not be underestimated.

In the introduction to his *Allgemeine Geschichte der Musik*, Johann Nikolaus Forkel neatly summarizes the inherently problematical relationship between pedagogy and practice, harmony and melody:

In good musical composition, harmony and melody are as inseparable as the truth of ideas and the correctness of expression are in language. Language is the garb of ideas, just as melody is the garb of harmony. In this respect, one can call harmony a logic of music, for harmony stands in approximately the same relationship to melody as does logic, in language, to expression . . . Clearly, correct thinking is a prerequisite to learning the correct expression of an idea. And in just this way, experience has truly taught us that no clean, correct, and flowing melody is possible without prior knowledge of harmony. All skilled teachers of composition—of which there are admittedly only very few—have sensed this, on the basis of experience, and they have advised their pupils not to attempt any melodic expression of musical ideas before they have sufficiently sharpened their feeling for the truth and correctness of harmony through knowledge of the same. In the meantime, both [harmony and melody] must be bound inseparably. They mutually elucidate each other, and while no one is capable of providing rules for the crafting of a good, cohesive melody, without deriving such rules from the nature of harmony—just as no teacher of language can provide rules for good and correct expression without resorting to the art of correct thinking—no harmonic progression, on the other hand, can be good if it is not at the same time melodic. Dry harmony without melodic connection is like a logic that lacks linguistic expressions.[89]

88. See Lars Ulrich Abraham and Carl Dahlhaus, *Melodielehre* (Cologne: Hans Gerig, 1972), p. 16.

89. Forkel, *Allgemeine Geschichte der Musik*, 2 vols. (Leipzig: Schwickert, 1788–1801), I, 24.

Forkel's image of music as a language, as will be seen in Chapter 2, provides the basis for a more historically accurate metaphor of form. Ratner's image of a harmonic framework and thematic superstructure, by contrast, establishes a false dichotomy, for it is based on pedagogical methods that eighteenth-century theorists themselves recognized to be heavily weighted toward the more teachable of the two elements. And while pedagogical manuals remain an invaluable source for reconstructing concepts of form, we should interpret these sources within a broader context that can also accommodate more aesthetically oriented perspectives. Thus, even though Mattheson, Riepel, and Koch all emphasize the use of small-scale dance forms (especially the minuet) in teaching composition, all three ultimately deprecate the aesthetic value of such forms.[90] Pedagogically, it makes good sense to begin by emphasizing those qualities of periodicity that all forms have in common. This is the context of Riepel's assertion that a minuet differs from a symphony or a concerto only in the "working out"*(Ausführung)* of its basic ideas. Riepel's approach is a pedagogically sound effort to boost the confidence of the beginner, one that emphasizes the commonality of different forms: the distinctions between metrically regular, small-scale movements like the minuet and metrically irregular, large-scale movements like a symphonic allegro, after all, can be taught later—or, as is more likely the case, can be learned through the careful study of paradigmatic compositions.

But Riepel's approach is not, by extension, a sound basis for theory and analysis, at least not by itself. A sonata-form movement can indeed be viewed as an "expanded Classical phrase," to use Rosen's formulation; yet so can many other conventional movement-length patterns. As we have seen, there is clearly more to the structure of an extended movement than the expansion of a phrase.

4. *The failure to provide the basis for a broader concept of form.* Even if one were to accept the premise that "large-scale Classic form" is indeed "fundamentally harmonic in its structure,"[91] this lowest-common-denominator approach still leaves open the question of how to deal with any number of other specific forms. If the basis of Classical sonata form lies in its harmonic plan, we must look for different parameters of form to account for such structural conventions as the rondo, the fantasia, the fugue, or the theme and variations. Harmony *is* in fact the lowest common denominator among

90. Mattheson, *Capellmeister*, p. 224; Riepel, *Anfangsgründe . . . De rhythmopoeïa*, p. 1; Koch, *Versuch*, III, 155. See also Johann Samuel Petri, *Anleitung zur praktischen Musik*, 2nd ed. (Leipzig: J. G. I. Breitkopf, 1782; rpt. Giebing: Emil Katzbichler, 1969), p. 266.
91. Leonard Ratner, "Key Definition: A Structural Issue in Beethoven's Music," *JAMS*, 23 (1970), 472.

sonata-form movements; but it does not necessarily follow that harmony therefore constitutes the basis for all forms. No one would deny that a set of variations on a theme is a particular type of form, yet it would be difficult to define this convention in any meaningful way as a harmonic construct, particularly at the level of a complete movement. In the effort to define Classical sonata form, scholars have too often lost sight of what the term "form" itself means.

5. *The imposition of an anachronistic dichotomy between "inner" and "outer" form.* Ratner's original model, it should be emphasized, was never intended to represent anything more than a lowest common denominator for Classical sonata form. As he himself points out, its level of detail is not really great enough to tell us very much about formal detail.[92] And this is the crux of the problem: the potential applications of a harmonic schema in analysis are limited. Such an outline can help delineate general proportions, and no adequate analysis can ignore the relative weight of the various sections that constitute a complete movement. But beyond this rather broad consideration, the schematization of these various sections seldom illuminates issues on a more local level. The identification of large formal units is an essential element of description, yet it fails to address important questions of detail. For this reason, the harmonic concept of sonata form, with its I - V :|: X - I schema, necessarily entails a conformational approach to large-scale form: the schema is used as a basis of comparison with the work at hand. The problem, as noted before, lies not so much in the legitimacy of deriving abstract formal types from a large body of works as in the fact that the application of these schemas to specific pieces seldom offers any true insights. Analytically, such a model can serve as little more than a heuristic device, a "bridge," to use Carl Dahlhaus's image, "that one dismantles as soon as one has succeeded in making the transition" from describing general formal elements to describing the individuality of the work at hand.[93]

This tendency to dismiss the external conventions of form is due not so much to the nature of any one particular pattern as to prevailing attitudes toward the idea of convention itself. There has long been an attitude of implicit disdain in musical scholarship toward the study of convention.[94] Most writers have preferred to focus instead on the qualities of novelty and innovation, attributes of more immediate and obvious interest. Conformity is too often taken to be a foil that is of importance only for the irregularities against which it can be compared. And while this predisposition is gradu-

92. Ratner, *Classic Music,* p. 219.
93. Dahlhaus, "Zur Theorie der musikalischen Form," p. 21.
94. See Janet M. Levy, "Covert and Casual Values in Recent Writings about Music," *Journal of Musicology,* 5 (1987), 3–27, esp. 23–27.

ally beginning to wane,[95] the traditional prejudice against convention has tended to inhibit efforts to come to terms with what at any given time are the common and widespread practices of the day. More than twenty-five years ago, Jan LaRue cited the need "to list in one place the statistically predominant formal types or variants occurring in sonata movements. What is the commonest intermediate form between polythematic binary and fully differentiated sonata form? What are the favorite tonalities for contrasting episodes in rondos?"[96] The need remains today.

The prejudice against convention is subtle but pervasive. For Ratner, "each composer could work within the familiar and accepted [harmonic] framework and modify [it] to express his unique personal message."[97] The "unique personal message" is implicitly that which makes a work aesthetically distinctive and appealing. Even for Dahlhaus, musical form in the late eighteenth and early nineteenth centuries is a "dialectic between the general and the specific, between a tonally based framework and individualized melodic ideas."[98]

An aesthetic distinction between the general and the specific is not yet evident in earlier accounts of form. It is not only the theory of sonata form that has changed since the late eighteenth century, but our fundamental outlook toward the nature and purpose of form in general. To think of conventional forms as diagrammable models based on lowest common denominators inevitably leads us toward an essentially conformational perspective that perpetuates the aesthetic dichotomy between "inner" and "outer" form. To ignore the conventions of large-scale structures like sonata form, on the other hand, is to ignore the reality of the musical repertoire. The conceptual metaphor of the musical work as an oration, as we shall see, offers an alternative that more nearly reflects the eighteenth century's approach to the paradox of musical form.

---

95. Recent writings that use the concept of convention to good advantage include Tilden Russell's essay on Beethoven's scherzos, "On 'looking over a ha-ha'," *MQ*, 71 (1985), 27–37; Jürgen Neubacher's monograph on movement-endings in Haydn's music, *Finis coronat opus: Untersuchungen zur Technik der Schlussgestaltung in der Instrumentalmusik Joseph Haydns* (Tutzing: Hans Schneider, 1986); Harold S. Powers's essay on Verdi's arias, "'La solita forma' and 'The Uses of Convention'," *Acta musicologica*, 59 (1987), 65–90; Anatoly Leikin, "The Dissolution of Sonata Structure in Romantic Piano Music (1820–1850)" (Ph.D. diss., U.C.L.A., 1986); and Jeffrey Kallberg, "The Rhetoric of Genre: Chopin's Nocturne in G Minor," *19th-Century Music*, 11 (1988), 238–261.

96. LaRue, review of *The Sonata in the Classic Era* by William S. Newman, *MQ*, 50 (1964), 405. Even LaRue himself appears to have reversed his opinion on the need for such surveys; see above, p. 25.

97. Ratner, *Classic Music*, p. 208.

98. Carl Dahlhaus, *Klassische und romantische Musikästhetik* (Laaber: Laaber-Verlag, 1988), p. 12.

CHAPTER 2

Rhetoric and the Concept of Musical Form in the Eighteenth Century

Rhetoric is not a term that is today ordinarily associated with the concept of movement-length form. Yet in his *Musikalisches Lexikon* of 1802, Heinrich Christoph Koch relates the two quite closely:

Rhetoric. This is the name given by some teachers of music to that body of knowledge belonging to composition by which individual melodic sections are united into a whole, according to a definite purpose. Through grammar, the material contents of artistic expressions are made correct; rhetoric, by contrast, determines the rules by which the artistic expressions within a particular work are concatenated, according to the end to be achieved. Although a great deal about rhetoric may be found scattered here and there in writings on music, and in writings devoted to the fine arts in general, it has nevertheless not yet been the fortune of the human spirit to bring these writings together in a systematic order and thereby fill those gaps that continue to exist. For this reason, the composer must in the meantime attempt to gather what fragments are available and substitute a sensitive artistic feeling for the lack of coherence in these writings.[1]

Far from representing an idiosyncratic, isolated view of either rhetoric or form—the manner in which "individual melodic sections are united into a whole"—Koch's definition is but one of many witnesses to a long tradition that associates the two. It is part of an important line of thought that includes virtually every major writer of the eighteenth century who addresses the broader conceptual issues of large-scale form. The instrumental work was seen as a wordless oration, and its form was viewed not so much as a harmonic or thematic plan but as an ordered succession of thoughts. In the interests of intelligibility, these musical ideas—an amalgam of melodic, harmonic, and rhythmic elements—tended to be arranged within a limited number of conventional patterns.

1. Koch, *Musikalisches Lexikon,* "Rhetorik."

The rhetorical concept of form continued well into the nineteenth century and was by no means limited solely to didactic treatises. It extended to the aesthetics of music, in writings directed not only toward the aspiring composer but toward the informed listener as well. The successive ordering of a work's individual sections was seen as a function of the manner in which the composer could effectively present a series of ideas to his audience and thereby elicit an intended emotional response.

Koch was nevertheless correct to note that contemporary writings on rhetoric in music, although plentiful, were widely scattered. With the possible exception of Forkel, no one theorist of the eighteenth century dealt with this issue comprehensively or systematically, and even Forkel's account represents only an outline of his wide-ranging ideas. At the same time, few writers who dealt with issues of movement-length form were completely silent on the matter. References to rhetoric typically appear within the context of other topics, such as periodicity, the compositional process, the aesthetic doctrine of "unity in variety," the nature of melody, or the relationship between genius and convention. Accordingly, the account that follows is arranged neither chronologically nor by author; instead, it approaches the rhetorical concept of form from some of the more important perspectives used by eighteenth-century writers themselves: the manner in which contemporary aestheticians viewed the relationship between rhetoric and the arts in general; the perceived parallels between verbal language and instrumental music; the distinction between musical grammar and musical rhetoric; the identity of the "melodic sections" that combine to make a whole; and the nature of the "end" to be achieved by the composer.

Rhetoric and the Pragmatic Orientation of Eighteenth-Century Aesthetics

Both the generative and conformational approaches to analysis tend to focus on the work itself. In so doing, they overlook a perspective basic to virtually all eighteenth-century analyses of specific works of music: that of the audience. The predominant critical orientation of all the arts in the eighteenth century, as M. H. Abrams points out in his influential study of early English Romantic literature, assigned a central role to the intended recipient of a work. The arts, including music, were considered a means toward an end, and that end was to elicit an emotional response in the beholder. Abrams labels this critical orientation "pragmatic" on the grounds that it considers art to be "an instrument for getting something done." This view, as Abrams observes, has its origins in classical antiquity and has "characterized by far the greatest part of criticism from the time of Horace through the eighteenth century. Measured either by its duration or the number of its adherents, . . . the pragmatic view, broadly conceived, has been the principal aesthetic attitude of the Western world."[2]

This orientation toward the audience distinguishes the pragmatic view of art from the later "expressive" theories that are more characteristic of Romanticism. Wordsworth, in an oft-cited phrase, considered poetry to be "the spontaneous overflow of powerful feelings."[3] In the expressive orientation, the recipient of these feelings plays a far smaller role in the aesthetic equation.

Some degree of self-expression is inherent in most Western art, at least since the Renaissance, and few artists have failed to take their anticipated audience into account to at least some extent, even if only to reject that audience as a factor in the shaping of a work.[4] The spectrum that lies between the extremes of the pragmatic and expressive orientations consists largely of gray. The concepts do, however, provide useful points of reference by which to gauge critical outlooks and make broad comparisons between contrasting eras. In this respect, there are clear distinctions between the relationship of audience to composer in 1750 and that in 1850.[5]

2. Abrams, *The Mirror and the Lamp: Romantic Theory and the Critical Tradition* (New York: Oxford University Press, 1953), pp. 15, 20–21. In some respects, the pragmatic orientation actually intensified over the course of the eighteenth century. See Gordon McKenzie, *Critical Responsiveness: A Study of the Psychological Current in Later Eighteenth-Century Criticism* (Berkeley and Los Angeles: University of California Press, 1949); P. W. K. Stone, *The Art of Poetry, 1750–1820: Theories of Poetic Composition and Style in the Late Neo-Classic and Early Romantic Periods* (London: Routledge and Kegan Paul, 1967); and Klaus Dockhorn, "Die Rhetorik als Quelle des vorromantischen Irrationalismus in der Literatur-und Geistesgeschichte," in his *Macht und Wirkung der Rhetorik* (Bad Homburg: Gehlen, 1968), pp. 46–95.

3. Abrams, *Mirror and the Lamp*, p. 21.

4. Wayne C. Booth, in *The Rhetoric of Fiction*, 2nd ed. (Chicago: University of Chicago Press, 1983), traces the continuation of pragmatic elements in literature beyond the eighteenth century and into the twentieth. On the rise of "self-expression" in music, see Hans Heinrich Eggebrecht, "Das Ausdrucks-Prinzip im musikalischen Sturm und Drang," *DVjs*, 29 (1955), 323–349; and Ludwig Finscher, "Das Originalgenie und die Tradition: Zur Rolle der Tradition in der Entstehungsgeschichte des Wiener klassischen Stils," in *Studien zur Tradition in der Musik: Kurt von Fischer zum 60. Geburtstag,* ed. Hans Heinrich Eggebrecht, Max Lütolf (Munich: Katzbichler, 1973), pp. 165–175.

5. Both Bellamy Hosler, in *Changing Aesthetic Views of Instrumental Music in 18th-Century Germany* (Ann Arbor: UMI Research Press, 1981), pp. xiv–xix, and John Neubauer, in *The Emancipation of Music from Language*, pp. 5–7, raise valid objections to the wholesale applicability of Abrams's concepts to eighteenth-century instrumental music, but in both instances the objections revolve around distinctions between the expressive orientation and a third outlook, the "mimetic." Pragmatic and mimetic views do share many features, but the essential element of the former—a predominant orientation toward the audience—is not necessarily to be associated with the latter. As Hosler herself points out, early Romantic writers on music like Tieck, Wackenroder, and E. T. A. Hoffmann all devote considerable attention to the effect of music upon the listener. The key issue is whether these effects are seen as an end in themselves, as in the pragmatic theory, or as a by-product, so to speak, of the artist's outpourings, as in the expressive theory.

This change manifests itself in a number of ways. The enormous growth of musical criticism and analysis in the early nineteenth century occurred in large part as a response to the growing desire of audiences to understand an ever more demanding repertoire. An essay along the lines of Schumann's review of Berlioz's *Symphonie fantastique,* advocating and elucidating a difficult work to a potentially skeptical public, would have been as unthinkable in the eighteenth century as the *Symphonie fantastique* itself, a work whose original title ("Episode in the Life of an Artist") had announced the composer/artist himself to be its focal point.

The social status of the composer also changed fundamentally between 1750 and 1850. Throughout most of the eighteenth century, the composer was generally seen as a craftsman; but by the middle of the nineteenth, the most esteemed composers were perceived (and on occasion idolized) as independent artists. The standard format of the printed opera libretto reflects this change with special clarity. If the composer of an opera in the mid-eighteenth century was identified at all, it was almost always in very small type, often not even on the title page. By the mid-nineteenth century, the composer enjoyed undisputed top billing.

Exceptions to these very broad generalizations abound in both centuries, of course, and in reality, the shift from the pragmatic to the expressive outlook was quite gradual. Haydn's celebrated remark to his biographer Griesinger about working conditions at Esterháza contains elements of both perspectives:

> My Prince was satisfied with all of my works and I received applause. As the director of an orchestra, I could make experiments, observe what elicited or weakened an impression, and thus correct, add, delete, take risks. I was cut off from the world, no one in my vicinity could cause me to doubt myself or pester me, and so I had to become original.[6]

From an expressive standpoint, Haydn implies that any composer, given the proper material support and left to his own devices, would be in a position to "become original." The image of the artist as an independent genius was an increasingly important concept in the second half of the eighteenth century, and by the middle of the nineteenth, it would become a *sine qua non.*[7] Equally noteworthy in Haydn's statement is his open acknowledgment of the crucial role played by the listener: "Ich konnte . . . beobachten, was den Eindruck hervorbringt und was ihn schwächt, also verbessern, zusetzen, wegschneiden, wagen." Haydn's formulation is sig-

---

6. Georg August Griesinger, *Biographische Notizen über Joseph Haydn,* ed. Karl-Heinz Köhler (Leipzig: Philipp Reclam, 1975; 1st ed. 1810), p. 28.

7. See Edward E. Lowinsky, "Musical Genius: Evolution and Origins of a Concept," *MQ,* 50 (1964), 321–340, 476–495.

nificant: later generations would interpret these comments in terms of artistic self-expression, but the composer himself was more concerned with what would "elicit" or "weaken" an impression in the minds and spirits of the audience he envisioned for the work at hand. The concept of *Eindruck* is central to the pragmatic outlook. Koch defines *Eindruck* as "one of the more common words used to designate the effect that a work of music has upon our spirits when we hear it performed."[8] On another occasion, Koch even uses the same verb as Haydn (*hervorbringen,* to elicit), emphasizing once again the process by which an impression is evoked in an audience: "Through the use of this word [*Eindruck*], one often means, in general, that the performance or the act of hearing a piece of music has either elicited a certain effect from us, or has left a certain echo of this effect in us."[9] Vernon Gotwals's widely used translation ("I could . . . observe what enhanced an effect, and what weakened it")[10] focuses on the work itself and does not convey the composer's concern for his anticipated audience. The critical orientation of Gotwals's translation, in other words, is expressive rather than pragmatic. The difference is a subtle one, but it is important if we are to reconstruct eighteenth-century attitudes toward the nature and function of musical form.

The pragmatic orientation is reflected even more directly in other accounts relating Haydn's views on his own music. According to Griesinger, the composer considered the commission for a purely instrumental setting of Christ's Seven Last Words to be "one of the most difficult challenges" of his career, for it required him to write "seven adagios, all in a row, that would not tire the listener and that would awaken in him all the sentiments inherent in each of the words spoken by the dying Saviour."[11] Again, the formulation is significant: Haydn saw his task not so much in terms of expressing the sentiments themselves as in terms of arousing the sensation of these sentiments within his anticipated audience. In a lighter vein, the famous drum-stroke in the slow movement of the Symphony No. 94 represents perhaps the best known manifestation of Haydn's pragmatic orientation. The composer, by his own account, had intended to "surprise the public with something new."[12] To some extent, this attitude is self-expressive in its own right; but on a more fundamental level, the surprise drum-stroke was inspired by Haydn's anticipation of the effect this device would have upon his audience.

8. Koch, *Musikalisches Lexikon,* "Eindruck."

9. Koch, *Kurzgefasstes Handwörterbuch der Musik,* "Eindruck."

10. Gotwals, ed. and trans., *Joseph Haydn: Eighteenth-Century Gentleman and Genius* (Madison: University of Wisconsin Press, 1963), p. 17.

11. Griesinger, *Biographische Notizen,* pp. 32–33.

12. Ibid., p. 45.

Mozart maintained a similar attitude toward his listeners. Writing to his father from Paris in 1778, the young composer described his calculated manipulation of an audience's expectations for the premiere of a new symphony (K. 297):

The symphony began . . . and just in the middle of the first Allegro there was a passage which I felt sure must please. The audience was quite carried away—and there was a tremendous burst of applause. But as I knew, when I wrote it, what effect it would surely produce, I introduced the passage again at the close—at which point there were shouts of "Da capo." The Andante also found favor, but particularly the last Allegro, because, having observed that all last as well as first Allegros begin here with all the instruments playing together and generally unisono, I began mine with two violins only, piano for the first eight bars—followed instantly by a forte; the audience, as I expected, said "hush" at the soft beginning, and when they heard the forte, began at once to clap with their hands.[13]

Like Haydn, Mozart was able to appeal to the less musically literate while simultaneously providing the *cognoscenti* with a wealth of innovations. His oft-quoted comment about the Piano Concertos K. 413–415 offers valuable insight into the composer's belief that an audience could be simultaneously charmed and challenged:

These concertos are a happy medium between what is too easy and too difficult; they are very brilliant, pleasing to the ear, and natural, without being vapid. There are passages here and there from which the connoisseurs alone can derive satisfaction; but these passages are written in such a way that the less learned cannot fail to be pleased, though without knowing why.[14]

Beethoven's attitude toward his audiences is more difficult to decipher. The popular image of his utter disregard for his contemporaries is largely without foundation, as is the notion that the majority of contemporary listeners found his music too difficult to comprehend.[15] The late works are an exception, of course, for they clearly placed unusual demands upon audiences. Yet it is in the favorable reviews of these late works that we see the clearest manifestations of a relatively new attitude, one that places the responsibility for understanding a work of art on the listener rather than on the composer. As in E. T. A. Hoffmann's celebrated review and analysis of the Fifth Symphony, one senses that it is now the audience's obligation to educate itself, to extend its aesthetic sensibilities, and to come to terms with the composer and his work.

13. Letter of 3 July 1778 to his father; translation adapted from Emily Anderson's edition, *The Letters of Mozart and His Family,* rev. ed. (New York: Norton, 1985), p. 558.

14. Letter of 28 December 1782 to his father; ibid., p. 833.

15. On the latter point, see especially Robin Wallace, *Beethoven's Critics: Aesthetic Dilemmas and Resolutions During the Composer's Lifetime* (Cambridge: Cambridge University Press, 1986).

This expressive, work-oriented perspective provides the aesthetic context for most analysis today. The pragmatic orientation, by contrast, with its emphasis on the composer's responsibility to make a work intelligible, has not been nearly so conducive to analysis. And in point of fact, analyses of specific works were quite rare up until approximately 1800. This is not to say that a pragmatically oriented framework is inhospitable to analysis; instead, we must reconsider the nature of this framework and its implications for understanding eighteenth-century attitudes toward analysis.

In its decided orientation toward the audience, the eighteenth century's aesthetic outlook was most often discussed in terms of rhetoric. Just as it was the goal of rhetoric to persuade the audience, so it was the goal of music to move the listener. Rhetoric was perceived as an instrument of persuasion, and so, too, in its own way, was music. Johann Joseph Klein, in his *Versuch eines Lehrbuchs der praktischen Musik* of 1783, sums up an attitude reflected over and over again by eighteenth-century theorists: "Rhetoric and poetics are so closely related to the art of music that anyone wishing to study music seriously cannot afford to remain ignorant of them. All of these arts work toward a common goal: to master our feelings, and to give our passions a certain direction."[16]

In our own time, rhetoric is a term that is used pejoratively more often than not. Yet its much longer tradition as one of the seven liberal arts has been of far greater historical consequence, not only in the fields of law and politics, but in the arts as well.[17] Rhetoric has long been associated with poetics—so much so, in fact, that the two remained virtually inseparable for many centuries.[18] It was only logical, as a result, that rhetoric should be closely allied to the emerging concept of aesthetics in the mid-eighteenth century. Johann Georg Sulzer, in his influential and widely quoted encyclopedia of the fine arts, first published in 1771–1774, points to the central role of rhetorical eloquence for the fine arts in general:

Eloquence. According to the general concept of the fine arts on which this entire work [his *Allgemeine Theorie der schönen Künste*] is based, the fine arts, through their works, make lasting impressions upon the spirit of man that elevate the powers of the soul. Eloquence, in the broadest sense, seems capable of fulfilling this stipulation. Eloquence perhaps does not create such spiritually penetrating or lively impressions as those arts whose true immediate goal is the stimulation of the exter-

---

16. Klein, *Versuch eines Lehrbuchs der praktischen Musik* (Gera: C. F. Bekmann, 1783), p. 15.

17. The best and most recent survey of the history of rhetoric and its influence on a wide variety of fields is Brian Vickers's *In Defence of Rhetoric* (Oxford: Oxford University Press, 1988).

18. See Brian Vickers, "Rhetoric and Poetics," in *The Cambridge History of Renaissance Philosophy,* ed. Charles B. Schmitt (Cambridge: Cambridge University Press, 1988), pp. 715–745.

nal senses; on the other hand, it can awaken every possible variety of those clear images that are beyond the scope of the more sensuous arts. This art [eloquence] therefore deserves to be considered with the greatest attention, in its true nature, in its origins and effects, in its manifold applications, and in the various external transformations it has sustained.[19]

Sulzer's view is typical of his time, for the leading aestheticians of the eighteenth century consistently equated rhetoric with poetics.[20] Alexander Gottlieb Baumgarten, for one, stressed the importance of "aesthetic persuasion," and Georg Friedrich Meier considered "rhetoric, in the broadest sense," to be "an undeniable element of aesthetics."[21] Large portions of the latter's treatise on aesthetics, in fact, read very much like a treatise on rhetoric. According to Meier, all aesthetic objects, to varying degrees, exhibit a basic outline consisting of an *Eingang* ("exordium, introitus"), a *Vortrag der Hauptvorstellung* ("thesis, thema, propositio per eminentiam"), an *Abhandlung* ("tractatio"), and a *Beschluss* ("conclusio, peroratio"). These are the "general laws by which thoughts, in all aesthetic elaborations, must be ordered."[22] The only real distinction between aesthetics, on the one hand, and rhetoric and poetics, on the other, rests on the specificity of their respective applications: "[But] as there are so many different kinds of aesthetic elaboration—prosaic and poetic, theatrical, epic, etc.—it therefore cannot be denied that these laws, in their particular applications, should be subject to various additions and limitations. These investigations, however, belong to rhetoric and poetics."[23]

The art of rhetoric, first codified in classical antiquity, was renewed with special vigor in eighteenth-century Germany. The works of Johann Christoph Gottsched, in particular, exerted enormous influence and inspired numerous imitators.[24] His most important work on rhetoric, the

19. Sulzer, *Allgemeine Theorie,* "Beredsamkeit."
20. See Wolfgang Bender, "Rhetorische Tradition und Ästhetik im 18. Jahrhundert," *Zeitschrift für deutsche Philologie,* 99 (1980), 481–506; Uwe Möller, *Rhetorische Überlieferung und Dichtungstheorie im frühen 18. Jahrhundert: Studien zu Gottsched, Breitinger und G. Fr. Meier* (Munich: W. Fink, 1983); Gerd Ueding and Bernd Steinbrink, *Grundriss der Rhetorik: Geschichte, Technik, Methode* (Stuttgart: J. B. Metzler, 1986), p. 138 ("Für das 18. Jahrhundert gilt noch . . . die Einheit von Rhetorik und Poetik"); Robert S. Leventhal, "Semiotic Interpretation and Rhetoric in the German Enlightenment, 1740–1760," *DVjs,* 60 (1986), 223–248.
21. Baumgarten, *Aesthetica,* 2 vols. (Frankfurt/Oder: I. C. Kleyb, 1750–1758; rpt. Hildesheim: Olms, 1970), II, 569–624; Meier, *Anfangsgründe aller schönen Wissenschaften,* 3 vols. (Halle: C. H. Hemmerde, 1748–1750), III, 341 ("Diese Redekunst im weitern Verstande ist unleugbar ein Theil der Aesthetik"). See also Johann Gotthelf Lindner, *Kurzer Inbegriff der Aesthetik, Redekunst und Dichtkunst,* 2 vols. (Königsberg and Leipzig, 1771; rpt. Frankfurt/Main: Athenäum, 1971).
22. Meier, *Anfangsgründe,* III, 293–332.
23. Ibid., III, 332.
24. See Eric A. Blackall, *The Emergence of German as a Literary Language, 1700–1775*

Ausführliche Redekunst, first published in 1736, went through many editions over the course of the century. By 1754, Gottsched felt obliged to begin his more modest *Vorübung der Beredsamkeit* with an apology for yet another work on a subject in an already crowded field.[25]

Nor was interest in rhetoric limited to northern Germany or to academicians. Leopold Mozart used Gottsched's *Deutsche Sprachkunst* (1748) in preparing his violin tutor and eventually requested a copy of each of the writer's major works, including the *Versuch einer critischen Dichtkunst* and the *Ausführliche Redekunst.*[26] And Gottsched's writings, in general, are known to have enjoyed wide distribution throughout southern areas of the German-speaking realm.[27]

Among German music theorists and aestheticians in particular, this renewed interest in rhetoric gave fresh impetus to the reexamination of an old idea: that music is a language.

Music as a Language

The idea of music as a rhetorical art rests on the metaphor of music as a language. While this image can be traced back to classical antiquity and appeared commonly throughout the Middle Ages and the Renaissance, it began to take on new importance in the sixteenth and early seventeenth centuries with the concept of *musica poetica.* In describing how the composer, the *musicus poeticus,* could create a work of music, theorists including Nicolaus Listenius, Gallus Dressler, Joachim Burmeister, and Johannes Lippius all drew upon the analogy of the orator manipulating verbal language in order to create a persuasive presentation of ideas.[28]

(Cambridge: Cambridge University Press, 1959), esp. chs. 4 and 5. John A. McCarthy, in his *Crossing Boundaries: A Theory and History of Essay Writing in German, 1680–1815* (Philadelphia: University of Pennsylvania Press, 1989), emphasizes the role of rhetoric in prose writing, especially the essay. A slightly later renewal of interest in rhetoric is also evident in Great Britain in the works of Hugh Blair, George Campbell, James Beattie, and others; see James Engell, *Forming the Critical Mind: Dryden to Coleridge* (Cambridge, Mass.: Harvard University Press, 1989), pp. 194–219.

25. Gottsched, *Vorübung der Beredsamkeit* (Leipzig: B. C. Breitkopf, 1754), p. i.

26. See Leopold Mozart's letters of 9 June and 28 August 1755 to his publisher in Augsburg, Johann Jakob Lotter.

27. See Roswitha Strommer, "Die Rezeption der englischen Literatur im Lebensumkreis und zur Zeit Joseph Haydns," in *Joseph Haydn und die Literatur seiner Zeit,* ed. Herbert Zeman (Eisenstadt: Institut für österreichische Kulturgeschichte, 1976), pp. 125–126.

28. See Carl Dahlhaus, "Musica poetica und musikalische Poesie," *AfMw,* 23 (1966), 110–124; Claude Palisca, "Ut oratoria musica: The Rhetorical Basis of Musical Mannerism," in F. W. Robinson and S. G. Nichols, eds., *The Meaning of Mannerism* (Hanover, N.H.: University Press of New England, 1973), pp. 37–65; Benito Rivera, *German Music*

This image continued throughout the seventeenth century in the writings of theorists like Mersenne and Kircher, particularly in relation to vocal music. But it was not until the mid- to late eighteenth century that the idea of music as a language in its own right, independent of any text, began to find widespread acceptance. Once established, this metaphor would remain a commonplace until well into the nineteenth century.[29] And, in certain respects, it is still with us today.[30]

Throughout the eighteenth century, the issue of whether music actually constituted a language revolved around the question of whether or not instrumental music was capable of expressing any kind of meaning. There was no question about the capacity of vocal music to convey specific ideas: thanks to the text, the purpose and meaning of the music could be made evident. The notes, in effect, served to amplify and illuminate the words. But instrumental music posed a more difficult problem. How could wordless music express any particular meaning? And how was a listener to make sense of it all? Gottsched's view of the matter is representative of his generation: "Music alone, unassociated with words, lacks a soul and is incomprehensible; words must speak for it if one would know what it is that music intends to say."[31] In a similar vein, the celebrated question attributed to Fontenelle—"Sonate, que me veux-tu?"—found enormous resonance throughout the continent for many decades.[32]

Other critics held that instrumental music did have its own expressive power, but attributed this quality to the notion that instrumental music was essentially an imitation of vocal music. Writing on the symphony in 1785, La Cepède, a contemporary of Mozart, maintained that

---

Theory in the Early 17th Century: The Treatises of Johannes Lippius (Ann Arbor: UMI Research Press, 1980).

29. The most comprehensive review of this *topos* is Fritz Reckow's "'Sprachähnlichkeit' der Musik als terminologisches Problem: Zur Geschichte des Topos Tonsprache" (Habilitationsschrift, Freiburg i.B., 1977), which unfortunately has yet to be published but which is summarized in his 1979 entry on "Tonsprache" in Hans Heinrich Eggebrecht's *Handwörterbuch der musikalischen Terminologie* (Wiesbaden: Steiner, 1972–). George Buelow's article "Rhetoric and Music" in the *New Grove* provides a useful introduction to the subject and a selective bibliography. Brian Vickers, in his essay "Figures of Rhetoric/Figures of Music?" *Rhetorica*, 2 (1984), 1–44, offers an overview of the secondary literature in the field from the perspective of a historian of rhetoric. For a broad review of the musico-rhetorical tradition in a variety of cultures, see Harold S. Powers, "Language Models and Musical Analysis," *Ethnomusicology*, 24 (1980), 1–60.

30. As reflected, for example, by the titles of such works as Olivier Messiaen's *Technique de mon langage musicale* (1944), Deryck Cooke's *The Language of Music* (1959), and Donald Mitchell's *The Language of Modern Music* (1963).

31. Johann Christoph Gottsched, *Auszug aus des Herrn Batteux Schönen Künsten* (Leipzig: B. C. Breitkopf, 1754), p. 207.

32. See Maria Rika Maniates, "'Sonate, que me veux-tu?': The Enigma of French Musical Aesthetics in the 18th Century," *Current Musicology*, no. 9 (1969), 117–140.

the musician will compose each of these three movements specifically as though he were writing a grand aria in which one or more voices were trying to express emotions that are more or less vivid: he will substitute for these voices the first violin, or other instruments that are easily distinguished; from time to time he will seek to imitate the inflections of the human voice by means of instruments capable of sweet or pathetic inflections.[33]

Christian Friedrich Daniel Schubart, writing in Germany at approximately the same time, shared this attitude, commenting that "all instruments are but imitations of the voice."[34] And to a certain extent, even Koch expressed variations on this same idea, noting that an instrumental concerto could be viewed as an imitation of an aria, and that a symphony was comparable to a full chorus.[35]

But Koch's views on instrumental music went far beyond this simple analogy, as we shall see, and increasingly throughout the century, critics came to concede that instrumental music was indeed capable of conveying meaning of at least some kind. Even Fontenelle's compatriot *philosophes,* whose opposition to the notion of meaningful instrumental music was especially strong, eventually conceded, if only grudgingly, that a textless work could embody meaning, however vague that meaning might remain at times. D'Alembert, who argued that vocal music was superior to instrumental music on the grounds that the latter was "a language without vowels," tacitly acknowledged that instrumental music was a language nevertheless.[36] Diderot, too, eventually concluded that "after all, even if one does not speak as distinctly with an instrument as with the mouth, and even if musical sounds do not portray one's thoughts as clearly as discourse, they nevertheless do say something."[37]

Composers, on the whole, accepted the image of music as a language still more readily. Mattheson, in his *Der vollkommene Capellmeister* of 1739, calls a work of music a "Klang-Rede," an oration in sounds.[38] Quantz, writing in 1752, declares music to be "nothing other than an artificial language by which one makes one's musical thoughts known to the listener."[39] Scheibe,

33. Bernard Germain, Comte de La Cepède, *La poëtique de la musique,* 2 vols. (Paris: Imprimerie de Monsieur, 1785), II, 331.

34. Schubart, *Ideen zu einer Ästhetik der Tonkunst* (Vienna: J. V. Degen, 1806; rpt. Hildesheim: Olms, 1969), p. 335. Schubart originally wrote his treatise in 1784–1785.

35. Koch, *Musikalisches Lexikon,* articles "Concert," "Symphonie."

36. Jean Lerond d'Alembert, "Fragment sur la musique en général et sur la notre en particulier" (ca. 1752), in his *Oeuvres et correspondances inédites,* ed. Charles Henry (Paris: Garnier frères, 1887; rpt. Geneva: Slatkine, 1967), pp. 182–184.

37. Denis Diderot, "Lettre sur les sourds et muets," in his *Oeuvres complètes,* 20 vols., ed. J. Assézat (Paris: Garnier frères, 1875–1877), I, 358.

38. Mattheson, *Capellmeister,* p. 180 and passim. Mattheson's idea of the *Klangrede* will be discussed in detail below.

39. Quantz, *Versuch einer Anweisung,* p. 102.

Riepel, Blainville, Vogler, and numerous other writers would repeat this metaphor throughout the remainder of the century.[40]

Functionally, a good deal of instrumental music throughout the seventeenth and eighteenth centuries did in fact serve as a replacement for vocal music. A large repertoire of diverse genres, including the ricercar, canzona, sonata da chiesa, and concerto grosso, had developed in part as instrumental substitutions or supplements for elements of the liturgy, especially in Mass and Vespers. Mozart's "Epistle" Sonatas, for example, are believed to have functioned in place of the reading of the epistle.[41] And as Neal Zaslaw has demonstrated, a number of early symphonies by Haydn and Mozart, particularly those with slow opening movements, also played a role within the liturgy, either replacing or supplementing spoken texts.[42] The original instrumental version of Haydn's *Seven Last Words of Christ,* each of whose movements opens with a wordless "setting" of Christ's final utterances, is a late example of this tradition. By virtue of their function, then, such works served to varying degrees as an "*ersatz* for the art of rhetoric."[43]

In Germany, the *redendes Prinzip*—the "speaking" or "oratorical" principle in music—enjoyed special favor during the middle decades of the century and further strengthened the perception of music as a language.[44] Specifically within the realm of instrumental music, Vogler made a categorical distinction between dance and military music, on the one hand, and "speaking music, the sovereign mistress of our hearts," on the other.[45] The notion that instrumental music must "speak" in order to be effective is particularly evident in the works of Carl Philipp Emanuel Bach. A reviewer in Leipzig's *Allgemeine musikalische Zeitung* summed up an attitude shared by many of

40. Scheibe, *Critischer Musikus* (1745), pp. 86–87, 91; Riepel, *Anfangsgründe . . . Grundregeln zur Tonordnung,* pp. 76–77, 99, 104; Charles-Henri Blainville, *L'esprit de l'art musical* (Geneva: n.p., 1754), p. 86; Georg Joseph Vogler, *Betrachtungen der Mannheimer Tonschule,* 1 (1778), 286–287, 311; idem, *Zwei und dreissig Präludien für die Orgel und für das Fortepiano. Nebst einer Zergliederung in ästhetischer, rhetorischer und harmonischer Hinsicht* (Munich: Falter, 1806), pp. 37, 47. See Reckow, "'Sprachähnlichkeit'," for numerous further citations to this *topos.*

41. See Stephen Bonta, "The Uses of the Sonata da Chiesa," *JAMS,* 22 (1969), 54–84.

42. Zaslaw, "Mozart, Haydn, and the *Sinfonia da chiesa,*" *Journal of Musicology,* 1 (1982), 95–124.

43. Wilibald Gurlitt, "Musik und Rhetorik: Hinweise auf ihre geschichtliche Grundlageneinheit," in his *Musikgeschichte und Gegenwart,* ed. Hans Heinrich Eggebrecht, 2 vols. (Wiesbaden: Franz Steiner, 1966), I, 64.

44. Arnold Schering, "Carl Philipp Emanuel Bach und das 'redende Prinzip' in der Musik," *Jahrbuch der Musikbibliothek Peters für 1938,* pp. 13–29. See also Helmut Rösing, "Musik als Klangrede. Die französische Nachahmungsästhetik und ihre Auswirkungen bis hin zur musique concrete," *Musicologica Austriaca,* 1 (1977), 108–120.

45. Vogler, *Betrachtungen,* I, 287.

the composer's contemporaries in calling him "another Klopstock," but one who used "notes *instead* of words."[46]

The perception of a "speaking" quality in C. P. E. Bach's instrumental music is further reinforced by such openly programmatic works as his trio-sonata representing a "Dialogue between a *Sanguineus* and a *Melancholicus.*" In the preface to this wordless discourse between two violins, Bach writes that he has tried "to express as much as possible with instruments something for which one could more easily use the singing voice and words."[47] These rhetorical tendencies in C. P. E. Bach's music derive in part from the influence of the composer's father—Johann Sebastian Bach's knowledge of rhetoric and his applications of its principles in his music have been well documented[48]—but they need not be seen merely as a relic of previous generations. C. P. E. Bach's fundamental attitude toward music as a language is characteristic of the *empfindsamer Stil* in general and altogether typical of many composers in the second half of the eighteenth century. In addition to programmatic works by other composers (for example, Dittersdorf's symphonies on Ovid's *Metamorphoses* and Haydn's trilogy of early symphonies depicting morning, noon, and night), one also finds programmatic analyses of instrumental works (for example, a fantasia by C. P. E. Bach interpreted as the celebrated monologue from *Hamlet*)[49] as well as instrumental recitatives (for example, in Haydn's String Quartet Op. 17, No. 5, and the Symphony No. 7, "Le midi"). Haydn, late in his life, is said to have revealed that one of his early symphonies—the composer could no longer recall which one—depicted a dialogue between God and a frivolous sinner.[50] And the contemporary *topos* of the string quartet as a conversation among four rational individuals adds still further credence to the concept of

46. [Johann Karl Friedrich] Triest, "Bemerkungen über die Ausbildung der Tonkunst in Deutschland im achtzehnten Jahrhundert," *AMZ*, 3 (1801), cols. 300–301.

47. C. P. E. Bach, "Vorbericht" to *Zwey Trio* (Nürnberg, 1751), quoted from the partial facsimile edition of Wq. 161/1 by Klaus Hofmann (Neuhausen-Stuttgart: Hänssler, 1980), p. 8.

48. See, for example, Birnbaum's report on Bach in Scheibe's *Critischer Musikus*, p. 997; Ursula Kirkendale, "The Source of Bach's Musical Offering: The *Institutio oratoria* of Quintilian," *JAMS*, 23 (1980), 99–141; and Arno Forchert, "Bach und die Tradition der Rhetorik," in *Alte Musik als ästhetische Gegenwart. Bericht über den internationalen musikwissenschaftlichen Kongress, Stuttgart, 1985*, 2 vols. (Kassel: Bärenreiter, 1987), I, 169–178.

49. This and other programmatic interpretations of seemingly nonprogrammatic works will be discussed in more detail in Chapter 4.

50. Albert Christoph Dies, *Biographische Nachrichten von Joseph Haydn*, ed. Horst Seeger (Berlin: Henschel, 1962; 1st ed. 1810), p. 131; Griesinger, *Biographische Notizen*, p. 80. Hartmut Krones believes that the movement in question is the Recitative and Adagio of the Symphony No. 7; see Krones, "Rhetorik und rhetorische Symbolik in der Musik um 1800," *Musiktheorie*, 3 (1988), 122–123.

instrumental music as a language independent of words.[51] To varying degrees, all of these phenomena rest on the fundamental assumption that instrumental music is capable of "speaking" to the listener through the vehicle of a musical language.

The metaphor of music as a language was often tempered by the qualification that music was a language of sentiment, of the passions. Instrumental music, by its very nature, could not express specific, rational ideas; as such, it was perceived to be a rather vague language, capable of expressing only general emotions, such as fear, joy, rage, or sorrow. But a few writers, most notably Mattheson, Batteux, Rousseau, and Forkel, recognized this vagueness as a potential advantage for instrumental music rather than a liability. The expression of the passions was seen as a more elemental—and thus more "natural"—form of expression.

Mattheson, while maintaining the traditional view of the inherent superiority of vocal music over instrumental, nevertheless suggests that the true power of music lies in the notes themselves and not in any text to which they might be set:

If I hear a solemn symphony in church, a devout shudder comes over me; if a strong choir of instruments joins in, it arouses a great admiration in me; if the organ begins to roar and thunder, a divine fear grows in me; and if everything closes with a joyful Hallelujah, my heart jumps within my body, even if I do not know the meaning of this or any other word, be it due to the distance [from which I hear it] or for other reasons—indeed, even if there were no words at all, merely through the contribution of the instruments and the speaking sonorities.[52]

In his celebrated and influential *Les beaux arts réduits à un même principe* of 1746, Batteux, in turn, identifies three means by which man can express his ideas and feelings: word, tone, and gesture. The first of these is the most specific; but the latter two are in many respects the more powerful. Music and gesture, because they lie "closer to the heart," transcend the conventional languages of individual nationalities, and in this sense are superior to verbal language:

I have cited the word first because it possesses the highest rank and because it is ordinarily given the most attention. Nevertheless, the tones of the voice and gestures have many advantages over the word. Their use is more natural; we have recourse to them when words fail us. Moreover, they are a universal interpreter that can take us to the ends of the earth and render us intelligible to the most barbaric nations and even to animals. Finally, they are devoted to sentiment in a special man-

---

51. This image, often attributed to Goethe, is in fact part of a much older tradition that has been traced back as far as 1773. See Ludwig Finscher, *Studien zur Geschichte des Streichquartetts* (Kassel: Bärenreiter, 1974), pp. 285–289.

52. Mattheson, *Capellmeister,* pp. 208–209.

ner. The word instructs us, convinces us: it is the medium of reason. But tone and gesture are media of the heart; they move us, win us over, persuade us. The word expresses passions only by means of the ideas with which the sentiments are associated, as though a reflection of them. Tone and gesture reach the heart directly, without any detour.[53]

Rousseau, in his "Essai sur l'origine des langues," argues that the function of melody is not merely to imitate the passions—one of the dominant beliefs of the century—but also to "speak" in its own right:

Melody, in imitating the inflections of the voice, expresses laments, cries of pain or joy, threats, or groans; all the vocal significations of the passions are within its domain. It imitates the inflections of different languages, and the rise and fall caused in each idiom by certain movements of the soul. It does not merely imitate, it speaks; and its language—inarticulate but vivid, ardent, passionate—has a hundred times more energy than speech itself.[54]

Rousseau's views are based in part on the widely held assumption that music and language shared a common origin in earlier societies. Writers of the day never tired of reminding their readers that the two arts had been virtually indistinguishable in classical Greece. Rousseau's specific point here, however, is that melody, in the guise of inarticulate cries, preceded articulate language. As such, it is closer to the essence of human nature and therefore superior.

In the Introduction to his *Allgemeine Geschichte der Musik* of 1788, Johann Nikolaus Forkel makes a similar distinction between the musical language of sentiments and the verbal language of ideas. Music is

a universal language of sentiments . . . whose scope can be and in fact is as great as the scope of a developed language of ideas. In a language of ideas, the highest degree of development is manifested in an abundance of expressions for all possible thoughts and their concomitant relationships; in correctness and order in the concatenation of these thoughts with one another; and in the possibility of manipulating and using all these expressions according to the various ends and goals that an orator can bring to bear upon them. In just this manner, the language of notes must also have (1) an abundance of combinations among notes; (2) correctness and order in the concatenation of the same; and (3) a specific goal. These are the three chief characteristics of a true, good, and authentic music.[55]

Once again, an anecdote reported by one of Haydn's early biographers sums up a broader attitude of the times. When Haydn was planning his first

53. Charles Batteux, *Les beaux arts réduits à un même principe* (Paris: Durand, 1746), pp. 253–255.
54. Jean-Jacques Rousseau, "Essai sur l'origine des langues," in his *Écrits sur la musique* (Paris: Stock, 1979), p. 229.
55. Forkel, *Allgemeine Geschichte,* I, 19.

visit to England, he was nearing the age of sixty and had traveled very little in his life. Although warned by his friends about the hazards of travel, he would not be dissuaded from his trip. According to Dies, it was Mozart who finally pointed out to the elder composer: "You have had no training for the wide world, and you speak too few languages." "Oh!" Haydn is said to have replied, "my language is understood throughout the entire world."[56]

Regardless of the anecdote's authenticity, its very formulation reflects the broader belief of the Classical era that music—including even purely instrumental music—was a language. The myth of music as a "universal language" has of course long since been exposed, but the very recognition of instrumental music as a language in its own right is one of the most significant developments in musical thought over the course of the eighteenth century. The precise nature of this language was (and still is) a matter of ongoing debate, but by the end of the century there was no longer any question that its power could rival and in some respects even surpass the capacities of conventional, verbal language.

This gradual change laid the foundation for the rhetorical concept of form. For the parallels that were perceived to exist between music and language did not end with their common function: they extended to issues of form as well.

Musical Grammar and Musical Rhetoric

Within the conceptual metaphor of music as a language, eighteenth-century theorists and aestheticians recognized that the language of music had its own grammar and rhetoric. Much of the basic terminology used to describe music reflects the traditionally close historical association between the verbal and the musical arts. Meter, rhythm, cadence, period, theme, even composition: all of these terms are grammatical or rhetorical in origin.[57]

In both verbal and musical language, grammar encompasses the rules of composition, the manner in which a discourse can be constructed in a technically correct fashion. Rhetoric, on the other hand, cannot be codified nearly so precisely or categorized according to correct or incorrect procedures. A work can be considered rhetorically "correct" only to the extent that it is aesthetically persuasive: two listeners can easily disagree as to whether a particular oration has been persuasive or not. In spite of rhetoric's many precepts, the listener, in the end, is the only true arbiter.

56. Dies, *Biographische Nachrichten,* pp. 77–78.
57. For a more detailed discussion of terminological borrowings from rhetoric, see Gurlitt, "Musik und Rhetorik," p. 65.

Rhetoric, then, is at least in part an aesthetic category. Musical grammar, as Gotthilf Samuel Steinbart points out, can ensure the technical correctness of a work, but not its aesthetic value:

[One often] says of musical compositions that they are correct in their construction [*Satz*] if nothing appears in them that would be offensive to the ear or contrary to the rules of harmony, even if in such pieces there is often neither melody nor spirit. According to this point of view, the *Satz* is nothing other than that which grammar is in language. A person can speak clearly and correctly as far as grammar is concerned, and yet say nothing that is worthy of our attention.[58]

Friedrich Wilhelm Marpurg makes a similar distinction between rhetoric, which deals with the actual "application" *(Ausübung)* and "concatenation" *(Zusammensetzung)* of notes in the process of composition, and grammar, which in its turn explains the more mechanical "rules of rhetorical music."[59]

This distinction between the mechanical rules of grammar and the more aesthetic qualities of rhetoric recurs throughout the writings of eighteenth-century music theorists and aestheticians. It is also one of the main reasons why so few musical treatises of the Classical era deal with the question of how one can construct a movement-length work into the shape of an aesthetically satisfying whole. Other aspects of the art—notation, figured bass, harmony, counterpoint—lend themselves far more readily to distinctions between correct and incorrect practice. But insofar as treatises on these subjects present a body of more or less fixed rules, they are all essentially grammars of music. And while Koch is absolutely correct that "a great deal about rhetoric may be found scattered here and there in writings on music, and in writings devoted to the fine arts in general," he is equally correct in pointing out that there are no systematic treatments of musical rhetoric. Forkel's account, to be considered later in this chapter, comes closer to a systematic treatment of the subject than any other, but his presentation is only an outline and necessarily lacking in detail.

Koch was not the first to express disappointment at this lopsided state of affairs, in which the grammar of music was an object of countless treatises, while rhetoric garnered only scant notice. An anonymous review of Christian Kalkbrenner's *Theorie der Tonkunst* (1789) takes the author to task for not presenting more material on the rhetoric of music and concentrating

---

58. Steinbart, *Grundbegriffe zur Philosophie über den Geschmack. Erstes Heft, welches die allgemeine Theorie sämtlicher schönen Künste, und die besondere Theorie der Tonkunst enthält* (Züllichau: Waysenhaus- und Frommanische Buchhandlung, 1785), p. 192.

59. Marpurg, *Anfangsgründe der theoretischen Musik* (Leipzig: J. G. I. Breitkopf, 1757), p. 2. Similar distinctions between musical grammar and rhetoric may be found in August F. C. Kollmann, *A New Theory of Musical Harmony* (London: Author, 1806), p. i; idem, *An Essay on Practical Musical Composition*, 2nd ed., p. v; and other treatises, cited below.

instead on such issues as periodicity, the use of figures, and the distinction among various styles, topics already "known to every amateur who wishes to judge the art correctly."[60] Johann Adam Hiller had similarly noted several years before that

as valuable as mathematical, arithmetical, and systematic knowledges may be in and of themselves, it is nevertheless to be wished that less fuss be made about such things; and that one should not thrust so much of them upon music toward its putative illumination. For to conceive of notes as quantities; to represent their relations in lines and numbers; to wrap intervals, like a thread, into a ball—this is a far cry from that which is required to bring forth a good melody and clean harmony. It would be better to cultivate the rhetorical or aesthetic part of music more, and to cultivate it more diligently, just as capable men have already done with music's grammatical part.[61]

Stefano Arteaga voiced similar complaints in his *Le rivoluzioni del teatro musicale italiano* of the mid-1780s. Teachers feel satisfied with themselves if they have taught their pupils the basics of harmony and musical accompaniment, Arteaga points out; but this is really nothing more than "the grammar of music," which is "more concerned with not committing errors than with producing something truly beautiful." Such methods do not teach students "the rhetoric of the art."[62]

In France, François Arnaud had announced a treatise on the rhetoric of music as early as 1754, proposing to show that rhetoric could serve as a common ground between two factions: that majority of artists who considered composition to be a matter of instinct and habit and who never spoke of anything other than music's "grammatical part," and those *philosophes* concerned only with music's "proportions, combinations, and mysteries, in a word, its scientific part."[63]

But nothing would ever come of Arnaud's project, and d'Alembert later expressed regret that the proposal had remained unfulfilled. Such a treatise, as d'Alembert pointed out, was

greatly needed, as up to the present, one has written almost exclusively about the *mechanics* of this art, that is to say, about its *material* part. There has been almost nothing said regarding taste and expression that one could call *intellectual*. It seems

60. Anonymous, review of Kalkbrenner, *Theorie der Tonkunst* (Berlin: Hummel, 1789), *Musikalische Real-Zeitung,* 9 June 1790, col. 178.

61. Hiller, preface to Georg Friedrich Lingke's *Kurze Musiklehre* (Leipzig: J. G. I. Breitkopf, 1779), p. vii.

62. Arteaga, *Le rivoluzioni del teatro musicale italiano,* vol. 2 (Bologna: Carlo Trenti, 1785), p. 79.

63. Arnaud, "Lettre sur la Musique, à M. le Comte de Caylus" (1754), in Jean Benjamin de Laborde, *Essai sur la musique ancienne et moderne,* 4 vols. (Paris: Onfroy, 1780), III, 551.

to me that one could throw a good deal of light on this subject by considering music from the perspective of painting and eloquence, particularly poetic eloquence.[64]

This distinction between the mechanical and rhetorical elements of music brings us closer to the connections between rhetoric and form. Koch associates the "formal" elements of music with "the ability to create works of music"; an idea is "formal" in the sense that it deals with how a composer actually brings forth—forms or formulates—a work. This process, ultimately based on the act of *inventio (Erfindung)*, is the province of genius and cannot be taught.[65] The "material" elements of music, on the other hand, constitute "a science that can be taught and learned." In practice, this body of knowledge should be divided into two parts, grammar and rhetoric; but because the available writings on rhetoric are so fragmentary and diverse, rhetoric is most often treated in conjunction with grammar. There are, as Koch observes, virtually no works dealing specifically with that aspect of composition dependent upon genius, "unless one wishes to include works on aesthetics . . ."[66] Rhetoric, in this view, is a mediating element between the teachable and the unteachable, between the mechanical and the aesthetic.

In spite of its subordinate role, the importance of grammar as a basis for aesthetics should not be underestimated. Grammar provides a foundation for all the rhetorical arts: a work must be correct before it can be eloquent. In linguistic terms, grammar encompasses both morphology—the construction of individual words—and syntax, the arrangement of these individual words into the larger units of phrase and sentence. Syntax, in turn, is closely allied to the practice of punctuation, by which individual units of thought are set off and related to one another. Musical grammar, in the eyes of eighteenth-century theorists, follows this same pattern. It begins with individual notes and chords, which join to form small-scale units, which in turn combine to form units of ever-increasing size.

This concept of periodicity—small-scale units concatenated into increasingly larger ones—provides a key link between the grammar and rhetoric of both language and music. On the smallest scale, periodicity falls within the realm of syntax, for it is concerned with the construction of brief and relatively discrete units. On the largest scale, it merges into the broader idea of rhetoric, for it addresses the totality of an oration or movement, that is,

64. Jean Lerond d'Alembert, "Fragment sur l'opéra" (undated, probably from the late 1750s), in his *Oeuvres et correspondances inédites*, pp. 157–158.

65. Koch, *Musikalisches Lexikon*, "Komposition, Setzkunst." The eighteenth century's theory of the compositional process, dealing with the concepts of *inventio, dispositio,* and *elaboratio,* will be dealt with in more detail below.

66. ". . . or the musical novel Hildegard von Hohenthal" (ibid.). Heinse's novel provides a framework for a series of aesthetic discourses by its various characters.

the ordering and disposition of all the periods that together constitute the whole. Forkel makes this point in the introduction to his *Allgemeine Geschichte* of 1788:

In concatenating musical expressions into a coherent whole, one must attend to two points in particular: first, the connection of individual notes and chords into individual phrases, and second, the successive connection of multiple phrases . . . The precepts for joining individual notes and chords into individual phrases are part of musical grammar, just as the precepts for joining multiple individual phrases are a part of musical rhetoric.[67]

Forkel, along with other writers, suggests that grammar and rhetoric, although closely related, operate on different hierarchical levels and maintain their own distinct qualities. While grammar provides the essential building blocks of music, it is rhetoric that governs the large-scale concatenation of these units into a complete movement—or as Koch would put it, the manner in which "individual melodic sections are united into a whole."

Periodicity is treated in a variety of eighteenth-century sources, and while theorists almost inevitably disagree on matters of detail and terminology, there is consensus on several basic points.[68] All authors stress that a hierarchy of cadences articulates various degrees of rest within a melody: authentic cadences are generally reserved for the conclusion of a major section or an entire movement, while half, deceptive, and inconclusive cadences articulate closures of ever-decreasing strength and importance. Almost every writer makes some kind of comparison between this hierarchy of cadences and the conventions of verbal punctuation: the full, authentic cadence is the equivalent of a period; the half cadence is like a colon or semicolon; and weaker points of articulation are analogous to commas. There is, moreover, a consistent emphasis on the underlying need for such points of articulation. Without them, individual phrases would be indistinguishable from one another; a movement consisting of unintelligible phrases would be unintelligible as a whole. And the ease with which a work's ideas can be comprehended by the listener is one of the most important qualities in any rhetorical art. The effective expression of ideas and the concomitant arousal of sentiments both rest upon the ability of the orator or composer to articulate the constituent elements of their respective arguments.

Saint-Lambert's *Principes du clavecin* of 1702 includes the earliest extended application of the imagery of verbal punctuation for musical periodicity in a purely instrumental work:

The melody of a piece is not composed without order and reason; it is made up of many small segments, each of which has its own complete sense; and a piece of

67. Forkel, *Allgemeine Geschichte*, I, 21.
68. For recent summaries of these ideas, see above, Chapter 1, note 21.

music somewhat resembles an oration, or rather, it is the oration that resembles the piece of music: for harmony, rhythm, meter, and the other similar things that a skilled orator observes in the composition of his works belong more naturally to music than to rhetoric. Be this as it may, just as an oration has its whole, composed most often of many sections; as each section is composed of sentences [*périodes*], each of which in turn has its own complete meaning; as each of these sentences is composed of phrases [*membres*], these phrases of words, and the words of letters— so, in the same way, does the melody of a piece of music have its whole, which is always composed of several reprises. Each reprise is composed of [units demarcated by] cadences, each of which has its own complete sense, and which often constitute the sentences [*périodes*] of the melody. These units are often composed of phrases; the phrases of measures, and the measures of notes. Thus, the notes correspond to letters, the measures to words, the [units demarcated by] cadences to sentences, the reprises to parts [*parties*], and the whole to the whole. But these divisions within the melody are not perceived by all those who hear someone singing or playing on an instrument. With the exception of those [divisions] that are so obvious that everyone can grasp them, one must know the idiom in order to hear them; nevertheless, they are marked in the tablature by the bar-lines that separate the measures and by several other characters, each of which I shall discuss in its proper place.[69]

Johann Mattheson, in his *Kern melodischer Wissenschaft* of 1737, and then again in *Der vollkommene Capellmeister* of 1739, provides a detailed account of "The Sections and Incisions within a Musical Oration" ("Von den Ab- und Einschnitten der Klang-Rede"): "Every proposition, oral or written, consists . . . of certain word-sentences or periods; but every such sentence in turn consists of smaller incisions up to the division [punctuated by] a period. Out of such sentences grows an entire concatenation or paragraph, and from various such paragraphs grows ultimately a main section or a chapter."[70] Musical compositions exhibit the same hierarchy of articulations. A "Periodus," for example, is "a brief statement that incorporates a full idea or a complete verbal sense in itself. Now whatever does not do this, but instead includes less than this, is not a period, not a sentence; and whatever does more than this is a paragraph, which can and by all rights should consist of various periods."[71] This definition of "Periodus," as Mattheson himself acknowledges, is derived from Quintilian, whose formulation was in fact the basis for most contemporary definitions of a sentence.[72]

69. M. de Saint-Lambert, *Les principes du clavecin* (Paris: Christophe Ballard, 1702), pp. 14–15.

70. Mattheson, *Capellmeister,* p. 181.

71. Ibid., p. 182.

72. Ibid., p. 183. See, for example, Johann Christoph Gottsched, *Versuch einer critischen Dichtkunst* (Leipzig: B. C. Breitkopf, 1730), p. 235: "a brief oration, incorporating one or more ideas, and which provides a complete sense in and of itself."

Smaller units, as Mattheson goes on to explain, are articulated by points of punctuation comparable to the comma and the colon. Using an aria as an example, Mattheson derives the musical "resting points," logically enough, from the sense of the text to be set. By relating the disposition of musical cadences to the text, Mattheson continues a long tradition going back as far as monophonic chant and extending throughout the Renaissance and Baroque. Zarlino, writing in 1558, had already observed that the "cadence is of equal value in music as the period in oratory," and that "the period in the text [to be set to music] and the cadence should coincide."[73]

Mattheson, however, goes on to note that purely instrumental music must follow these same principles of articulation. Instrumental music, "without the aid of words and voices, strives to say just as much" as vocal music. Mattheson's subsequent account of instrumental genres includes numerous references to the articulation of sentences, paragraphs, and the like.[74]

These same ideas of periodicity appear repeatedly throughout the eighteenth century as part of almost all contemporary accounts of movement-length form. This is largely in response to important changes in musical style that are characterized by units of increasingly smaller size and slower harmonic rhythm: short, more or less symmetrical phrases replace the long, spun-out melodies of earlier generations. While this kind of periodic construction was by no means a new technique in the second half of the eighteenth century, it did achieve unprecedented prominence at this time.

No single theorist is particularly succinct in presenting these various elements of periodicity, and the problem of terminology further confuses the issue. Kirnberger, writing in Sulzer's *Allgemeine Theorie,* recognized this even at the time, noting that "the names one gives to the smaller and larger sections of a melody have been somewhat indefinite up to now. One speaks of *Perioden, Abschnitten, Einschnitten, Rhythmen, Cäsuren,* etc., in such a way that one word sometimes has two meanings and two different words sometimes the same meaning."[75]

Nevertheless, these basic ideas are present, with varying degrees of clarity, in virtually all contemporary accounts that attempt to describe how a composer actually goes about constructing a work of music. And these accounts almost invariably emphasize the central importance of intelligibility. In his own *Kunst des reinen Satzes,* Kirnberger observes that

73. Gioseffo Zarlino, *Le istitutioni harmoniche* (Venice, 1558), p. 221.
74. Mattheson, *Capellmeister,* p. 209. On musical punctuation, see ibid., pp. 224–234.
75. Sulzer, *Allgemeine Theorie,* "Einschnitt (Musik)." See also Koch, *Musikalisches Lexikon,* "Periode"; and Carl Dahlhaus, "Satz und Periode: Zur Theorie der musikalischen Syntax," *Zeitschrift für Musiktheorie,* 9 (1978), issue 2, pp. 16–26.

it is immediately apparent to everyone that the most moving melody would be completely stripped of all its power and expression if one note after another were performed without precise regulation of speed, without accents, and without resting points, even if performed with the strictest observance of pitch. Even common [i.e., verbal, as opposed to musical] speech would become partly incomprehensible and completely disagreeable if a proper measure of speed were not observed in the delivery, if the words were not separated from one another by the accents associated with the length and brevity of the syllables, and finally if the phrases and sentences were not differentiated by resting points. Such a lifeless delivery would make the most beautiful speech sound no better than the letter-by-letter reading of children.

Thus tempo, meter, and rhythm give melody its life and power . . . Melody is transformed into a comprehensible and stimulating oration by the proper combination of these three things.[76]

These factors combine to make individual units within a movement understandable, and the same process applies to the larger-scale ordering of these units:

In speech one comprehends the meaning only at the end of a sentence and is more or less satisfied by it depending on whether this meaning establishes a more or less complete statement. The same is true in music. Not until a succession of connected notes reaches a point of rest at which the ear is somewhat satisfied does it comprehend these notes as a small whole; before this, the ear perceives no meaning and is anxious to understand what this succession of notes really wants to say. However, if a noticeable break does occur after a moderately long succession of connected notes (providing the ear with a small resting point and concluding the meaning of the phrase), then the ear combines all these notes into a comprehensible unit.

This break or resting point can be achieved either by a complete cadence or simply by a melodic close with a restful harmony, without a close in the bass. In the first case, we have a complete musical statement that in the melody is equivalent to a full sentence in speech, after which a period is placed. But in the other case, we have a phrase that is indeed comprehensible, yet after which another or several more phrases are expected to complete the meaning of the period.[77]

A "series of such periods, of which only the last closes in the main key, forms a single composition," and a cadence in the tonic signals the end of "the complete musical oration" *(die ganze musikalische Rede).*[78]

One of the most extensive eighteenth-century accounts of periodicity appears in the first and second volumes of Joseph Riepel's *Anfangsgründe zur*

76. Kirnberger, *Die Kunst des reinen Satzes in der Musik,* 2 vols. (Berlin and Königsberg: G. J. Decker and G. L. Hartung, 1771–1779), pt. 2, sct. 1, p. 105. Translation adapted from David Beach and Jurgen Thym's edition, *The Art of Strict Musical Composition* (New Haven: Yale University Press, 1982), p. 375.

77. Ibid., p. 138. Translation adapted from Beach and Thym's edition, pp. 404–405.

78. Ibid., p. 139.

musicalischen Setzkunst (1752–1755). Riepel presents composition essentially as a process of expansion: small phrases grow into larger ones, which in turn combine with other units to produce a movement-length whole. The composer can begin with a unit between two and nine measures in length, but a unit with an even number of measures—particularly two and four— is by far the most common. Regardless of its size, this basic unit can be expanded by the techniques of repetition, extension, interpolation, and a "doubling of cadences," that is, a varied repetition of a closing formula. Again, even-numbered units predominate in practice, as groupings of "four, eight, sixteen, and even thirty-two measures are so rooted in our nature, that it seems difficult to listen (with pleasure) to a different arrangement."[79] The relative strength of closure for any given unit is determined by the strength of its cadence. A perfect tonic cadence is ordinarily reserved for the end of a movement, while a dominant cadence normally articulates an internal resting point of some kind. Cadences on other scale degrees are correspondingly weaker. In this sense, the various units that constitute a movement are set off from one another both harmonically and rhythmically.[80]

Koch adopted this same basic outlook some thirty years later, and his account of periodicity is by far the most comprehensive of his time. Koch's techniques of expansion are derived from Riepel (repetition, extension, and doubling of cadences), but he goes into considerably more detail in explaining how these units can be combined into increasingly larger forms, and he relies much more heavily on rhetorical imagery than does Riepel. When Koch first introduces the concept of periodicity, he compares a short verbal sentence *(enger Satz)* to a short musical sentence. Both have a subject and a predicate (Example 2.1). The former establishes the "main idea" of the sentence, while the latter gives it a "certain direction, a certain mood." The nature of the sentence as a whole, then, is established by the subject, but can be modified by the use alternative predicates (Example 2.2). Both subject and predicate can be expanded by means of elaboration (Example 2.3).

2.1   Koch, *Versuch,* II, 352

79. Riepel, *Anfangsgründe . . . De rhythmopoeïa,* p. 23.
80. Riepel's concept of periodicity is described in greater detail in the works cited in Chapter 1, note 21.

2.2   Koch, *Versuch*, II, 353

This very simple example incorporates the essence of Koch's approach to periodicity. A two-measure unit, the subject, is complemented by the predicate, a succeeding unit of the same size. The resulting four-measure unit, in turn, can be expanded through juxtaposition with related or contrasting units into a still larger unit of eight measures. This same process of expansion, concatenating eight- and sixteen-measure units, ultimately applies to the construction of a movement-length whole as well.

The intelligibility of a complete movement depends on the clear articulation of large-scale units from one another:

Certain resting points of the spirit, perceptible to varying degrees, are generally necessary in speech and thus also in the products of those fine arts which attain their goal through language, namely poetry and rhetoric, if the subject they present is to be comprehensible. Such resting points of the spirit are just as necessary in melody if it is to affect our feelings. This is a fact which has never yet been called into question and therefore requires no further proof.

By means of these variously perceptible resting points of the spirit, the products of these fine arts can be broken up into larger and smaller units. Speech, for example, breaks down into various sections [*Perioden*] through the most readily perceptible of these resting points; through the less readily perceptible [of these resting points], a section, in turn, breaks down into separate sentences [*Sätze*] and parts of speech. And just as in speech, the melody of a composition can be broken up into

2.3   Koch, *Versuch*, II, 355

sections by means of analogous resting points of the spirit, and these, again in turn, into individual phrases [*einzelne Sätze*] and melodic segments [*melodische Theile*].[81]

This structural principle is evident throughout the repertoire of the Classical era. At one point in his treatise, Koch even reproduces a reduced score of almost the entire second movement from Haydn's Symphony No. 42, using this Andante as a paradigm of the manner in which phrases can be extended, repeated, combined, and articulated.[82]

The importance of these articulations for the performer is addressed in several of the eighteenth century's most important manuals on instrumental technique. In his *Violinschule* of 1756, Leopold Mozart enjoins violinists to observe the *Abschnitte* and *Einschnitte* of melody, adding that composers and performers alike should be sensitive to the *incisiones* observed by grammarians and rhetoricians.[83] Daniel Gottlob Türk, in his *Klavierschule* of 1789, similarly notes that it is not enough for the composer alone to articulate the various sections of a composition: it is incumbent upon the performer to bring out the hierarchy of these divisions in his own playing. Otherwise, the weight and clarity of the individual units will be unintelligible to the listener.[84] Quantz, almost forty years earlier, had already pointed to the advantage of the performer's understanding the rhetorical art, invoking a still earlier, complementary idea, borrowed from Quintilian: that the orator has much to learn from the musician.[85]

The central importance of periodicity and its correlative for the listener—intelligibility—were emphasized repeatedly throughout the century and across the continent in numerous accounts of large-scale form. The Spanish theorist Antonio Eximeno, writing in 1774, argued that

with cadences one creates musical sentences, as in a discourse with periods and commas. One ends a [musical] sentence with a perfect cadence as with a period.

81. Koch, *Versuch*, II, 342. Translation adapted from Nancy K. Baker's edition, *Introductory Essay on Composition: The Mechanical Rules of Melody, Sections 3 and 4* (New Haven: Yale University Press, 1983), p. 1. Koch's repeated references to the *Ruhepuncte des Geistes* may reflect an earlier association of *Geist* with "breath" (Latin, *spiritus*).

82. Koch, *Versuch*, III, 179–190. See Sisman's essay, cited in Chapter 1, note 21.

83. Leopold Mozart, *Versuch einer gründlichen Violinschule* (Augsburg: J. J. Lotter, 1756), pp. 107–108.

84. Türk, *Klavierschule* (Leipzig: Schwickert, 1789), pp. 343–344.

85. Quantz, *Versuch einer Anweisung*, p. 100; Quintilian, *Institutio oratoria*, I.X.22–23. See also Schubart, *Ideen zu einer Ästhetik der Tonkunst*, p. 375: "The composer must know everything that the poet and orator know." In his *Elemente der Rede: Die Geschichte ihrer Theorie in Deutschland von 1750 bis 1850* (Halle/Salle: Max Niemeyer, 1931), pp. 83–102, Klaus Winkler points out that the parallels between music and rhetoric, particularly oratorical delivery, became especially important in German manuals of rhetoric between 1790 and 1820.

Therefore one may call the passage contained between two cadences a musical sentence . . .

In sum, a composition written precisely according to the fundamental rules of music is a discourse that is occasionally elegant but that neither moves nor persuades [the listener]; expressive music is an eloquent discourse that triumphs over the spirit of its audience.[86]

And in one of the few theoretical treatises published in Vienna during the Classical era, Johann Friedrich Daube noted that "the entire musical movement must consist above all of certain main sections, which in turn can be broken down into smaller subsidiary sections or elements, if the movement is to elicit a good effect. The alternation of harmony also belongs here."[87] Elsewhere, Daube urged composers to apply "judicious incisions, resting points, etc.," along with "good alternation of the rushing and the cantabile, or, to use the language of painting, of light and shadow. And in all of this, the rules of rhetoric must be taken into account."[88] In a later treatise, Daube encouraged composers to study carefully the works of great orators, including Cicero, Horace, and Seneca, and to emulate them in questions of "symmetry" and the "relationship of all a work's parts."[89]

The concept of periodicity offers an essentially generative approach to the question of form, with small-scale units expanding into larger ones. But Mattheson and other subsequent theorists, including Koch, sensed that this approach alone would not suffice to explain the multiplicity of movement-length forms then current. While the mechanics of constructing small-scale units could be (and were) described in relatively straightforward fashion, the creation of large-scale forms out of smaller units had long been considered a more difficult matter, in music as in rhetoric. Sulzer is typical of many other writers in pointing out that

the art of periodizing well is one of the most difficult elements in all of eloquence . . . Everything else can be attained more easily than this, through natural gifts and without back-breaking study. Work, industry, much deliberation, and great strength in language are required for this. It does not seem possible to provide methodical instruction in this area. The best that one could do in educating the orator in this area would be to provide him with a well-arranged collection of the

---

86. Eximeno, *Dell'origine e delle regole della musica* (Rome: M. Barbiellini, 1774), pp. 57–58. See also William Jones, *A Treatise on the Art of Music* (Colchester: Author, 1784), pp. i, 46.

87. Daube, *Der musikalische Dilettant: Eine Abhandlung der Komposition* (Vienna: Trattner, 1773), p. 82.

88. Daube, *Der musikalische Dilettant: Eine Wochenschrift* (Vienna: J. Kurtzböcken, 1770), pp. 10–11.

89. Daube, *Anleitung zur Erfindung der Melodie*, II, 58.

best periods, ordered according to the varying character of their contents, and to show him the value of each through their thorough dissection.[90]

Among music theorists, the concatenation of individual units into a larger whole could help to explain the construction of movement-length forms, but only up to a point. Neither Mattheson nor Koch, significantly enough, was content to conclude his treatment of large-scale form with a discussion of periodicity. For while this principle emphasizes the fundamental similarities among disparate stereotypical patterns, it cannot adequately account for their differences. Periodicity, moreover, focuses primarily on the articulation of ideas, as opposed to the aesthetic coherence of the ideas themselves over the course of an entire movement. It emphasizes, in other words, the framework of articulation at the expense of that which is to be articulated. Mattheson, Koch, and others viewed form not so much as a process of articulation—critical as that process may be for intelligibility—but as a process of elaboration. The eighteenth century's theory of the compositional process provides the conceptual context for this idea of form.

Rhetoric and the Theory of the Compositional Process

"Composition," as noted earlier, is one of the many terms that music has borrowed from rhetoric. And in eighteenth-century accounts of musical form, the manner in which a composer "puts together" his work is perceived as analogous to the manner in which an orator constructs an oration. The final products of these two processes, in turn, exhibit close structural similarities.

Throughout the eighteenth century, the act of composition, both for rhetoric and for music, is seen as an essentially three-stage process. The first step is what German writers call the *Erfindung* or creation *(inventio)* of basic ideas. These ideas, in the rudimentary sequence of their eventual order, constitute the *Anlage* or "groundplan" of the oration or musical movement. The second step is the *Anordnung* or *Ausführung* (the *dispositio* or *elaboratio*), in which these basic ideas *(Gedanken)* are ordered, elaborated, repeated, varied, and articulated in the sequence of their ultimate deployment over the course of an entire movement or speech. It is here that large-scale form is determined by the orderly arrangement of discrete units; it is at this stage that "individual melodic sections," to use Koch's terminology, are "united into a whole." In the third and final step, the *Ausarbeitung (elocutio)*, the orator or composer shapes all the remaining details of the argument.

90. Sulzer, *Allgemeine Theorie,* "Periode."

It should be emphasized that this very brief summary is a composite drawn from a number of different schemes proposed by a variety of writers throughout the eighteenth century.[91] Among music theorists, Mattheson alone presents at least three different versions over a period of some sixteen years.[92] Other writers extend the imagery to include the performance of the work as well, but this stage lies beyond the compositional process itself and need not be considered here. Yet while the terminology may be far from uniform, the basic concepts are quite consistent throughout the century.

Two points stand out consistently: (1) Form must be comprehensible if a work is to achieve its goal of moving the audience's passions. Large-scale intelligibility is a prerequisite for any composition that is to penetrate the mind and move the spirit of the listener. (2) The process of ordering, elaborating, and shaping ideas in an effective manner can be taught—this, indeed, is one of the basic premises of the discipline of rhetoric—but the process of creating these ideas cannot. A composition, as Mattheson notes in his *Das neu-eröffnete Orchester* of 1713,

demands three elements: Inventio *(Erfindung)*, Elaboratio *(Ausarbeitung)*, Executio *(Ausführung* or *Aufführung)*, which together represent a rather close relationship to oratory or rhetoric. The last two elements can be learned; the manner of learning the first has never occurred to any diligent master, but rather, so to speak, only to larcenous pupils . . . .[93]

Scheibe, in his characteristically more concise fashion, confirms that "we can give no rules for invention, whereas we can appropriately reduce, expand, and bring into general order that which has already been invented."[94] There are, to be sure, numerous techniques to aid the composer in the pro-

---

91. Mattheson, *Vorrede* to *Capellmeister*, pp. 25–26, and text, pp. 121–132, 235–244; Meinrad Spiess, *Tractatus musicus compositorio-practicus* (Augsburg: J. J. Lotters Erben, 1745), pp. 133–135; Ernst Gottlieb Baron, *Abriss einer Abhandlung von der Melodie* (Berlin: A. Haude & J. C. Spener, 1756), pp. 8–9; Ignatz Franz Xaver Kürzinger, *Getreuer Unterricht zum Singen mit Manieren, und die Violin zu spielen* (Augsburg: J. J. Lotter, 1763), p. 77; Johann Nikolaus Forkel, *Ueber die Theorie der Musik* (Göttingen: Wittwe Vandenhöck, 1777); idem, intro. to *Allgemeine Geschichte*, I; Sulzer, *Allgemeine Theorie* (e.g., "Anordnung," "Ausarbeitung," "Instrumentalmusik"); Koch, *Versuch*, II, 68; idem, *Musikalisches Lexikon* ("Anlage," "Ausführung," etc.); Ernst Wilhelm Wolf, *Musikalischer Unterricht* (Dresden: Hilscher, 1788), pp. 71–73. Most of these works will be discussed in greater detail below.

92. Ian Bent examines some of the differences in terminology between Mattheson and Koch in "The 'Compositional Process' in Music Theory, 1713–1850."

93. Johann Mattheson, *Das neu-eröffnete Orchestre* (Hamburg: Schillers Wittwe, 1713), p. 104. On contemporary views of *inventio*, see Wulf Arlt, "Zur Handhabung der 'inventio' in der deutschen Musiklehre des frühen achtzehnten Jahrhunderts," in *New Mattheson Studies*, ed. George J. Buelow and Hans Joachim Marx (Cambridge: Cambridge University Press, 1983), pp. 371–391.

94. Scheibe, *Critischer Musikus*, p. 80; see also Koch, *Versuch*, II, 94.

cess of invention, also borrowed from rhetoric, such as the *loci topici* and the various devices of *ars combinatoria,* by which very small ideas, through processes of permutation, can be expanded into larger ones. In his *Der vollkommene Capellmeister,* Mattheson himself reviewed these techniques in unprecedented detail.[95] But on the whole, the *loci topici* and *ars combinatoria* were widely recognized to be devices for beginning or struggling composers.

Nevertheless, these techniques do illustrate the extent to which *inventio* and *elaboratio* are intertwined, for the former is not limited to the creation of a theme *ex nihilo;* it also incorporates the process by which an idea can be varied, including even the derivation of an apparently new idea out of an existing one.[96] But in the end, true invention was held to be the province of genius and thus outside the manner in which composition—including form—could be taught.

It is against this theory of the compositional process that Mattheson's celebrated parallel between musical form and the six parts of an oration is best understood. First presented in his *Kern melodischer Wissenschaft* of 1737 and then again two years later (with minor changes and additions) in *Der vollkommene Capellmeister,* Mattheson's account is one of the earliest and yet most fully developed of the various attempts to relate musical form and rhetoric. Even though few subsequent writers embraced the specificity with which Mattheson spelled out these connections, his basic ideas exerted a demonstrable influence on subsequent discussions of form throughout the eighteenth century.

Unfortunately, Mattheson's treatment of large-scale form has been widely misunderstood. His rhetorical imagery has often been dismissed as willful and idiosyncratic. It is neither. The historical importance of Mattheson's account for later eighteenth-century theorists becomes quite clear when considered within its broader rhetorical and pedagogical context.

Just as Mattheson's interpretation of the compositional process is framed in terms of rhetoric, his method of teaching composition is deeply rooted in the traditional pedagogy of rhetoric and poetics. His didactic method, like the process of composition itself, consists of three stages: (1) a presentation of rules and precepts, including the conventions of periodicity, followed by (2) a description of genres, and concluding with (3) specific ex-

95. *Capellmeister,* pp. 121–132. See Leonard Ratner, "*Ars Combinatoria:* Chance and Choice in Eighteenth-Century Music," in *Studies in Eighteenth-Century Music,* ed. Roger Chapman and H. C. Robbins Landon (London: George Allen & Unwin, 1970), pp. 343–363; idem, *Classic Music,* pp. 98–102; and Arlt, "Zur Handhabung der 'inventio'."

96. See, for example, Friedrich Andreas Hallbauer, *Anweisung zur verbesserten teutschen Oratorie* (Jena: J. B. Hartung, 1725; rpt. Kronberg: Scriptor, 1974), pp. 271–272.

amples of actual works. This approach ultimately derives from poetics. Gottsched's *Versuch einer critischen Dichtkunst* encapsulates this same basic outline in its subtitle: . . . *darinnen erstlich die allgemeinen Regeln der Poesie, hernach alle besondere Gattungen der Gedichte, abgehandelt und mit Exempeln erläutert werden* . . . (". . . in which first the general *rules* of poetry, then all particular *genres* of poems, are treated and illuminated with *examples* . . ."). This three-step process appears repeatedly in pedagogical works throughout the eighteenth century, both for rhetoric and for music. Mattheson's *Kern melodischer Wissenschaft* and Koch's *Versuch einer Anleitung zur Composition*, as we shall see, are two of the more important music treatises that follow this pattern.

It seems all but certain, in fact, that Mattheson used contemporary manuals of rhetoric and poetics as methodological models for his *Kern melodischer Wissenschaft*. He makes at least one specific reference to the methodology of such treatises in his discussion of *inventio*, pointing out that the subject of *inventio* usually comprises the first or second chapter of rhetorical manuals.[97] And in the *Capellmeister*, Mattheson explicitly cites Christoph Weissenborn's *Gründliche Einleitung zur teutschen und lateinischen Oratorie wie auch Poesie* of 1713 in conjunction with the *loci topici*.[98] But it is Gottsched's *Versuch einer critischen Dichtkunst* and his later *Ausführliche Redekunst* that offer the most striking structural precedents for Mattheson's treatise. Published in the years just before the *Kern*, Gottsched's manuals, as noted earlier, were among the most comprehensive and influential works of their kind. Both works trace the process by which small-scale units of thought can be expanded into larger periods, which in turn are concatenated into still larger sections; and both treatises conclude with a review of specific genres. In his *Critische Dichtkunst*, Gottsched considers the following points (among others) in this order: (1) the character of the poet; (2) the nature and use of individual words; (3) the construction of small and large periods; (4) the nature and structure of various genres (ode, idyll, elegy, tragedy, comedy, and so on). The *Ausführliche Redekunst* follows much the same pattern. From a musical perspective, Mattheson's *Kern melodischer Wissenschaft* considers essentially these same points in much the same sequence: (1) the qualities that a music director and composer must possess beyond the field of music; (2) the structure of musical periods; and (3) the nature and structure of specific genres (chorale, aria, symphony, sonata, and so on). Mattheson does not follow the details of Gottsched's outline precisely, for poetics and music each have their own peculiar elements, but the general outline of thought is strikingly similar.

97. Mattheson, *Kern*, p. 33; *Capellmeister*, pp. 139–140.
98. (Frankfurt/Main: C. Pohl, 1713). Mattheson's reference is in *Capellmeister*, p. 123n.

While Mattheson was by no means the first to comment on the parallels between rhetoric and musical composition, he was one of the first to develop a theory of musical composition within a rhetorical framework. Regarding periodicity, he notes somewhat sarcastically in the *Kern* that

some years ago a great poet believed that he had discovered something quite unusual: that music and oratory share an almost identical set of circumstances in this respect. What a wonder! Composers may well be ashamed that they have been so negligent in this regard. For although some of them, here and there, may have come upon sound ideas, guided by the light of nature, these good gentlemen have nevertheless remained merely on the periphery of things and have not been able to penetrate to the core of the matter, much less to order it, either openly or privately, within an appropriate artistic fashion.

Now to help us overcome this deficiency to at least some extent, we must make the effort to take the hand, as it were, of dear Grammar and of esteemed Rhetoric and Poetics.[99]

Mattheson goes on to describe the manner in which a larger-scale unit, the paragraph *(paragraphum)*, is constructed out of smaller-scale units, which he calls sentences *(periodi)*. These smaller units, in turn, are articulated internally by elements of cadential punctuation that are analogous to the comma, the semicolon, and the colon. On a larger scale, the same kind of punctuation also serves to articulate paragraphs from one another. In its hierarchical structuring of grammatical and syntactical units, Mattheson's methodology is once again appropriated from the rhetorical manuals of the day.

When it comes time to elucidate the construction of still larger units, however—those built up out of *paragrapha*—Mattheson shifts gears, as it were, and adopts a new methodology. He abandons the units which up to that point had been the focus of his attention and turns instead to a discussion of genres, describing the typical construction first of vocal genres (aria, arioso, cantata, recitative, duet, trio, chorus, opera, oratorio, concerto, motet, and so on), followed by instrumental genres, beginning with "a little minuet, so that everyone may see what the structure of such a little thing consists of, when it is not a monstrosity, and so that one might learn to make a sound judgment by moving from the trifling to the more important."[100] He then proceeds to other dance types (gavotte, rigaudon, gigue, and so on) and concludes with the larger categories of sonata, concerto, sinfonia, and overture. This strategy is once again taken directly from manuals of rhetoric, in which discussions of periodicity are followed by ac-

99. Mattheson, *Kern*, p. 71. A slightly different version of this passage appears in *Capellmeister*, p. 181.

100. Mattheson, *Kern*, p. 109. See also *Capellmeister*, p. 224.

counts of large-scale form ordered according to specific genres: sermons, funeral orations, panegyrics, and so on.

It is highly significant that this change of methodology occurs precisely at the point at which generative and conformational approaches to form meet—or do not meet, as is in fact more often the case. All forms, regardless of length, are concatenations of individual periods; but this alone does not explain the variety of ways in which these periods tend to be organized in practice. Mattheson recognized the limitations of explaining form solely through the concept of periodicity, and he attempted to bridge this gap by adopting the methodology of conventional rhetoric, moving from a predominantly prescriptive account of periodicity to an essentially descriptive account of individual genres.

The close connection between genre and form will be addressed later in this chapter; for the moment, suffice it to say that Koch, some fifty years later, follows precisely this same sequence of ideas in the teaching of composition: small-scale ideas expanding into larger-scale units (of which the largest would be the minuet), followed in turn by a review of genres. In contrast to Mattheson, Koch incorporates considerably more details of specific forms into these later discussions of genre: his most extended account of sonata form, for example, occurs within his description of the symphony.[101] And while Koch returns to the concept of periodicity at the conclusion of his treatise with some general comments on the construction of the first and second halves of larger forms, his accounts of each of these halves conclude once again with a review of the procedures characteristic of specific genres.[102]

Mattheson, too, had rounded out his discussion of genres by returning to the broader principles of large-scale forms. But his focus at this point is quite unlike Koch's. It is here in the seventh chapter of the *Kern*—"On Invention, Elaboration, and Embellishment in Composition"—that Mattheson first presents his celebrated image of musical form as a function of rhetoric. He calls the musical work a *Klangrede,* an oration in notes, and draws direct attention to the rhetorical equivalents of *dispositio, elaboratio, decoratio* in music:

Regarding now the Disposition, it is, first of all, a *proper ordering of all the sections and elements in the melody, or in an entire musical work,* almost in the manner in which one arranges a building and sketches out a draft or an outline, a ground-plan, in order to show where, for example, a hall, a room, a chamber, etc., should be placed. Our musical Disposition differs from the rhetorical arrangement of an ordinary [i.e., verbal] speech only in the subject, the matter at hand, the Object. Hence it [the

101. Koch, *Versuch,* III, 304–311. See above, pp. 41–42.
102. Ibid., III, 381–386, 420–430.

musical Disposition] must observe the same six parts that are normally prescribed for the orator, namely: the *introduction,* the *narration,* the *proposition,* the *proof,* the *refutation,* and the *closing,* otherwise known as: Exordium, Narratio, Propositio, Confirmatio, Confutatio, & Peroratio.[103]

The imagery of the building or house in the construction of an oration is yet another *topos* of rhetoric, deriving ultimately from Quintilian's *Institutio oratoria.*[104] Gottsched, in his *Ausführliche Redekunst,* introduces his chapter on "the ordering or arrangement of an oration" with precisely the same imagery, noting that "stones, wood, and lime do not constitute a building, no matter how good they are in and of themselves. They must be joined together and connected in a certain manner if they are to make a house."[105]

But in proposing this outline of *dispositio,* Mattheson is careful to note that its application is intended to be quite flexible:

In spite of all correctness, things would often turn out quite pedantically if one were to bind oneself all too anxiously to this line and constantly measure one's works against it. Nevertheless, it cannot be denied that the diligent examination of good orations, as well as of good melodies, will certainly reveal the presence of these sections, or some of them, in an apt sequence—even if in some instances the composers of these works thought sooner of their deaths than of this kind of guide.[106]

Even the insistence that this scheme is flexible and by no means fixed is taken from rhetoric. Gottsched prefaces his account of this same general six-part structure (exordium, narratio, and so on) with the following:

It is of course not the general opinion that everything in a model must be applied without exception in all complete orations; or that no more can be added than what has been presented here. No, an orator certainly reserves the freedom to add something according to his opinion, and to omit something, how and wherever he may be required to do so by the circumstances of his main idea [*Hauptsatz*] and by his listeners.[107]

Sure enough, Mattheson's subsequent analysis of an aria by Marcello follows his proposed order only loosely. Yet rather than weaken his argument, this application illustrates all the more graphically that his proposed outline is to be applied with great flexibility:

Thus, whoever . . . would make use of the method described above, *in a certain, unforced way,* should sketch out, perhaps on a sheet of paper, his entire concept,

103. Mattheson, *Kern,* p. 128. See also *Capellmeister,* p. 235.
104. Quintilian, *Institutio oratoria, Proemium* to book VII; see also XI.II.17–20.
105. Gottsched, *Ausführliche Redekunst* (Leipzig: B. C. Breitkopf, 1736), "Von der Anordnung oder Einrichtung einer Rede," p. 193.
106. Mattheson, *Kern,* p. 128. See also *Capellmeister,* p. 235.
107. Gottsched, *Ausführliche Redekunst,* p. 204.

outline it in the roughest form, and arrange it in an orderly fashion, before he proceeds to the *elocutio* . . .

Invention demands fire and spirit; Disposition order and measure; Elaboration cold blood and circumspection.[108]

Mattheson's imagery drew almost immediate criticism from Lorenz Mizler, who, in an otherwise essentially favorable review of the *Kern,* decried Mattheson's rhetorical imagery of form as forced:

I do not know if the admirable Marcello would wish to apply the six parts of an oration here, in so much as it is not at all necessary to apply everything in every section of a piece. Rather, it is highly likely that the incomparable composer of this aria, while writing it, did not think about exordium, narratio, confutatio, confirmatio, or the order of how the said parts should follow upon one another. The matter thus seems forced, because Herr Mattheson uses one and the same phrase [*Satz*] for the introduction, the narration, and the proposition.[109]

Without citing Mizler by name, Mattheson rebutted this attack in the preface to *Der vollkommene Capellmeister* of 1739. He begins by refuting what has since come to be known as the "intentional fallacy":

Marcello, to be sure, has given as little thought to the six parts of an oration in composing the aria I quoted in the *Kern,* as in his other works; but one concedes that I have *quite plausibly* shown how they must be present in the melody. That is enough. Experienced masters proceed in an orderly manner, even when they do not think about it. One can observe this in everyday writing and reading where no one gives spelling a second thought.

But it does not follow that students must regard such a declaration and its commentary as similarly objectionable, and that no benefit can be drawn therefrom. This is the principal aim, and if it is attained, then all is well.[110]

Mattheson then calls attention to the careful qualifications he had appended to his original comments:

The fifth paragraph of the seventh chapter in the *Kern* is directed against constraint in these matters so explicitly and precisely that it would be very pedantic indeed if one were to look anxiously for all these elements in their particular order in every melody and seek to apply them. That is not the intent. We are distant from that . . .

The ways and means of elaboration and application are not nearly so diverse and varying in rhetoric as in music, where one can vary things much more frequently, even though the theme seems to remain the same to some degree. A musical oration

---

108. Mattheson, *Kern,* pp. 137, 139. See also *Capellmeister,* pp. 240, 241.

109. Mizler, review of Mattheson's *Capellmeister,* in Mizler's *Neu eröffnete musikalische Bibliothek,* 1 (1738), pt. 6, pp. 38–39.

110. Mattheson, *Vorrede* to *Capellmeister,* p. 25. Translation adapted from Ernest C. Harriss's edition, *Johann Mattheson's "Der vollkommene Capellmeister": A Revised Translation with Critical Commentary* (Ann Arbor: UMI Research Press, 1981), pp. 62–63.

has a great deal more liberty and compatible surroundings than a different [i.e. verbal] kind of oration; hence in a melody there might be something similar among the exordium, the narratio, and the propositio, so long as they are made different from one another by keys, by being made higher or lower, or by similar marks of distinction (of which ordinary rhetoric is ignorant).[111]

These important qualifications to Mattheson's account have been largely ignored, and as a result, the thrust of his ideas has been widely misinterpreted. His proposed parallels between musical and rhetorical form have been either embraced too literally or, more often, rejected outright.[112] Mattheson's central point here is not so much the six-part schema itself as the idea of thematic elaboration. His approach to form begins with the theme or *Hauptsatz*—the subject of the *Klangrede*—and proceeds with its subsequent elaboration. The numerous musical examples accompanying his discussion all illustrate the manipulation of the aria's opening idea. Mattheson's rhetorical concept of form views the musical movement as an oration in which a basic idea is presented, developed, and examined again in the light of other ideas derived from it. The emphasis in our interpretation of this account should not be directed so much toward the schematic nature of the form as toward the idea that a central theme can and should be varied in different ways at different points within a musical oration.

But, by your leave, I also have not used (as I have been further accused) one and the same statement for the exordium, for the narratio, and for the propositio, in such a way that one and the same entity was retained in a uniform manner. For first of all the disputed phrases are as different as minor and major; besides, transposition and reiteration give them a completely different aspect. High and low are not the same. None of this can be evaluated by the standards of an ordinary [i.e. verbal] oration, in which such things are not found.

. . . I myself acknowledge, in the *Kern,* that the narratio in our aria sounds almost

111. Ibid., pp. 25–26. Translation adapted from Harriss's edition, p. 63.

112. For example by Rolf Dammann, who speaks of Mattheson's "dogmatisches Aufbauschema" in *Der Musikbegriff im deutschen Barock* (Cologne: Arno Volk, 1967), p. 126; Ritzel, *Die Entwicklung der "Sonatenform,"* pp. 23–28; Baker, "Koch and the Theory of Melody," p. 3 ("the reader learns a good deal more about oratory than he does about the musical structure of a composition"); Günther Wagner, *Traditionsbezug im musikhistorischen Prozess zwischen 1720 und 1740 am Beispiel von Johann Sebastian und Carl Philipp Emanuel Bach* (Neuhausen-Stuttgart: Hänssler, 1985), pp. 164–167. At the other extreme, Hans-Heinrich Unger *Die Beziehungen zwischen Musik und Rhetorik im 16.-18. Jahrhundert* (Würzburg: K. Triltsch, 1941; rpt. Hildesheim: Olms, 1979), pp. 53–54, offers an extended but ultimately unconvincing application of the six-part schema to the first movement of Bach's Brandenburg Concerto No. 3. See also Leona Jacobson's "Musical Rhetoric in Buxtehude's Free Organ Works," *Organ Yearbook,* 13 (1982), 60–79; and Daniel Harrison's perceptive analysis of Bach's Toccata, BWV 915, in "Rhetoric and Fugue: An Analytical Application," *Music Theory Spectrum,* 12 (1990), 1–42.

the same as the exordium . . . [but] the exordium differs [from the narratio] in five ways[:] . . . in pitch, text, elaboration, in its instruments, and in its voices, and this is not at all one and the same statement, nor one and the same thing. Similar is not identical.[113]

Mattheson's passing reference to the text is striking, for at no point does he provide the words to Marcello's aria. He does not even give a text incipit.[114] Clearly, it is the music—and specifically, the elaboration of the basic theme—that Mattheson considers central to the *dispositio*. In any event, he felt sure enough of his imagery to publish it again, with some minor changes and additions, in chapter 14 of *Der vollkommene Capellmeister.*

In addition to criticism, Mattheson's rhetorical imagery also found support. Mizler himself, in a subsequent review of the same basic material in *Der vollkommene Capellmeister,* conceded that in spite of his previous criticisms, he would "by no means deny that this newly proposed guide could lead to order and good ideas."

Music is an oration in notes [*Klangrede*] and seeks to move listeners just as an orator does. Why, then, should the rules of oratory not be applicable to music? But understanding and wit [i.e., the ability to see similarities in seemingly disparate objects] are required if no school-like tricks and pedantry are to come out of this. It is a cunning device of orators to give their strongest proofs at the beginning [of an oration], their weaker ones in the middle, and their strongest ones brought together once again at the end. This can also provide a good artifice for musical composition. Above all, a successful composer must well consider everything before he advances to his work; he must, so to speak, outline his concept in the broadest way on a piece of paper and order it neatly before he proceeds to elaborate it. The elaboration [*Ausarbeitung*] then follows much better. He who has disposed well is already halfway toward elaboration.[115]

And no less an authority than Johann Adolph Scheibe singled out Mattheson's pioneering treatment of the rhetorical basis of large-scale form with particular enthusiasm. Scheibe calls Mattheson's "clear and pleasing" treatment of the *Klangrede* an "important service," even if few musicians would have previously thought it "necessary to observe all the small and large divisions one finds in a well-ordered oration."

113. Mattheson, *Vorrede* to *Capellmeister,* pp. 25–26. Harriss (p. 63) interprets the last sentence of the first paragraph quite differently.

114. A comparison of Mattheson's analysis with Marcello's original work would be most revealing, but it has proven impossible to identify this particular aria. See Eleanor Selfridge-Field, *The Music of Benedetto and Alessandro Marcello: A Thematic Catalogue* (Oxford: Clarendon Press, 1990), p. 197.

115. Mizler, review of Mattheson's *Capellmeister,* in Mizler's *Neu eröffnete musikalische Bibliothek,* 2 (1742), pt. 3, pp. 104–105.

The seventh chapter [of the *Kern*] deals at last with one of the most important issues to be considered in the art of musical composition. Is it not equally important in the elaboration [*Ausarbeitung*] of musical pieces to be both circumspect and spontaneous, as in rhetoric and poetics? If the elaboration of the main idea [*Hauptsatz*] deviates from the beginning in so noticeable a way that one no longer knows what the subject is, there arises in the listener or reader an uncertainty vis-à-vis the subject being dealt with, and one experiences a disdain for the author when one perceives such a disorderly elaboration.[116]

Mattheson's *Capellmeister* eventually became one of the most widely used manuals of composition in eighteenth-century Germany. The young Haydn was among the many composers who used it, and late in his life he would recall "its basic premises" as having been "no longer new, but nevertheless good."[117] Beethoven, too, owned a copy and is known to have used it on more than one occasion.[118]

But one need not trace the reception of *Der vollkommene Capellmeister* in order to establish the influence of this rhetorical view of form, for the essence of Mattheson's approach appears repeatedly in later treatises by other authors. Subsequent writers were reluctant to take up Mattheson's precise and perhaps overly detailed imagery of the six parts of an oration. But it is equally clear that his basic imagery and methodology—both derived from the principles of traditional rhetoric—retained their appeal throughout the eighteenth century and well into the nineteenth. Mattheson's rhetorical metaphors emphasize that form is essentially thematic—not in the sense that certain themes must appear at certain junctures, but in the sense that a movement's form is determined by the manner in which its thematic material is presented and elaborated. His rhetorical methodology also emphasizes the close relationship between a work's form and the genre to which it belongs. Both of these ideas, as we shall see, are central to virtually all eighteenth-century accounts of large-scale form.

Melody and the Thematic Basis of Form

Mattheson's idea of form as the unfolding of a work's central idea is part of a broader contemporary view that closely associates form with the concepts

---

116. Scheibe, "Sendschreiben an Sr. Hoch Edl. Herrn Capellmeister Mattheson, über den Kern melodischer Wissenschaft," in *Gültige Zeugnisse über die jüngste Matthesonisch-Musicalische Kern-Schrifft . . .* (Hamburg: n.p., 1738), p. 14.

117. Dies, *Biographische Nachrichten*, p. 41. See also Griesinger, *Biographische Notizen*, p. 20, where Mattheson's *Capellmeister* is cited along with Fux's *Gradus ad Parnassum*. Haydn also owned a copy of the *Kern:* see H. C. Robbins Landon, *Haydn: Chronicle and Works*, 5 vols. (Bloomington: Indiana University Press, 1976–1980), V, 402.

118. See Richard Kramer, "Notes to Beethoven's Education," *JAMS*, 28 (1975), 94–95.

of melody and theme. Among German theorists, the term *Melodie* carried many meanings and connotations throughout the eighteenth century,[119] one of the most important of which relates it to the outline of an entire movement. Whereas today we routinely equate "melody" with "theme," eighteenth-century theorists seldom used these two terms interchangeably. *Thema* and *melodischer Theil* were the more usual designations for smaller units; melody itself was perceived to be broader and more general, encompassing the trajectory of a complete movement.

In the *Kern melodischer Wissenschaft,* for example, Mattheson notes that "a melody must not be hindered or noticeably interrupted in its natural progress for the sake of a theme."[120] He speaks of "the musical work"; but with no significant change in context, the same phrase becomes "the melodic work" two years later in *Der vollkommene Capellmeister.* Elsewhere, he speaks of "the form . . . of a given work, of a given melody."[121] His discussions of musical punctuation, incisions, sentences, and periods all occur under the rubric "Von der Melodie." And his treatment of genres does not fall under the heading of merely "Gattungen," but rather "Gattungen der Melodien." Koch, writing some fifty years later, notes that a "melody, like an oration, must consist of various periods, which in turn can be divided into individual sentences."[122] This view similarly emphasizes the idea that melody is a unit extending throughout an entire movement or work.

While *Melodie* and *Thema* are seldom interchangeable for Koch, *Melodie* and *Tonstück* often are. Midway through his definition of melody in his *Lexikon,* yet without a break of any real kind, Koch switches from discussing the structure of a melody to the structure of a movement as a whole. There is, in fact, little distinction to be made between the two. The modulatory conventions he describes here function as a means of providing melody with the necessary balance of variety and unity, but it is melody that provides the basic structural perspective of any musical movement or work. "Thus it follows that melody is the essential element of any work of music, and that harmony, in spite of its great importance and however much it increases the artistic means of expressivity, must nevertheless be subordinate."[123]

Koch's views, which echo those of both Mattheson and Scheibe from earlier in the century, were shared by many of his contemporaries. Johann

---

119. See Ratner, *Classic Music,* pp. 81–82.

120. *Kern,* p. 36; see also *Capellmeister,* p. 141.

121. *Kern,* p. 128, and *Capellmeister,* p. 235; *Capellmeister,* p. 129.

122. Koch, *Musikalisches Lexikon,* "Melodie." See also the previously cited quotation from the *Versuch,* II, 342 (pp. 77–78) as well as Saint-Lambert's observation that "the melody of a piece . . . is made up of many small segments," including units as large as a period (pp. 72–73); and Daube, *Der musikalische Dilettant: Eine Wochenschrift,* p. 10.

123. Koch, *Musikalisches Lexikon,* "Melodie."

Joseph Klein, in his *Versuch eines Lehrbuchs der praktischen Musik* of 1783, clearly considers *Melodie* to be the largest structural unit within a movement:

A melody consists . . . of sentences [*Sätze*], each of which is a series of successive notes that together constitute a musical thought or sense. These *Sätze* may consist of one, two, or more measures, or they may also comprise only a part of a single measure; they are analogous to [units delineated by] a comma in language. The *Satz* that constitutes the main idea of a melody is called the *Hauptsatz* (Thema, subjectum) . . .

A melody can also be divided into sections or periods, which are analogous to the [units delineated by] larger points of articulation in language, and which in themselves can be considered to be smaller melodies.[124]

Except in the case of a strictly monophonic work (for example, a composition for solo flute), *Melodie* is not synonymous with the work or movement as a whole, for it represents only a single line. But as the predominant voice, it is capable of at least representing a complete outline of a movement by establishing the basic elements of a movement's overall structure. The *Hauptsatz,* in turn, is the "main idea" of this melody—literally the "sentence at the head"—and as such stands for the identity of the melody as a whole.

French theorists express similar views on the connection between the main idea and the large-scale structure of a movement or work by using *sujet* and *dessein,* terms borrowed from the visual arts.[125] In his *Dictionnaire de musique,* Rousseau defines the latter as

the invention and deportment [*conduite*] of the subject, the disposition of each part [i.e., voice], and the general ordering of the whole.

. . . This idea of the general *dessein* of a work applies particularly to each of its movements. It is thus that one designs an aria, a chorus, etc. Having thought up a subject, one distributes it according to the rules of good modulation in each of the parts [voices] in which it should be heard, in such a way that it cannot escape the attention of the audience . . . It is a fault of *dessein* to let the subject be forgotten; and it is an even greater fault to pursue it to the point of tedium.[126]

Like so many other theorists both before and after, Rousseau emphasizes the central importance of the main theme—and specifically, its disposition and elaboration—in establishing the structure of a movement. Rousseau himself would probably not have wished to call this view of form "rhetor-

---

124. Klein, *Versuch eines Lehrbuchs,* pp. 59–60.
125. See Peter Eckhard Knabe, *Schlüsselbegriffe des kunsttheoretischen Denkens in Frankreich* (Düsseldorf: Schwann, 1972), pp. 165–173. For other relevant excerpts from contemporary music theorists, see Ritzel, *Die Entwicklung der "Sonatenform,"* pp. 76–83.
126. Jean-Jacques Rousseau, *Dictionnaire de musique* (Paris: Veuve Duchesne, 1768), "Dessein."

ical," but its origins in earlier French theory are evident as far back as Mersenne, who in 1627 had noted that "rhetoric teaches one how to order [*disposer*] a musical subject."[127]

This same imagery is still evident in the last quarter of the eighteenth century in Jean Baptiste Mercadier's definition of *dessein* as

> the manner of directing the harmony, the melody, the rhythm, and the modulation in such a way that everything relates to one central idea and only one; for in dramatic music and all music of expression, one must treat a subject as in the art of oratory and in all the other fine arts, that is to say, without deviating from the rules of unity that all these arts share.[128]

The manner in which this "central idea" *(idée commune)* is elaborated ultimately determines the structure of a movement. All other ideas must stand in some logical relationship to this idea. It provides the basic material of the movement, and it governs not only the nature of subsequent ideas but also the process by which individual units will be concatenated into a whole. "Before taking pen in hand," Mercadier observes, "the musician must have a *motif,* that is to say, a basic and principal idea that will determine the melody, the harmony, the modulation, the tempo, the meter, and the arrangement of the voices, and in general everything that he must do."[129]

Jean Benjamin de la Borde, writing in 1780, endorses Rousseau's definition of *dessein,* adding that it is "a theme one wishes to have predominate in the piece one is writing, and which one is careful to recall in the various voices and in the different tonalities through which one passes . . . The great art of the composer consists in designing first on a large scale, in establishing his motive firmly, and in reiterating it from time to time for his listeners."[130]

This idea of a connection between a main theme, its elaboration, and the structural outline of a movement extends throughout the century and transcends nationalities. Scheibe, in 1737, notes that "a *Hauptsatz* is necessary in all musical works; the entire course [of a work] must ineluctably result from it."[131] Riepel, in 1752, speaks of the "theme or draft, according to which the entire musical piece is constructed."[132] Elsewhere, in a revealing exchange, Riepel's *discantista* confesses that his "heart" tells him "that the

127. Marin Mersenne, *Traité de l'harmonie universelle* (Paris: Guillaume Baudry, 1627), p. 21.

128. Jean Baptiste Mercadier de Belesta, *Nouveau systême de musique théorique et pratique* (Paris: Valade, 1776), pp. 247–248.

129. Ibid., p. 169.

130. Laborde, *Essai sur la musique,* II, 49. See also J. J. O. de Meude-Monpas, *Dictionnaire de musique* (Paris: Knapen, 1787), "Dessein" and "Sujet."

131. Scheibe, *Critischer Musikus,* p. 82.

132. Riepel, *Anfangsgründe . . . De rhythmopoeïa,* p. 13.

first solo in a concerto should contrast with the idea of the opening theme." The *praeceptor's* response is brief and cutting: "Then your heart does not know what *Thema* means." The teacher goes on to provide numerous examples of themes that contrast with an opening idea and yet at the same time share with it certain elements.[133] The quality of formal coherence, in this view, clearly depends on the technique of thematic elaboration.

In Italy, Salvatore Bertezen also emphasizes the primacy of the theme, not only for the compositional process, but for the final product itself. "In composing, the first object must always be a melody . . . For example, in composing a minuet, a solfeggio, or a sonatina," one must keep in mind "the principle of sustaining the theme, as in a discourse."[134] Francesco Galeazzi makes a direct comparison between the structure of a musical movement and that of an oration on the grounds that both represent the elaboration of a central idea. "The *motive* is nothing other than the principal idea of the melody; it is the subject, the theme, so to speak, of the musical discourse around which the entire composition must revolve."[135]

In France, Alexandre Choron sums up this "law of sustaining the theme" in his *Principes de composition* of 1808 by invoking "the doctrine of Zarlino and all masters, be they ancient or modern," who maintain that "in every composition *there is one subject* without which the work cannot exist . . . Viewed in this manner, composition is the art of discoursing upon a subject."[136]

Significantly, it is in the entry "Hauptsatz" that Kirnberger (in conjunction with Sulzer) comes closest to defining musical form:

A *Hauptsatz* is a period within a musical work that incorporates the expression and the whole essence of the melody. It appears not only at the beginning of a piece, but is repeated frequently, in different keys and with different variations. The *Hauptsatz* is generally called the "theme," and Mattheson compares it not inappropriately to the [biblical] text [that provides the basis] of a sermon, which must contain in a few words that which the discourse will develop more fully.

Music is actually the language of sentiment, whose expression is always concise, for sentiment in itself is something simple, something that can be presented in a few utterances. Thus, a very short melodic phrase of two, three, or four measures can express a sentiment so definitely and correctly that the listener understands exactly

133. Riepel, *Anfangsgründe . . . Grundregeln zur Tonordnung,* pp. 105–107.

134. Bertezen, *Principj di musica teorico-prattica* (Rome: Salomoni, 1780), pp. 341–342. Vincenzo Manfredini uses similar imagery in his *Regole armoniche,* 2nd ed. (Venice: Adolfo Cesare, 1797), p. 103.

135. Galeazzi, *Elementi,* II, 254. Elsewhere (I, 230), Galeazzi cites Haydn, Boccherini, Vanhal, and Pleyel as among the best composers of instrumental music whose works are available in Italy.

136. Choron, *Principes de composition des écoles d'Italie,* 3 vols. (Paris: Le Duc, 1808), I, xviii. Emphasis in the original.

the emotional state of the person who is singing. If, then, a musical work had no other purpose than to present a sentiment clearly, such a brief phrase, if well thought out, would suffice. But this is not the goal of music; it should engage the listener for a period of time in the same emotional state. This cannot be achieved through the mere repetition of the same phrase, no matter how splendid it may be, for the repetition of the same thing becomes boring and destroys the attentiveness of the listener. Therefore, one had to invent a type of melody in which one and the same sentiment, with appropriate variety and in different modifications, could be repeated often enough to make the appropriate impression upon the listener.

It is in this manner that the form of most of our usual current musical works has arisen: concertos, symphonies, arias, duets, trios, fugues, etc. They all have this in common: that they are based on a *Hauptsatz* presented in a main period, brief and appropriate to the expression of a sentiment; that this *Hauptsatz* is supported or interrupted by smaller, interpolated ideas [*Zwischengedanken*] appropriate to it; that this *Hauptsatz* and these *Zwischengedanken* are repeated often enough, in different harmonies and keys, and with small melodic variations, so that the spirit of the listener is sufficiently captivated.[137]

In general, then, the musical work or movement was considered analogous to an oratorical argument; its purpose was to move, persuade, and delight the listener. The subject of this argument, in turn, was equated with its main theme, the *Hauptsatz* or *sujet*. Once established, it was essential that this idea remain the focal point of the discourse; the thread of the argument would otherwise be lost. At the same time, discourses of any substantial length required variation and contrast; subordinate or interpolated ideas must therefore stand in some appropriate relationship to the sentiment embodied in the *Hauptsatz*. The coherence of the argument, finally, was seen to be embodied in melody. Koch, after all, had specifically equated rhetoric, the art by which an argument could be made both coherent and persuasive, with the manner in which "individual *melodic* sections" could be "united into a whole."[138]

Throughout the eighteenth century, form was considered to be primarily an aesthetic category, a concept having more to do with qualities of coherence and persuasiveness than with diagrams or lowest common denominators. In one of the very few eighteenth-century definitions of the term "form" as applied to music, in fact, an anonymous lexicographer of the late 1760s calls it "the manner in which the thoughts within an entire melody

---

137. Sulzer, *Allgemeine Theorie*, "Hauptsatz." According to J. A. P. Schulz, "Ueber die in Sulzers Theorie der schönen Künste unter dem Artikel Verrückung angeführten zwey Beispiele von Pergolesi und Graun . . . ," *AMZ*, 2 (1800), cols. 276–280, Kirnberger was responsible for the musical articles through "Modulation," at which point Schulz himself began to assist Kirnberger. Schulz then assumed sole responsibility from the letter "S" onward.

138. See above, p. 53.

or period follow one another."[139] In another entry, the same author defines "The Whole" (*das Ganze*) as

a general dependence of the sections [of a movement] upon one another, by means of which all sections contribute to a single effect alone. The art of constructing a whole resides in the concatenation of main, subsidiary, and connective ideas, in the agreement of rhythms within the main voice, in the juxtaposition of the secondary voices that duly support the main voice, draw the ears to it and delight them. It is not enough that the sections of a composition, each considered on its own, have succession, correctness, and due proportion; above and beyond this, these sections must all agree with one another and constitute a harmonious whole. A single section can include mistakes, e.g., parallel octaves or fifths, and the whole can nevertheless be well put together.[140]

The final comment implicitly reinforces the traditional distinction between musical grammar and musical rhetoric. Form is the province of the latter.

While periodicity, as we saw earlier, is a means of fostering intelligibility, it is important to remember that the object of this articulation is a movement's thematic ideas. Numerous theorists of the eighteenth century stress the importance of presenting and elaborating thematic ideas in such a way that they can be perceived clearly. In his *Abriss einer Abhandlung von der Melodie* of 1756, Ernst Gottlieb Baron devotes considerable attention to the manner in which a melody—a coherent series of themes—can be grasped by the listener:

A melody must have certain incisions. Thus, where there are no incisions (commas, semicolons, periods, etc.), as in an oration, the sense and understanding become muddled; this impedes one from grasping what is intended, especially if one cannot distinguish beginning, middle, and end from one another, or perceive any symmetry among these parts. Would one not laugh at an orator who spoke in one continuous flow, without such distinctions, without distinguishing a preceding thought from a subsequent one? For the main idea intended for the oration—and a clear and distinct understanding of this idea—would be missing altogether.[141]

This same emphasis on intelligibility is present throughout Sulzer's *Allgemeine Theorie der schönen Künste,* which equates the structure of musical and rhetorical discourse in many of its entries.[142] Daube, writing in Vienna in the early 1770s, similarly attributes the success of any given work not to the variety of its contents but to the "proper ordering of a few melodic

---

139. Anonymous, "Beytrag zu einem musikalischen Wörterbuch," in Johann Adam Hiller's *Wöchentliche Nachrichten und Anmerkungen die Musik betreffend,* no. 39 (27 March 1769), p. 302.

140. Ibid., p. 303.

141. Baron, *Abriss einer Abhandlung von der Melodie,* p. 8.

142. See, for example, the entries for "Anordnung," "Hauptsatz," "Satz; Setzkunst."

elements, their manipulation, and their correct placement."[143] And Carl Ludwig Junker, writing in 1778, also relies on rhetorical imagery to emphasize the quality of intelligibility:

Theme. (Motif, principal idea, concentrated sentiment.) Without a theme, there would be no unity in variety. The composer has his plot, just as in the plastic and rhetorical arts. Thus—predominant sentiment, in the case of the composer; interest in the hero, in the case of the painter; concentrated moral truth or speculation, in the case of the poet. Key, motion, division, and length are all formed according to the theme . . . Every musical piece is an extension, an alteration, a contrasting of the theme. The theme must therefore always be prominent, so that the sentiment can always be conveyed, so that I always understand the composer and grasp the expression without confusion.[144]

Grétry, in his *Mémoires* of 1797, extends the imagery of rhetoric to the point of calling for "proofs" of a movement's "propositions":

The first part of a sonata, duo, trio, or quartet can contain elements that are highly characteristic; and after a pause on the dominant . . . these same elements are taken up again, brought in differently, and varied in their own manner, in their melody and in their harmony; and this is, so to speak, like supplying proofs to the propositions one has made at the outset; this would be according to nature.[145]

While "proofs" may at first seem inappropriate within a language as vague and nonreferential as that of instrumental music, Grétry is in fact drawing upon an established distinction between two different kinds of rhetorical proofs: those which are logical and rational, that is, persuasive; and those which are psychological and emotional, that is, moving.[146] Proofs, in effect, are ideas that either grow out of or reflect directly upon the subject of a discourse. It is in this sense that Grétry's musical proofs are to be understood, as reflections upon a movement's central idea or ideas. One is reminded here of Kollmann's "propositions" and their subsequent "elaborations."

143. Daube, *Der musikalische Dilettant: Eine Abhandlung der Komposition*, p. 162.

144. Junker, *Betrachtungen über Mahlerey, Ton-und Bildhauerkunst* (Basel: K. A. Serini, 1778), pp. 82–83. See also Junker's *Tonkunst* (Bern: Typographische Gesellschaft, 1777), pp. 25–26.

145. André Ernest Modeste Grétry, *Mémoires, ou essais sur la musique*, 3 vols. (Paris: Imprimerie de la République, 1797), III, 357.

146. See, for example, Hallbauer, *Anweisung*, pp. 257–260. The distinction between these two categories of proofs is discussed by Roland Barthes in *The Semiotic Challenge*, trans. Richard Howard (New York: Hill and Wang, 1988), pp. 53–75. Other writers referring to the "proofs" of a musical work include Forkel (see below, p. 123), Carpani (p. 138), and Friedrich August Kanne, who in his analyses of some of Mozart's piano sonatas in the *Wiener allgemeine musikalische Zeitung* of the early 1820s used extensive rhetorical imagery. On Kanne, see Krones, "Rhetorik und rhetorische Symbolik," pp. 125–127.

Georg Joseph Vogler, in the last decade of the eighteenth century, observes that the technique of variation is itself an essentially rhetorical procedure. In his "Improvements" upon Forkel's earlier set of variations on "God Save the King," Vogler asserts that

> variations are a kind of musical rhetoric, in which the same idea is presented in various turns, with the difference that the limitations in music are much more precise than in verbal rhetoric . . . In spite of this strict adherence to the theme, which one may never lose from one's sight, there is, on the other hand, if one is speaking of the manner of presentation, an opening to the widest possible field.[147]

The process of elaboration, in other words, is more strict within the genre of theme and variations, but the rhetorical concept of elaboration itself is applicable to virtually all genres.[148]

Yet a great many—indeed most—instrumental works from the Classical era incorporate more than a single theme. Hiller's anonymous lexicographer, working in the late 1760s, had already alluded to a hierarchy of ideas within a single work: a main idea, supported by subordinate and connecting ideas. This concern reflects a stylistic change in music around the middle of the eighteenth century. Whereas individual instrumental movements of the Baroque era had in fact tended to elaborate a single theme, more and more mid-century composers were beginning to explore the use of overt thematic contrasts within a single movement. It was no longer deemed aesthetically necessary for a single passion or a single idea to dominate throughout. The disposition and elaboration of the main theme would remain essential to the structure of the movement as a whole, but subsidiary themes could now be taken into account as well.

Contemporary theorists often justified the presence of contrasting themes within a movement by the doctrine of "unity in variety," one of the most important aesthetic doctrines of the eighteenth century, not only in music, but in all the arts.[149] Variety provides the diversity necessary to sustain a movement-length whole; but the predominance of a main theme, a central idea, also ensures the unity necessary to sustain a coherent whole.

---

147. Vogler, *Verbesserung der Forkel'schen Veränderungen über das englische Volkslied God Save the King* (Frankfurt/Main: Varentrapp und Wenner, 1793), pp. 5–6. I am grateful to Elaine Sisman for calling this passage to my attention. See also Jones, *A Treatise on the Art of Music,* p. 46.

148. On the relationship between variation technique and the genre of variation, see Elaine Sisman, "Haydn's Variations" (Ph.D. diss., Princeton University, 1978).

149. See Sulzer, *Allgemeine Theorie,* articles "Einheit" and "Mannichfaltigkeit"; Johann Christoph Adelung, *Über den deutschen Styl,* 3 vols. (Berlin: C. F. Voss und Sohn, 1785; rpt. Hildesheim: Olms, 1974), I, 522–530; F. Fleischmann, "Wie muss ein Tonstück beschaffen seyn, um gut genannt werden zu können?" *AMZ,* 1 (1799), cols. 209–213, 225–228.

For contemporary writers on music, rhetoric played a central role in rationalizing the coherence of thematic diversity within a movement. Riepel's *discantista*, who, as we have seen, at one point argues in favor of variety, elsewhere criticizes an overabundance of contrast in another composition, maintaining that the composer must adhere to his theme, just as a preacher must adhere to the Gospel text that provides the basis for his sermon. The *praeceptor* corrects his pupil once again: just as an orator will often delay the introduction of an important point, a composer is free to present contrasting or subordinate themes after the *Hauptsatz:* "The master has indeed stayed with the theme. A preacher cannot constantly repeat the Gospel and read it over and over; instead, he must interpret it. He in fact makes transitions, etc. In addition to the thesis [*Satz*], he has at the very least an antithesis [*Gegensatz*]."[150]

Marpurg, writing in 1761, notes that a movement's predominant idea, its *Hauptsatz,* must give birth to other ideas (*Gedanken*) that "flow out of it" and as such are necessarily related:

Will not an idea soon come flowing out of the main idea [*Hauptsatz*] of a piece? In every musical work there must certainly be something that projects slightly above the rest. This something, whether it appears immediately at the beginning, in the first section, or in the second, I call the *Hauptsatz,* which through repetitions, transpositions, imitations, and fragmentations must be manipulated. The passages that arise in different fashions from these processes serve to preserve the unity of the musical work. If one alternates the *Hauptsatz,* or the ideas that flow out of it, with a new secondary idea, according to an established, rational plan, and if one manipulates this secondary idea in the same manner as the earlier one, within appropriate proportions—there arises from this connection of the *Hauptsatz* with the secondary idea (as well as of the respective sections arising out of these ideas, which are, so to speak, so many new movements [*Sätze*] in their own way) the variety of a musical work.[151]

The anonymous author of the *Musikalisches Handwörterbuch* published in Weimar in 1786 also uses the image of ideas "flowing" out of the *Hauptsatz.*[152] Jacob Schubak, writing in 1775, describes the relationship between a melody's main theme and its "secondary" ideas in much the same way, again emphasizing the primacy of the *Hauptsatz:*

150. Riepel, *Anfangsgründe . . . Grundregeln zur Tonordnung,* p. 76. The image of the preacher and his sermon is repeated on pp. 99 and 104. In the article "Hauptsatz" in the *Allgemeine Theorie,* Sulzer (assisted by Kirnberger) cites with approval Mattheson's earlier use of this same image.

151. Friedrich Wilhelm Marpurg, *Kritische Briefe über die Tonkunst,* no. 85 (7 November 1761), p. 161.

152. *Musikalisches Handwörterbuch* (Weimar: Carl Ludolf Hoffmanns seel. Wittwe und Erben, 1786), "Thema."

Every composer who has a thorough understanding of how to write for instruments knows that one chooses a certain proposition or theme, which one allows to be heard first at the beginning, then especially in the elaboration of the piece, and then once again at or near the end. Certainly, there are exceptions to this; but I am not speaking of them. There are also certain secondary propositions, or secondary themes [Neben-Themata], which are elaborated in approximately the same manner, and which at the very least are not to be omitted from consideration once they have been presented. I am not speaking here of the contrapuntal countersubject, of which much could be said . . . instead, I continue to refer to that which a single voice must accomplish.[153]

Johann Nepomuk Reichenberger, in 1780, similarly uses rhetorical imagery to describe the nature and function of secondary ideas. Just like the orator, the composer

introduces his *Satz,* or theme, early on; and he repeats it briefly once or twice at this point, in order that it be well understood. He continues . . . until he finally brings together everything announced earlier. And often, after he has fought his way through passages and progressions that may at first have seemed contradictory to his intentions, after he has aroused, by means of the most refined harmonies and rhythms, all affects and passions that are useful to his intention—after all these routes, he finally arrives once again at his sentence and goal in the original key.[154]

Even works as rich in thematic variety as Mozart's piano concertos, sonatas, and serenades consistently reveal a process of unfolding and elaboration. Charles Rosen has convincingly demonstrated the remarkable economy of material and the central importance of thematic continuity in the opening movement of the Concerto in E-flat, K. 271: each seemingly new idea is in fact a new elaboration, spun out of preceding ones.[155] Economy is not a virtue in and of itself, nor is it in any respect "natural"; but the process of thematic elaboration does contribute to the coherence of the whole and prevents a work from becoming a mere potpourri of ideas.[156] Christoph Wolff, in a similar fashion, has shown how the succession of ideas within the first movement of the Piano Sonata in F Major, K. 533/494, is based on an ongoing elaboration of thematic material.[157] And as

153. Schubak, *Von der musicalischen Declamation* (Göttingen: Vandenhoecks Wittwe, 1775), pp. 41–42.

154. Reichenberger, *Die ganze Musikkunst,* 3 vols. (Regensburg: Hochfürstlich- bischöfliches Schulhaus bey St. Paul, 1777–1780), III, 160–161.

155. Rosen, *The Classical Style,* pp. 199–211.

156. On the covert assumption that "economy" is an inherently positive and "natural" attribute in works of music, see Levy, "Covert and Casual Values"; and Leonard B. Meyer, *Style and Music: Theory, History, Ideology* (Philadelphia: University of Pennsylvania Press, 1989), pp. 193–195.

157. Wolff, "Musikalische 'Gedankenfolge' und 'Einheit des Stoffes': Zu Mozarts

Joseph Kerman has argued in his brief analysis of the opening movement of *Eine kleine Nachtmusik, K. 525*, even as light and unpretentious a genre as the serenade can exhibit these same qualities of elaboration and coherence, albeit to a somewhat lesser degree.[158] Thus, we should not be so quick to approach Mozart's less assuming genres as "garlands of song-like melodies."[159] The garland-like quality of these works is superficial.

Postulating connections among seemingly diverse ideas need not degenerate into the kind of theme-mongering so common in quests for *Substanz-gemeinschaft*. The search for such connections, as Dahlhaus points out, can become obsessive, as it unquestionably has in the work of certain analysts.[160] But the rhetorical concept of musical form, it should be remembered, does not insist that a single idea be omnipresent, either within a movement or across an entire cycle of movements. On the contrary, the metaphor of the musical work as an oration allows for—indeed demands—digressions, secondary ideas, and even genuine contrasts, provided that these ideas are presented within a wider framework of thought that is sufficiently coherent.

Unfortunately, there are no accepted criteria for determining the thematic "coherence" or "unity" of any given work. Connections that are obvious to one analyst may seem preposterous to another. Perhaps the only true criterion for evaluating the legitimacy of such an approach, as Peter Kivy suggests, is to consider the extent to which such an analysis can be integrated into subsequent hearings of the work at hand.[161] Much of the problem lies in the fact that one's evaluation of the relationship among thematic ideas in any individual work or movement depends largely upon one's broader belief in (or skepticism toward) the very legitimacy of such connections. The evidence presented in this chapter suggests that, from a historical perspective, the search for such links is entirely justified. It must, however, be approached with the understanding that even two analysts

---

Klaviersonate in F-Dur (KV 533 & 494)," in *Das musikalische Kunstwerk . . . Festschrift Carl Dahlhaus zum 60. Geburtstag,* ed. Hermann Danuser et al. (Laaber: Laaber-Verlag, 1988), pp. 441–453.

158. Kerman, "Theories of Late Eighteenth-Century Music," pp. 236–239.

159. Walter Wiora, "Die historische und systematische Betrachtung der musikalischen Gattungen," *Deutsches Jahrbuch der Musikwissenschaft für 1965,* p. 8.

160. Dahlhaus, "Zur Theorie der musikalischen Form," pp. 26–29. See also Dahlhaus's "Unité de Mélodie," in *Aufklärungen: Studien zur deutsch-französischen Musikgeschichte im 18. Jahrhundert,* II, ed. Wolfgang Birtel and Christoph-Hellmut Mahling (Heidelberg: Carl Winter Universitätsverlag, 1986), pp. 23–29.

161. Kivy, *Music Alone: Philosophical Reflections on the Purely Musical Experience* (Ithaca, N.Y.: Cornell University Press, 1990), p. 143; see pp. 130–145 for a critique of the theories of Rudolf Réti, one of the most extreme advocates of *Substanzgemeinschaft.*

convinced of the basic legitimacy of this idea and dealing with the same work are likely to produce at least three different opinions.[162]

The brief analysis that follows, dealing with the first movement of Mozart's String Quartet in C Major, K. 465 ("The Dissonant," 1785: see Example 2.4), is offered in this spirit, in an attempt to elucidate what Marpurg and others might have meant in speaking of ideas that "flow" out of the *Hauptsatz*. The slow introduction to this movement, with its extreme and sustained dissonances, is justly celebrated as one of the most demanding passages in the entire Classical repertoire, for performers and listeners alike; its harmony and voice-leading have been the object of analysis on many occasions.[163] Here, however, I would like to take a somewhat different approach and consider the slow introduction and exposition of the Allegro from the perspective of how the *Hauptsatz* is elaborated.

The theme or *Hauptsatz* of the first movement is not a single melodic line, but the polyphonic network of all four voices at the beginning of the introduction. The pitches, rhythms, and harmonies of these opening measures all figure in the subsequent course of the movement. Thus the form of this movement cannot be explained solely on the basis of any one of these instrumental lines or any one of these elements in isolation, but only through their coordination. What follows these opening measures can be interpreted either as derivatives or counterideas to the *Hauptsatz*—or as a fulfillment of both functions at one and the same time, as is in fact most often the case.

Given its dense polyphonic texture, it is scarcely surprising that the *Hauptsatz* at the very opening cannot be divided into a simple texture of melody and accompaniment. But it is surprisingly difficult to draw such distinctions even in the more homophonic Allegro that follows. For while the middle voices in mm. 23–30 do indeed function as an accompaniment to the first violin, they also represent a diatonic reinterpretation of the cello's pedal point C and descending chromatic line in mm. 1–12. What seems to function "merely" as accompaniment at the opening of the Allegro, in other words, represents the elaboration of an important idea presented within the opening measures of the work. In this manner, certain basic elements of the *Hauptsatz* are reinterpreted within an utterly contrasting manifestation: a

162. James Webster's forthcoming monograph on Haydn's "Farewell" Symphony includes an extended and judicious discussion of this problem. Webster makes the important point that while the "discovery" of thematic connections depends in large part upon one's faith in the existence of such connections ("Seek and ye shall find"), fundamental skepticism in this regard may be as unwarranted as fundamental belief.

163. See Julie Ann Vertrees, "Mozart's String Quartet K. 465: The History of a Controversy," *Current Musicology*, no. 17 (1974), 96–114; Françoise Lacour, *Les quatuors de Mozart dédiés à Haydn. Etude analytique et ésthétique* (Paris: Maîtrise, 1985).

descending line (motive "a," chromatic in the introduction, diatonic in the Allegro) beneath an ascending line (motive "b," a tritone in the introduction, a perfect fifth in the Allegro) that moves by sequence (down a step in the introduction, up a step in the Allegro). The basic rhythms of these two lines from the opening measures are also preserved in the Allegro: a steady pulse of eighth notes in the lower voices, and a longer note-value followed by a series of shorter ones in the ascending line. The underlying pulse of the introduction's opening makes the rhythmic vagueness of the upper voices there all the more pronounced, while the similarly steady but faster pulse of the Allegro underscores the two-plus-two periodic regularity of the first violin above it (mm. 23–30). The imitative counterpoint that plays such an important role in the introduction figures prominently throughout much of the Allegro at later points as well (mm. 32–36, 44–47, 75–76, 79–83, 91–99, and so on), as do the chromatic elements that have been the focus of so much attention surrounding this work (mm. 73–75, 93–94, 227–232, 242–244 of the Allegro, and more powerfully still in subsequent movements).

Within the Allegro itself, what might be considered the "reconstituted" *Hauptsatz* (mm. 23ff.) provides a new starting point for the subsequent ideas that flow out of it. Motive "b" is restated in m. 31, transposed down an octave and with a new "accompaniment" in imitative counterpoint. The extension of this statement in mm. 35–39 articulates the previously tied eighth-note figure within "b," creating a new rhythm of ♩♪♪♪ out of ♪♪♪♩ . The origins of this figure in the three-note grouping of "b" is recalled in the *sforzando* markings of mm. 36–37. This rhythmic figure is further manipulated in mm. 40–43: the three-note grouping of eighths returns, but now preceded by eighth-note rests (♪♪♪♩ becomes 𝄾♪♪♪).

In m. 44, we arrive at a root-position cadence on the tonic, which is elided to begin the transition to the dominant. Once again, Mozart elaborates his material by varying ideas derived from "b."

In mm. 47–50 of the first violin, we hear one of those phrases that at first strike us as an elegant but not terribly significant variation of a previous idea. The triad D-B-G (♪♪♩·) is diminuted to become D-B-D-B-G (♬♬♩·). This initially unobtrusive variant becomes a springboard for a great deal that follows. For a time, the forward motion of the movement seems to be "stuck" on this four-note sixteenth-figure, which continues (in various guises) almost unabated until the cadence on V/V at m. 55.

Later analysts would call the idea in the dominant beginning in m. 56 the "second theme," and it does indeed contrast with the opening of the Allegro: it has a wide range, against the opening's rather narrow ambitus; detached articulation (as opposed to the legato phrasing in m. 23ff.); it is

2.4 Mozart, String Quartet, K. 465, first movement, mm. 1–112. From Wolfgang Amadeus Mozart, *Neue Ausgabe Sämtlicher Werke,* series VIII, workgroup 20, pt. 1, v. 2, ed. Ludwig Finscher (Kassel: Bärenreiter, 1962). Used by permission.

2.4   continued

2.4   continued

2.4   continued

2.4 continued

2.4 continued

loud rather than soft. But there are important points of continuity here as well: the downbeat attack, the repeated notes in the cello (broken off after the third beat in m. 56 but more significant than most performances of this work would lead one to believe); and the continuation of the bustling sixteenth-note rhythm across the three upper instruments, a procedure clearly derived from mm. 50–55.

The countersubject to this sixteenth-note figure that appears in m. 60, like the sixteenth-note embellishment of m. 50, also enters unobtrusively; but it, too, will have an important role to play in the remainder of the movement. Its consequent shows a strong rhythmic resemblance to "b," and it is this consequent that Mozart chooses to elaborate.

After a full cadence at m. 71, the pace slackens (nineteenth-century analysts, if consistent, would have had to have called this the "'second' second theme"), and Mozart now returns to the opening of the countersubject introduced eleven measures before. The two quarter-note pick-ups on the same pitch followed by a half-step descent derive from m. 60; the triplet rhythm and accompanimental texture provide variety, while the chromatic line in the second violin (mm. 73–74) and the chromatic countersubject in the first violin provide a further point of continuity with the movement's slow introduction. A new triplet rhythm figures prominently in the subsequent passage (mm. 79–83), while the sixteenth-note passagework of mm. 84–90 is reminiscent of mm. 56ff. At m. 91, the reconstituted *Hauptsatz* returns yet again, this time with a pedal-point harmony that recalls both the opening of the slow introduction and the opening of the Allegro.

There is ample room for disagreement as to the details of this or any comparable analysis that seeks to show "the manner in which the thoughts within an entire melody or period follow one another"—the definition of "form" according to Hiller's anonymous lexicographer. But there seems little doubt that these are the kinds of procedures that Riepel, Marpurg, and others are referring to when they speak of a movement's unity or coherence. In the case of K. 465, the overt and repeated use of the *Hauptsatz* in a variety of guises to fulfill three different functions within the exposition alone— opening (mm. 23ff.), transitional (mm. 44ff.), and closing (mm. 91ff.)— illustrates this principle in a particularly striking fashion.

Even this brief review of the matrix of melodic ideas, rhythms, harmonies, textures, instrumentation, and dynamics within a single section of a single movement suggests that it would be pointless, in one respect, to ascribe conceptual primacy to any one of these elements in the construction of form. It is only through the coordination of these various factors that a work achieves coherence and shape. Each of these elements offers a very different perspective on the nature of form, and all of them are legitimate and necessary to its understanding.

It may thus seem misleading at first to describe the eighteenth century's concept of form as essentially "thematic." But the eighteenth century's understanding of form is "thematic" in a manner that is quite different from the nineteenth century's preoccupation with the character and placement of specific melodic ideas within a movement. It is "thematic" in that it confers primacy to the unfolding and elaboration of a work's thematic ideas, beginning with, and to a large extent deriving from, the *Hauptsatz*. These "themes" are not to be equated with the nineteenth century's idea of "melodies"; instead, they are best understood in the rhetorical sense, as the subjects of a discourse, regardless of whether they are monophonic, homophonic, or polyphonic in texture.

Describing the eighteenth century's conceptual basis of form as "thematic" also has the advantage of retaining the era's perception of the link between the fabric of a polyphonic idea and the leading melodic voice within that idea. According to context, a *Satz* can be interpreted as a monophonic phrase, a multi-voiced phrase, a complete melody (in the eighteenth-century's sense of the term), or an entire movement as polyphonic whole. As a particular type of *Satz*, a *Hauptsatz* can be either monophonic or polyphonic. The terminological coincidence is significant, for it manifests the deeply rooted associations of theme and melody with form. While a "theme" as a single melodic line within a polyphonic texture cannot express the full nature of the work's central idea, it can and more often than not does embody the essence of that idea. By the same token, a movement's leading melodic line (which, it should be recalled, can migrate from voice to voice throughout), usually incorporates the most important elements of pitch and rhythm that constitute the polyphonic whole. Harmony, although not explicitly present within a single line, tends to be strongly implied. Melody alone is capable of synthesizing, however imperfectly, the variety of elements that go into a work of music: rhythm—small-scale periodic structures as well as larger-scale cadential articulations—almost always plays a prominent role in a movement's leading melodic line; and harmony, by the same token, is likely to be implied within that same line. Clearly, there are exceptions to these tendencies; but melody, on the whole, provides a framework of form that other elements do not.

The relationship of the theme or *Hauptsatz* to melody helps explain why eighteenth-century accounts of movement-length formal coherence, few as they may be, are most often found within the larger context of *Melodielehren*. Indeed, it is only from the perspective of form as the concatenation of melodic ideas—Koch's "individual melodic sections united into a whole"— that a larger theory of musical form can be developed in such a way as to accommodate large-scale stereotypical patterns and yet at the same time avoid the nineteenth century's aesthetic dichotomy between "inner" and "outer" form. To consider form only from the perspective of large-scale harmony or rhythm (that is, periodicity) only perpetuates the idea of form as a framework different from and thus necessarily inferior to a work's "true" substance. Harmony and rhythm, working in tandem, can and do help to articulate the melodic unfolding of a movement, but they constitute at best only an external kind of form in which the essence of a work—that which makes it different from all others—remains to be "filled in." The harmonic view of form, as seen in Chapter 1, represents a lowest-common-denominator approach resulting in a framework for the "thematic super-structure" of some (but by no means all) forms. And while the concept of form as a series of concatenated periods articulated by cadences represents a more flexible approach to the problem, it, too, equates form with the process of articulation. Cadences—Koch's "resting points of the spirit"— are an undeniably important factor in the matrix of elements that give a movement its form, but an outline of a movement's cadential structure tends to emphasize the process of articulation at the expense of that which is being articulated.[164] Like the harmonic concept of form, this view per-petuates a dichotomy between content and form in which the latter plays an aesthetically inferior role.

If we are to accord any meaning to the term "form" beyond "the shape of a musical composition as defined by *all* of its pitches, rhythms, dynam-ics, and timbres,"[165] then we must focus our attention on a substratum of the work, a level that represents something less than its totality. Likewise, if we are to avoid the aesthetic disparity of the form/content dichotomy, we must assign form-giving powers to an element that is neither static (such as large-scale areas of harmonic stability) nor present only at isolated junctures (such as cadences). The trajectory of thematic events within the course of a melody provides such an element. It is an analytical substratum that can be expanded through the process of elaboration and not merely "filled in."

Moreover, it is only melody—in the eighteenth-century sense of the term—that can represent the identity of a musical work or movement un-ambiguously. Clearly, the first violin part in the slow introduction to the Quartet K. 465, to return to our example, cannot by itself provide the basis for a comprehensive analysis; but it can, at the very least, establish the uniqueness of this work in a way that even the most detailed harmonic or cadential outline could not. The first violin part here incorporates the es-sence of the melodic, harmonic, and rhythmic events that will prove central to the movement as a whole. The opening gesture is highly chromatic and

164. In explicating the importance of rhythmic articulation in Koch's view of form, Dahlhaus tends to underestimate the importance of thematic events within the course of a movement. See his "Der rhetorische Formbegriff H. Chr. Kochs und die Theorie der Sonatenform," *AfMw*, 35 (1978), 155–177.

165. See above, p. 28.

melodically dissonant, especially in the tritone motion from G to D♭ in mm. 4–5: it projects in linear fashion the pronounced vertical dissonances that figure so prominently between the four voices as a whole. The contour and rhythms of the Allegro's opening, as already noted, are also inherent in the opening five measures of this same voice. And while this single line by its vary nature cannot embody all of the elements that must constitute the focus of analysis, it does in fact incorporate a sufficient number of those elements to project the basic sequence of the movement's most important events, "the manner in which the thoughts within an entire melody or period follow one another."

To the extent that anything less than the full score can project the identity of a movement, then, it is the melodic trajectory of that movement that comes closest to preserving its individuality. Melody, after all, is the most readily intelligible of vehicles for the listener's apprehension of musical events; and intelligibility, as we have seen, is a vital requisite of coherence and aesthetic value throughout the eighteenth century. In his late (1811) *Handbuch bey dem Studium der Harmonie,* Koch elaborates on an idea he had hinted at earlier in both the *Versuch* and in the *Lexikon:* the melody of a work embodies "the ideal of the composer, or at the same time the sketch of the musical picture." Such a melody, often called the *Hauptmelodie,* is the essence of the *Tonrede,* for it is the element of music that more than any other "addresses our spirits in the act of performance."[166]

The melody of a movement also represents most closely the product of *dispositio* or *Anordnung,* that stage of the compositional process, as interpreted by eighteenth-century theorists, which establishes the large-scale structure of a musical whole. A composer's sketches might range from random, fragmentary thoughts (the product of *inventio*) to a complete movement just short of a finished realization of the final score (the product of *elocutio*). What lies in between can cover a very wide range, but somewhere around the middle of this spectrum lies a realization in which melodic ideas will be predominant. The preserved sketches of Haydn, Mozart, and Beethoven all confirm that what we now think of as a "continuity draft"—a preliminary version of the score showing the general disposition of ideas and the succession of events, albeit without considerable detail—consists largely of melodic ideas. Harmonies can certainly be indicated throughout, and Koch, among others, urged composers to "think of melody harmonically" *(die Melodie harmonisch denken).*[167] But the vehicle for conveying the

---

166. Koch, *Handbuch bey dem Studium der Harmonie* (Leipzig: J. F. Hartknoch, 1811), pp. 8–9.

167. Koch, *Versuch,* II, 81. On Vogler's similar formulation of this concept, see Jürgen Neubacher, "'Idee' und 'Ausführung': Zum Kompositionsprozess bei Joseph Haydn," *AfMw,* 41 (1984), 197.

larger-scale coherence of the movement lies in its melody. Griesinger, for one, reported that "Haydn completed his compositions in one outpouring; for each section he set down the plan of the main voice by noting the prominent passages with a few notes and figures." Only later did the composer "breathe spirit and life into this dry skeleton by means of the accompanying voices and through artful transitions."[168] Koch and Daube describe the compositional process in much the same terms.[169]

Haydn's "prominent passages," as noted earlier, often correspond to what we would now identify as the opening of the exposition, development, and recapitulation of a sonata-form movement, and it is significant that the "plan" of each of these sections was conveyed with a single melodic line. It is also significant that Riepel, Galeazzi, and later Reicha, among others, either intentionally chose or at the very least were able to illustrate the construction of large-scale forms with musical examples that consist of only a single melodic line.

Musical form in the Classical era was thus conceived of thematically in both the musical and rhetorical senses of the term: the elaboration of a central idea was seen to shape the trajectory of subsequent ideas (including the recurrence of the central idea) throughout a movement. Leonard Ratner is certainly correct to point out that "classic sonata form has something of the character of a forensic exercise, a rhetorical discourse," but it is not "the opening keys" that constitute the "premises to be argued." For Ratner, the "forces" of these key areas "are *represented* by their respective thematic material," and the large-scale harmonic units are "colored" by their "rich thematic content."[170] But from the theorists surveyed in this chapter, it is clearly the themes themselves, particularly the *Hauptsatz*, that provide the central premises to be argued in any form, and not merely sonata form alone.

The eighteenth century's understanding of form as a process of thematic elaboration can accommodate a movement's adherence to, or deviation from, stereotypical patterns of form. The thematically oriented concept of form is applicable to virtually all forms from the period under consideration here, for with the possible exception of the fantasia and the closely related capriccio, there are no truly "athematic" genres. In point of fact, the fantasia and the capriccio prove to be revealing exceptions that further help elucidate

168. Griesinger, *Biographische Notizen*, p. 79.

169. Koch, *Versuch*, II, 79–83; Daube, *Anleitung zur Erfindung der Melodie*, II, 38. See also Ratner, *Classic Music*, p. 81; Schafer, "'A Wisely Ordered Phantasie'"; Neubacher, "'Idee' und 'Ausführung'," pp. 187–207.

170. Ratner, *Classic Music*, p. 246. See also his "Key Definition: A Structural Issue," p. 472. I am aware of only one eighteenth-century writer, not cited by Ratner, who likens the key-areas of a movement to the propositions of a discourse. In his *Musical Dictionary* of 1740 (London: J. Wilcox), James Grassineau uses this analogy in defining the term "Key."

the thematic basis of form, for within the realm of instrumental music, these are the only genres that can legitimately claim to be wholly unrelated to any kind of stereotypical pattern. They are the two "forms" (if the term may be applied to a work whose essence is a complete lack of any predictable pattern) that are based on the variety of their thematic ideas rather than on the manipulation and development of a single theme or a limited number of related ideas.[171] Elaboration can certainly be present within a fantasia and indeed often is; but this quality is not essential, whereas it is to all other forms in the period under consideration here.

Mattheson, like most theorists before the nineteenth century, treats the fantasia as a style rather than as a genre, for it is not, in Mattheson's terms, a *Melodie-Gattung*. It is the "freest and least constrained manner of composing, singing, and playing imaginable, for one sometimes lights upon a sudden idea, and then another, as one is bound neither to words nor a melody, . . . without a formative *Hauptsatz* and outline, without a theme or subject that is to be elaborated."[172]

One of the distinguishing characteristics of the fantasia, for Mattheson, is the lack of a formal—that is, form-shaping—*Hauptsatz*. This basic idea recurs throughout the century. Klein, for example, notes in 1783 that "a melody that binds itself to neither a *Hauptsatz* nor a distinct rhythm is called a *fantasia* or capriccio."[173]

Thus the fantasia's melody—in the eighteenth-century sense of the term—does not unfold through the elaboration of its constituent elements. It is determined, instead, by the *inventio* of the composer. Koch, in his *Lexikon* of 1802, defines the "Capriccio" as a type of work in which the "composer does not adhere to the conventional forms and modulations, but instead gives rein to the prevailing mood of his fantasy, rather than to a thought-out plan."[174] At the same time, Koch points out, this approach does not mean that such a work is chaotic; rather, the concatenation of its ideas does not follow conventional patterns, and the *Hauptsatz* need not necessarily play the predominant role it does in other forms. Elsewhere, in describing his view of the compositional process, Koch similarly notes that one's own fantasy, if given excessively free rein, will lead to subsidiary ideas (*Nebenideen*) that are "too far removed" from the movement's central ideas embodied in the *Anlage*.[175]

---

171. Hugo Riemann, in his *Grundriss der Kompositionslehre,* 2 vols. (Berlin: M. Hesse, 1905), II, 120, calls the fantasia a "Nicht-Form."

172. Mattheson, *Capellmeister,* p. 88. Harriss's translation (p. 217) of "ausgeführt" as "performed" distorts much of the sense of this passage.

173. Klein, *Versuch eines Lehrbuchs,* p. 61.

174. Koch, *Musikalisches Lexikon,* "Capriccio."

175. Koch, *Versuch,* II, 97. See also Czerny's similar comments from as late as ca. 1840 in *School of Practical Composition,* I, 35.

This distinction between "conventional forms," on the one hand, and the fantasia and capriccio, on the other, is borne out in the contemporary repertoire. C. P. E. Bach's "free" fantasias in particular—those notated without bar-lines—are thought to be the best available evidence of their composer's widely acclaimed improvisational abilities. They often move from idea to idea with little or no apparent sense of continuity or predictability. Mozart's and Beethoven's fantasias, although more tightly organized, exhibit strong elements of this improvisatory character, with a degree of harmonic and thematic freedom not found in the sonatas. Haydn's infrequent use of the term is somewhat more problematic, in that his few works labeled as such are very much dominated by a *Hauptsatz*. On the other hand, the second movement of the Quartet in C Major, Op. 20, No. 2, labeled "Capriccio," exhibits the kind of thematic discontinuity traditionally associated with this genre. The opening section in C Minor breaks off abruptly in m. 33, only to be supplanted by a cantabile section in E-flat that is of a completely contrasting character. And although the two halves of the movement are related by subtle thematic connections, there is no articulated return to the opening theme.[176]

Nevertheless, the term *fantasieren,* for Haydn, is demonstrably associated with the process of *inventio* and the free succession of ideas. Near the end of his life, he described the initial stages of his own compositional method in just these terms:

I sat down [at the keyboard] and began to fantasize, according to whether my mood was sad or happy, serious or playful. Once I had seized an idea, my entire effort went toward elaborating and sustaining it according to the rules of art . . . And this is what is lacking among so many of our young composers; they string together one little bit after another, and they break off before they have barely begun, but nothing remains in the heart when one has heard it.[177]

The traditional distinction between *inventio* and *elaboratio* is clearly evident here. The original ideas are the product of the composer's fantasy and in one sense beyond his control: the shape in which they come to him depends upon his mood. But once *an* idea—not a series of ideas, but *"eine* Idee," the *Hauptsatz*—has been established, the composer begins to apply the technique of his craft and elaborates *(führt aus)* that idea "according to the rules of art."[178]

176. For a useful discussion of Haydn's concept of the fantasia and capriccio, see A. Peter Brown, *Joseph Haydn's Keyboard Music: Sources and Style* (Bloomington: Indiana University Press, 1986), pp. 221–229.

177. Griesinger, *Biographische Notizen,* p. 78.

178. For further commentary on this and other passages relating to Haydn and the term "fantasiren" in the early biographies of Griesinger and Dies, see Schafer, "'A Wisely Ordered *Phantasie*'," I, 138–197, and II, 1–3.

In noting the failure of younger composers to elaborate a main idea sufficiently, Haydn might well have added that such a procedure could be condoned for the genres of fantasia and capriccio; but these genres do not represent the mainstream of composition, and Haydn's views on the importance of thematic elaboration are shared by many of his contemporaries.[179]

In his *Handbuch der Aesthetik,* published shortly before 1800, the aesthetician Johann Heinrich Gottlieb Heusinger sums up this fundamental distinction between the fantasia—the product of the process of *fantasieren*—and what might be called the more "elaborative" categories of form. Heusinger notes that an "entirely free fantasia" has "neither a theme nor an intention," and it "sometimes surprises artists when its imagination flees the reins of understanding."[180] Clearly, neither Mattheson nor Heusinger nor any other theorist of the day means to imply that the fantasia lacks themes, but rather, that it lacks a *central* theme, a *Hauptsatz* that governs the remainder of the work. The emphasis in nonelaborative works centers on *Erfindung* rather than *Ausarbeitung; inventio* takes center stage at the expense of *elaboratio.* Heusinger's comment—"when [the fantasia's] imagination flees the reins of understanding"—is particularly revealing, for it touches on the necessity of making the product of *inventio* intelligible through the more calculated process of *elaboratio.* Klein similarly makes a clear distinction between musical fantasias and the "well-ordered *chreia* and artful discourses of our best spiritual and secular orators."[181]

This is not to say that notated fantasias are in fact the product of little or no reflection, but rather that as a genre they enjoy the option of giving the impression that they are free of all deliberation. Indeed, the lack of any structural stereotype, and the fact that elaboration is at best an optional quality for the fantasia, require this genre to be judged by standards different from all others. As Heusinger points out, anyone would concede that "one can say more about a large piece, e.g., a symphony, than about a free fantasia." Yet "no critic has ever thought to criticize the latter, while the former are rigorously criticized, even if unfortunately only seldom in print."[182]

This distinction between two broad categories of form—the free and the elaborative—is based at least in part on a distinction between genres, and as such touches on the crucial link between genre and form. To some extent, all elaborative genres and forms can be viewed from the generative per-

179. See Daube, *Anleitung zur Erfindung der Melodie,* I, 25; Koch, *Versuch,* II, 131–133; Galeazzi, *Elementi,* II, 253.

180. Johann Heinrich Gottlieb Heusinger, *Handbuch der Aesthetik,* 2 vols. (Gotha: Justus Perthes, 1797), I, 153.

181. Johann Joseph Klein, *Lehrbuch der theoretischen Musik* (Offenbach/Main: Johann André, 1800), p. iv.

182. Heusinger, *Handbuch der Aesthetik,* I, 155.

spective: the composer begins with a single idea, and the movement grows out of this germinal unit. But this, as noted before, is a process common to all elaborative genres and forms. The various conventional forms, such as the rondo, theme and variations, and sonata form, are differentiated by the manner in which they elaborate their thematic ideas.

Genre, Formal Convention, and Individual Genius

Our modern-day concept of form as an abstract pattern tends to be divorced from specific genres. A rondo or a sonata-form movement can appear within any number of different kinds of works, from a concerto to a symphony to a sonata. But to eighteenth-century theorists and aestheticians, the form of a work, be it an oration or a musical composition, is strongly influenced by the genre to which it belongs. The conventions of traditional rhetoric dictate that the nature and effective ordering of ideas in a funeral oration, for example, will necessarily differ from those of a sermon, a panegyric, or a university lecture. Within a work of music, the nature of a *Hauptsatz* and its subsequent elaboration similarly vary from genre to genre. Eighteenth-century theorists conceived of genres not only on the basis of their function and instrumentation but also according to the manner in which their thematic ideas are elaborated. Genre, in other words, is determined in part by melody, at least in the eighteenth-century sense of the term.

The connection between melody, genre, and form is most clearly evident in the methodology by which Mattheson, Koch, and other contemporary theorists introduce their accounts of specific large-scale forms within discussions of genre, which in turn appear under the still broader rubric of melody. Mattheson entitles the second part of *Der vollkommene Capellmeister* "The True Crafting of a Melody, or a Single Line, Together with its Circumstances and Characteristics," and it is in the thirteenth chapter of this part that he deals with "Genres of Melodies and Their Particular Marks of Distinction."[183] The entire second half of Koch's *Versuch* is devoted to "The Mechanical Rules of Melody," and the whole of the third volume deals with "The Concatenation of Melodic Segments, or the Construction of Periods." It is in the fourth chapter of this volume, addressing the manipulation of periods at the largest level, that Koch describes specific genres: "On the

---

183. Mattheson, *Capellmeister*, pt. 2, "Darin die wirckliche Verfertigung einer Melodie, oder des einstimmigen Gesanges, samt dessen Umständen und Eigenschafften, gelehret werden," ch. 13, "Von den Gattungen der Melodien und ihren besondern Abzeichen."

Concatenation of Melodic Segments into Periods of Larger Dimensions, or On the Ordering of Larger Musical Movements."[184]

This same general methodology is also found in Ernst Wilhelm Wolf's *Musikalischer Unterricht* of 1788, which concludes its discussion of periodicity with "Something on the Ordering of Musical Movements," an account organized according to genre.[185] The fifth part of Jean Baptiste Mercadier's *Nouveau système de musique* of 1776, "Which Deals with Practical Music," includes a chapter on constructing an entire movement ("The Manner of Dealing with a Harmonic Whole") that also ends with a discussion of such specific genres as sonata and symphony.[186] This basic pattern is evident once again in the second volume of Francesco Galeazzi's *Elementi teorico-pratici di musica* of 1796. Under the heading "On Melody" (part 5, section 2), Galeazzi moves from *inventio* (articles 1 and 2) to *dispositio,* (article 3), deals briefly with the issue of large-scale modulation (article 4), and concludes with a description of various genres (articles 5 and 6).

The tradition of treating movement-length form as a function of genre continued well into the nineteenth century. In his *Lehrbuch der allgemeinen Musikwissenschaft* of 1840, Gustav Schilling directly equates *Formenlehre* with the concept of genre (section 5, "Musical *Formenlehre,* or a Brief Description of Individual Works That Can Be Named").[187] And Ferdinand Hand, in his *Aesthetik der Tonkunst* (1841) moves from "The Laws of [Melodic] Elaboration" directly into a review of genres.[188] For much of the nineteenth century, in fact, the distinction between form and genre is far from clear.[189]

It is a striking testimony to the strength of didactic tradition that Johann Christian Lobe, as late as 1850, adhered to the same basic pedagogical method as Johann Mattheson in the 1730s. Lobe explains the structure of a

184. Koch, *Versuch,* sect. 4, "Von der Verbindung der melodischen Theile, oder von dem Baue der Perioden," ch. 4, "Von der Verbindung der melodischen Theile zu Perioden von grösserem Umfange, oder von der Einrichtung der grössern Tonstücke." Note the similarity of these formulations with Koch's definition of rhetoric (see above, p. 53).

185. I, 74–76: "Etwas von der Einrichtung musikalischer Tonstücke."

186. Mercadier, *Nouveau système,* pt. 5, ch. 3.

187. Karlsruhe: Christian Theodor Groos, 1840, pt. 5: "Musikalische Formenlehre, oder kurze Beschreibung der einzelnen namhaften Tonstücke."

188. Hand, *Aesthetik der Tonkunst,* vol. 2 (Jena: Carl Hochhausen, 1841).

189. See Friedrich Blume, "Die musikalische Form und die musikalischen Gattungen," in his *Syntagma musicologicum: Gesammelte Reden und Schriften,* ed. Martin Ruhnke (Kassel: Bärenreiter, 1963), pp. 480–504; Wiora, "Historische und systematische Betrachtung der musikalischen Gattungen"; and Thomas S. Grey, "Richard Wagner and the Aesthetics of Musical Form in the Mid-19th Century (1840–1860)" (Ph.D. diss., University of California, Berkeley, 1987), pp. 75–76.

minuet as a concatenation of individual units, but he turns to a description of genres in accounting for more sophisticated forms. The periodic nature of the minuet, Lobe notes, cannot adequately explain the structure of the first movement of Beethoven's String Quartet in F Major, Op. 59, No. 1; if one applies the model of a Classical minuet in this particular case, "a few things will have remained unclear" regarding the movement's form.[190] Lobe's acknowledgment is a magnificent understatement, for the structure of the first movement of Beethoven's F Major Quartet is indeed far removed from that of a minuet. Something similar to Lobe's recognition of these methodological limitations, as we have already seen, is tacitly present in many earlier accounts of form as well.

By Lobe's time, conventional forms were widely viewed as something to be either avoided or overcome; too close an adherence to convention smacked of academicism. *Formenlehre,* as Dahlhaus points out, would eventually come to be equated with anatomy: it could describe the physical structure but not the inner nature of a musical composition.[191] The essence of a work, its moving spirit, remained beyond explication. Yet it was only toward the end of the eighteenth century, as musical form began to be described with increasing specificity, that such attitudes began to emerge. At least some theorists were already troubled by the apparent conflict between the genius of the individual composer and the persistent use of a relatively small number of formal schemes. Theorists of the Classical era gradually acknowledged a widening gulf between innate genius, which could not be taught or learned, and the mechanical rules of composition, which could.

Two theorists of the late eighteenth century distinguish themselves from all others by addressing this issue with unusual clarity. Unlike their predecessors and contemporaries, Heinrich Christoph Koch and Johann Nikolaus Forkel both confront the difficult question of how to reconcile the concept of form as an abstract, stereotypical pattern with the concept of form as the manifestation of a unique work. Forkel and Koch both provide evidence to suggest that the dichotomy between "inner" and "outer" form in the Classical era is itself misleading unless framed within the larger issue of intelligibility—that is, within a rhetorical concept of form. These two writers are also the last to propose an aesthetic view of large-scale musical form that sees no fundamental distinction between inspired genius and an adherence to convention. It is convention, in fact, that ensures the intelligibility of genius.

---

190. Lobe, *Lehrbuch der musikalischen Komposition,* vol. 1 (Leipzig: Breitkopf und Härtel, 1850), p. 305.
191. Carl Dahlhaus, "Gefühlsästhetik und musikalische Formenlehre," pp. 505–506.

At the small-scale level, this intelligibility, as we have already seen, rests on the principle of periodicity. Incisions of varying degrees generate units that correspond to the phrases, sentences, and paragraphs of verbal discourse. At the larger level, this intelligibility rests on the unfolding of a movement's *Hauptsatz* by means of repetition, variation, and contrast. The disposition of thematic events within conventional structures, as both writers suggest, is ultimately also a function of intelligibility.

In discussing the mechanics and aesthetics of music, Forkel relies more heavily on the imagery of language than most of his contemporaries. Nevertheless, his ideas on form remain well within the mainstream of late-eighteenth-century musical thought. In his *Ueber die Theorie der Musik* (1777), and again in the introduction to the first volume of his *Allgemeine Geschichte der Musik* (1788), he calls music an *Empfindungssprache,* a language of sentiments or emotions that exhibits distinct (although not always direct) parallels with the conventional "Ideensprache" of verbal language.[192] As such, music has its own rules and conventions, which Forkel, like other theorists of his day, divides into the categories of grammar and rhetoric. Grammar governs the relationship between individual notes and chords and their concatenation into periodic units *(Sätze)*. Rhetoric, in turn, governs the joining and successive ordering of these various small-scale units into a large-scale whole. Forkel goes out of his way, however, to stress that the distinction between musical grammar and rhetoric is not always clear: "In many respects, musical rhetoric differs from grammar only in that the former teaches on a large scale what the latter had taught only on a small scale."[193]

But because all manuals on musical composition until his time had amounted to "nothing more or less than musical grammars,"[194] Forkel was determined to present a systematic outline of musical rhetoric. He divides the field into six broad areas:

1. Periodicity *(Periodologie)*

2. Styles *(Schreibarten):* for church, theater, or chamber

3. Genres *(Gattungen)*

4. The ordering of musical ideas *(Die Anordnung musikalischer Gedanken)*

---

192. Forkel, *Ueber die Theorie der Musik, insofern sie Liebhabern und Kennern nothwendig und nützlich ist* (Göttingen: Wittwe Vandenhöck, 1777); idem, *Allgemeine Geschichte,* I. The first of these works, a prospectus for a series of lectures, was later reprinted in Carl Friedrich Cramer's *Magazin der Musik,* 1 (1783), 855–912.

193. Forkel, *Allgemeine Geschichte,* I, 21 and I, 39.

194. Ibid., I, 38. Forkel cites Kirnberger's *Kunst des reinen Satzes* as an exception.

5. The performance or declamation of musical works

6. Musical criticism.[195]

The fourth of these categories is of particular interest for the issue of large-scale form. *Anordnung,* as noted before, refers to the process within the act of artistic creation by which individual units are arranged in their proper sequence.[196] Under the rubric of "Aesthetic Ordering" *(Die ästhetische Anordnung),* Forkel sets forth the elements by which large-scale form can be described:

a. Exordium

b. Thema (Hauptsatz)

c. Nebensätze

d. Gegensätze

e. Zergliederungen

f. Widerlegungen

g. Bekräftigungen

h. Conclusion.

The influence of Mattheson's schema is immediately obvious. Forkel explicitly acknowledges the earlier theorist's efforts in this direction, noting that it was the music of Mattheson's time, and not his theory, that was in need of emendation:

Yet in his day—or rather in the time when *Der vollkommene Capellmeister* first appeared—music was not yet of such a nature that it permitted a coherent musical rhetoric to be abstracted from it. Music lacked not only refinement and taste but above all the coherence of its individual segments that make it into a formed oration of sentiments—in part through the development of ideas out of one another, in part through the unity of the style, etc. It attained this highest degree of perfection only after his [Mattheson's] time, at the hands of a few of our leading composers.[197]

195. Ibid., I, 66–68. Forkel's ideas on musical rhetoric are discussed in more detail in Wilibald Gurlitt, "Hugo Riemann und die Musikgeschichte," *Zeitschrift für Musikwissenschaft,* 1 (1918/1919), 574–578; Heinrich Edelhoff, *Johann Nikolaus Forkel: Ein Beitrag zur Geschichte der Musikwissenschaft* (Göttingen: Vandenhoeck & Ruprecht, 1935), pp. 47–52; and Ritzel, *Die Entwicklung der "Sonatenform,"* pp. 106–111.

196. This concept, it should emphasized, is not peculiar to music. See, for example, Sulzer's definition of "Anordnung" in his *Allgemeine Theorie:* "Anordnen means to assign each element to its place . . . in a work of art."

197. Forkel, *Allgemeine Geschichte,* I, 37.

Forkel unfortunately does not name the more recent composers he has in mind, but the few musical examples he presents in his discussion of periodicity feature the antecedent-consequent structure basic to the Classical style. And like Mattheson, he preserves the reversed sequence of the *refutatio* and *confirmatio* to reflect more closely the reiteration of the tonic (and usually the principal theme) toward the end of a movement in most forms.

Like many earlier theorists, Forkel emphasizes the quality of intelligibility in the construction of large-scale form:

An orator would behave unnaturally and contrary to the goal of edifying, persuading, and moving [his audience] if he were to give a speech without first determining what is to be his main idea [*Hauptsatz*], his secondary ideas [*Nebensätze*], his objections and refutations of the same, and his proofs . . .

As musical works of any substantial length are nothing other than speeches for the sentiments by which one seeks to move the listener to a certain empathy and to certain emotions, the rules for the ordering and arrangement of ideas are the same as in an actual oration. And so one has, in both, a main idea, supporting secondary ideas, dissections of the main idea, refutations, doubts, proofs, and reiterations. Similar means to our end (in the musical sense) must be used. This order and sequence of the individual sections is called the aesthetic ordering of the ideas. A musical work in which this ordering is so arranged that all thoughts mutually support and reinforce one another in the most advantageous way possible, is well ordered.[198]

That Forkel should offer no specific application of his system in the *Allgemeine Geschichte* is scarcely surprising. He could not, after all, afford to be overly specific, for his outline was intended to serve as a kind of prolegomenon and glossary to a history of music. His terms, accordingly, had to be broad enough to be applicable to a variety of forms from a variety of periods.

But in his *Musikalischer Almanach für Deutschland auf das Jahr 1784,* Forkel does apply elements of this outline to a specific piece of music, C. P. E. Bach's F Minor Sonata for keyboard, Wq. 57/6, from the third set of the *Clavier-Sonaten nebst einigen Rondos fürs Forte-Piano für Kenner und Liebhaber* (Leipzig, 1781). In reviewing this work, Forkel observes that

one of the main points in musical rhetoric and aesthetics is the ordering of musical ideas and the progression of the sentiments expressed through them, so that these ideas are conveyed to our hearts with a certain coherence, just as the ideas in an oration are conveyed to our minds and follow one another according to logical principles . . .

Accordingly, this is the basis of the necessity, that in a work of art (1) a main sentiment, (2) similar subsidiary sentiments, (3) dissected sentiments, i.e., senti-

198. Ibid., I, 50.

ments broken up into individual segments, (4) contrasting and opposed sentiments, etc., must all obtain. When ordered in an appropriate manner, these elements are thus in the language of sentiments the equivalent to what in the language of ideas (or in actual eloquence) are the well-known elements still preserved by good, genuine orators and based on our own nature—that is, *exordium, propositio, refutatio, confirmatio,* etc.[199]

Forkel thus clearly intended that his flexible image of form be applied to a wide variety of music, including what would eventually come to be known as sonata form, for the first movement of C. P. E. Bach's F Minor Sonata follows this conventional pattern quite closely.[200] Although Forkel does not state so explicitly, the opening idea in the tonic presumably conforms to the *Hauptempfindung,* the contrasting ideas in the relative major to the *Nebenempfindungen.* The extended development presents the *zergliederte* and *widersprechende Empfindungen,* and the full recapitulation is analogous to the *Bekräftigung,* a "certain kind of reiteration of the *Hauptsatz,* by which the interpolations and doubt that had preceded it are repudiated."[201]

This interpretation is further supported by a suppressed passage at the end of paragraph 103 in the autograph manuscript of the *Allgemeine Geschichte,* a passage that was originally intended to follow immediately after a discussion of *Widerlegung, Bekräftigung,* and *Conclusion.* Here, Forkel applies his rhetorically inspired outline to a sonata-form movement directly and unambiguously:

If one wanted to apply all of this to, say, a sonata, then its aesthetic ordering would be approximately as follows:
1. The *Hauptsatz,* the theme.
2. Then secondary themes derived from it.
3. Strengthening contrasting themes [*Gegensätze*], followed by
4. A conclusion to support the *Hauptsatz,* and the close of the first part.

As the first part of a sonata is ordinarily much shorter than the second, there is no true elaboration [*Ausarbeitung*], fragmentation [*Zergliederung*], etc., in the first part; instead, it comprises, just as in the introduction to an oration, only a preliminary presentation and mention of the main intention and goal of a musical work. The second part, on the other hand, comprises:
1. The *Hauptsatz* transposed, or in the key of the dominant.
2. Fragmentation of the *Hauptsatz.*

199. Forkel, "Ueber eine Sonate aus Carl Phil. Emanuel Bachs dritter Sonatensammlung für Kenner und Liebhaber, in F moll, S. 30. Ein Sendschreiben an Hrn. von ✶ ✶," in his *Musikalischer Almanach für Deutschland auf das Jahr 1784* (Leipzig: Schwickert), pp. 31–32.

200. Ritzel, in *Die Entwicklung der "Sonatenform,"* p. 128, maintains that Forkel's comments apply only to the sonata as a whole and not to the individual movements. But it is clear from Forkel's concluding remarks in his review that the same standards apply to individual movements as well as to the complete work.

201. Forkel, *Allgemeine Geschichte,* I, 53.

3. Various doubts against it, along with a refutation and resolution of the same.

4. Yet another confirmation through the presentation of the *Hauptsatz* once again in a varied form [*Gestalt*], as in a secondary key related to the tonic.

5. A Conclusion that now moves to the tonic, just as the harmony had moved to the dominant in the first part. The movement ends in this fashion.[202]

This hitherto unnoted description of sonata form assumes a decidedly thematic orientation. Its concern with thematic events is quite different, however, from nineteenth-century accounts, which almost invariably focus on the nature and function of the "second theme." The function of secondary themes in Forkel's account is not so much one of contrast as one of elaboration, based on the nature of the original theme itself.

Why did Forkel suppress this passage? He may have felt that it was too specific to the music of his own time and inappropriate for the broader purposes of the introduction to his *Allgemeine Geschichte*. He was almost certainly aware of the controversy surrounding Mattheson's earlier, related account, and perhaps he hoped to avoid raising similar discord over an issue that plays a relatively minor role within a lengthy introduction. Forkel had in fact already made similar specific equations some ten years before in his review of the rondo from C. P. E. Bach's Keyboard Sonata, Wq. 90/2.[203] But the important point is not so much the application of any one specific pattern—sonata, rondo, minuet, theme and variations, and so on—as the fact that each of these formal patterns is considered to be a function of thematic elaboration. Forkel viewed the structure of any given movement as a sequential presentation of individual units that begins with a main idea and proceeds to elaborate this idea, either by variation, contrast, repetition, or some combination of these techniques.

It would be simple to dismiss Forkel's approach as yet another of his many anachronisms: he is, after all, one of the last writers to offer an elaborate defense of the doctrine of affections, long after this kind of thinking had gone out of fashion, and his musical ideal was embodied in J. S. Bach, a composer of a previous generation who toward the end of his own life was already considered somewhat old-fashioned. But Forkel first presented these ideas before he had come to perceive a decisive break in the musical tradition between J. S. Bach and the composers of subsequent generations. On the basis of his own public concerts, in fact, Forkel's favorite composer

202. Forkel, autograph manuscript of the *Allgemeine Geschichte,* Deutsche Staatsbibliothek, Berlin, paragraph 103. Edelhoff alludes to this deleted passage in his *Johann Nikolaus Forkel,* p. 50 and p. 125n143. I am very grateful to Kirsten Beisswenger for her transcription of this passage from Forkel's original manuscript.

203. *Musikalisch-kritische Bibliothek,* 2 (1778), 281–294. For a discussion of this review, see Malcolm S. Cole, "The Vogue of the Instrumental Rondo in the Late 18th Century," *JAMS,* 22 (1969), 427–432.

at the time of the *Allgemeine Geschichte* appears to have been Dittersdorf. Forkel's own sonatas, the earliest of which date from 1771, are stylistically typical for their day and in their opening movements adhere rather consistently to the structural conventions of sonata form.[204] And it should be remembered that the examples he used to illustrate musical periodicity are decidedly up-to-date for his generation. Forkel's rhetorical conception of form, although unusual in the extent of its detail, is on the whole quite representative of his time and part of an established tradition that would persist, as we shall see, well into the nineteenth century.

Koch, too, was a part of this tradition, even though he himself did little to redress the "lack of coherence" he perceived in contemporary accounts dealing with the rhetoric of form. Throughout his writings, in fact, Koch exhibited no small degree of ambivalence and uncertainty on the issue of form. His massive *Lexikon* of 1802, as noted earlier, contains no entry under the term, even though it appears repeatedly within the context of other entries and throughout his earlier *Versuch*. The abridged *Kurzgefasstes Handwörterbuch der Musik* of 1807, on the other hand, provides a new and entirely original entry on the subject. It is here that Koch sums up—unfortunately within the limited space of this later, more modest work—his own scattered attempts to deal with the paradox of inner and outer form:

Form. In music, as in the other fine arts, there is much discussion about the form of art-works. By the form of a musical work, one understands the manner in which the work is brought before the soul of the listener.

Daily experience certainly teaches us that the various genres of musical works differ only in their form; the symphony has a form different from that of a concerto, the aria has one different from that of a song. Yet when the aestheticians maintain that what one calls the beauty of a musical work resides in its form, then there certainly must also be an external [*zufällige*, literally "accidental"] form in which the beautiful is included, and which may or may not be present. Otherwise, for example, every rondo that corresponds to the usual form would have to be granted the character of beauty without any further qualification.

If, then, one is speaking of the form of art-works in the sense by which the content is appropriated to beauty, then one is not referring to that external form of art-works by which genres differ, but rather to the particular manner in which variety is bound to unity, or the particular manner in which the composer has transferred into a work the moments of pleasure inherent in his ideal.[205]

Koch makes a clear distinction here between external, conventional forms and the specific *(besondere)* form of an individual work by implicitly invok-

---

204. On Forkel's earlier musical tastes and on his sonatas, see Edelhoff, *Johann Nikolaus Forkel*, pp. 27, 120.
205. Koch, *Kurzgefasstes Handwörterbuch der Musik*, "Form."

ing the Aristotelian distinction between "accidental" and "essential" characteristics. But only if read in conjuction with a particular passage in the earlier *Versuch* does the more technical nature of the relationship between these two different ideas of form become clear.

Under the rubric "On the Intention and the Internal Structure of Musical Works, and Especially the Manner in Which They Are Composed," Koch deals at length in the *Versuch* with the distinction between "mechanical" and "aesthetic" concepts of form. The "mechanical aspects of elaboration [*Ausführung*]" normally embrace a movement's "large-scale plan of modulation [*Tonausweichung*] and its form." And while "the latter" (external form) "is determined largely by the former" (the plan of modulation) the two are not to be equated. "Form depends in part on the particular number of main periods, in part on the tonality in which this or that period is directed, but also in part on the junctures at which one or another main section [*Haupttheil*] is repeated."[206] But Koch is quick to emphasize once again that this concept of form is restricted to its "mechanical" elements. Periodicity, large-scale harmony, and large-scale thematic repetition determine the external form of a work but do not address the more aesthetic issues of form and formal coherence. In elaborating the ideas of the *Anlage,* "we must attend to two things: that which concerns the spirit or inner character of the piece, and that which concerns its mechanical elements."[207] Koch's own subsequent account in the *Versuch,* as he repeatedly emphasizes, is devoted primarily to the mechanical aspects of melody and form. Dahlhaus's interpretation—that Koch assigns the "soul" of a work to its *Anlage,* its "body" or external form to the unfolding of these ideas—is misleading, in that it overlooks Koch's emphasis on the two very different types of elaboration: the mechanical, which develops ideas through periodicity and large-scale modulation, and the aesthetic, which is concerned with issues of thematic coherence and continuity.[208] Unfortunately, Koch did not deal with the issue of aesthetic elaboration in any sustained way in the *Versuch;* his *Melodielehre* within that treatise, as he repeatedly reminds the reader, is concerned with "the mechanical rules of melody."

Koch's ideas concerning the more aesthetic process of elaboration are scattered and fragmentary. He does, however, address the functional link between "inner" and "outer" form in one particularly important passage in the *Versuch* by asking how the genius of the individual composer can be reconciled with the conventions of large-scale form:

206. Koch, *Versuch,* II, 103.
207. Ibid., II, 97.
208. Dahlhaus, "Gefühlsästhetik," pp. 509–510.

I now come to the form of the various sections [*Sätze*] of a piece. It cannot be denied that form is something rather incidental, something that actually has little or no influence on the inner character of a piece. On the other hand, one has little reason to object to the [conventional] form of our various sections, in larger as well as in smaller works. And this, presumably, is the reason why many great masters have constructed their arias, for example, almost entirely according to one and the same form. It is equally difficult to deny that a great deal of the beauty of a movement can be lost through the constant use of one form and one form only. When one has heard so many arias, for example, constructed according to the same form, this form ultimately becomes so impressed upon the mind that after hearing only the first period [of a new aria], one often knows with certainty precisely where the modulation is going to go, and what main thematic ideas will be repeated at which points. And the movement will necessarily lose much of its strength, unless the composer can enliven his work with a particularly unusual expressive turn . . .

But in piecing together these various sections, what attitude must one then maintain vis-à-vis form? Is it better to construct sections always according to the common form, or is it better to begin by trying to construct new forms? The first approach would impose unnecessary shackles upon genius and compel it to forgo some of the beautiful turns of expression that it [genius] gives rise to, lest these effects spoil the form. The second approach might produce too much nonsense, if one is set on creating new forms for no particular reason—for how often would it not happen that the essence of art would be lost from view by a preoccupation with form, the newly created form thereby losing more than it gains? The best approach, therefore, is to choose a rational middle ground. If one is putting together in the conventional form a movement whose content possesses sufficient aesthetic power, or if one can discover beautiful turns of expression that correspond to the standard form, why should one consider altering the conventional form? But if one has a text to set that calls for a unique form and unusual turns of expression, . . . or if one discovers out of thin air (and this can also happen in purely instrumental movements as well) an unusual turn of expression, one should not bind oneself timidly to the known form, but rather construct it in the manner that the movement demands, provided one is certain that this will ensure a true perfection of the movement, and provided that no other accidental infelicities thereby arise.[209]

Koch's reconciliation of external conventions with internal imperatives rests on compromise. The various conventions serve a purpose—intelligibility—but they also carry within them the potential to stifle originality. Form and content are distinguishable, and novel content necessitates novel form. A conventional form can nevertheless provide a framework within which the shape of a movement can be better apprehended by the listener; deviations from this norm must be justified by the material at hand.

Forkel and Koch were among the last writers to comment extensively on the nature of large-scale form before its codification in the *Formenlehren* of

209. Koch, *Versuch,* II, 117–119.

the nineteenth century. As such, they were also among the last theorists not to be handicapped by the perceptions of later generations that would draw increasingly sharper distinctions between the internal, genetic "spirit" of a work and its external, conventional "form."

Forkel's writings are particularly unusual in that they are directed primarily at the listener, rather than the composer. In addressing the connoisseur (or would-be connoisseur) of music, he notes that a sense of large-scale form is in fact one of the most important prerequisites for an understanding of the art:

But the mere amateur of music has no reason to want to know how he himself might actually create and construct musical sections according to the rules of rhetoric; instead, he wishes to know only how they should be put together once they have already been created. Accordingly, a correct knowledge of the ordering of musical ideas is more important for him [the amateur] than a knowledge of all those means and ways so often prescribed to facilitate creativity . . . The proper ordering of sections . . . by which every unit is placed in the most appropriate spot . . . can be specified quite clearly; and this ordering must necessarily be known to any friend of music who wishes to be a connoisseur and who desires to derive a part of his pleasure from the inner workings of the art.[210]

The listener who has no concept of formal conventions, according to Forkel, is like the viewer of a painting who has no knowledge of the conventions of perspective, or like someone who listens to an oration but who understands neither grammar nor the construction of sentences, much less the concatenation of these sentences into larger units of thought.[211] To the composer, in turn, the proper ordering of these elements is the most reliable course by which to ensure that the audience will perceive the structure of a work in the intended manner:

In rhetoric or in poetry, a great deal depends upon the ordering of these proofs, persuasions, or refutations. It is just this way in music as well, for it is of the utmost importance that everything be arranged in such a way that the listener is led toward or away from a sensation step by step and in the most natural way possible. From this arises a particular ordering of musical ideas that I might call the "aesthetic ordering" (if it were allowed me to give this object a distinct name), an object that until now has been sensed by few, but which has nevertheless been accorded to the teaching of periodicity.[212]

Forkel and Koch both recognize that internal imperatives, if they are to be comprehended by the audience, must necessarily coexist with external

210. Forkel, *Ueber die Theorie*, p. 21.
211. Ibid., pp. 8–9.
212. Ibid., pp. 25–26.

conventions. This approach to large-scale form directly confronts the nature of the relationship between the composer and convention. Forkel explicitly states that the conventions for the arrangement of units within a movement are abstractions drawn from "musical-classical masterworks."[213] The "genius" composer, although unrestricted by any set of rules, nevertheless ordinarily works within a convention of such rules:

At the same time, one has to abstract the rules from Genius, and no one will maintain that the rules precede Genius . . . Yet how were these first utterances of Genius created? Were there not at first the most deformed monstrosities, and was it not necessary that hundreds of such deformed monstrosities had to be brought into this world before one began to notice that they were not yet that which they should have been, that the intentions they were meant to fulfill had not yet been achieved? Genius therefore always precedes the rules of experience . . . and thus it is truly Experience alone that clears the path of Genius, that protects it against mistakes, that helps Genius achieve its intentions among a choice of so many means and to reach its goal, to show it the one true path, and to guide it toward the most efficient, appropriate means.[214]

Form is thus viewed as both a process and a plan, or more specifically, as a process that can be made more intelligible through the application of certain conventional plans. It is both generative and conformational, and these two perspectives are united by the concept of musical rhetoric. A work's form is generative in the unfolding of its ideas, and specifically its central idea. But in order to be made more readily intelligible to the listener, the sequence of these ideas must ordinarily follow at least the outlines of a conventional pattern. Specific schemata serve to make the unfolding of a movement's ideas more readily comprehensible to the listener. And only an intelligible presentation of these ideas—through repetition, elaboration, and variation—can produce a coherent form, the shape of a satisfying whole.

As a metaphor, rhetoric is necessarily imperfect. Not all elements of musical structure, as even Mattheson acknowledged, can be explained in such terms. Grétry, too, recognized the imperfection of the metaphor of rhetoric in his *Mémoires* of 1797, when he criticized the still-common practice of repeating both halves of a binary movement:

A sonata is an oration [*discours*]. What are we to think of a man who, dividing his discourse in half, repeats each half? "I was at your house this morning; yes, I was at your house this morning to talk with you about something; to talk with you about

213. Ibid., p. 26 ("musikalisch-classische Meisterstücke").
214. Forkel, *Allgemeine Geschichte*, I, 61. Forkel's comments on J. S. Bach's earliest compositions reflect this same outlook: see his *Ueber Johann Sebastian Bachs Leben, Kunst und Kunstwerke* (Leipzig: Hoffmeister und Kühnel, 1802), p. 23.

something" . . . I speak above all of the long reprises that constitute the halves of an oration. Reprises may have been good at the birth of music, at a time when the listener did not comprehend everything until the second time around. I know that an oration is often divided into two sections; but without a doubt, one does not present each one twice.[215]

Grétry's dissatisfaction is directed not at the imagery of rhetoric but at the conventions of contemporary sonatas themselves. The problem, in Grétry's view, is that the conventional structure of a sonata-form movement, with its literal repetition of extended sections, is not *enough* like an oration: "There are also orations that are divided into more than two parts, and it is these that we must imitate."[216]

Grétry's remarks remind us that the metaphor of rhetoric alone cannot explain the nature of musical form. Yet it would be mistaken to underestimate the significance of a metaphor as widely used as this one, no matter how imperfect it might be. It would be especially unfortunate to view this particular metaphor merely as a holdover from Baroque thought. The rhetorical concept of large-scale form was in fact a fundamentally new concept in the eighteenth century, and it actually intensified toward the beginning of the nineteenth. It represents the best efforts of eighteenth-century theorists to come to grips with what remains a troublesome issue even today, for it attempts to reconcile both the similarities and the differences inherent in a substantial repertoire of music. With its fundamentally thematic orientation, the rhetorical concept of form offers a framework that can integrate the generative and the conformational approaches to form.

215. Grétry, *Mémoires,* III, 356–357. The term *discours* in this well-known passage is usually translated as "discourse." But the English "discourse" is more general than the French cognate, which is more closely associated with an oration, particularly during this period. See, for example, the first definition given in the *Dictionnaire de l'Académie françoise,* 5th ed., 2 vols. (Paris: J. J. Smits, 1798–1799), I, 428: "Propos, assemblage de paroles pour expliquer ce que l'on pense." See also Karl Spazier's translation of this passage in *Gretry's Versuche über die Musik* (Leipzig: Breitkopf & Härtel, 1800), p. 223: "Eine Sonate ist als eine Rede zu betrachten."

216. Grétry, *Mémoires,* III, 357. The trend of repeating both halves of a movement was already in decline by this time, but the practice of repeating the first half was still widespread. See Broyles, "Organic Form," pp. 340–341, for statistics from a wide sample of music from the period 1760–1810.

CHAPTER 3

Continuity and Change in Later Metaphors of Form

Over the first half of the nineteenth century, the metaphor of the musical work as an oration gradually gave way to a new image, that of the biological organism. This shift reflects important changes in the perceived nature of form: an organism, after all, is structured according to principles that are necessarily different from those governing an oration.

At the same time, this new metaphor reveals a certain degree of continuity between eighteenth- and nineteenth-century concepts of musical form. For in spite of their differences, the two images have a good deal in common, and it is largely for this reason that rhetoric could continue to function as a useful metaphor of form until well into the nineteenth century. In many later accounts of form, in fact—most notably in the writings of Arnold Schoenberg—the two metaphors are evoked side by side in such a way as to emphasize their common basis.

The Continuity of Rhetorical Imagery in the Nineteenth Century

As an academic discipline, rhetoric experienced a remarkably precipitous decline during the early decades of the nineteenth century. While it never disappeared entirely from secondary schools and universities, its importance in the curriculum diminished substantially. Many of the university professorships that had long been designated as chairs of rhetoric were reassigned to other disciplines such as history, literature, and in some cases even the natural sciences.[1]

---

1. On the decline of rhetoric in Germany around 1800, see Dieter Breuer, "Schulrhetorik im 19. Jahrhundert," in Helmut Schanze, ed., *Rhetorik: Beiträge zu ihrer Geschichte in Deutschland vom 16.–20 Jahrhundert* (Frankfurt/Main: Fischer, 1974), pp. 145–179; Heinrich

Nor was rhetoric's decline merely academic. While the discipline has never been entirely free from the suspicion of sophistry, antirhetorical sentiment reached new heights in the early nineteenth century. Numerous writers sought to deprecate the art of persuasion as empty technique, devoid of substance.[2]

The shift from a pragmatic to a predominantly expressive critical orientation toward the arts around this same time was one important correlative of this phenomenon. With the growing view of art primarily as a vehicle of self-expression, the quality of persuasion inevitably began to relinquish its central role in aesthetic criticism.

It is thus all the more striking that the tradition of rhetoric in musical thought should continue so vigorously and for so long into the nineteenth century. The use of rhetorical imagery in dealing with the problem of form continued unabated not only in contemporary dictionaries of music and manuals of composition, but in broader, more aesthetically oriented treatises as well.

Dictionaries tend to be among the most conservative (and derivative) genres in the literature of almost any field, and numerous nineteenth-century music lexicographers simply quote or paraphrase the work of earlier writers on rhetoric, particularly Forkel and Koch. But the very fact that such accounts persist into the third, fourth, and fifth decades of the century is in itself significant. Johann Daniel Andersch, for example, writing in 1829, preserves the traditional distinction between musical grammar ("the first main division of composition, containing the rules according to which notes and chords are to be joined in succession") and rhetoric ("the theory that shows how multiple individual musical units [*Sätze*] are to be brought together into a whole").[3] Echoing Koch, in particular, Andersch goes on to note that rhetoric is "that portion of musical science that teaches one how to concatenate melodic sections into a whole consistent with the purpose at hand."[4]

August Gathy, in his *Musikalisches Conversations-Lexikon* of 1840, calls rhetoric "the theory of the rhythmic, logical, and aesthetic ordering and

---

Bosse, "Dichter kann man nicht bilden: Zur Veränderung der Schulrhetorik nach 1770," *Jahrbuch für internationale Germanistik*, 10 (1978), 80–125; Manfred Fuhrmann, *Rhetorik und öffentliche Rede. Über die Ursachen des Verfalls der Rhetorik im ausgehenden 18. Jahrhundert* (Konstanz: Universitätsverlag, 1983). A convenient summary is available in Ueding and Steinbrink, *Grundriss der Rhetorik*, section E, "Ubiquität der Rhetorik. Vom Verfall und Weiterleben der Beredsamkeit im 19. Jahrhundert."

2. On the historical conflict between rhetoric and other disciplines, particularly philosophy, see Vickers, *In Defence of Rhetoric*.

3. Andersch, *Musikalisches Wörterbuch* (Berlin: W. Natorff, 1829), "Grammatik" and "Musikalische Rhetorik."

4. Andersch, *Musikalisches Wörterbuch*, "Rhetorik."

concatenation of homophonic or polyphonic sections into a whole."[5] And Gustav Schilling, writing around the same time, points out that while rhetoric is "only an image," it is "an established concept" nevertheless. Synthesizing elements of both Koch's definition and Forkel's elaboration on the subject, Schilling explains that

by rhetoric of music one understands that body of knowledge pertaining to composition by which individual melodic sections are united into a whole according to a particular goal and standard. One distinguishes it from grammar, which deals with the more material nature of music, the elementary phrases of composition. Rhetoric determines the rules for the concatenation of these same phrases into a complete, expressive (oratorical) whole. At the same time, grammar and rhetoric overlap each other in an inseparable manner.[6]

The continuing presence of such imagery in these works cannot be ascribed solely to the inherent conservatism of lexicographers. The persistence of these metaphors, as we shall see, reflects their continuing use in compositional pedagogy throughout the early nineteenth century.

The demand for textbooks aimed at aspiring composers increased substantially around this time, largely in response to the growing number of musical conservatories. One of the earliest and most detailed of these manuals, for the *Conservatoire* at Paris, was Jérome-Joseph de Momigny's *Cours complet d'harmonie et de composition* of 1803–1806.[7] Momigny maintains the traditional distinction between grammar and rhetoric and interposes the third member of the trivium, logic:

Musical grammar . . . is the art of subordinating ideas to one another, and of forming propositions or cadences.

. . . Logic is the art of arranging the ideas, the cadences, in an order that is confirmed by good sense or proper reason. It falls entirely within the realm of judgment.

The oratorical art consists of arranging thoughts in a manner that will produce the greatest impression on the mind and on the heart.[8]

Momigny's approach to composition and analysis reflects an essentially rhetorical view: "The art of composing an oration lies in concatenating a

---

5. 2nd ed. (Leipzig: Schuberth & Neumeyer, 1840), "Rhetorik."

6. Schilling, *Universal-Lexicon der Tonkunst,* 7 vols. (Stuttgart: Köhler, 1841), "Rhetorik."

7. On the pedagogical tradition of the Paris *Conservatoire's* textbooks, see Renate Groth, *Die französische Kompositionslehre des 19. Jahrhunderts* (Wiesbaden: Franz Steiner, 1983), and Cynthia Marie Gessele, "The Institutionalization of Music Theory in France: 1764–1802" (Ph.D. diss., Princeton University, 1989).

8. Momigny, *Cours complet d'harmonie et de composition,* 3 vols. (Paris: Author, 1803–1806), I, 145.

certain number of propositions according to grammatical, logical, and oratorical order. The art of composing a piece of music lies in concatenating
a certain number of cadences or musical propositions according to these
same relationships."[9]

Like so many of his contemporaries, Momigny considers the instrumental music of his own day to have reached heights of unparalleled greatness.
And the greatest of these instrumental composers is Joseph Haydn, whose
works Momigny likens to the orations of Bossuet:

> Considering the immense number of masterpieces produced by these immortal men
> in all genres, can one, in good faith, doubt any longer that music has acquired this
> pronounced character of truth, energy, and charm, which has established it in an
> irrevocable manner as any language, and above all, as a language that is natural? Is
> it not a language that abounds in noble locutions, harmonious and touching? The
> sentences [périodes] of Haydn, so eloquent and numerous—do they concede any-
> thing, in their own idiom, to those of *Bossuet* and other great orators? We dare to
> say that all great men, in dramatic art and in oratorical art, have their true counter-
> parts in the celestial language of sounds. If it were otherwise, all the heart and spirit
> of man would not have passed through the pen of our composers; music would not
> yet have arrived at its present degree of maturity.[10]

Momigny's analysis of the first movement of Haydn's Symphony No.
103 ("Drumroll") reflects this rhetorical perspective at almost every turn.
He divides the movement into an introduction and three large sections, each
of which consists of a series of *périodes*. In the introduction, a section of
"admirable simplicity," Haydn presents a subject that "may be called the
plain-chant" (Example 3.1).[11]

3.1   Haydn, Symphony No. 103, first movement, mm. 1–7

9. Ibid., I, 134.

10. Ibid., I, "Discours préliminaire," 20–21.

11. Ibid., II, 586. Whether or not Momigny is alluding here to the often-noted similarity
of this theme with the opening of the *Dies irae* chant is unclear. Momigny's separate, programmatic analysis of this same movement, to be discussed below, places the opening of
the symphony in a church, but makes no reference to any chant in particular.

3.2 Haydn, Symphony No. 103, first movement, mm. 14–19

"Always faithful to *Variety,* without compromising *Unity,*" Haydn does not subsequently "take up a different motive." Instead, the second *période,* beginning in m. 14, produces a "new effect" on the listener by means of varied accompaniment and a new orchestration of the original theme (Example 3.2).

When Haydn introduces the Allegro con spirito, he first presents his subject *piano,* so that the subsequent *période de verve* (mm. 48ff.) "will achieve

3.3 Haydn, Symphony No. 103, first movement, mm. 79–93

its fullest effect." Following a *période mélodieuse* in mm. 8off., Haydn then concludes the opening section with a period that is "a kind of refrain, or, as one might wish to call it, a *gloria patri,* and thus a commonplace [*lieu commun*]." But the composer avoids banality by connecting this ending thematically with material previously heard: he avoids introducing an idea "foreign to the preceding discourse" (Example 3.3).

Momigny's analysis of the "second part"—the development section—is full of remarks about thematic manipulations of the opening idea and their effect upon the listener. In commenting upon the return of the introduction's bass line in this section's third *période* (mm. 112–120), for example, he notes that Haydn is "always measured in what he does . . . [He] abandons counterpoint here, so as not to lose his audience; but he does not leave it for something unrelated to his subject. Haydn always has something to say concerning his subject" (Example 3.4).

Admittedly, Momigny's analysis of this movement is far from thorough, for he overlooks many of the thematic elaborations he might have pointed out: the repeated use of the half-step auxiliary linking the opening portions of the two themes that begin the introduction and the Allegro con spirito, respectively; or the similarity in contour between the second half of the introduction's principal theme and the *période mélodieuse* (rising sixth, descending third, and so on). The "unity in variety" within this movement is far deeper than Momigny even begins to suggest: few pieces better illustrate the manner in which a composer can begin with a simple subject—so simple that in this particular case it is in unison, without any underlying harmony—and explore its implications in a moving and satisfying progression over the course of an entire movement. But the important point here is not so much Momigny's ultimate degree of analytical success as his focus upon

3.4 Haydn, Symphony No. 103, first movement, mm. 111–118

the continuing elaboration of the "subject at hand" and the very premise of his effort to show the essentially rhetorical motivation behind the structure of the movement.[12]

Momigny's outlook is by no means isolated, nor is it a mere holdover from eighteenth-century thought. A number of subsequent writers likened Haydn to an orator and his instrumental works, particularly the symphonies, to orations. These comparisons first began to appear only in the nineteenth century. Ignaz Theodor Ferdinand Arnold, in an early biography of Haydn, notes that the composer achieves his effects in his instrumental music

in the manner of a clever orator, who, when he wants to convince us of something, proceeds from the basis of a sentence that is universally recognized to be true, one with which everyone agrees, one that everyone must be able to understand; but he [Haydn] knows so cunningly just how to use this idea, that he can soon convince us of anything he wishes to, even if it is the very contrary of the original idea.

In this way, Haydn's music enters our ears quite smoothly, for we have a sense that we are hearing something that is easily perceived and already familiar to us; but we soon find that it is not that which we had thought it was or which we thought it should become. We hear something new and are amazed at the master, who knew so cunningly how to offer us, under the guise of the well known, something never before heard.[13]

Giuseppe Carpani, another early biographer of Haydn, expounds on this imagery at length, emphasizing once again the importance of thematic intelligibility over the course of a movement.

A musical composition is an oration that is made with figurative sounds instead of words. The *motive* is the proposition, the assumption one sets out to prove. In the same manner as the orator, who, having proposed his theme, develops it, presents proofs, presses the argument forward, and, recapitulating what he has already said, leads it to its conclusion—in this same manner, the composer must proceed with his work. He returns to the *motive* every so often and allows it to be heard again, in order that the listener be penetrated with it quite thoroughly. If this *motive* is such that it brings pleasure to the ear, it is then quite likely that by returning to the fore, it will renew, confirm, and increase that initial pleasure. But the true distinction of the genius is [the ability to] give the theme an air of novelty each time it is recalled, not being content simply to repeat it docilely, passing from one key to another, as do mediocre intellects, but instead, to reinvigorate it, make it more astringent at

12. Many other aspects of this analysis are considered by Malcolm Cole, "Momigny's Analysis of Haydn's Symphony No. 103," *Music Review*, 30 (1969), 261–284.

13. Arnold, *Joseph Haydn. Seine kurze Biographie und ästhetische Darstellung seiner Werke* (Erfurt: J. C. Müller, 1810), pp. 101–102.

times, vary it, manipulate it with learning and with grace, always embellishing it further. In this I appeal to those who have heard the symphonies of *Haydn*.[14]

"Only in instrumental music," Carpani adds, "can the composer be an Orator; in vocal music, he can do no more than translate into musical language the discourse of the poet, and therefore he cannot and must not be anything other than a translator, an imitator, or a paraphrast."[15]

Even as late as 1828, the Würzburg *Kapellmeister* and Professor of Music Joseph Fröhlich (1780–1862) cites Haydn's "tellingly developed musical oratory" as one of the composer's most outstanding characteristics. "In his symphonies, one hears a gathering of skilled orators who, using noble language before an educated audience, give evidence of their powers to grasp and elaborate an idea."[16]

Within the realm of more strictly technical accounts of form, Alexandre Choron's *Principes de composition des écoles d'Italie* of 1808 includes an extended treatment of "rhétorique musicale," beginning with a discussion of the "formation de la phrase et du discours musical."[17] The same writer's *Nouveau manuel complet de musique* of 1838, co-authored with Juste-Adrien de La Fage, borrows heavily from Koch's *Versuch* and incorporates an even greater number of explicit references to the art of oratory.[18]

In Germany, Gottfried Weber's widely used *Versuch einer geordneten Theorie der Tonsetzkunst* (1817–1821; second edition 1830–1832) also retains the traditional division between musical grammar and rhetoric. Under the rubric "Theory of Composition," Weber notes that

the first and as it were lowest requirement for the connection of notes and the construction of a musical phrase is that it above all does not sound wrong or repugnant to the ear . . . This is somewhat like the first and lowest requirement of the arts of oratory and poetry, to avoid grammatical mistakes. This part of the study of composition, devoted merely to the technical or grammatical correctness of combining notes, merely to the purity of the language of notes, is therefore called the study of correct [*rein,* literally "clean"] composition, or also the grammar of the language of notes. It concerns itself with the rules according to which notes, like musical letters or the sounds of speech, shape themselves into syllables, then into words, and finally into a musical sense . . .

14. Carpani, *Le Haydine, ovvero lettere su la vita e le opere del celebre maestro Giuseppe Haydn* (Milan: C. Buccinelli, 1812), pp. 43–44. See also pp. 64–66.
15. Ibid., p. 66.
16. Fröhlich, *Joseph Haydn,* ed. Adolf Sandberger (Regensburg: Gustav Bosse, 1936), p. 28; orig. pub. in the *Allgemeine Encyklopädie der Wissenschaften und Künste* (Leipzig, 1828).
17. 3 vols. (Paris: LeDuc, 1808), book 6.
18. 3 vols. (Paris: Roret, 1838). Nancy K. Baker discusses Koch's influence on this treatise in her translation of Koch's *Versuch,* p. xxii.

The study of the correctness of composition is followed by the study of artful composition, encompassing artistic or more complicated manipulation and elaboration of musical phrases, of fragmentation comparable to that of oratory, of the many-sided illumination and development of individual musical phrases and ideas comparable to a musical rhetoric, or, if one prefers, *syntaxis ornata,* the study of the connection of melodies or of the interweaving of melodies. This includes the study of so-called double counterpoint, of fugue and canon and all that is pertinent to them, as well as the study of the ground-plan [*Anlage*] and shaping of musical works as a whole.[19]

The vocabulary of eighteenth-century theory remains essentially unchanged here. Weber preserves the contrast between the mechanical rules of grammar and the more aesthetic elements of rhetoric and large-scale form, and he continues to view form as a function of melodic structure, regardless of whether a work's texture is homophonic or polyphonic.

Georg Joseph Vogler, in his *System für den Fugenbau* (ca. 1811) similarly argues that the fugue, like other genres, must be intelligible to the listener, and he goes on to provide a relatively detailed analysis of a fugue from a rhetorical perspective.[20] Vogler's analysis testifies that even the structure of a "strict" composition can be explained according to its rhetorical elaboration *(rhetorische Ausführung)* of the main idea.

The association of rhetoric and large-scale form is even more explicit in Siegfried Dehn's *Theoretisch-praktische Harmonielehre* of 1840, in which "musical rhetoric" is directly equated with *Formenlehre.*[21] As late as 1852, Ernst Friedrich Richter continues to distinguish between grammar and rhetoric, equating the latter with *Compositionslehre.* Richter, much like earlier theorists, emphasizes the original sense of the term "composition" from the Latin "componere." Musical composition, in this sense, is the process of "putting together" units of musical thought. In retaining the image of mu-

---

19. 2nd ed., 4 vols. in 2 (Mainz: B. Schott's Söhne, 1830–1832), I, 19. Weber reiterates the division between grammar and rhetoric at the very end of his treatise (IV, 149).

20. Vogler, *System für den Fugenbau als Einleitung zur harmonischen Gesang-Verbindungs-Lehre* (Offenbach/Main: Johann André, n.d.). The preface is dated 1811; the work was published posthumously "from manuscripts left behind at the author's death" in 1814. For a more detailed discussion of rhetoric in this treatise, see Floyd Grave and Margaret G. Grave, *In Praise of Harmony: The Teachings of Abbé Georg Joseph Vogler* (Lincoln: University of Nebraska Press, 1987), pp. 94–97, 115–118. See also Vogler's "aesthetic, rhetorical, and harmonic analyses" of his own *Zwei und dreissig Präludien für die Orgel . . .* (Munich, 1806), especially of numbers 3 and 25, in which he meticulously traces the derivation of almost every measure from each prelude's opening idea.

21. Berlin: W. Thome, 1840, p. 308: "die musikalische Rhetorik oder Formenlehre." Dehn's remarks come at the end of his treatise; rhetoric, or large-scale form, is not a topic he addresses in any further detail.

sical works as orations, Richter emphasizes the importance of the listener's ability to grasp the succession of ideas, which must be presented "simply and precisely" before they are elaborated.[22]

In all of these composition treatises, form is still viewed as the manner in which a movement's ideas are presented and elaborated, and the listener still plays a critical role in the evaluation of a work's aesthetic quality. Aestheticians, too, preserve this line of thought. Gustav Schilling's *Versuch einer Philosophie des Schönen in der Musik* of 1838 follows the same basic methodology found in Mattheson's *Kern melodischer Wissenschaft* and in Koch's *Versuch einer Anleitung zur Composition,* both of which had in turn been derived from traditional manuals of rhetoric.[23]

Ferdinand Hand's *Aesthetik der Tonkunst* (1837–1841) is heavily influenced by Forkel's theories of musical rhetoric. In outlining the "laws of artistic musical representation," Hand cites with approval the earlier author's rhetorical analysis of C. P. E. Bach's F Minor Sonata, Wq. 57/6, and applies the traditional sequence of *inventio, dispositio,* and *elocutio.* He concludes his discussion with a review of genres. Mattheson would surely have been pleased to know that his basic ideas and methodology would still be in use more than a hundred years later.

The Metaphor of the Organism and the Emerging Paradox of Musical Form

In spite of its continuing influence, the metaphor of the musical work as an oration did eventually disappear over the course of the nineteenth century. Although isolated references to the rhetorical concept of form continued for many years afterwards,[24] the tradition associating rhetoric and musical form lost its central role during the period between approximately 1820 and 1850.

It is no small coincidence that the paradox of form—the seemingly irreconcilable dichotomy between the conformational and generative

---

22. Richter, *Die Grundzüge der musikalischen Formen und ihre Analyse* (Leipzig: Georg Wigand, 1852), p. 51.

23. Schilling, *Versuch einer Philosophie des Schönen in der Musik, oder Aesthetik der Tonkunst* (Mainz: B. Schott's Söhne, 1838), pp. 359–360. See above, pp. 83, 118–120.

24. As, for example, in Vincent d'Indy's *Cours de composition musicale,* 2nd ed., 2 vols. (Paris: Durand, 1902–1909). Donald Francis Tovey may have arrived at the image of the sonata-form recapitulation as a "peroration" independently; but it seems likely that the idea of this metaphor came to him from some of his older German friends and colleagues. See also the discussion of Schoenberg's writings below.

perspectives—should emerge during precisely this period. Only with the decline of rhetoric does the conceptual basis of large-scale form become fragmented.

This fragmentation, although gradual, had a profound influence on subsequent accounts of form. The early stages of this change are particularly subtle, for the basic concept of rhetoric, as we have seen, did not disappear suddenly; it was first supplemented and only later superseded by the organic-generative concept of form.

The Organic-Generative Concept of Form

The organic-generative concept of form, as noted in Chapter 1, has been central to much analysis since the nineteenth century.[25] According to this outlook, the component elements of every successful work of art must articulate in a manner analogous to the constituent parts of a living organism. The process of growth within a work, moreover, must be internally motivated. The shape of an organic whole is often held to be inherent in its germinal unit, with the whole existing in the part just as the part exists in the whole.[26] The oak, to use one of the favorite images of this line of thought, grows out of the acorn.

Elements imposed externally upon a work do not threaten its organic unity: they destroy it. Beethoven's first two "Razumovsky" quartets, according to Adolf Bernhard Marx, fall short of being "unified organisms" on the grounds that each features a Russian folk-song theme—that is to say, an element supposedly either suggested or dictated to the composer by its dedicatee, Count Razumovsky.[27]

In the absence of such extraneous influences, however, a musical work will "develop in the realm of artistic genius according to organic laws," as

---

25. On the rise of the organic outlook in music theory and aesthetics, see Ruth A. Solie, "The Living Work: Organicism and Musical Analysis," *19th-Century Music,* 4 (1980), 147–156; Broyles, "Organic Form"; Thaler, *Organische Form;* Kerman, "Theories of Late Eighteenth-Century Music," esp. pp. 219–224; and Meyer, *Style and Music,* pp. 189–205. Broader studies of organicism include James Benzinger, "Organic Unity: Leibniz to Coleridge," *PMLA, 66* (1951), 24–48; Abrams, *Mirror and the Lamp,* esp. chs. 7 and 8; and G. S. Rousseau, ed., *Organic Form: The Life of an Idea* (London: Routledge & Kegan Paul, 1972). Murray Krieger, in his *A Reopening of Closure: Organicism Against Itself* (New York: Columbia University Press, 1989), refutes many of the arguments commonly directed against organic theories of art.

26. See, for example, the anonymous review of Beethoven's Second Symphony in the *AMZ,* 6 (1804), col. 542: "the individual in the whole and the whole in the individual."

27. Marx, *Ludwig van Beethoven: Leben und Schaffen,* 2 vols. (Berlin: Otto Janke, 1859; rpt. Hildesheim: Olms, 1979), II, 42–43.

one anonymous writer notes in 1827: "it desires nothing other than to become, to grow, to unfold, to bloom."[28] What grows and blooms in a musical movement is its central idea, usually the opening theme. It is this germinal unit that gives the movement its generative force.

In this sense, the metaphor of the organism preserves an essential component of the earlier metaphor of the oration. The process of growth shares with the process of elaboration the basic premise of internal motivation, with one thought or part leading or growing into the next. Indeed, the metaphor of the oration as a living organism can be traced back at least as far as Plato, and it recurs in the writings of Cicero, Horace, and many subsequent authors dealing with rhetoric.[29]

Nevertheless, it is the organic image of form that provides the central conceptual metaphor for numerous textbooks on composition from the second third of the nineteenth century onward. Arrey von Dommer's mid-century account of the close relationship between the nature of a movement's basic thematic material and its form is typical of its time:

Just as the blossom and the fruit lie dormant in the bud, so too does the further development of a musical movement reside . . . in the theme, and more specifically, within the theme's individual motives . . . Accordingly, it is obvious that a work of art (if it is to be worthy of the name) must always be a free creation of the spirit, the product of an inner drive rather than the result of some intentional, rational combination, or of the "mechanical achievement of imposed demands." Otherwise, this work of art would be merely a technical artifice.[30]

Johann Christian Lobe, another influential theorist of the same period, also stresses the intimate connection between form and the unfolding of a germinal thematic idea. His *Compositions-Lehre* of 1844 bears the alternate title *Umfassende Theorie von der thematischen Arbeit und den modernen Instrumentalformen*.[31] The elaboration of a theme, in Lobe's view, is the basis of composition in general and of the creation of modern instrumental forms in particular. In his later *Lehrbuch der musikalischen Komposition* (1850), Lobe reproduces in facsimile excerpts from Beethoven's sketchbooks in an attempt to show how an entire movement can grow from a single, germinal idea.[32]

28. Anonymous, "Soll man bey der Instrumental-Musik Etwas denken?" *AMZ*, 29 (1827), col. 550.

29. *Phaedrus*, 264C. On the image of the oration as an organism, with citations to other texts from classical antiquity, see Vickers, *In Defence of Rhetoric*, pp. 16 and 344–345.

30. Dommer, *Elemente der Musik* (Leipzig: T. O. Weigel, 1862), pp. 169–170.

31. Weimar: Bernhard Friedrich Voigt, 1844.

32. Leipzig: Breitkopf & Härtel, 1850.

Even Ferdinand Hand, who had been influenced so strongly by Forkel's notion of rhetoric, ultimately opts for the image of an organism in describing the essence of a musical work:

If, then, invention gives an art-work its basic idea [*Grundgedanke*] and spiritual animation, the work can achieve its existence only when its individual sections are ordered and arranged into a whole, and when the work in this shape impresses the basic idea completely and clearly, so that the spirit beholding it is satisfied and delights in the appearance of something that is beautiful. The musical art-work should also embrace a world in miniature and constitute an organic structure in which all the parts are in keeping with the whole and the whole is reflected in each of the parts.[33]

Phrases like "spiritual animation" and "organic structure," virtually non-existent in the eighteenth century, become commonplaces in nineteenth-century accounts of form and composition. Yet Hand's remarks also illustrate how closely the images of the oration and the biological organism are linked: both metaphors emphasize the need for functional unity among an entity's individual elements.[34]

The images of the organism and the oration are similarly intertwined throughout Dommer's *Elemente der Musik*. Biological and rhetorical metaphors are presented side by side when Dommer claims that

every musical work, like any other art-work, is an *organism* that is full of meaning and that has grown out of the conditions of inner life. Its parts stand in *inner necessity* to one another and in relation to the whole. *Truth and unity of idea, correctness in the sequence of its development and the perceptibility of its expression and representation*—these are definitive conditions just as much for a musical work as for a painting or a poem.[35]

Dommer's organic imagery is overt, but his emphasis on the quality of perceptibility betrays a lingering allegiance to the pragmatic, rhetorical orientation as well. Perceptibility and intelligibility may perhaps be desirable qualities in a living organism, but they are scarcely essential to its existence. And while Dommer does not evoke the image of the oration explicitly, he apparently finds the quality of organic wholeness insufficient to ensure a work's artistic value. The individual elements that make up the whole must relate to a central idea, and the whole must rest on the basis of inner necessity, but the elaboration of this central idea must be presented intelligibly, in a proper sequence.

33. Hand, *Aesthetik der Tonkunst*, II, 188.
34. For another example of Hand's mixing of organic and rhetorical metaphors concerning form, see ibid., I, 180–181.
35. Dommer, *Elemente der Musik*, p. 169.

To a certain extent, then, the change in imagery used to describe form masks an underlying continuity. Even Koch, in one of his last published treatises, could use phrases like "organische Bildung" and "organische Form" alongside the earlier image of rhetoric.[36] In the end, however, the new metaphor reflects a profound shift in aesthetic outlook. As an organism, the musical work is an object of contemplation that exists in and of itself. As an oration, the musical work is a temporal event whose purpose is to evoke a response from the listener. We can be moved by both modes of experience; but the metaphor of the oration necessarily emphasizes the temporality of the work, the role of the listener, and the element of aesthetic persuasion, whereas the model of the biological organism has no need to account for a work's effect upon its intended audience. Indeed, the audience, for all practical purposes, is irrelevant to the organic model. The organic metaphor implies that the standards by which any given work is to be judged will be found within the work itself. This kind of thinking further reinforces the conceptual autonomy of both the work of art and the process of its creation, for the biological metaphor tacitly encourages us to see the artist as a life-giving force.[37] The nineteenth century's "religion of art" is manifest in the very metaphor of the art-work as a living creation.

The rise of organic imagery in the early nineteenth century, as Michael Broyles points out, also coincides with an important change in the musical repertoire itself.[38] Literal repetition of large sections in binary movements—often the exposition, and sometimes the development and recapitulation as well—was a practice that declined sharply toward the end of the eighteenth century. By the 1820s and 1830s, such extended repetition was the exception rather that the rule. Grétry's exhortation, that sonata-form movements should be organized more like orations, had largely been fulfilled.

The technique of thematic "metamorphosis," to use another term borrowed from the biological sciences, also becomes more widespread around this time. Inter-movement connections are certainly present in the Classical style, but they are not nearly so obvious, nor do they play so central a role as in later works like Schubert's "Wanderer" Fantasy, or the symphonies of Schumann and Bruckner. Once again, the image of the organism reflects changing ideas of what devices and elements can give coherence to the musical work.

36. Koch, *Handbuch bey dem Studium der Harmonie,* pp. 3, 6, 7.

37. On the concept of the artist as a creator-god, see Abrams, *Mirror and the Lamp;* Tzvetan Todorov, *Theories of the Symbol,* trans. Catherine Porter (Ithaca, N.Y.: Cornell University Press, 1982), pp. 153–154.

38. Broyles, "Organic Form."

The Mechanistic-Conformational Concept of Form

Fertile in its own right, the organic concept of form also gave rise to its antithesis—or more precisely, provoked the need for a sharpened formulation of an outlook already inherent in the earlier rhetorical concept. August Wilhelm Schlegel, in his lectures on drama and literature delivered in Vienna in 1808, contrasts organic form with mechanical form and extends these images to the fine arts:

> Form is mechanical when it is imparted to any material through an external force, merely as an accidental addition, without reference to its character . . . Organic form, on the contrary, is innate; it unfolds from within, and achieves that for which it was destined simultaneously with the fullest development of the seed . . . In the fine arts, just as in the province of nature—the supreme artist—all genuine forms are organic, i.e., determined by the content of the work of art.[39]

Schlegel's view of organic form comes very close to denying any essential distinction between form and content, for it is the content that determines the form. In this respect, the organic view differs fundamentally from the rhetorical view, which consistently upheld this distinction without making "outer" form aesthetically inferior to "inner" form. The form-content debate, in other words, did not emerge until the organic image of form began to establish itself as the only "genuine" kind of form.

Koch's acknowledgment of the conflict between genius and external conventions in the 1790s is a harbinger of things to come; but for Koch and other eighteenth-century writers, the rhetorical concept of form encompasses not only the generative process of thematic elaboration but also the application of conventional patterns as a means toward achieving artistic intelligibility. In acknowledging a distinction between form and content, the rhetorical concept of form had already implicitly embodied the mechanistic-conformational approach in its own right. Large-scale structural conventions were recognized as such; but these conventions had been seen as a vehicle for making a movement's central idea intelligible to an audience. With the open emergence of the form-content debate in the early nineteenth century, however, theorists were forced to rethink the nature of these large-scale structural conventions. Theorists eventually began to look upon these patterns as a qualitatively different (and lesser) category of form, something to be learned but ultimately overcome.

Within the rhetorical concept of musical form, the primary function of conventional large-scale harmonic patterns had been to enhance the unfold-

39. Schlegel, *Vorlesungen über dramatische Kunst und Literatur,* in his *Kritische Schriften und Briefe,* vol. 6, pt. 2, ed. Edgar Lohner (Stuttgart: W. Kohlhammer, 1967), 109–110. Translation (in part) from Abrams, *Mirror and the Lamp,* p. 213.

ing of thematic ideas. But by the 1820s, these harmonic patterns themselves began to emerge as a conceptual basis for form, or at least for certain forms. Heinrich Birnbach, writing in 1827, was the first writer to equate the concept of form directly to the modulatory pattern of a work:

We must first pose the question: by what means is the form of a musical work actually determined? Or what, altogether, is the form of a musical work? . . . Because a particular key is established as the tonic at the beginning of any musical work and because the modulations to other keys in any given work must have a certain relationship to the tonic if the work is to be good—for this reason, the various different arrangements of modulation within a given musical work constitute the criterion by which one might recognize the genre to which a composition belongs, according to established rules of modulatory arrangement . . . It is through the modulations present in a work that its form is established, and it is through the manipulation of the corresponding fundamental themes that the relative gradation of a work's value is determined.[40]

Birnbach's approach is remarkably similar to more recent efforts to reconstruct eighteenth-century concepts of form. He explicitly identifies form with large-scale harmonic structure, the lowest common denominator among a large number of works. The nature of any given work's thematic material, as he implies, is too variable to provide such a framework. And it is only in the unique qualities of an individual work, Birnbach argues, that the aesthetic value of a work can be judged.

Many earlier writers had noted these large-scale harmonic conventions, of course, but these modulatory patterns had never been equated exclusively with the concept of form; nor had they ever been separated entirely from an account of thematic events; nor, above all, had they ever been relegated to second-class aesthetic status. The eighteenth century, it should be remembered, lacked any single term to describe what we now think of as patterned form (among German writers, the most common terms were *Anlage, Anordnung,* or simply *das Ganze*). Birnbach, by contrast, explicitly applies the term "form" to an abstract concept: the structural conventions shared by large number of works.

Divorced from rhetoric, the mechanistic-conformational approach also tends to foster a view of form that is more spatial and synoptic in perspective than temporal. The very idea that a structural stereotype can be represented schematically necessarily undermines the fundamentally temporal nature of the convention. And while earlier accounts of specific forms (for example, sonata form as described by Koch or Galeazzi) can be translated into schematic representations, it is significant that the first actual diagram of a form did not appear until 1826, in the second volume of Anton Reicha's

40. Birnbach, "Über die verschiedene Form," p. 269.

Traité de haute composition musicale. Reicha's concept of form, to be discussed in greater detail below, rests on the concept of the *coupe,* which in the literal sense denotes a receptacle or a container, in this case for musical thoughts. He conceives of form, in a word, as a mold, as a pattern that can be represented synoptically, rather than through time. Leonard Ratner's I - V :|: X - I model, described in Chapter 1, is a more recent application of the synoptic perspective to the Classical repertoire. But insofar as all schemas necessarily represent form from a synoptic perspective, they reflect a historical shift of aesthetic interest away from the process of temporality and the listener.

Both the generative and the conformational perspectives of form, previously united by rhetoric, lose their common thread with the rise of *Formenlehre* and the detailed codification of external conventions based on lowest common denominators. It is scarcely coincidental that Koch, the first writer to present a detailed account of what we now know as sonata form, should also have been the first in a long line of theorists to address the potential conflict between the external conventions of form and the internally generated demands of the individual work. It is precisely because he describes specific conventions in such detail that he feels the need to clarify the relationship between genius and convention. Koch, significantly enough, is also the last theorist to reconcile the two convincingly, for his account is the last serious attempt that is firmly based on a rhetorical foundation. With the emerging idea of form as an aggregate of lowest common denominators, later writers could not resolve (or in many cases, simply did not acknowledge) the paradoxical coexistence of two disparate concepts of form without deprecating one of them as "outer" form.

The issue of intelligibility, central to so much critical thought in the eighteenth century, became increasingly less important over the course of the nineteenth, and by the time of Adolf Bernhard Marx's *Die Lehre von der musikalischen Komposition* (1837–1847), the rift between the generative and the conformational approaches to form was openly acknowledged. Marx is one of the few nineteenth-century writers who made a sustained effort to reconcile the two, and his *Lehre* includes repeated pleas to his readers not to equate the use of stereotypical patterns with the process of artistic creation. Nevertheless, his efforts focus on the act of creation rather than on the act of reception. Koch, as we have already seen, was still capable of reconciling this conflict through the conceptual metaphor of rhetoric by emphasizing the role that conventional structures play in facilitating the listener's comprehension of the composer's ideas. Marx, on the other hand, was not nearly so concerned about the listener and the processes by which intelligibility could be facilitated, and in the end, his efforts to reconcile the divergent senses of the term "form" were unsuccessful. The present-day aesthetic dichotomy between the two is a legacy of rhetoric's decline.

Three Case Studies: Reicha, Marx, Schoenberg

It is beyond the scope of this book to trace the historical development of the organic and mechanistic concepts of form throughout the nineteenth century and into the twentieth. But two composer-theorists already mentioned—Anton Reicha and Adolf Bernhard Marx—illustrate a critical stage in the emerging paradox of musical form in the early nineteenth century. And the writings of a third, Arnold Schoenberg, help demonstrate the manner in which rhetorical concepts have persisted well into our own century in nonrhetorical guises.

Reicha

Anton Reicha (1770–1836) is the pivotal figure in the emerging dichotomy of form. A native of Prague who spent his early life in Bonn, Hamburg, and Vienna before emigrating to Paris in the early 1800s, Reicha was a proficient composer as well as the author of numerous treatises. He was a personal friend of both Haydn and the young Beethoven, and his theoretical works consistently extol the music of Haydn and Mozart as stylistic paradigms. His writings, as a whole, survey virtually the entire field of composition, including treatises on harmony, melody, counterpoint, and orchestration. Carl Czerny's extensive translation of many of these works, published in Vienna in the early 1830s, helped ensure Reicha's international renown as a theorist.[41] Reicha's treatises in fact represent the only systematic corpus of theoretical writings to emanate from a representative of Viennese Classicism—in spite of the fact that almost all of them were written in French, after his move to Paris.

In one of his earliest published treatises, the *Traité de mélodie* of 1814, Reicha adopts a fundamentally rhetorical outlook, citing with approval the Abbé Arnaud's intention to prepare a work on musical rhetoric. In describing the purpose of melody, Reicha evokes the celebrated triad of the orator's three duties: *movere, docere, delectare*. A melody, according to Reicha, must "strike the listener, move him, or please him" *(frapper, émouvoir, ou flatter)*; melody cannot "teach," at least not in the traditional sense, but the deriva-

---

41. Reicha, *Cours de composition musicale. Vollständiges Lehrbuch der musikalischen Composition*, 4 vols., ed. and trans. Carl Czerny (Vienna: Anton Diabelli, preface dated 1832).

tion of the other two categories from rhetoric is unmistakable. The princi-ples by which one composes a good melody, then, are "somewhat compa-rable to those by which one constructs an oration or a poetic narrative. Melody, moreover, incorporates the theory of rhythm, with its points of repose or cadences; the art of concatenating and elaborating ideas in order to make a whole; and the knowledge of periodicity and the manner in which periods can be combined with one another."[42]

Methodologically, Reicha follows much the same strategy as Mattheson and Koch. He begins his discussion of melody by considering invention and the nature of musical genius; he then moves on to review the periodic structure of melody, the expansion of individual units within each period, and the concatenation of successive periods into a whole. For Reicha, the term "melody" generally retains its eighteenth-century sense, referring to the span of a complete movement. A melody—a movement—can consist of one, two, three, or more periods, and there are any number of ways of combining these periods. He illustrates one such large-scale combination by analyzing in some detail the melody of the Adagio from Haydn's Symphony No. 44 in E Minor. Koch, it will be remembered, had also il-lustrated the concatenation of periods by analyzing the slow movement from a middle-period Haydn symphony (No. 42).

But instead of treating the conventions of large-scale form within a dis-cussion of genres, as Mattheson and Koch had done, Reicha steps back to consider form as a more abstract idea. He introduces the concept of the "cadre, coupe, ou dimension," terms he uses interchangeably to describe the various large-scale constructs common to a variety of genres. A move-ment—a melody—consisting of two periods alone is a *coupe de la romance* or a *petite coupe binaire.* If the melody consists of three principal periods, of which the third is a literal repetition of the first, it is a *coupe du rondeau,* or a *petite coupe ternaire.* A melody divided into two large halves, each of which consists of multiple periods, is *la grande coupe binaire;* and if divided into three multi-period sections with a *da capo* third section, it represents *la grande coupe ternaire.*

Because of its importance in the contemporary repertoire, the *grande coupe binaire* occupies the bulk of Reicha's subsequent discussion of these conven-tions. The second half of this *coupe* is never shorter than the first, for "the first half is the exposition, while the second is the development." The ter-minology seems strikingly modern, yet the metaphor of the oration is never far beneath the surface, for in a footnote Reicha observes how "remarkable

42. Reicha, *Traité de mélodie,* p. 9. Numerous other references or allusions to rhetoric occur throughout Reicha's treatise (pp. iii, 1, 85, 93, 100, etc.) For Arnaud, see above, p. 70.

it is that our feelings follow a law here that the spirit adopts; for in an oration, there must be an exposition whose ideas can be developed in another section."[43]

Reicha then goes on to describe the modulatory conventions of the *grande coupe binaire*, noting that this framework is used for "grand arias and bravura arias; and in instrumental music for the first movement of sonatas, duos, trios, quartets, overtures, symphonies, and large concertos."[44] The basic perspective is still rhetorical, however, for once again the listener provides the ultimate justification for these procedures. One must not modulate too much in the first half, for example,

in order not to contradict the movement's exposition, which must always be clear and distinct—otherwise the second half will lose its interest, for it would no longer be connected to the first in an obvious manner. If the exposition is defective, all the rest will be defective, too, as in an oration, for the attention of the listener will be distracted or lost, or will be engaged too weakly to be able to appreciate the rest.[45]

Later in his treatise, Reicha offers further observations on these "coupes, cadres et dimensions mélodiques": "The *coupe* is the master of the melody and of a movement of music in general; and just as an outline [*cadre*] can be square or round, or triangular, so too can the melody vary in its outline. The study of these outlines is very important for the composer, and yet no one has yet spoken of them in the art of music."[46]

Reicha is not the first to use the term *coupe* in connection with structural conventions—Momigny had earlier defined a *fantaisie* as a "morceau dans lequel le Compositeur sort de la coupe ordinaire des morceaux"[47]—but he is the first to elaborate upon the concept at any length. Once introduced, the concept of the *coupe* or *cadre* takes on increasing significance within Reicha's treatise. More and more, the *coupe* begins to resemble a "jelly mold," a framework for individual themes. Reicha goes on to expand the concept of the *coupe* in order to include forms that are neither binary nor ternary. The result is the earliest taxonomy of form as an abstract concept. Genres no longer constitute the organizational principle for the elucidation of conventional constructs; instead, abstract formal types represent specific genres. These include:

1. the *petite coupe variée* for a set of variations on a single theme;

43. Ibid., p. 46.
44. Ibid., p. 48.
45. Ibid., p. 47.
46. Ibid., p. 58.
47. Momigny, *Cours complet,* II, 679.

2. the *grande coupe variée* for variations on two different themes, one in major and one in minor ("double variations");

3. the *coupe arbitraire* for "fantasias and preludes";

4. the *coupe libre ou indéterminée,* in which one presents many periods, without dividing them into two, three, or more sections, as in *airs déclamés;*

5. the *coupe de retour,* in which one "repeats the main theme often, but each time after a new period, as in many *rondeaux.*"[48]

The fluctuation in Reicha's terminology is problematic. His alternating use of *coupe* and *cadre* with the much vaguer *dimension* is symptomatic of the broader problems that arise when an external parameter becomes the primary criterion for the definition of specific forms. His original definition of the *coupe* rests on the concept of periodicity, but his subsequent application of the term to the "fantasia or prelude" is less satisfactory: the *coupe arbitraire* seems a contradiction in terms. Can a "free form," by this line of thought, really be a form at all? Reicha, moreover, ignores the conceptual problems of form posed by such contrapuntal constructs as the fugue and the canon. And while he emphatically denies that a *coupe* is the basis of a musical composition, he also asserts that it is the "patron de la Mélodie." The *coupe,* for Reicha, is clearly an organizing force at a level above the period. For the most part, in fact, it supplants the concept of rhetoric as the organizing force for the trajectory of a melody—which is to say, for the structure of a movement. The imagery of a musical movement as an oration is most clearly present in the earlier portions of the *Traité de mélodie,* but it gradually gives way to the idea of the *coupe.*

Reicha's *Traité de haute composition musicale* of 1824–1826 continues in this direction, with fewer references to the metaphor of the oration and even greater stress on the concept of the *coupe.* The *coupe* is still viewed as a means for developing a a melody's ideas, for Reicha introduces the term under the rubric "Sur les coupes ou cadres des morceaux de musique qui sont le plus avantageux au développement des idées." And the importance of the *grande coupe binaire* is stressed once again, not only because it is the most common structure in music, but because the student, once he has mastered this form, "will have no great difficulty in composing in the other *coupes.*"[49]

In the *Traité de haute composition,* Reicha introduces a new category, the *coupe du menuet,* but the most significant additions to his treatment of form are the schematic diagrams that represent large-scale conventions synoptically (see Figure 3.1). The use of schematic diagrams, as noted earlier, ex-

48. Reicha, *Traité de mélodie* pp. 58–60.
49. Reicha, *Traité de haute composition musicale,* 2 vols. (Paris: Zetter, 1824–26), II, 296.

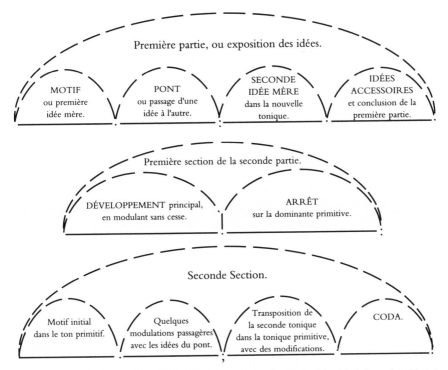

Figure 3.1 Reicha's schematization of the "Grande coupe binaire," from his *Traité de haute composition* (1824–1826), II, 300

ercises a subtle but significant influence on the manner in which form is perceived. In its search for lowest common denominators, Reicha's *grande coupe binaire* suggests that the tonal outline of a movement is the constant element in the equation, that harmony is now the basis of form, and that the *coupe* is a vessel for melodic ideas. Reicha argues against this interpretation at several points: the notion of an *idée mère* evokes organic imagery, but his concept of the *coupe,* as we have seen, is ambiguous at best. It is more useful for defining specific forms than it is in providing a broader basis for a theory of form.

Reicha's schematic representations, with the synoptic perspective they foster, also tend to emphasize a shift in aesthetic and analytical emphasis from the act of listening to the work itself. His diagrams make no reference to the listener, and however detailed or refined his prose may be, it is the visual schematization that inevitably provides the most concise and memorable representation of the concept of form. The perspective is now squarely centered on the work itself, viewed as an external, autonomous object.

Marx

This work-oriented perspective is integral to the writings of Adolf Bernhard Marx (1795–1866). Composer, author, and founding editor of the *Berliner allgemeine musikalische Zeitung,* Marx also relied on schematic diagrams (albeit less elaborate ones), and he described specific musical forms in unprecedented detail.[50] Like Reicha, Marx begins his account of musical form by reviewing the principles of periodicity. In going beyond the limited model of the minuet, Marx follows the traditional precept of urging the student to study the works of great composers. His detailed accounts of specific forms represent an important additional device by which to bridge the gap between student and master.

To an even greater extent than Reicha, Marx treats form from the perspective of the composer rather than that of the listener. He is the first theorist in whose writings the paradox of musical form becomes explicit. To his credit, Marx openly acknowledges this conceptual dichotomy and confronts a problem that Koch had raised only briefly and that Reicha had more or less avoided altogether. Marx's solution to the problem is to distinguish between *Form* and *Kunstform.* The former is "the manner in which the content of the work—the composer's concept, feeling, idea—becomes an external whole [*Gestalt*]." This essentially generative view sees form as the *Aeusserung* (literally the "externalization" and figuratively the "expression") of its content. Thus, there can be "as many forms as there are works of art."[51]

Kunstform, on the other hand, is Marx's term for those "essential features shared by a large number of individual artistic works." The number of *Kunstformen* is also limitless, at least in theory; in practice, however, a relatively small number of patterns provide the basis for all others. *Formlehre* is the teaching of these *Kunstformen.*[52]

This terminological distinction between the mechanistic-conformational *(Kunstform)* and the organic-generative *(Form)* confirms the establishment of a dichotomy that is still very much a part of theoretical thought today.

---

50. For Marx's diagrams, see his *Lehre,* III, 206, 213, etc. In the preface to volume one of his *Lehre,* Marx explicitly acknowledges Reicha's contributions to the theory of melody.

51. Ibid., II, 5. Marx issued a second edition of volumes one (1841) and two (1842) of the *Lehre* before publishing volume three (1845). In the second edition of volume two, he deleted his original explication of sonata form, moving it to volume three (1845) and presenting it there in considerably greater depth. His general approach to the concept of form is essentially consistent in both editions, however. All citations to volume two of the *Lehre* here are to the second edition.

52. Marx, *Lehre,* II, 5. Marx vacillates between *Formlehre* and *Formenlehre,* apparently without any significant distinction in meaning (e.g., between the study of "form" and the study of "forms").

In some respects, Marx's definition of *Form* comes quite close to Koch's ("the manner in which the art-work is brought before the soul of the listener").[53] But Marx's concept of *Kunstform,* like Reicha's diagrams, ignores the destination of the work—the listener—and emphasizes instead the process by which the composer shapes the structure of his "concept, feeling, and idea." Thus, although earlier theorists had recognized the existence of conventional structures, Marx is the first to make a consistent terminological distinction between stereotypical patterns and the broader concept of form in general.

Other terms used by Marx preserve rhetorical categories under the guise of a nonrhetorical vocabulary. The traditional distinction between what earlier writers had called grammar—the mechanical rules of music—and rhetoric—the art of combining smaller units into an aesthetically satisfying whole—is now expressed through more neutral terminology. Marx calls the former the "pure theory of the composition," the latter "applied."[54] The change in vocabulary only masks the continuity of a pedagogical tradition that distinguishes between that which is technically correct and that which is aesthetically moving.

The widening gulf between pure and applied theory, *Kunstform* and *Form,* made the need to distinguish between genius and convention all the more acute. Forkel and Koch had already addressed this issue briefly, but Marx attacked it with unprecedented vigor and directness. His hierarchical codification of forms, as noted earlier, is balanced by his deep concern that the student not confuse pedagogical necessity with the act of true artistic creation. He repeatedly reminds his readers that *Kunstformen* are not to be viewed as matters of mere technique, divorced from content.

The true purpose of *Formenlehre* for Marx, in fact, is to teach the student mastery of all forms in order that he be slave to none. Only with the fantasia, the "formless" form, does the aspiring composer reach the true goal of *Formenlehre.* He must give up every "fixed form" and give himself over to "the freedom of the spirit, which knows no law other than itself."[55] In the end, the value of *Kunstformen* is essentially heuristic for Marx: the very purpose of mastering specific, conventional forms is to transcend them. It is thus all the more ironic that Marx himself has since come to be so closely associated with the "textbook" concept of form.

Nevertheless, it is the classification and description of specific conventional forms in *Die Lehre von der musikalischen Komposition* that have re-

---

53. See above, p. 126.
54. Marx, *Lehre,* I, 4–5; III, 4. See also Marpurg's equation of rhetoric with the "applied" elements of composition, above, p. 69.
55. Marx, *Lehre,* III, 326.

mained the work's most enduring legacy. This in itself is a tribute to Marx's method, for the pedagogical usefulness of such a taxonomy has proven itself repeatedly over more than a century. But Marx's simultaneous derogatory attitude toward conventional forms has gone largely unrecognized, even though it, too, persists in present-day pedagogy and analysis.

Marx's treatise went through multiple editions throughout the nineteenth century, and no less an authority than Hugo Riemann revised the last of these editions before preparing his own *Grosse Kompositionslehre* of 1902. Marx's framework has since provided the basis for numerous composition treatises down to the present day: specific forms are described, sometimes in considerable detail, but ultimately deprecated. Much of the present-day ambivalence toward conventional forms I outlined in Chapter 1 has its origins in this pedagogical tradition. With the possible exception of Czerny—who seems to have been imbued with a particularly strong pedantic streak—no serious theorist has adopted a mechanistic viewpoint other than for didactic purposes.

Schoenberg

As a composer, Arnold Schoenberg (1874–1951) took great pride in viewing his own music within the historical tradition of Haydn, Mozart, Beethoven, and Brahms.[56] As a theorist, Schoenberg did not claim his place in a corresponding heritage, but he would have been perfectly justified had he done so. Certain aspects of his writings, in fact, exhibit much closer ties to the eighteenth than to the nineteenth century.

In what is perhaps his single best-known essay, "Brahms the Progressive," Schoenberg never uses the word "rhetoric," but his stance throughout is thoroughly rhetorical. He views music as a language in its own right; intelligibility is an essential quality of form; and each work must observe what rhetoricians call decorum: its style must stand in proper relationship not only to its content but also to its intended audience.

Form in Music serves to bring about comprehensibility through memorability. Evenness, regularity, symmetry, subdivision, repetition, unity, relationship in rhythm and harmony and even logic—none of these elements produces or even contributes to beauty. But all of them contribute to an organization which makes the presentation of the musical idea intelligible. The language in which musical ideas are expressed in tones parallels the language which expresses feelings or thoughts in words, in that its vocabulary must be proportionate to the intellect which it ad-

---

56. See esp. "Brahms the Progressive" in Schoenberg's *Style and Idea,* ed. Leonard Stein (Berkeley and Los Angeles: University of California Press, 1984), pp. 398–441.

dresses, and in that the aforementioned elements of its organization function like the rhyme, the rhythm, the meter, and the subdivision into strophes, sentences, paragraphs, chapters, etc. in poetry or prose.

The more or less complete exploitation of the potency of these components determines the aesthetic value and the classification of the style in respect to its popularity or profundity . . . Even Antony, when addressing the Roman people, realizes that he must repeat his ". . . and Brutus is an honourable man" over and over, if this contrast is to penetrate into the minds of simple citizens.[57]

The purpose of form in both verbal and musical language, as Schoenberg suggests, is to facilitate intelligibility. He goes on to cite the recurring rhythmic pattern of a Johann Strauss waltz as a vehicle by which a musical thought can be made intelligible. But Schoenberg's own goal as a composer was to reach a more sophisticated audience, one that could grasp complex ideas at a single hearing. "This is what musical prose should be—a direct and straightforward presentation of ideas," without the aid of the "patchwork" or "mere padding and empty repetitions" that characterize a popular waltz.

Mature people think in complexes, and the higher their intelligence the greater is the number of units with which they are familiar. It is inconceivable that composers should call "serious music" what they write in an obsolete style, with a prolixity not conforming to the contents—repeating three to seven times what is understandable at once. Why should it not be possible in music to say in whole complexes in a condensed form what, in the preceding epochs, had at first to be said several times with slight variations before it could be elaborated?[58]

Schoenberg's complaint is a twentieth-century echo of Grétry's comments more than one hundred fifty years before ("I was at your house this morning; yes, I was at your house this morning . . ."). Both composers, in essence, are arguing for a rhetoric of music that more nearly reflects "an oration," to use Grétry's term, or in Schoenberg's terminology, "musical prose":

I wish to join ideas with ideas. No matter what the purpose or meaning of an idea in the aggregate may be, no matter whether its function be introductory, establishing, varying, preparing, elaborating, deviating, developing, concluding, subdividing, subordinate, or basic, it must be an idea which had to take this place even if it were not to serve for this purpose or meaning or function; and this idea must look in construction and in thematic content as if it were not there to fulfil a structural task. In other words, a transition, a codetta, an elaboration, etc., should not be

57. Ibid., p. 399. Schoenberg draws on Antony's celebrated oration from *Julius Caesar* once again in his essay "For a Treatise on Composition," in *Style and Idea*, p. 265.
58. "Brahms the Progressive," p. 408.

considered as a thing in its own end. It should not appear at all if it does not develop, modify, intensify, clarify, or throw light or colour on the idea of the piece.[59]

"Rhetoric," in its debased sense, is probably the last term Schoenberg would have wished to use in this context, redolent as it is with the very notions of "empty repetition" and "padding" he sought to avoid. Yet it is precisely rhetoric, in its traditional and more elevated sense, that Schoenberg is evoking here, for he seeks a "logic" by which to connect the presentation of his ideas.[60] The formulation in the last of the passages cited above offers a particularly striking parallel with Mattheson's image of a musical movement as an oration. Within his listing of the various functions of musical ideas, Schoenberg incorporates the traditional categories of rhetoric almost verbatim ("introductory" = exordium; "establishing" = narratio and propositio; "varying," "elaborating," and "developing" = confirmatio; "deviating" = confutatio; "concluding" = peroratio). There can be no doubt that Schoenberg was aware of the rhetorical source of these categories, even if he was not specifically aware of Mattheson's or Forkel's earlier applications of these terms.

Closely related to the idea of "musical prose" is Schoenberg's celebrated—if rather vaguely formulated—concept of "developing variation." Its object is the unfolding, the elaboration of a work's central idea or "basic shape," its *Grundgestalt*.[61] Developing variation can also be seen as an essentially rhetorical concept, for the metaphor of the musical work as an oration encompasses not only the expansion and elaboration of small-scale units but also the broader coherence of the whole, the manner in which one idea follows another.[62] By giving priority to the elaboration of a central idea,

59. Ibid., p. 407. The term "musical prose" is not original with Schoenberg, although he used it in his own peculiar way: see Hermann Danuser, *Musikalische Prosa* (Regensburg: G. Bosse, 1975).

60. See, for example, Johann Joachim Eschenburg's *Entwurf einer Theorie und Literatur der schönen Redekünste*, 3rd ed. (Berlin: F. Nicolai, 1805), in which rhetoric is defined as the basis for a "successive and coherent presentation of ideas" (p. 319), and in which music, poetry, and oratory are classed together as "sounding" ("tonische") arts (p. 4).

61. Schoenberg used the term *Grundgestalt* in a variety of contexts, and it is a term that poses special problems for translators: see David Epstein, *Beyond Orpheus* (Cambridge, Mass.: MIT Press, 1979), pp. 17–21. For a convenient summary of Schoenberg's scattered uses of the term, see Reinhold Brinkmann's appendix to "Anhand von Reprisen," in *Brahms-Analysen: Referate der Kieler Tagung, 1983,* ed. Friedhelm Krummacher and Wolfram Steinbeck (Kassel: Bärenreiter, 1984), pp. 116–118. See also Patricia Carpenter, "*Grundgestalt* as Tonal Function," *Music Theory Spectrum,* 5 (1983), 15–38; and Carl Dahlhaus, "What Is 'Developing Variation'?" in his *Schoenberg and the New Music,* trans. Derrick Puffett and Alfred Clayton (Cambridge: Cambridge University Press, 1987), pp. 128–133.

62. On the distinctions between "thematic-motivic manipulation" and developing variation, see Carl Dahlhaus, *Die Musiktheorie im 18. und 19. Jahrhundert, erster Teil: Grundzüge einer Systematik* (Darmstadt: Wissenschaftliche Buchgesellschaft, 1984), pp. 135–136.

embodied in what eighteenth-century theorists would have called the *Hauptsatz*, Schoenberg embraces a concept of form that is perhaps even more traditional than he realized. Vogler's description of variations on a theme as "a kind of musical rhetoric" is a direct anticipation of Schoenberg's formulation.

There is in fact a revealing parallel between Schoenberg's idea of musical prose and Ernst Ludwig Gerber's essay on the symphony that appeared in the *Allgemeine musikalische Zeitung* of 1813. Gerber gives Haydn credit for having established a new kind of symphonic style, in which an entire movement is based on a single *Hauptsatz*.[63] But in spite of its clear superiority, Gerber argues, this manner of writing poses certain difficulties for the composer, the orchestra, and the listener. The problem, according to Gerber, lies in the issue of intelligibility and

the receptivity of the public in hearing such complex and artful music. Only someone with an ear educated through much practice and the repeated pleasure of hearing great works of art, and with an enlightened artistic sense of the same, is in a position to absorb and enjoy such beauties and magnificent works, especially in light of the racing tempos that are now common. If one adds to all this the currently predominant mania for modulation and instability, by which no idea is actually allowed to be elaborated, and in which the participation of the ear and heart is often disturbed and torn away—then it could not be any wonder at all if in hearing such an artwork, one should find it, as did the Parisian public, according to its own spokesmen, remarkable but *fatiguing*.[64]

The public's ability to assimilate the concentrated expression of Haydn's music, Gerber implies, is limited. And even listeners familiar with the idiom will be challenged by a work that, while based on a single idea, elaborates and develops that idea in a dense, demanding fashion. Considered from the perspective of his contemporaries, Haydn's music elaborates ideas in a manner that seems much closer to musical prose than to poetry. In the early years of the nineteenth century, it should be recalled, Haydn was consistently compared not to a poet, working in fixed meters and rhyme schemes, but to an orator, who expresses ideas in prose. What constitutes "empty padding," in other words, changes with the perceptions of successive generations.

In this light, Schoenberg's concept of the *Grundgestalt* appears less revolutionary than it is often made out to be. The idea, in fact, shares a direct link to A. B. Marx, who speaks of "the sensuous representation of the idea that the artist carries within himself, more or less clearly in his conscious-

63. Gerber, "Eine freundliche Vorstellung über gearbeitete Instrumentalmusik, besonders über Symphonien," *AMZ*, 15 (1813), cols. 457–463.
64. Ibid., col. 459.

ness . . . Thus every part of the sensuous form of a work of art must stem from the artist's internal idea, and must be recognizable and demonstrable" throughout the course of that work.[65]

And like Schoenberg, Marx hints at, but never clearly formulates, a theory that all works (and thus by extension all *Kunstformen*) are based on a deeper, fundamental idea, which Marx calls the *Grundgedanke*. Early in the second volume of his *Lehre*, Marx notes that he can "at this point touch only briefly on the concept of *Grundgedanke*, which is manifested in all forms that are not only already known but are also likely to evolve in the future. The idea can be explained and proven only when the *Formenlehre* has been presented in its entirety."[66] Unfortunately, Marx would in fact never spell out precisely what he meant by the term. From the context of other writings, however, it is clear that the term refers to the central idea that unifies a movement or work. In his later biography of Beethoven, Marx uses the same word to describe the organic growth of the first movement of the Seventh Symphony: "A life has unfolded out of the seed of the *Hauptsatz*. It began lightly, happily, and delightfully idyllically, then raised itself up energetically and combatively, disputatious and inflamed to anger; even its *Grundgedanke* is incandescent with warlike turbulence."[67]

Ferdinand Hand uses the term *Grundgedanke* in a similar context at almost the same time: musical works whose various ideas are not unified by a generative, germinal idea are without shape *(gestaltlos)*.[68] Hand, Marx, and Schoenberg all use nonrhetorical vocabulary to express an essentially rhetorical concept: the elaboration of a central idea in such a way that it will be intelligible to the listener.

Carl Dahlhaus is thus only partly correct in asserting that Schoenberg's concept of developing variation is based on the metaphor of the biological organism.[69] Developing variation does in fact rest on the process of growth, but in describing the nature of that growth, Schoenberg consistently mixes metaphors. At the very outset of his *Fundamentals of Musical Composition*, he notes that "form," used "in the aesthetic sense . . . means that a piece is organized, i.e., that it consists of elements functioning like a living organism." But he then goes on to observe that "without organization music would be an amorphous mass, as unintelligible as an essay without punctuation, or as disconnected as a conversation which leaps purposelessly

---

65. Marx, *Die Kunst des Gesanges, theoretisch-praktisch* (Berlin: A. M. Schlesinger, 1826), pp. 240–241.

66. Marx, *Lehre*, II, 2nd ed. (1842), 6. This passage does not appear in the first edition.

67. Marx, *Beethoven*, II, 198.

68. Hand, *Aesthetik der Tonkunst*, II, 188. See also Dommer, *Elemente*, p. 170.

69. Dahlhaus, "Entwicklung und Abstraktion," *AfMw*, 43 (1986), 91–108.

from one subject to another."[70] Schoenberg's juxtaposition of organic and rhetorical metaphors reflects the essential compatibility and historical continuity of these two images. Like so many composers since the early nineteenth century, Schoenberg saw himself as a godlike artist, his works as living creations; but like his eighteenth-century counterparts, he ultimately appealed to such categories as logic, coherence, and above all intelligibility. "The presentation of ideas rests on the laws of musical coherence," he wrote elsewhere; and the art of presentation is measured in terms of "comprehensibility" *(Fasslichkeit)*[71]—scarcely a prerequisite of organic life.

By whatever name it may be known—*Grundgestalt,* thematic transformation, or metamorphosis—the concept of thematic elaboration is a fundamental element of much analysis today, particularly for music since the time of Beethoven. Yet the earlier theoretical basis for this kind of thinking has long been somewhat obscure, particularly as regards the music of the Classical era. There is a vague if largely unspoken sense that the idea of thematic transformation is a quintessentially nineteenth-century concept, and that it plays at best only an occasional role in earlier repertoires.[72] The nineteenth century did in fact view form as a thematic process, but this was an idea inherited from the eighteenth. Richard Wagner's equation of melody with form is part of a much longer tradition that stretches back more than a hundred years before.[73] Some of the basic elements of Schoenberg's thinking, in turn, can similarly be traced back to the venerable tradition of rhetoric, which ultimately provides a mediating link in concepts of form across the centuries.

70. Schoenberg, *Fundamentals of Musical Composition,* ed. Gerald Strang and Leonard Stein (London: Faber and Faber, 1970), p. 1.

71. Quoted in Jonathan Dunsby and Arnold Whittall, *Music Analysis in Theory and Practice* (New Haven: Yale University Press, 1988), p. 75.

72. One notable exception is Karl H. Wörner's *Das Zeitalter der thematischen Prozesse in der Geschichte der Musik* (Regensburg: Gustav Bosse, 1969), a work that has received scant critical attention to date.

73. Grey, in "Richard Wagner and the Aesthetics of Musical Form," convincingly demonstrates that theorists of the mid-nineteenth century viewed form as an essentially melodic construct. But this view is not, as Grey (pp. 77–79) and other scholars have argued, original to the nineteenth century.

CHAPTER 4

Rhetoric and the Autonomy of Instrumental Music

Before 1800, instrumental music was widely considered aesthetically inferior to vocal music. This attitude is reflected throughout Johann Georg Sulzer's encyclopedic *Allgemeine Theorie der schönen Künste* of 1771–1774. Instrumental music, according to Sulzer, can be pleasing and at times moving, but its "meaning" is relatively obscure. Music without a text cannot specify the precise nature of the emotion it expresses or arouses within the listener. Vocal music, on the other hand, can make its emotional motivation explicit through the vehicle of the text. Music therefore "achieves its full effect only when it is united with poetry."[1] This same attitude is evident even in the writings of Koch and Forkel, who adopt Sulzer's position with only minor modifications. Unlike instrumental music, vocal music can affect both the mind and the heart.[2]

Many eighteenth-century writers, including Sulzer, Forkel, and Koch, do in fact extol the power of instrumental music; but not until well into the nineteenth century was it widely recognized as aesthetically equal or superior to vocal music. In certain circles, however, this change was anticipated as early as the 1790s. In the view of the early German Romantics, instrumental music was actually superior to vocal music. Novalis, for one, could observe at the end of the eighteenth century that "music for singing and music for dancing are not really true music, but only derivatives of it. Sonatas, symphonies, fugues, variations: this is real music."[3]

---

1. Sulzer, *Allgemeine Theorie,* "Musik" and "Instrumentalmusik."
2. Koch, *Musikalisches Lexikon,* "Instrumentalmusik"; see also his *Versuch,* II, 33. Johann Nikolaus Forkel, "Genauere Bestimmung einiger musicalischen Begriffe," in C. F. Cramer's *Magazin der Musik,* 1 (1783), 1067–1068.
3. Novalis, *Schriften,* 4 vols., ed. Paul Kluckhohn (Leipzig: Bibliographisches Institut, n.d.), III, 349.

This change in perception is due in no small part to changes in the music itself: Haydn's and Mozart's late symphonies, to take but one example from a specific genre, are far more ambitious in scope than comparable works by such earlier composers as Giovanni Battista Sammartini or Johann Stamitz—or by Haydn and Mozart themselves, for that matter. Nevertheless, all of these works lack a verbal text, and it is a transformation of attitudes toward what had previously been considered instrumental music's vagueness of meaning that lies at the heart of the new Romantic outlook. The absence of specific images, long considered a liability to instrumental music, was now held to be its greatest asset. Precisely because it transcended the representational limits of the word, a number of influential critics came to see instrumental music as the most demanding and mysterious, and thus the highest and most rewarding, medium of artistic expression.[4]

This new attitude is a common element in the writings of such critics as Wackenroder, Tieck, Novalis, the Schlegels, and E. T. A. Hoffmann. While the individuality of each writer should not be underestimated, there is a remarkable degree of unanimity among the early Romantics that instrumental music, and the symphony in particular, embodies a higher, transcendental language.

This reversal in aesthetic status among the German Romantics is all the more striking in light of the apparent speed with which it took place. The concept of a "paradigmatic shift" has been invoked to account for this change;[5] but such an explanation obscures important elements of continuity between the Romantics and preceding generations. Most previous attempts to interpret the Romantic view of instrumental music have tended to emphasize the movement's innovations at the expense of its more traditional views. Early Romantic writings on music, moreover, are seldom considered in light of the more technical concepts of late-eighteenth-century musical theory.

The Romantic aesthetic does indeed represent a revolution, but it is a revolution in the older sense of the term: a 180-degree turn accomplished by a transformation of ideas, not an abrupt upheaval. Early Romantic theories of instrumental music are in fact deeply rooted in the traditional imagery of music as a language and musical works as orations. The Romantic understanding of instrumental music's "meaning" develops out of the earlier premise that the structure, if not the content, of instrumental music is

---

4. The transformation of aesthetic views in the writings of the early Romantics can be outlined in only the broadest terms here. For more detailed discussions of this phenomenon, see Carl Dahlhaus, *Die Idee der absoluten Musik* (Kassel: Bärenreiter, 1978), trans. by Roger Lustig as *The Idea of Absolute Music* (Chicago: University of Chicago Press, 1989); Hosler, *Changing Aesthetic Views;* and Neubauer, *The Emancipation of Music from Language*.

5. See Dahlhaus, *Die Idee der absoluten Musik*, pp. 12–13.

analogous to that of verbal discourse. And rhetoric, as we shall see, was an important element of continuity in the emerging aesthetic of an autonomous instrumental music. The concept of the "musical idea" that appears for the first time in the second half of the eighteenth century is a direct outgrowth of rhetorical thought, as are the programmatic interpretations of absolute music that first began to appear around this same time. Both represent transitional stages on the path from early-eighteenth-century attitudes toward instrumental music, which are largely condescending, to those of the early nineteenth century, which are nothing short of reverential.

Rhetoric and the "Musical Idea"

The image of music as a language, as seen in Chapter 2, took on special importance over the course of the eighteenth century, particularly in connection with instrumental music. Mattheson's analysis of Marcello's aria as a *Klangrede,* significantly enough, had provided neither the text nor any indication of the aria's dramatic context. Music accompanying a verbal text was seen as an amplification of that text; music without any text at all was considered a wordless oration embodying a language in its own right.

This kind of imagery helped lay the foundation for later interpretations of instrumental music as a meaningful, autonomous art. Whether this "meaning" is representational or nonrepresentational is a basic issue that remains a matter of dispute even today. But from a historical perspective, the very notion that untexted music can have a significance of any kind is an idea that first gained widespread acceptance during the eighteenth century.

The belief in instrumental music's expressive power in the first half of the eighteenth century rested primarily on the idea of music as a language of representational, if rather vague, ideas like sorrow, joy, and anger. But by the end of the century, the Baroque concept of *Affekt* had been largely eclipsed. Even though it continued well into the Classical era, this doctrine was for the most part no longer a vital aesthetic concept by the early years of the nineteenth century. The equation of a movement's theme with an intrinsically musical, nonrepresentational idea, on the other hand, became increasingly prevalent over the second half of the eighteenth century. The perception of *Thema* as *Gedanke* reflects the growing belief in an inherent, self-referential meaning within musical works that have no text.

The concept of an intrinsically musical idea is implicit in the writings of virtually all of the theorists cited in Chapter 2. Scheibe, C. P. E. Bach,

Quantz, Riepel, and Türk all speak repeatedly of "musical ideas."[6] Within the conceptual metaphor of the musical work as an oration, the themes of an instrumental work were seen as units of complete and self-contained thought. The anonymous but perceptive author of the musical dictionary published serially in Hiller's *Wöchentliche Nachrichten* of 1769 emphasizes this quality, particularly for a movement's *Hauptsatz:*

> *Ideas, musical,* are small sections of a melody that nevertheless must have their own sense. One distinguishes among *main, secondary,* and *connective* ideas . . .
>
> The ideas are the first things one writes down according to an established plan for their elaboration. Here one abandons one's self to the fire of imagination and only later brings the proposed piece to the perfection it should have. Ideas are emphasized if the preceding and succeeding ones exhibit less liveliness, beauty, and elaboration. These secondary ideas must nevertheless contribute by emphasizing the main idea and by giving it greater importance. Thus it should not be assumed that secondary ideas are to be neglected. Rather, the composer must know how to elevate the main idea in such a way that it enters the listener's ears most prominently and makes the strongest impression both upon his hearing and upon his spirit.[7]
>
> The main idea [*Hauptgedanke*] is the most important [idea] within the melody. Therefore, it must be presented within every section, for in just this way, one knows that the sections belong together, and because the unity of the melody [i.e., the movement] is determined through the main idea.[8]

Johann Nepomuk Reichenberger, in the third volume of his *Die ganze Musikkunst* (1780), similarly views a work's theme as its leading idea:

> By the word "theme," we mean a brief musical passage consisting of a few notes, or a musical idea, as one calls it, presented in a few notes, much as one generally makes known the content or essence of a sermon with a word or two. This idea is subsequently the ongoing object, the continually recurring material and goal of either the musical work or the oration.[9]

The representational, affective qualities of a theme, in these accounts, are no longer central. What is basic to the musical idea is its potential for subsequent elaboration, its ability to provide an intrinsically musical focus for

6. Scheibe, *Critischer Musikus;* C. P. E. Bach, *Versuch über die wahre Art das Clavier zu spielen,* I (Berlin: Author, 1753), 117, 132–133, etc.; Quantz, *Versuch,* pp. 13, 17, 102, 104–105, 115–116, 304 ("gute Ordnung der Gedanken"), etc.; Riepel, *Anfangsgründe;* Türk, *Klavierschule,* pp. 340–341. For other similar citations, see Ulrich Leisinger, "Was sind musikalische Gedanken?" *AfMw,* 47 (1990), 103–119.

7. Anonymous, "Beytrag zu einem musikalischen Wörterbuch," in Johann Adam Hiller's *Wöchentliche Nachrichten,* no. 39 (27 March 1769), p. 303.

8. Ibid., no. 40 (3 April 1769), p. 313.

9. Reichenberger, *Die ganze Musikkunst,* III, 175.

an entire movement. It is within this broader tradition that Friedrich Schlegel's celebrated aphorism on instrumental music is best understood:

Many a person tends to find it strange and ridiculous that musicians should talk about the thoughts [*Gedanken,* i.e., themes] in their compositions; and indeed, it often happens in such a way that one perceives musicians to have more thoughts in their music than about it. But whoever has a sense for the wonderful affinities among all the arts and sciences will at least not consider the issue from the flat perspective of so-called naturalness, according to which music is supposedly only the language of sentiment; and this person will not find it inherently implausible that there is a certain tendency of all purely instrumental music toward philosophy. Must not purely instrumental music create its own text? And is the theme [of an instrumental work] not developed, confirmed, varied, and contrasted in the same manner as the object of meditation in a philosophical sequence of ideas?[10]

Far from being a "fleeting spark of anticipation" of an idea that would not be fulfilled for another half-century, Schlegel's views represent the continuation of a well-established tradition.[11] Schlegel himself explicitly acknowledges that musicians had already begun to talk in terms of "musical ideas." Carl Dahlhaus has interpreted this passage as a basis for the notion of the thematic process as a "sequence of ideas . . . that would represent the epitome of musical form in the nineteenth century,"[12] and it is certainly this. But it is also the basis for the eighteenth century's understanding of form. The concept of the *Ideenreihe* had been advanced as early as the 1730s by Mattheson and subsequently amplified by Forkel, Koch, and a number of other eighteenth-century writers. Schlegel himself had heard Forkel's lectures in Göttingen and was familiar with the *Allgemeine Geschichte der Musik.*[13]

10. Schlegel, Athenäums-Fragment 444, in *Kritische Friedrich-Schlegel-Ausgabe,* II, ed. Hans Eichner (Munich: Ferdinand Schöningh, 1967), p. 254.

11. Dahlhaus, *Die Idee der absoluten Musik,* p. 110: "flüchtig aufblitzende Antizipation" (Lustig trans., p. 108). Dahlhaus cites this very passage as being in opposition to Forkel's concept of harmony as the "logic" of music. But this interpretation ignores Forkel's broader concept of musical rhetoric, particularly the central role Forkel assigns to thematic ideas and their elaboration. Only a few years later, Karl Spazier, in his annotated translation of Grétry's *Mémoires,* all but quotes the better part of Schlegel's comments, obliquely attributing them to a "recent writer" (Spazier, *Gretrys Versuche,* pp. 183–184).

12. Dahlhaus, *Die Idee der absoluten Musik,* p. 112 (Lustig trans., p. 111). See also Dahlhaus's *Between Romanticism and Modernism,* trans. Mary Whittall (Berkeley: University of California Press, 1980), pp. 43–44.

13. See Edelhoff, *Johann Nikolaus Forkel,* pp. 31–33, 120–121. This is not to suggest that Schlegel's ideas are necessarily based on Forkel's concept of musical rhetoric: his comments on the elder theorist are for the most part derogatory ("he understands as much about music as a castrato does about love"), but his exposure to Forkel's ideas is well documented.

Schlegel's "meditation," moreover, is not to be understood as a kind of transcendental self-communion, but rather in the more traditional sense of contemplating a single object from all possible perspectives. *Meditatio,* as numerous writers on rhetoric point out, is the true source of invention, as opposed to the more mechanical *ars combinatoria* or the *loci topici,* which provide, in effect, a template for *meditatio.*[14] The content of an instrumental work consists of a musical idea and its elaboration; the content of a "philosophical sequence of ideas" differs only in that the idea is verbal rather than musical.

Yet it is also important to recognize that the aesthetic orientation in Schlegel's formulation is no longer pragmatic. The musical oration, a public event directed to the listener, has now become a philosophical discourse, a private act that requires no audience, and indeed probably functions better without any audience at all. Coherence is still important, but now primarily as a validation of the work's autonomous integrity, rather than as a prerequisite for moving an audience. Persuasion has relinquished its central role in the aesthetic equation: the composer is no longer a musical orator but a musical philosopher, and his ideas are to be interpreted on their own terms. The language of music, if referential at all, is now self-referential.

The decline of rhetoric in the late eighteenth century coincides with the rising tendency of the Romantics to see all works of art, including music, as nonreferential. The art-work, in this view, is symbolic rather than allegorical, a vehicle of "intransitive signification": the signifier is also the signified.[15] Even language itself began to be seen from this perspective: "If only one could make clear to people," Novalis laments, "that the condition of language is like that of mathematical formulas," which "constitute a world in and of themselves, express nothing beyond their own wonderful nature, and are therefore all the more expressive. It is precisely for this reason that they reflect in themselves the remarkable play of relationships among things."[16]

But attempts at "absolute poetry," as Dahlhaus has noted, would remain unrealized for almost another century.[17] Instrumental music, on the other hand, could be compared to poetry in its syntactic structure yet at the same time transcend the referential limitations of verbal language. In calling C. P. E. Bach "another Klopstock, who used notes *instead* of words," Triest

14. See, for example, Hallbauer, *Anweisung,* pp. 212–216, 403.
15. See Todorov, *Theories of the Symbol,* p. 162.
16. Novalis, *Schriften,* ed. Kluckhohn, II, 430–431.
17. See esp. the final chapter of Dahlhaus's *Idee der absoluten Musik,* "Absolute Musik und poésie absolue."

argued in 1801 that Bach "showed that pure [i.e., instrumental] music is not merely a cloak for applied [i.e., vocal] music, or abstracted from it, but rather strives to elevate itself to the level of a *poetry* that would be all the more pure if it were drawn less into the region of common thought through the use of words, which always have their secondary connotations."[18] A few years later, Michaelis similarly argued that "pleasure in music does not necessarily derive from the significance of melodies or modulations, which is often indeterminate . . . We usually do not contemplate the sounds of music as symbols at all, but rather derive pleasure directly from the harmonious interplay of their variety."[19] This is essentially the same conviction that Johann Gottfried Herder had expressed in his *Kalligone* of 1800, that "every moment of this art [music] is and must be transitory. For precisely the longer and shorter, the louder and softer, higher and lower, the greater and lesser is its meaning, its impression. The victorious power of the note and of sentiment lies in its coming and going, its becoming and having been."[20]

The prevailing emphasis of these views has little to do with the earlier mimetic concept of *Affekt*. It is the process of artistic elaboration itself that now becomes the focus of attention. Herder does not concern himself with the representational associations of a musical work's prevailing idea, but rather with its treatment.

Novalis makes much the same argument for the arts in general. The true interest in a work of art lies not in its main idea per se, but in its elaboration. And although he does not evoke the concept of rhetoric explicitly, his vocabulary is decidedly rhetorical:

Ideas interest us either for their content—their new, striking, and correct function— or for their origins, their history, their circumstances, their multiple dispositions, their various application, their utility, their different formations. In this manner, a very trivial idea can allow itself to be manipulated in a quite interesting fashion . . . Here it is the method, the procedure, the process that is of interest and agreeable to us . . . That which is new interests us less, for one sees that so much can be made out of the old. In short, the more one has a feeling for the infinity of the particular, the more one loses one's desire for variety. One learns how to do with one single instrument something for which others need hundreds, and one is altogether *more interested in elaboration than in invention.*[21]

18. See above, pp. 64–65. Triest, "Bemerkungen," *AMZ*, 3 (1801), col. 301.

19. C. F. Michaelis, "Ein Versuch, das innere Wesen der Tonkunst zu entwickeln," *AMZ*, 8 (1806), col. 677.

20. Herder, *Kalligone. Von Kunst und Kunstrichterei* (1800), in his *Sämtliche Werke*, vol. 22, ed. Bernhard Suphan (Berlin: Weidmann, 1880; rpt. Hildesheim: Olms, 1967), p. 187.

21. Novalis, *Gesammelte Werke*, ed. Hildburg and Werner Kohlschmidt (Gütersloh: S. Mohn, 1967), p. 427. Emphasis added.

Schlegel, Herder, Triest, and Novalis, in spite of the variety of their imagery, all agree that the essential element of instrumental music is not its content but its form—and specifically, its form in the eighteenth-century sense of the term, as the elaboration of a central idea. Hanslick's later formulation of music as "tönend bewegte Formen," as we shall see, was in large measure the continuation of a tradition that emphasizes the process of elaboration over the process of representation.

Rhetoric and Analysis in the Late Eighteenth and Early Nineteenth Centuries

A similar transformation of traditional ideas regarding the process of thematic elaboration can be seen in the growing number of analyses of instrumental music that began to emerge in the late eighteenth century. Two basic approaches can be discerned in these writings. The first and far more common is the technique of interpreting instrumental music through a program of some kind. The second is what we today recognize as more typical of "mainstream" analysis: the technical description of a work's elements and an account of their functional coordination within the musical whole. On the surface, these two approaches would seem to have little or nothing in common. At a deeper level, however, they are united by the idea of thematic elaboration.

Programmatic Analyses of Nonprogrammatic Music

The idea of program music—instrumental music that attempts to depict or narrate an extra-musical object or event—was a well-established tradition by the beginning of the eighteenth century. Programmatic interpretations of absolute music, on the other hand, did not begin to appear in any real quantity before approximately 1780. To a considerable degree, they are manifestations of the growing effort to explicate instrumental music's "meaning." The form of these works, in turn, rests upon the elaboration of a main idea.

Carl Friedrich Cramer, in one of the earliest of such accounts, notes, "It is difficult . . . to say anything specific about instrumental pieces. Nevertheless, in order to account for my sentiments at least somewhat, I will try to imagine some kind of character that could correspond to a particular piece." He then proceeds to describe the first rondo in a collection of pieces by C. P. E. Bach through the imagery of "a young girl who has gotten an idea into her head" and is "determined to get her way through humor and pleasing persistence." Another sonata in the same set is interpreted as an "innocent maiden sitting beside a stream on a summer evening," and so on.[22] The details of Cramer's account are of little import here. What is significant is his attitude that the music at hand does convey a meaning of some kind, and that intrinsically musical events, including the elaboration of the work's central idea (for example, the repeated return of the rondo's main theme) can be related to extra-musical scenarios.

Many subsequent attempts to explicate instrumental music go well beyond Cramer's relatively vague imagery. And while it would be outside the scope of this book to provide any systematic or detailed account of the programmatic and quasi-programmatic analyses of this period, the examples presented below offer some sense of the scope and nature of such interpretations.[23] These range from the association of a poetic text with a specific work (August Apel, Johann Friedrich Reichardt) to the application of a narrative plot (Momigny, A. B. Marx) to the underlaying of a specific literary text (Herdenberg, Momigny).

ASSOCIATION WITH A POETIC TEXT

In an essay published in 1806, the poet August Apel points out that music and poetry have in common the "presentation of an idea." To "transpose a symphony into poetry," then, requires that one separate the idea and its characterization from its original medium of expression. Apel proceeds to illustrate his point through a poetic interpretation of Mozart's Symphony in E-flat, K. 543. The first movement's introductory *Largo maestoso,* for example, is interpreted thus:

> Praise, honor and renown to the immortal
> First children of the old, chaotic night!
> Eternally begotten and begetting, birth and bearer,
> Never separated, each calling forth the other;
> Praise to thee, Eros, and to thee, Anteros, praise!
>
> You bring the gifts of the gods
> to humans below;
> etc.[24]

22. Review of C. P. E. Bach's *Sonaten . . . für Kenner und Liebhaber,* 4th book, in Cramer's *Magazin der Musik,* 1 (1783), 1243–1245. Cramer quotes with approval Forkel's earlier description of the rondo as consisting of a *Hauptgedanke, Nebengedanken,* etc.

23. Robin Wallace, in *Beethoven's Critics,* presents a good overview of this practice and argues persuasively for its historical significance in the emerging aesthetic of program music in the nineteenth century. The first chapter of Arnold Schering's highly problematic *Beethoven und die Dichtung* (Berlin: Junker und Dünnhaupt, 1936) provides a more detailed compendium of such interpretations from the early nineteenth century. See also Krones, "Rhetorik und rhetorische Symbolik."

24. Apel, "Musik und Poesie," *AMZ,* 8 (1806), cols. 449–457, 465–470. For a more detailed discussion of Apel's analysis, see Gernot Gruber, "Johann August Apel und eine

A change of mood and meter sets in with the *Allegro moderato* ("Spielend durchschwärmt, unbekümmert von Sorgen, / fröhlich der Knabe des Lebens Morgen . . ."), and corresponding verses are provided for subsequent movements as well.

Johann Friedrich Reichardt, in 1782, attempts to associate a poetic text with the creation of one of his own compositions. He confides that reading a "great or beautiful" passage of literature can inspire him to compose. "Filled by such a passage, I set the book aside, turn to the clavier, and fantasize, staying within certain emotions, then afterward write down that which has remained."[25] He then provides a specific example: a sonnet by Petrarch in the original Italian and in German translation, together with the keyboard work it had inspired. Although Reichardt's account is more directly concerned with the compositional process than with analysis per se, there is an implication that the poetic inspiration of the work must necessarily play an important role in its analysis.

ASSOCIATION WITH A NARRATIVE

In addition to the rhetorical analysis of Haydn's Symphony No. 103, discussed in Chapter 3, Momigny presents an "analyse pittoresque et poétique" for the same movement.[26] A brief excerpt from its beginning should give a sufficient sense of its method:

The scene takes place in the country.

A frightful storm may be imagined to have raged for so long that the inhabitants of a village have gathered in the church. After a thunderclap, played by the timpani, we hear the prayer begin.

In the fifth and sixth measures, an exclamation is portrayed by the flute and the oboes. It seems to emanate from the hearts of some young maidens who say only two words: *Great God!*[27]

A. B. Marx's interpretation of Beethoven's "Eroica" Symphony includes an attempt to trace the work's Napoleonic associations in a surprisingly literal fashion. The opening chords are a call to attention ("Hört! Hört!"), the harmonic deflection away from the tonic in m. 7 a cry of "Not yet!" "How often Napoleon said just this in the heat of battle, when his generals

---

Diskussion um die Ästhetik der Sinfonie im frühen 19. Jahrhundert," in *Studien zur Instrumentalmusik: Lothar Hoffmann-Erbrecht zum 60. Geburtstag,* ed. Anke Bingmann, Klaus Hortschansky, Winfried Kirsch (Tutzing: Hans Schneider, 1988), pp. 267–281.

25. Reichardt, "Instrumentalmusik," in his *Musikalisches Kunstmagazin,* 1 (1782), 64. Note the similarity of Reichardt's account of his compositional procedure (after setting aside his book) with Haydn's, as reported by Griesinger (see above, p. 116).

26. A more detailed discussion of this analysis is available in Cole, "Momigny's Analysis of Haydn's Symphony No. 103."

27. Momigny, *Cours complet,* II, 600–601.

called too early for reinforcements!" The first movement of the Seventh Symphony, in turn, conjures up images of a rural folk in valleys and vineyard-covered hills, "to whom battle and war is a game."[28] Marx goes on to distance himself somewhat from this kind of interpretation, but he does not deny its validity altogether, and it is clear that there was at least limited room for it in his aesthetic outlook.

TEXT UNDERLAY

In 1767, the poet and playwright Heinrich Wilhelm Gerstenberg provided the C Minor Fantasia from C. P. E. Bach's *Versuch über die wahre Art das Clavier zu spielen* with not one but two texts: Hamlet's monologue "To be or not to be," and an original text based on the last words of Socrates.[29] Momigny carried out a similar plan in his *Cours complet* of 1803–1806, underlaying the first movement of Mozart's String Quartet in D Minor, K. 421, with a text based on a scene from the legend of Dido and Aeneas.[30]

From our perspective today, all of these efforts—especially the underlaying of a text to an instrumental work—seem rather naive and simplistic, and in one respect, they represent attempts to impose meaning where none is explicit. But most critics of the time perceived no essential contradiction between a musical analysis and a corresponding verbal "translation." Momigny's "Analyse pittoresque et poétique" for the first movement of Haydn's Symphony No. 103, for example, is presented as a complement to his previous, more technical "analyse musicale" of the same movement. In his *Cours complet,* Momigny was attempting to reach a wide audience (nothing less than "tout le monde," according to the work's subtitle), and his programmatic analysis would clearly have been more appealing to the musically nonliterate. The two approaches are complementary, not contradictory: both are consistent with the view that "music is a language, and each work of music is an oration of greater or lesser dimension."[31] One of these interpretations simply pursues the consequences of this imagery in a more literal manner.

28. Marx, *Beethoven,* I, 258–259; II, 197.

29. See Eugene Helm, "The 'Hamlet' Fantasy and the Literary Element in C. P. E. Bach's Music," *MQ,* 58 (1972), 277–296; and Peter Schleuning, *Die freie Fantasie: Ein Beitrag zur Erforschung der klassischen Klaviermusik* (Göppingen: Alfred Kümmerle, 1973), pp. 153–226. More recently, Wolfgang Wiemer has suggested that this fantasia is a lament on the death of Johann Sebastian Bach. See "Carl Philipp Emanuel Bachs Fantasie in c-Moll—ein Lamento auf den Tod des Vaters?" *Bach-Jahrbuch 1988,* pp. 163–177.

30. See Albert Palm, "Mozarts Streichquartett d-moll, KV 421, in der Interpretation Momignys," *Mozart-Jahrbuch 1962/63,* pp. 256–279. For an illustration of this analysis from Momigny's treatise, see Ian Bent's "Analysis" article in the *New Grove.*

31. Momigny, *Cours complet,* II, 405.

None of these efforts, moreover, is wholly without justification from composers themselves. On occasion, Beethoven made explicit reference to extra-musical ideas in his works, such as the Piano Sonata in E-flat Major, Op. 81a ("Les Adieux"), the Pastoral Symphony, or the "Muss es sein? Es muss sein!" of the String Quartet in F Major, Op. 135. According to Anton Schindler, Beethoven's plan to supervise a new edition of his piano sonatas in 1816 was based in part on the composer's desire to indicate the "poetic idea" at the "core" of many of his works, in order to "facilitate their comprehension" by listeners.[32] This and similar references by other contemporaries led Arnold Schering, in the 1930s, to pursue literary allusions in Beethoven's instrumental works, often to unfortunate extremes. More recently, Owen Jander has pursued similar connections that rest on more convincing evidence.[33] Almost all of the composer's hints remain cryptic: Beethoven was doubtless leery of interpretations that would be too literal. But there is sufficient evidence to indicate that, for certain of his instrumental works, literary programs are more than a mere possibility.

Haydn, too, blurred the distinction between absolute and program music on more than one occasion, as in the *Seven Last Words of Christ,* the instrumental depiction of Chaos at the beginning of *The Creation,* and the trilogy of Symphonies Nos. 6–8 ("Le matin," "Le midi," and "Le soir").

Composers even occasionally sanctioned the more extreme idea of underlaying a literary text to a complete movement. Haydn endorsed and improved upon Joseph Frieberth's vocal arrangement of the *Seven Last Words of Christ,* and Beethoven apparently approved of Franz Wegeler's poetic underlay (entitled "Die Klage") to the Adagio from the F-Minor Piano Sonata, Op. 2, No. 1. The composer is reported to have subsequently commissioned Wegeler for another text to the theme of the variations in the Piano Sonata in A-flat Major, Op. 26.[34]

Late in the eighteenth century, Grétry proposed a similar undertaking for Haydn's symphonies: "What devotee of music has not been filled with admiration upon hearing the beautiful symphonies of Haydn? A hundred times I have given them the words they seem to demand. And why not give them?"[35] In his annotated translation of Grétry's *Mémoires,* Karl Spazier argued that Grétry's suggestion had not been to underlay a specific text to

32. Schindler, *Biographie von Ludwig van Beethoven* (Münster: Aschendorff, 1840), p. 195.

33. Schering, *Beethoven und die Dichtung;* Owen Jander, "Beethoven's 'Orpheus in Hades': The *Andante con moto* of the Fourth Piano Concerto," *19th-Century Music,* 8 (1985), 195–212. See also Myron Schwager, "Beethoven's Programs: What is Provable?" *Beethoven Newsletter,* 4 (1989), 49–55.

34. Wegeler and Ferdinand Ries, *Biographische Notizen über Ludwig van Beethoven* (Koblenz: K. Bädeker, 1838), pp. 47–48, 69.

35. Grétry, *Mémoires,* I, 348.

an instrumental work in the "literal, syllabic sense"; but on the whole, he concurred with the essence of Grétry's comments. In Spazier's view, it was "to the credit" of instrumental music that a symphony could be capable of sustaining an association with a literary text.[36]

In one respect, Grétry's idea of setting words to purely instrumental works represents the antithesis of all the German Romantics stood for. Schlegel, Wackenroder, Tieck, and Hoffmann consistently emphasize that the very essence of instrumental music is its transcendental quality, its ability to touch the emotions in a way that words cannot. The addition of a literary text to a purely instrumental work, from this perspective, denies music's true essence and its capacities for subtlety and fluidity. In their own way, however, these programmatic and quasi-programmatic interpretations of absolute music represent an important intermediate step in the elevation of the status of instrumental music above that of vocal music.

All of these programmatic analyses emphasize the idea of thematic elaboration. The "story" of an instrumental composition, as one writer notes in 1826, is "the story of one and the same musical thought."[37] The gulf between programmatic and more strictly musical analysis is not nearly so wide as it may seem to us today. The differences in interpretation are issues of form rather than content, for the form of each work continues to be seen as the unfolding of the work's central idea.

Gerber's essay of 1813 on the symphony, cited earlier, illustrates the close relationship of these two approaches. Among other works, Gerber analyzes Haydn's Symphony No. 104 in D Major, breaking down the opening theme of the first movement into its constituent units and commenting on the manner in which Haydn bases virtually the entire movement on a relatively small quantity of seemingly simple material (see Example 4.1a). "One divides this statement [Satz] into four phrases," Gerber observes (see Example 4.1b). All of these units, as Gerber points out, are elaborated at various points throughout the first movement. This technique of motivic analysis, by which larger units are dissected into smaller ones, is familiar to us today; indeed, it is a basic element of many technical analyses. Yet almost without transition, Gerber slips into a quasi-programmatic account of the symphony, comparing it to an individual's feeling of joy through a variety of circumstances, ending with a "true dance of joy" in the finale. He interprets the main theme of the first movement as a series of statements ("Now

36. Spazier, *Gretrys Versuche*, p. 187. For a summary of the critical debate raised by Grétry's original remarks, see Wallace, *Beethoven's Critics*, pp. 79–81. From a somewhat different perspective, Wallace demonstrates the close relationship between the "symbolic" (representational) and "descriptive" (analytical) analyses of this period.

37. Franck, "Ueber das Verhältnis der Form zum Inhalte in der neueren Musik," *BAMZ*, 3 (1826), 326.

I am happy! all cares cease; joy smiles; what more could I wish?") that in the original German could easily be underlaid to his four units of the opening theme (see Example 4.1b). Over the course of the movement, these "happy ideas" are occasionally presented in a "somewhat darkened" fashion, but in every instance, they "soon become joyful again."[38] Gerber's fusion of a programmatic interpretation with a more technical, motivically oriented account is based on the premise that the two approaches are in fact closely related.

In a similar fashion, Ludwig Tieck acknowledges the common procedural basis of vocal and instrumental music even while drawing a sharp distinction between the two:

Pure vocal music should move within its own force, without any accompaniment of instruments; it should breathe its own unique element, just as instrumental music follows its own path, without concerning itself about any text, about any underlaid poetry. It poeticizes for itself, it comments upon its own self poetically. Both kinds [of music] can exist pure and separate from each other.[39]

4.1a   Haydn, Symphony No. 104, first movement, mm. 1–8

4.1b   Gerber's division of the theme to Haydn's Symphony No. 104, first movement

38. Gerber, "Eine freundliche Vorstellung," *AMZ*, 15 (1813), col. 461–462.
39. Tieck, "Symphonien" (orig. pub. 1799), in Wilhelm Heinrich Wackenroder, *Werke und Briefe*, ed. Gerda Heinrich (Munich: Carl Hanser, 1984), p. 352.

Thus, although the notion of *adding* a text to a purely instrumental work is foreign to the aesthetic of the early German Romantics, there is a deeper parallel between the processes of the verbal arts and of music, in that a central idea functions as an object of elaboration. The course of a movement becomes a "poetic commentary on itself." The concept of the autonomous musical idea, independent of external reference, is an outgrowth of rhetorical thought and imagery and is essential to the early Romantics' view of music. Wackenroder emphasizes the self-referential quality of instrumental music in chiding those who would provide a program for every untexted composition:

What do they want, these timorous and doubting sophists, who ask to have hundreds and hundreds of musical works elucidated in words and yet who cannot acknowledge that not every one of these works has a nameable meaning like a painting? Do they strive to measure the richer language by means of the weaker and solve with words that which disdains words? Or have they never felt without words? Have they stuffed their hollow hearts with only descriptions of emotions? Have they never perceived in their souls the mute singing, the mummer's dance of unseen spirits? Or do they not believe in fairy-tales?[40]

A work of art, from this perspective, can only be understood through the same emotion that originally gave it birth, and emotions can only be understood in terms of emotions. Feelings can be expressed only in terms of themselves; ordinary, verbal language is wholly inadequate in describing the emotions raised by instrumental music.[41]

This of course did not prevent the Romantics from trying to do just that. Their rhapsodic musings have fostered the widespread misconception that the new and distinctive element of early Romantic musical aesthetics was its emphasis on the emotions. This notion, as Dahlhaus has observed, is one of the "most resilient prejudices of intellectual history."[42] More important to the early Romantic aesthetic is the abandonment of a fundamental belief in the need to justify instrumental music through extra-musical associations, and the corresponding acceptance of the notion that an idea can be expressed and elaborated in a purely musical fashion. Wackenroder, Tieck, Novalis, Herder, and Friedrich Schlegel had all expressed this new outlook in general terms; E. T. A. Hoffmann, as we shall see, was the first to translate this view into the more technical vocabulary of musical analysis.

40. Wackenroder, "Das eigentümliche innere Wesen der Tonkunst und die Seelenlehre der heutigen Instrumentalmusik" (orig. pub. 1799), in his *Werke und Briefe,* p. 326.
41. Ibid., p. 325.
42. Dahlhaus, *Die Idee der absoluten Musik,* p. 74.

Given the low esteem of rhetoric around the turn of the century, it is not at all surprising that the early Romantics would seldom use the term itself. Nevertheless, these writers were members of a generation whose formal education included a thorough grounding in rhetoric, and their writings, like those of Marx and Schoenberg later, frequently introduced rhetorical concepts outside an overtly rhetorical framework or under the guise of nonrhetorical terminology.

The unspoken framework of rhetoric is particularly evident in the music criticism of E. T. A. Hoffmann, whose reviews in the *Allgemeine musikalische Zeitung* incorporate analyses that are remarkably technical for their time. These essays have already been examined elsewhere at length;[43] the discussion here focuses primarily on the tradition of rhetoric in these writings, at the conscious expense of the many other novel and quite provocative issues they raise.

One of the basic premises of Hoffmann's music criticism is his distinction between the rational and irrational elements of music, which he associates with the qualities of *Besonnenheit* and *Genie,* respectively. Romanticism is not based entirely on irrational genius, but on the coordination of genius with the more rational, measured perspective that is the essence of *Besonnenheit.* Genius, while closely allied to *Besonnenheit,* cannot be taught; the more detached, rational qualities of reflection, on the other hand, can be fostered through the "diligent study of art."[44]

These categories, which Hoffmann probably appropriated from Jean Paul's *Vorschule der Ästhetik,*[45] are in fact little more than new designations for the rhetorical concepts of *inventio,* on the one hand, and *dispositio* and *elocutio,* on the other. The terminological preference for *Besonnenheit* over the more traditional *dispositio* and *elaboratio* is typical of the Romantics and anticipates Schoenberg's similar avoidance of overtly rhetorical terminology. But as with Schoenberg, the rhetorical origins of such categories are never far beneath the surface.

Hoffmann's traditionalism is further reinforced by the central importance he assigns to the quality of intelligibility. Like earlier critics, he is still very much concerned that a composition be constructed in such a way as to

---

43. Peter Schnaus, in his *E. T. A. Hoffmann als Beethoven-Rezensent der Allgemeinen musikalischen Zeitung* (Munich: Emil Katzbichler, 1977), presents an especially valuable survey of Hoffmann's views on a variety of issues. See also Wallace, *Beethoven's Critics.*

44. Hoffmann, review of Beethoven's Symphony No. 5, *AMZ,* 12 (1810); quoted from his *Schriften zur Musik,* ed. Friedrich Schnapp (Munich: Winkler, 1963), pp. 36–37.

45. See Schnaus, *E. T. A. Hoffmann,* pp. 81–82.

facilitate the listener's comprehension.[46] *Besonnenheit* emphasizes the objective side of art, the process by which the creator distances himself from his creation and exercises criticism upon it. For Hoffmann, the perspective of this objective process is that of the composer's intended audience.

Hoffmann's celebrated review of Beethoven's Fifth Symphony provides a good illustration of the rhetorical elements in his criticism. Hoffmann relies heavily on the organic metaphor of unfolding *(entfalten)*, yet in so doing he alternates, like so many later critics, between organic and rhetorical imagery.[47] With its recurring ideas throughout all four movements, Beethoven's Fifth Symphony is today recognized as one of the earliest manifestations of thematic organicism, and Hoffmann was the first to present this kind of account in such specifically musical detail. Speaking of the first movement, Hoffmann observes:

there is no simpler idea than that on which the master based the entire Allegro. It is with great admiration that one becomes aware of how he knew to order the sequence of all the secondary ideas and all the transitional passages through their rhythmic relationship to that simple theme, and in such a way that these ideas serve to unfold gradually the character of the whole, which that theme could only suggest. All the phrases are short, consisting of only two or three measures, and even these are divided by the constant alternation of the strings and winds. One might think that from such elements only something fragmentary could arise, something difficult to understand; but instead, it is precisely this ordering of the whole and the consistent, successive repetition of brief phrases and individual chords that grips one's feelings in an ineffable longing.[48]

Many traditional categories of rhetoric are preserved here: a central idea *(Gedanke)*, with derivative secondary and connective ideas *(Nebengedanken, Zwischensätze)*; the successive presentation of these ideas in the "ordering of the whole" *(anreihen, Einrichtung des Ganzen)*; and attention to the listener's ability to grasp the trajectory of the musical argument. "Longing" *(Sehnsucht)* is a new and quintessentially Romantic category, but the structural process is the same as in Schlegel's "meditation": a central idea is considered from many different perspectives and unfolds into a unified whole. The work is "*invented* with genius and *elaborated* with deep circumspection" ("genial *erfunden* und mit tiefer Besonnenheit *ausgeführt*—emphasis added)."[49] Here, even the vocabulary of rhetoric is retained: invention is the

46. On the importance of the listener in Hoffmann's music criticism, see ibid., pp. 63–67.

47. On Hoffmann's organic imagery, see ibid., pp. 72–80.

48. Hoffmann, review of Beethoven's Symphony No. 5; quoted from *Schriften zur Musik*, p. 43.

49. Ibid., p. 50. See also p. 43: "wie der Meister das Ganze . . . nicht allein im Geist auffasste, sondern auch durchdachte" (emphasis added).

domain of genius, while disposition and elaboration are products of circumspection. Hoffmann's categorization of the compositional process, then, is fundamentally no different from that of his predecessors and contemporaries. It is entirely consistent with Mattheson's view, echoed in various guises throughout the century, that "invention demands fire and spirit; disposition order and measure; elaboration cold blood and circumspection."[50]

Like Schoenberg almost a century and a half later, Hoffmann scrupulously avoids using the term "rhetoric" as a broader category; both Schoenberg and Hoffmann probably judged, with good reason, that reference to this much-maligned discipline would only confuse the issue.[51] As an art of deception or empty padding, rhetoric represented precisely the opposite of what both writers intended. But as the art of making an idea intelligible (and by extension persuasive), rhetoric provided an important context for both Hoffmann and Schoenberg.

The importance of intelligibility and its relationship to the idea of thematic elaboration are even more evident in Hoffmann's review of Beethoven's Op. 70 piano trios. Speaking of the composer's instrumental works in general, he observes that "a simple but fertile, cantabile theme, capable of the most varied contrapuntal turns, fragmentations, etc., lies at the heart of every movement. All other secondary themes and figures are intimately related to the main idea so that the greatest unity is inextricably entwined and ordered through all the instruments. Such is the structure of the whole."[52] Hoffmann emphasizes that it is the composer's responsibility to articulate the work's unity by bringing out the main idea clearly, in order that it impress itself sufficiently on the mind of the listener. He quotes the opening eight measures of Op. 70, No. 1, in score with the comment that

the first four measures contain the main theme, while the seventh and eighth measures in the violoncello contain the secondary theme. The entire Allegro is woven out of these two phrases, with the exception of a few secondary figures that are inserted between the elaboration of these main ideas. It was thus all the more appropriate to present the idea that predominates the entire movement in unison over four octaves. This idea is deeply and distinctly imprinted upon the listener, who does not lose it from his sight, like a bright silvery stream moving through the most remarkable contortions and turns.[53]

50. Mattheson, *Kern*, p. 139. See above, p. 87.
51. See, for example, the disparaging use of the term in an earlier issue of the same *AMZ* in which Hoffmann was writing, 10 (1808), col. 304, within an anonymous review of Ferdinand Ries's *Grand Trio Concertante,* Op. 2, which equates rhetoric with overladen figures of speech. This, of course, is rhetoric in the debased sense of the term.
52. Hoffmann, review of Beethoven's Piano Trios, Op. 70, *AMZ,* 15 (1813); quoted from *Schriften zur Musik,* p. 121.
53. Ibid., p. 122.

It is typical of Hoffmann's time that technical musical analysis should coexist with such typically Romantic visual images as "a bright silvery stream." And it is equally typical that both of these elements should function within an essentially traditional rhetorical framework, exemplified by Hoffmann's aesthetic categories and vocabulary; by his concern with the effect of an idea upon the listener; by the central importance of intelligibility; and by the understanding of form as a succession of events unified by the unfolding of a central idea.

This gradual transformation of rhetorical ideas provides an important link between theories based on the earlier representational, mimetic theory of *Affekt,* and the later, quintessentially Romantic idea of music as an autonomous, self-referential art. E. T. A. Hoffmann is a central figure in this changing perspective.

It is remarkable, in fact, how much of Hoffmann's—and in turn Mattheson's—thinking is present in that supreme mid-nineteenth-century manifesto of absolute music, Eduard Hanslick's *Vom Musikalisch-Schönen.* Hanslick accepts the traditional premise that music is a language, even if its semantic premises cannot be compared directly to those of a verbal language. He also acknowledges the importance of the intrinsically musical idea. His dictum that "music is a language that we speak and understand yet are not capable of translating" has often been quoted, but the explicitly rhetorical imagery of the sentences that immediately follow should not be overlooked:

That one also speaks of "thoughts" in musical [as well as in verbal] works represents a profound insight, and as in speech, a trained judgment easily distinguishes genuine thoughts from empty phrases. In just this way, we recognize the rationally self-contained quality of a group of notes in that we call this grouping a "sentence" [*Satz*]. We feel precisely where its sense is completed, just as in a logical sentence, even though the truths of the two propositions are entirely incommensurable. [54]

Hanslick's view here, in the light of eighteenth- and early-nineteenth-century discussions of musical rhetoric, is profoundly traditional. He emphasizes the form of music rather than its affective content. "The sole content and object of music," in his most famous statement, "is forms set in motion by sound" ("tönend bewegte Formen"). The forms constructed of musical sounds are free of associative content: their "meaning" is intrinsically syntactical. Their spirit is generated from within ("sich von innen heraus gestaltender Geist"), and in this sense, Hanslick allies himself with organic theories of form. But it is the intelligible elaboration of musical ideas that is, for Hanslick, the essence of autonomous music, the essence of form.

54. Leipzig, 1854; rpt. Darmstadt: Wissenschaftliche Buchgesellschaft, 1981, p. 35.

CHAPTER 5

Rhetoric and the Role of the Listener in the Analysis of Large-Scale Form

The eighteenth century's metaphor of the musical work as an oration and its form as a function of rhetoric anticipates several important trends in recent critical thought. With its focus on the role of the listener, the rhetorical perspective represents a historical forerunner of current listener-oriented approaches to form. And in emphasizing the functional, syntactical role of musical ideas within a small number of stereotypical constructs, the rhetorical concept of form also anticipates recent attempts to relate theories of plot to musical form.

It would be impossible to do justice here to these present-day approaches. Instead, I wish only to point out some of the historical foundations for these perspectives and suggest avenues for further investigation. I shall conclude with a brief analysis of the first movement of Haydn's Symphony No. 46 in B Major.

Listener-Oriented Theories of Form

The emergence of a dichotomy between "inner" and "outer" form in the first half of the nineteenth century led, as we have seen, to the establishment of two aesthetically disparate categories of form. The very theorists who described such conventional patterns as sonata form and rondo were the same writers who consistently disparaged the conformational view of form as categorically inferior to the generative. This attitude persists in current analysis.

One of the most important reasons behind this change in attitude toward large-scale conventions has been a change in attitude toward the role of the listener in analysis. Since around 1850, most serious analyses of form have tended to focus on the work itself. The eighteenth century's rhetorical concept of form, by contrast, had considered the technical structure of a work not so much in terms of the work itself as in terms of its effect upon the listener. Conventions of periodicity and large-scale harmony were seen as means toward the intelligible unfolding of a work's central idea—in a word, its form.

While not without its own problematic aspects, this listener-oriented approach to form offers a useful alternative to the work-oriented perspective. Recent reader-oriented theories of literary criticism can help ensure that a listener-oriented approach to musical analysis need not return to the impressionistic subjectivism that characterizes so much of eighteenth- and early-nineteenth-century analysis (see Chapter 4).

The chief value of the listener-oriented approach is heuristic, for it helps to focus attention not only on the text but on our responses, as analysts, to that text.[1] As Stanley Fish points out, there is no way to separate the process of describing a text from the process of analyzing it. We cannot, in other words, distinguish between the work being analyzed and our own reactions to it, for the process of description is itself based on an interpreter's "extension of an already existing field of interests." The very points to be singled out for analysis are shaped by the reader's or listener's previous experiences. In the absence of any preexistent guidelines, "there is no way of deciding either where to begin or where to end" a description, "because there is no way of deciding what counts." A pattern of repetition within a work, for example, has no meaning in and of itself. More important is what "a reader [or listener], as he comes upon that . . . pattern, is *doing,* what assumptions he is making, what conclusions he is reaching, what expectations he is forming, what attitudes he is entertaining, what acts he is being moved to perform."[2]

Openly or covertly, a good deal of musical analysis has long been based on the process by which an implicit listener reacts to a given work as it

1. For a survey of such theories, with an extensive annotated bibliography, see Susan Suleiman and Inge Crosman, eds., *The Reader in the Text: Essays on Audience and Interpretation* (Princeton: Princeton University Press, 1980); and Jane P. Tompkins, ed., *Reader-Response Criticism: From Formalism to Post-Structuralism* (Baltimore: Johns Hopkins University Press, 1980). On comparable issues in what Claudio Guillén calls the "generic process," see his "On the Uses of Literary Genre," in his *Literature as System* (Princeton: Princeton University Press, 1971), pp. 107–134. Peter J. Rabinowitz, "Circumstantial Evidence: Musical Analysis and Theories of Reading," *Mosaic: A Journal for the Interdisciplinary Study of Literature,* 13 (1985), 159–173, considers some of the problems associated with applying the literary concept of the reader to the field of music but is less informative about the potential benefits of such an approach.

2. Fish, "What Is Stylistics and Why Are They Saying Such Terrible Things about It?" in his *Is There a Text in This Class? The Authority of Interpretative Communities* (Cambridge, Mass.: Harvard University Press, 1980), pp. 94, 92.

unfolds. Leonard B. Meyer, in particular, has consistently emphasized that the "understanding of form is learned, not innate."[3] The perception of the relationship between small-scale events and the larger-scale whole, as Meyer points out, depends to a considerable degree upon the listener's competence within a particular musical idiom and his preconceived or evolving understanding of form. Repetition, for example, "has one meaning in a movement which is believed to be a fugue, another in one which is believed to be a theme and variations, and still another in one believed to be a sonata form."[4]

The listener's comprehension of a musical event is thus based in large measure upon his knowledge of a "set of conventional signs and schemata" and a "system of internalized probabilities" as to what will happen next at any given moment.[5] By extension, the understanding of movement-length form rests on the listener's internalized patterns of expectations derived from repeated exposure to a relatively small number of basic conventional constructs. Although Meyer generally limits his discussions to small- and middle-scale events, the basic elements of his approach could be applied profitably, *mutatis mutandis,* to issues of large-scale form as well.

Analysts have nevertheless been unwilling, for the most part, to extend these principles to issues of movement-length form. Eugene Narmour's "implication-realization model," based on the listener's knowledge and concomitant expectations of style, has much to say about the ever-changing horizon of the listener's expectations of style in general, yet very little regarding specific issues of large-scale form. Fred Lerdahl and Ray Jackendoff open their *Generative Theory of Tonal Music* by proclaiming that "the goal of a theory of music" is "a formal description of the musical intuitions of a listener who is experienced in a musical idiom."[6] But they, too, tend to concentrate on small-scale events, as does Robert O. Gjerdingen in his valuable recent study of phrase structure in the Classical era.[7]

3. Meyer, *Emotion and Meaning in Music* (Chicago: University of Chicago Press, 1956), p. 57.

4. Ibid., p. 153.

5. Meyer, *Music, the Arts, and Ideas,* p. 8. Since the publication of *Emotion and Meaning,* Meyer has distanced himself from the idea of "expectations," preferring instead to frame his inquiries in terms of the "implications" generated by a given musical event (see *Music, the Arts, and Ideas,* p. 8n). This change in terminology, according to Meyer, avoids the potential misunderstanding of "expectation" in a simplistic sense, for a single musical event may give rise to a variety of complex and even contradictory expectations. But the listener himself remains the source of these implications; in spite of his more recent terminology, Meyer's listener-oriented approach remains essentially unchanged.

6. Cambridge, Mass.: MIT Press, 1983, p. 1.

7. Gjerdingen, *A Classic Turn of Phrase: Music and the Psychology of Convention* (Philadelphia: University of Pennsylvania Press, 1988).

The absence of corresponding studies for movement-length structures is in part a reflection of the difficulties inherent in dealing with conventions and expectations that can cover as much as several hundred measures within a single movement. Those relatively few writers who have approached large-scale form from the perspective of the listener have tended, as a result, to be somewhat general in their level of detail. In the 1930s, Kurt Westphal, under the influence of his teacher Ernst Kurth, proposed that form be considered a *Verlaufskurve,* a processive act in which form is perceived not merely as the sum of a work's parts, but rather as the functional relationship of those parts to one another. Westphal further suggested that form be considered a phenomenon that becomes actualized only during the process of listening ("ein im Hörvorgang werdendes Phänomen"), thereby emphasizing the temporal elements of form rather than its synoptic "architecture." Form is not a given, nor an entity in itself, but a process the listener himself must create.[8] Unfortunately, Westphal did not go on to pursue these ideas, nor did he suggest the manner in which the listener's expectations might be established.

More recently, Carl Dahlhaus has also hinted at a theory of large-scale form based on listeners' expectations, asserting that "the anticipated whole is analogous to the visibly presented whole, and the anticipation may be defined more closely by a title announcing the whole as representative of a type—sonata form or rondo—so that a system of relations is specified in advance, and the listener's expectation can fasten onto it." If a work is to be perceived as a complete entity, rather than as a mere medley of ideas, according to Dahlhaus, any perceived detail must exist not in and of itself but as a consciously anticipated part of the whole.[9]

The idea of basing an analysis of large-scale form on the process of large-scale expectations is, as noted before, scarcely novel.[10] Almost any analysis of the finale to Haydn's String Quartet Op. 33, No. 2 ("The Joke"), must make at least some reference, if only tacitly, to the listener's *a priori* understanding of what the finale of a Classical-era work should sound like. Even someone with only a passing familiarity with the era's sense of form will recognize that this particular ending is atypical. In a similar vein, it is only

8. Westphal, *Der Begriff der musikalischen Form in der Wiener Klassik,* (Leipzig: Kistner & Siegel, 1935), p. 53: "Sie [Form] ist nicht ein Gegebenes, sondern ein Aufgegebenes."

9. Dahlhaus, *Musikästhetik* (Cologne: Hans Gerig, 1967); trans. adapted from William W. Austin, *Esthetics of Music* (Cambridge: Cambridge University Press, 1982), p. 78.

10. Three recent examinations of this methodology, each of which reviews substantial quantities of earlier literature on the subject, are Thomas Clifton, *Music as Heard: A Study in Applied Phenomenology* (New Haven: Yale University Press, 1983); David Lewin, "Music Theory, Phenomenology, and Modes of Perception," *Music Perception,* 3 (1986), 327–392; and Nicholas Cook, *Musical Analysis and the Listener* (New York: Garland, 1989).

because of our understanding of style that we recognize the drum-stroke early in the slow movement of Symphony No. 94 ("The Surprise") as the surprise it is, for this is not the way a set of variations on a theme (or for that matter any symphonic slow movement) usually begins. It is precisely because these procedures violate such clear conventions for endings and beginnings that they are so readily apparent.

But the application of a listener-oriented approach to more subtle points of movement-length structure has been limited primarily to comparable deviations from accepted norms, and has remained largely intuitive and unsystematic. Charles Rosen's success in analyzing Classical repertoire rests in part on his ability to relate a listener's expectations to the unfolding of musical events within a specific work; but his efforts to establish the basis of these extra-opus expectations are informal at best.[11] Other analysts have similarly been content to use formal archetypes as a foil to highlight the originality of works that deviate from the norm, such as Beethoven's oft-cited modulation to the mediant in the first movement of the Piano Sonata Op. 53 ("Waldstein"), or the return of the slow introduction in the opening movement of Haydn's Symphony No. 103 ("Drumroll"). It is, in any event, easier (although by no means easy) to establish a taxonomy of phrase structures covering a span of four to eight measures than it is to establish a comparable matrix of formal types encompassing the breadth of an entire movement.

Taxonomic surveys of defined movement-length repertoires, however, would be a welcome first step toward establishing a historically accurate theory of expectations for large-scale form. Jan LaRue cited the need for just such a survey of music from the Classical era more than twenty years ago, noting the need "to list in one place the statistically predominant formal types or variants occurring in sonata movements." Yet today, the prospect for such a listing seems remote; even LaRue appears to have reversed his opinion on the value of such surveys.[12]

Still, if our expectations are a product of remembering "various statistical recurrences of syntactic relationships" within a given style, then it would be to our benefit to have a more precise notion of what these statistical recurrences actually are.[13] Scholars have tended to shy away from this kind of taxonomic classification in the past on the grounds that it smacks too much of the "textbook" approach to form. But if applied carefully, such a

11. See above, p. 28.

12. LaRue, review of *The Sonata in the Classic Era* by William S. Newman, *MQ*, 50 (1964), 405; idem, review of *Sonata Forms* by Charles Rosen, *JAMS*, 34 (1981), 560. See above, pp. 25, 52.

13. Eugene Narmour, *Beyond Schenkerism: The Need for Alternatives in Musical Analysis* (Chicago: University of Chicago Press, 1977), p. 127.

categorization could be of considerable value in advancing our understanding of large-scale formal conventions. An instructive example of how difficult it is to assume an "informed listener's" expectations in the absence of such a survey is evident in Rudolf Kelterborn's recent attempt to apply a matrix of anticipations to the music of Mozart. Limiting himself principally to the piano sonatas, Kelterborn offers a series of analyses that are based on an implicit comparison of the listener's expectations of sonata form's "architectonic outline" with the individual works themselves. But the lack of an available census of techniques leads Kelterborn to call such devices as a "mirror" recapitulation (in which the general order of ideas is reversed in the recapitulation) "entirely unconventional," when in fact this procedure was not particularly unusual for Mozart (or other composers) as late as the 1770s.[14]

The most difficult conceptual task in compiling such a survey would be to establish the specific formal parameters on which expectations could be based. The foundations of a listener's expectations, as Narmour points out, are constantly shifting. How far back in time should one go? What geographic reach would be appropriate? How should the correlative limitations implied in a work's genre be treated? Should a work written by a composer acknowledged as a master (such as Haydn) be given more weight than a comparable work by a lesser composer?

These are not easy questions to answer, yet they represent the kinds of questions that analysts already answer routinely, if largely intuitively, in the very process of outlining the broad dimensions of a sonata-form movement's parts: exposition, development, and recapitulation. The important point, in any case, is to move away from an analytical methodology that distinguishes between the "mere" description of a movement—outlining its modulatory plan, identifying its moment of recapitulation, and so on—and the "true" (that is, generative) analysis that focuses on the more individualistic elements of that movement. By joining the two processes and recognizing the act of description itself as an act of interpretation, we can reconsider structural conventions as issues of more than merely secondary importance and begin to resolve the aesthetic dichotomy of form.

Listening for the Plot: The Rhetoric of Formal Archetypes

The idea of basing the analysis of large-scale forms on an informed listener's expectation of events suggests further parallels with recent literary theory,

14. Kelterborn, *Zum Beispiel Mozart: Ein Beitrag zur musikalischen Analyse*, 2 vols. (Basel: Bärenreiter, 1981), I, 11. See the review by Juliane Brand in *JMT*, 27 (1983), 306–313; for a more favorable account of Kelterborn's work, see Carl Dahlhaus's review in the *Mozart-Jahrbuch 1984/85*, pp. 232–233.

specifically as regards the idea of plot. A literary plot, as Peter Brooks argues, constitutes the "logic or perhaps the syntax of a certain kind of discourse, one that develops its propositions only through temporal sequence and progression." Plot is the "principle of interconnectedness . . . which we cannot do without in moving through the discrete elements—incidents, episodes, actions—of a narrative."[15] For eighteenth- and early-nineteenth-century theorists, as we have seen, form serves much the same function.

Yet it was not until the mid-nineteenth century that the image of the musical work as a drama or novel began to gain popularity. In describing sonata form in the 1840s, Carl Czerny mixes organic imagery with the metaphor of the musical work as "a romance, a novel, or a dramatic poem":

We perceive that this first movement has a well established form, and makes an organic whole; that its various component parts follow each other in a settled order, and must be entwined together; and that the whole structure presents a musical picture, in which a precise idea can be expressed, and a consequent character developed.

Just as in a romance, a novel, or a dramatic poem, if the entire work shall be successful and preserve its unity, the necessary component parts are: first, an exposition of the principal idea and of the different characters, then the protracted complication of events, and lastly the surprising catastrophe and the satisfactory conclusion:—even so, the first part of the sonata-movement forms the exposition, the second part the complication, and the return of the first part into the original key produces, lastly, that perfect satisfaction which is justly expected from every work of art.[16]

The metaphor of the novel or drama retains at least some of the elements basic to the metaphor of the oration, for it emphasizes the role of the audience and the temporal nature of the musical work. Like the organic metaphor, it tends to anthropomorphize the work: themes become "characters"; the central idea of a movement or work functions as a kind of protagonist, and the unfolding of this idea is the fate of that protagonist. To use Schoenberg's imagery, "a piece of music resembles in some respects a photograph album, displaying under changing circumstance the life of its basic idea—its basic motive."[17] But unlike the organic image, the idea of musical form as a plot avoids a dichotomy between "structure" and "expression" by positing form in the very process by which content is made intelligible.

15. Brooks, *Reading for the Plot: Design and Intention in Narrative* (New York: Knopf, 1984), p. xi.

16. Czerny, *School of Practical Composition*, I, 34. Czerny's reference to a "picture" is probably not a reference to painting (which would represent yet another mixed metaphor), but in all likelihood an overly literal translation of *Bild* ("image," "representation") in the original German text, now lost (see above, p. 32n39).

17. Schoenberg, *Fundamentals of Musical Composition*, p. 58.

If form is the unfolding of events or ideas, then stereotypical forms are analogous to archetypal plots. Czerny implies that the listener's familiarity with the "settled order" of sonata form will help to make the presentation of the various characters, the "complication of events," the "surprising catastrophe," and the "satisfactory conclusion" all the more intelligible. Adherence to the conventions of paradigmatic "plots" like sonata form, rondo, theme and variations, and so on, facilitates the listener's comprehension of events; deviation from them heightens his awareness of an exceptional turn of events. A relatively small number of widely used formal archetypes, such as sonata form, rondo, and theme and variations, function as the musical equivalent of plot archetypes. Just as we expect certain elements and a general sequence of events within specific literary genres, from the *Bildungsroman* to the murder mystery, so, too, do we expect certain thematic types and sequences of events within the various movements of a given musical genre. These expectations are fairly fluid, of course, but they provide important points of reference to the listener in his apperception of large-scale musical structures.

In recent years, several scholars have explored the analytical implications of viewing musical form as a plot, principally in connection with the repertoire of the nineteenth century.[18] This concept is equally valid for music of the Classical era. Even a schema as broad as Ratner's harmonic outline of sonata form fosters certain implications of plot. The pattern of I - V :|: X - I stipulates (among other things) a return to the tonic key at some point during the second half of the movement. This moment of recapitulation is an event that any informed listener of the late eighteenth century would have had reason to expect, particularly after a modulation from the tonic to the dominant (or relative major) in the opening allegro movement of such important genres as the symphony or string quartet. Yet the implications of this archetypal structure have gone largely unexamined to date. The preoccupation with defining sonata form, with identifying its lowest common denominators, has fostered a widespread suspicion that this particular construct is not really a form at all, or that eighteenth-century audiences, faced with such an immense diversity of procedures within this very broad framework, could not have entertained any substantial preconceptions about the form of a movement within any given work. But as far as the

18. Anthony Newcomb, "Sound and Feeling," *Critical Inquiry,* 10 (1984), 614–643; idem, "Once More 'Between Absolute and Program Music': Schumann's Second Symphony," *19th-Century Music,* 7 (1984), 233–250; idem, "Schumann and Late Eighteenth-Century Narrative Strategies," *19th-Century Music,* 11 (1987), 164–174; Siegfried Schmalzriedt, "Charakter und Drama: Zur historischen Analyse von Haydnschen und Beethovenschen Sonatensätzen," *AfMw,* 42 (1985), 37–66; Fred Everett Maus, "Music as Drama," *Music Theory Spectrum,* 10 (1988), 56–73.

moment of recapitulation is concerned, even a cursory review of the instrumental music of such composers as Haydn and Mozart reveals that a simultaneous return of the opening theme and the tonic key is extremely common, particularly in works written after 1770.[19]

Exceptions to this practice do exist, and it is for this reason that, as discussed earlier, the simultaneous double return cannot be considered a form-defining element. Yet if we consider more closely one of the works most often cited as an example of just why the moment of recapitulation cannot be defined in terms of its thematic material, we shall discover once again that expectations and definitions rest on two quite different bases.

In the first movement of Mozart's Piano Sonata in C Major, K. 545, the opening theme returns in the subdominant (m. 42); only in mm. 58–59 does the tonic reappear, with material first heard at mm. 13–14 of the exposition. The thematic recapitulation, in other words, begins in m. 42, while the harmonic return is delayed until mm. 58–59. But it is important to recognize just how unusual this technique of "bifocal recapitulation" really is. Mozart never used the device in any other movement of his entire output, and Haydn never used it at all. The only two composers who appear to have cultivated it with any regularity were Florian Leopold Gassmann (in his symphonies of the 1760s) and Muzio Clementi (in his piano sonatas of the 1780s).[20] That this technique existed cannot be denied; but its actual use is far too infrequent to have altered the nature of a listener's expectations of events—their understanding of the plot archetype—within the course of a sonata-form movement.

Similarly, the "binary recapitulation," in which the opening theme is omitted altogether from the recapitulation, becomes increasingly unusual in fast opening movements after about 1770. While not nearly as rare as the bifocal technique, this particular device is limited, in practice, primarily to slow movements (hence its occasional designation as "slow-movement sonata form").[21] Again, the existence of this procedure necessarily alters our definition of sonata form; but it need not therefore play a fundamental a role in our expectations of form, particularly in fast movements.

Most important, the concept of the paradigmatic plot offers a rationale by which we can integrate conventional and unconventional elements within a given work. Again, literary theory provides some useful parallels of methodology. Critics dealing with verbal discourse have long concerned

19. For a detailed study of the articulation of recapitulation in the works of Haydn, see Bonds, "Haydn's False Recapitulations."

20. George R. Hill, "Bifocal Recapitulations in 18th-century Sonata Forms" (paper read at the annual meeting of the American Musicological Society, Denver, 1980). I am grateful to Dr. Hill for sharing his findings with me in writing.

21. See Bonds, "Haydn's False Recapitulations," pp. 270–286.

themselves with questions of formal conventions, readers' anticipation of events within large-scale patterns, and the implications of both adherence to and deviance from these norms. Frank Kermode, in his interpretation of the Aristotelian concept of peripeteia, emphasizes the extent to which the unfolding of a plot depends upon a listener's familiarity with specific structural conventions:

> Peripeteia . . . is present in every story of the least structural sophistication. [It] depends on our confidence of the end; it is a disconfirmation followed by a consonance; the interest of having our expectations falsified is obviously related to our wish to reach the discovery or recognition by an unexpected and instructive route . . . The more daring the peripeteia, the more we may feel that the work respects our sense of reality . . . The falsification of expectations . . . obviously . . . could not work if there were not *a certain rigidity in the set of our expectations. The degree of rigidity is a matter of profound interest in the study of literary fictions.*[22]

Such an approach toward form in the arts of the late eighteenth century, based on the recipient's awareness and anticipation of structural archetypes, has ample historical validity as well. Sulzer, for one, notes three basic considerations for the overall plan of any artistic work: the precise connection among all the work's parts; sufficient contrast between the parts; and finally "a complication of events" ("Verwicklung der Vorstellungen") in order that "the unfolding of the essentials is suitably delayed, so as to provoke increasing curiosity, until at the end everything is unified once again into a single main idea."[23] The resolution of ideas is anticipated, but its arrival is intentionally delayed. The effect of Sulzer's "Verwicklung"—Aristotle's peripeteia—thus relies heavily on the audience's anticipation of a resolution toward the end of the work. Sulzer's comments, significantly enough, appear within his discussion of *Anordnung,* the most important stage within the compositional process for the construction of large-scale form.[24]

Kermode's interpretation of peripeteia provides a direct bearing on the two analyses I introduced in Chapter 1. The false recapitulation in Haydn's Symphony No. 41 is an unusually striking instance of a "disconfirmation followed by a consonance." Somewhat paradoxically, it respects the listen-

---

22. Kermode, *The Sense of an Ending* (New York: Oxford University Press, 1967), pp. 18–19. Emphasis added. See also Kenneth Burke, *Counter-Statement,* 2nd ed. (Berkeley: University of California Press, 1968), p. 124: "Form in literature is an arousing and fulfillment of desires. A work has form in so far as one part of it leads a reader to anticipate another part, to be gratified by the sequence."

23. Sulzer, *Allgemeine Theorie,* "Anordnung."

24. See above, p. 80.

er's understanding of conventional patterns by violating those very norms. Its "falsification of expectations" works precisely because the composer could assume a certain rigidity of expectations on the part of the listener regarding sonata form.

In the case of Beethoven's String Quartet Op. 59, No. 1, the same is true for another critical juncture of sonata form: the articulation between the exposition and development sections. As we have seen from the autograph score, Beethoven had already decided not to repeat the movement's first half (exposition) even while considering a repeat for most of its second half (development and recapitulation). For the opening movement of a string quartet in the first decade of the nineteenth century, the repeat of a movement's first half was still part of its "paradigmatic plot" even though this repeat was no longer as standard an element as in earlier decades.[25] In a work of such unprecedented dimensions, the composer was faced with a dilemma: a large-scale repeat would have been of great help to listeners in assimilating such an unusually large quantity of material; yet to repeat this particular exposition would have created a still larger and longer argument, which would also have taxed the attention of listeners, albeit in a different way. In the "Eroica" Symphony, Beethoven had already opted in favor of a literal repeat, in spite of the size of the first movement; in this first of the "Razumovsky" Quartets, however, Beethoven's solution was to avoid repetition by drawing attention to its very absence. In cutting short the exposition repeat and proceeding directly to the instability of the development section, he constructed an ingenious solution to the problems of both length and form—the unfolding of the movement's central idea—by playing upon the listener's understanding of large-scale structural conventions.

The concept of archetypal patterns as paradigmatic plots ultimately relates back to Mattheson's effort to compare musical structures to the outline of an oration. It was not the identity of the thematic material presented throughout a movement that Mattheson had tried to emphasize, but its function at any given juncture, be it introductory, expository, developmental, contradictory, or concluding. And while subsequent theorists of the eighteenth century avoided the precision of Mattheson's rhetorical analogy, they did promulgate the essence of his ideas, often using less overtly rhetorical vocabulary. The continuity of this tradition becomes clear when we conceive of form primarily as a process of thematic elaboration, in which conventional patterns function as a means to a pragmatic end.

25. See Broyles, "Organic Form."

Analyzing the Musical Oration: The First Movement of Haydn's Symphony No. 46 in B Major

One of the more troublesome issues associated with the theory of stereo-typical forms, as we have seen, has been the question of how to reconcile "inner" and "outer" form, the genius of the individual composer with the conventions of his day. But eighteenth-century theorists, as shown in Chapter 2, saw no real need for reconciliation, for they viewed form not so much from the perspective of the composer or even of the work itself as from the perspective of the listener. Conventional forms were seen as a means to an end: the intelligible elaboration of a movement's central idea.

At the same time, eighteenth-century theorists seldom engaged in what today would be considered technical analysis. How, then, might the theoretical perspectives of the Classical era be applied to current-day analysis? The following discussion of the first movement of Haydn's Symphony No. 46 in B Major for two oboes, two horns, and strings (1772: see Example 5.1) draws on the various accounts of form considered earlier in this book, with particular emphasis on the role of the listener in the understanding of form. It is not presented as a hypothetical eighteenth-century analysis, but rather as an analysis informed by eighteenth-century perspectives.

5.1   Haydn, Symphony No. 46, first movement, mm. 1–77

5.1   continued

5.1   continued

5.1 continued

The *Hauptsatz,* relatively straightforward on the surface, provides the impetus for virtually all that follows in the first movement. Haydn begins with an antecedent-consequent phrase, four measures in length, whose conventional rhythmic structure makes it readily intelligible:

5.2   Haydn, Symphony No. 46, first movement, mm. 1–8

The elements of this musical idea to be unfolded over the course of the movement are based on the contrasts inherent in the antecedent (a) and consequent (b) portions of this statement:

1. *Pitch:* disjunct (a) versus conjunct (b). The antecedent moves down a minor sixth (B–D♯) and up a major third (E–G♯), with a half-step (D♯–E) in between (mm. 1–2). The consequent moves principally in step-wise motion down a fifth (F♯–B, mm. 3–4)

2. *Rhythm:* slow and even (a) versus fast and uneven (b). The antecedent consists of two rhythmic units, each of which consists of two notes of equal value (♩ ♩ and ♩ ♩); both units begin on the downbeat. The two units of the consequent both begin on an upbeat, with the first marked by syncopation (♩ | ♫ ♩), the second by a dotted rhythm (♩ | ♫ ♩).

3. *Dynamics:* loud (a) versus soft (b).

4. *Texture:* unison (a) versus polyphony (b).

Together, these elements constitute the theme of this musical oration, its *Hauptsatz.* Haydn begins to "link ideas with ideas" (to use Schoenberg's phrase) as early as m. 6. He varies the opening half of the main idea by harmonizing it and providing it with a new, fuller instrumentation. But while mm. 5–6 represent a varied restatement of mm. 1–2, the idea of the original antecedent is followed by a new and quite different consequent. Koch might easily have used these opening measures as an example of how different predicates can be linked to an essentially identical subject within the same movement.

The new predicate (mm. 6–8, labeled "c" in Example 5.2) is in fact not entirely new, but derived from elements of the opening subject. The rhythm (♪ ♫♫ | ♩ ♩) serves as a new anacrusis, replacing the original antecedent's rhythm of two quarter-notes: ♩ ♩ | ♩ ♩ becomes ♪ ♫♫ | ♩ ♩ , with legato articulation replacing the original detached. The pitches of the ♪ ♫♫ figure, moreover, represent an inversion of the opening's distinctive minor sixth (G♯–E). But most important for the forward momentum of the movement, Haydn introduces here the idea of counterpoint: the figure of the new predicate (c) provides a contrapuntal answer to itself four times in succession (mm. 7–10) before returning to a unison restatement (mm. 10–11) with the full orchestra.

The contrast of textures, in fact, is an issue that is developed early on. Within the space of only ten measures, Haydn introduces three distinct kinds in order of increasing complexity, yet all in conjunction with material that ultimately derives from the same source: unison (mm. 1–2), followed by polyphony (mm. 3–6), and then imitative counterpoint (mm. 6–10), before finally returning to unison (mm. 10–11). This remarkable variety of textures, adumbrated in the opening four measures, will be expanded still further over the course of the movement.

The idea (d) that appears in m. 13 offers a strong contrast to what has gone before: an upward contour, a new drum-like figure in the bass, and a new rhythm (♩ ♫♩ ♩ | ♩) in the melody. But the underlying continuity of this moment—the *Zusammenhang,* the "interconnectedness" of the elements that constitute the whole—derives from the phrase's consequent in the winds (m. 14), which reiterates the all-important B–D♯ descending minor sixth. Rhythmically, this consequent is a variation of the original consequent (b), a relationship that becomes all the more explicit in m. 19 (see Example 5.3).

Even the connective tissue in m. 12 linking (c) with (d) is derived from the opening theme. The intervals F♯–A♯–B—again, a descending minor sixth, followed by an ascending half-step—correspond precisely to the transposed version of the (a) theme that will be heard at m. 22 (see Examples 5.4a and 5.4b). More important still is the broader connection illuminated here between the original subject and predicate presented in mm. 1–4. The F♯–A♯–B–D♯ in m. 12 is preceded by the interval of E–G♯, drawing the figure as a whole still closer to the movement's opening four

5.3   Haydn, Symphony No. 46, first movement, mm. 13–21

5.4a   Haydn, Symphony No. 46, first movement, mm. 10–17

5.4b   Haydn, Symphony No. 46, first movement, mm. 22–25

measures. The outlines of the two passages emerge as parallel to each other (see Example 5.5).

This parallel also calls attention to the presence of a descending minor sixth and rising half-step within the original (b) phrase, thus linking it to (a). What had appeared as a contrast between antecedent and consequent at the beginning is now revealed to have been based on the principle of elaboration. Thus within the brief space of three measures (11–13), Haydn not only elides two main contrasting (but related) themes by reinterpreting earlier material but also demonstrates the relationship of the two main elements of his original subject (mm. 1–2 and mm. 3–4).

These kinds of connections can be pursued throughout the remainder of the movement. Here, I would like to call attention to only a few of the more outstanding events as they relate to the broader eighteenth-century concept of form as a function of rhetoric. The move to the dominant at m. 22 is part of the archetypal "plot" of sonata form; and while the reappearance of the opening theme at this juncture is not necessarily common, neither is it altogether surprising. The opening theme here, moreover, is not really the same at all, as Mattheson would have argued ("similar is not the same"), for it is presented within a new texture (imitative, with a countersubject) and in a new key (F♯, the dominant). Thematic contrast had not yet established itself as a *sine qua non* within the archetype of sonata form by 1772; what *was* expected was a process of thematic elaboration, which could take the form of either variation or contrast—or, as is most often the case and as is seen here, a fusion of the two.

The contrast in mm. 22–25 is provided by the tonality, the reduced texture (violins only), and the counterpoint in the second violins. But once again, the variety masks the process of elaboration and continuity: the two rhythms of the counterpoint in m. 22 (⁷ ♫) and in m. 23 (♬♬ ♬♬) have been heard before (m. 6, m. 13), and the rhythms in mm. 26–27 (♩ ♩ | ♬♬) also relate to previous material. The running eighth-note figure in m. 31 covers the span of a major sixth; its contour is reminiscent of the counterpoint in m. 23, and its rhythm, although familiar from

5.5   Haydn, Symphony No. 46, first movement, mm. 2–4 and mm. 11–13

mm. 13, 23, and 29, acquires an air of novelty through its articulation, combining staccato and slurred notes with a decided accent on the leading note midway through the measure. The (c) rhythm returns once again as a kind of consequent phrase in m. 33.

The abrupt turn to the minor at m. 36 introduces yet another element of variety—mode—but within the context of familiar material, a reinterpretation of (d). The continuation of this section is similarly based on earlier material: the (c) rhythm returns in m. 42 and is subject to the same kind of imitations originally associated with the (c) motive as first introduced in mm. 7–10. In mm. 45–48, this motive is superimposed on the opening (a) rhythm. The abrupt entry of this entire minor-mode section is mirrored in the equally unanticipated resumption, in m. 52, of the very same material the minor-mode section had earlier interrupted. This kind of abrupt entrance and departure is not a part of the archetypal "plot" of sonata form; rather, it is a distinctive feature of this movement and an essential element of its form.

The return of the running eighth-note idea in m. 52 marks the unexpected reappearance of an entire unit of thought, unchanged. Even the orchestration is the same as in mm. 31–32: it is almost as if the utterly contrary, minor-mode interpolation of mm. 36–51 had never occurred. This, too, is a portent of future events. The juxtaposition of contrasts becomes even more remarkable when we realize that the "true" continuation of m. 56 takes us back to precisely the same idea of the minor-mode interpolation, but this time in the major mode. The exposition thus closes with an idea (d) that is being heard already for the third time within the exposition, fulfilling a very different function with each appearance: as a continuation of the opening idea (m. 13), a large-scale consequent, as it were; as a minor-mode contrast (m. 36); and as a closing theme (m. 57).

The opening of the development section follows the plot archetype of sonata form in exemplary fashion—so much so, in fact, that it can be said to represent a condensed, almost exaggerated manifestation of the kinds of techniques one expects at this point within a movement. The opening theme is not only fragmented but also subjected to stretto-like points of imitation. Within the idiom of the time, it could scarcely be more unstable harmonically, touching on several tonalities without ever settling on any one of them. But without warning, the music comes to a halt on V/vi in m. 68; the texture thins out to a single line of violins, and what sounds like the recapitulation sets in abruptly at m. 70. Just as the exposition had seemed to be heading for a premature close (m. 35), so now the development seems to be concluding in an even more summary fashion.

But the turn to the minor mode in m. 74 and the resumption of destabilizing, developmental techniques eradicates the sense of return established at m. 70 (see Example 5.1).[26] By this point, it is clear that interruption is one of the basic strategies of this movement (see Figure 5.1). Measures 70–74 constitute an interpolation, an interruption that is itself interrupted. This sudden and unexpected turn to the minor is, in effect, another manifestation of the procedure heard earlier in m. 36. The disconfirmation of our expectations has now become more than a merely local device: it is basic to the very idea of elaboration within this movement.[27]

Somewhat paradoxically, the remainder of this movement contains no comparable surprises of structure. Further destabilizing techniques would only have undermined the very basis on which the listener's expectations rest. The structural surprises already presented, moreover, create a certain tension that carries over into the more or less conventional continuation of events. At least part of the interest in the slow movement of the "Surprise" Symphony, it should be remembered, lies in our anticipation—unfulfilled, as it turns out—that the drum-stroke heard early on might return at some later point.

To say that this first movement of Haydn's Symphony No. 46 is in sonata form is to say very little. It shares the structural harmonic outline of |: I - V :|: X - I :| with a great many other movements, but from the perspective of eighteenth-century theorists, its form is the manner in which its *Hauptsatz* is elaborated. In this instance, the elaboration incorporates the large-scale harmonic outline of sonata form but goes beyond this to include techniques of thematic manipulation and the "aesthetic ordering" (Forkel's

26. Whether this passage represents a "false recapitulation" depends on how one defines that problematic term. This passage does not, in any event, represent the kind of perfunctory restatement of the main theme in the dominant and then briefly again in the tonic at the beginning of the development section as described by Koch (*Versuch*, II, 224 and III, 115, 396–397). In the works of Haydn, at least, such passages almost invariably have a formulaic quality: four measures in the dominant, followed by a retransition to the tonic by means of a descending bass line from the fifth to first scale degree; then a single restatement of the theme in the tonic, again covering four measures; and finally an abandonment of the tonic by means of a I⁷-IV or I⁷-ii progression (see Bonds, "Haydn's False Recapitulations," pp. 303–310). The opening of Haydn's development section here is anything but formulaic, and the fact that the opening theme and the tonic return too early to be heard as a recapitulation is consistent with the strategy of interpolation throughout this first movement.

27. There is an interesting counterpart to this device in this symphony's companion piece, the Symphony No. 45 in F-sharp Minor ("Farewell"), also written in 1772, and also in a highly unusual (and related) key. The new and seemingly contrasting D Major theme that appears in m. 108 and departs just as abruptly in m. 140 anticipates the bizarre events of the work's finale. James Webster deals with both the Symphony No. 45 and No. 46 (especially the last two movements) in his forthcoming monograph on the "Farewell" Symphony.

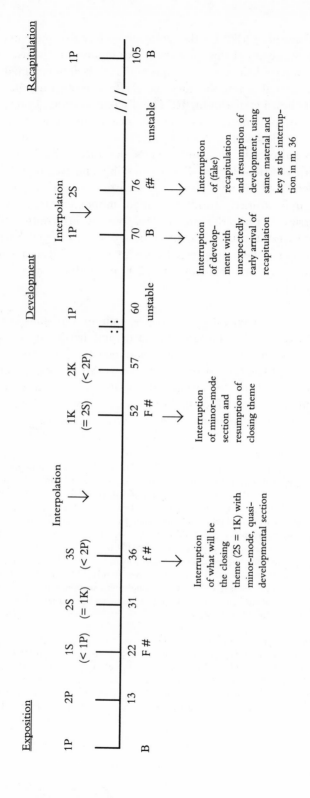

Figure 5.1 Haydn, Symphony No. 46: the strategy of interruption and interpolation in the first movement

5.6 Haydn, Symphony No. 46, third movement, mm. 15–20; first movement, mm. 1–4; fourth movement, mm. 1–4

phrase) of ideas. Perhaps the most important (and unusual) strategy of elaboration in this movement is the process of disruption and the concomitant interpolation of ideas heard previously in a different context. The very effect of disruption depends upon the listener's knowledge of convention, including the conventions of sonata form. If form is equated with the process of thematic elaboration, there is no need or reason to distinguish between the movement's "outer" form and its unique "inner" form. The listener's familiarity with the conventions of sonata form can be readily reconciled with—and indeed, is essential to an understanding of—the more unconventional aspects of this movement.

The strategy of interruption and the interpolation of material heard earlier in different contexts is even more readily apparent in the work's finale. The opening of this last movement is based on the same F♯–A♯–B figure so basic to the first movement (see Example 5.6), and the second consequent of the second restatement of this idea (mm. 7–8) makes use of the syncopated ♩ ♩ ♫ rhythm once again. The exposition, development, and recapitulation are repeatedly interrupted by sudden and unexpected silences (mm. 29, 70–71, 77–78, 152). The interpolation of earlier ideas does not begin until the recapitulation has more or less run its course, but when it appears, it arrives all the more forcefully. At m. 153, the meter and tempo of the minuet return within an almost exact repetition of mm. 15–26 of that movement. All of this is followed by a fuller statement corresponding to a repeat of the entire second half of the minuet. After yet another pause (m. 187), the original theme and meter of the finale return, and the movement ends—but not before still another series of interrupting silences (mm. 195–196, 198–200).

But why begin the interpolation of the minuet into the finale with a theme from the middle of the minuet and not its opening idea? Measures 15–20 represent an inversion of the movement's initial idea, and it is in this guise that the idea bears the closest resemblance not only to the opening of the finale but to the opening of the first movement as well.

Charles Rosen, who was the first to point out these resemblances, calls the "thematic logic" of this interpolation within the finale "isolated." But it is "isolated" only if we consider the work's thematic materials in isolation. When coupled with the broader strategy of interruption and interpolation, the return of the minuet within the finale (as well as its abrupt dismissal) marks the culmination of an attempt to create a coherence between movements that goes beyond the mere recycling of similar themes. This technique would become a basic element of much nineteenth-century music, particularly within the genres of the symphony and concerto, but also in the sonata and string quartet.

In the overtness of its cyclic integration, Haydn's Symphony No. 46 is admittedly unusual for its time, more than thirty years before Beethoven's Fifth Symphony. But it is by no means isolated in its attempt to apply specific principles of elaboration not only within a single movement but also among multiple movements.[28] Throughout this particular symphony, a germinal idea has been elaborated in a variety of ways, and both the conventional and the unconventional processes used to elaborate this idea have themselves become elements in the work's coherence.

The "meaning" of this symphony will necessarily vary from listener to listener, and the essentially formalistic analysis presented here suggests only one kind of analysis that in no way precludes others. One could, for example, argue that there are extra-musical associations in this particular work. At the same time, the "logic" of this musical oration need not be judged solely in relation to external ideas or emotions, nor in its deviation from an archetypal progression of ideas. Haydn's work exhibits the kind of qualities eighteenth- and early-nineteenth-century theorists had in mind when they used rhetoric as a metaphor of musical form.

28. See, in particular, Webster's forthcoming monograph, which deals at length with issues of cyclic integration in a number of Haydn's instrumental works, including the Symphony No. 46.

Originals of Quotations Given in Translation

Index

Originals of Quotations Given in Translation

1. The Paradox of Musical Form

At note 57: Per quanto la modulazione sia distante dal Tono principale della Composizione, deve a poco a poco ravvicinarsi fin tanto che cada naturalmente bene e regolarmente la Ripresa, cioè il primo Motivo della prima parte nel proprio natural Tono, in cui fu già scritto. Se il pezzo è lungo si riprende, come si è detto, il vero Motivo nel Tono principale, se poi non si voglia tanto allungar la Composizione basterà riprendere in sua vece il Passo Caratteristico nello stesso Tono Fondamentale trasferito.

At note 59: Im andern Theile fange ich an mit lauter Ausweichungen zu moduliren . . . Diese [Durdominante] führt mich also wieder ins D dur, den Hauptton, in welchem ich das Thema wiederhole, mich mit meinen schon in der Nebentonart . . . angebrachten Melodiearten und Wendungen nochmals hören lasse, darinnen bleibe und schliesse.

At note 62: Der letzte Periode unsers ersten Allegro, der vorzüglich der Modulation in der Haupttonart gewidmet ist, fängt am gewöhnlichsten wieder mit dem Thema, zuweilen aber auch mit einem andern melodischen Haupttheile in dieser Tonart an.

At note 63: Die Modulation wird . . . wieder zurück in die Haupttonart geleitet, in welcher der dritte Periode, und zwar gewöhnlich mit dem Thema wieder anfängt. Nach dem wiederholten Vortrage des Thema[s] werden einige in der ersten Hälfte des ersten Perioden enthaltene melodische Theile in eine andere Verbindung . . . gebracht.

At note 75: Anjezt will ich . . . dem angehenden Setzer zu zeigen suchen, wie ein Tonstück in der Seele des schaffenden Componisten entstehen muss, wenn es die Absicht der Kunst erreichen soll.

Gleich zu Anfange der Einleitung des ersten Theils versprach ich, zwischen der Harmonie und Melodie eine Linie zu ziehen, und die bekannte Streitfrage, ob die Harmonie oder die Melodie eher sey, ob sich ein Tonstück in Melodie oder in Harmonie auflösen lasse, so zu beantworten, dass man sich bey der Entscheidung beruhigen könne. Ich weiss nicht wie einige meiner Leser . . . auf den Gedanken haben kommen können, als hätte ich dadurch zu erkennen geben wollen, die Harmonie müsse bey der Entstehung eines Tonstücks in der Seele des Componisten zuerst entstehen . . .

. . . Weder die Melodie, noch die Harmonie kann den ersten Stoff eines Tonstücks ausmachen. Beyde tragen charakteristische Kennzeichen dessen, was vor beyde vorausgesezt werden muss, und dieses ist die . . . Tonart . . . Diese durch einen Grundton bestimmte Grösse aller musikalischen Töne, ist nun eigentlich der erste Stoff eines Tonstücks, das heisst, es ist dasjenige, woraus alle Theile des ganzen Tonstücks geformt sind. Wird nun dieser Stoff, werden diese Töne nach einander hörbar gemacht, so wird der Stoff melodisch bearbeitet; harmonisch aber wird er gebraucht, wenn einige dieser Töne woraus er besteht zusammen hörbar vereinigt werden . . .

Die Sache so betrachtet deucht mich, dass die Frage materiel betrachtet, gar nicht mehr statt finden kann; denn weder die Melodie, noch die Harmonie kann den lezten Grad der Auflösung eines Tonstücks ausmachen. Sie entstehen beyde aus einem und eben demselben Stoffe; dieser Stoff ist nur bey der Melodie anders behandelt als bey der Harmonie.

Hieraus ist klar, dass es meine Meinung ohnmöglich seyn konnte . . . zu erkennen geben zu wollen, als sollte der schaffende Componist zuerst Harmonie denken.

At note 86: Abbiamo infatti un'infinità di Autori, che hanno con vario successo scritto sull'Armonià ma un solo non ve n'ha, ch'io sappia, che abbia trattata la parte principale della moderna Musica, cioè la Melodìa. Ho tentato questa nuova carriera, e chieggo scusa al mio Lettore, se ho dovuto inventare de' nuovi vocaboli, e non ancora usitati in Musica.

At note 87: Le grand édifice de la Musique repose sur deux colonnes de même grandeur et d'une egale importance, la Mélodie et l'Harmonie. Depuis plusieurs siècles on a publié une quantité de Traités sur l'Harmonie et pas un seul sur la Mélodie.

At note 89: Harmonie und Melodie sind in einer guten musikalischen Zusammensetzung so unzertrennlich, als Wahrheit der Gedanken, und Richtigkeit des Ausdrucks in der Sprache. Sprache ist das Kleid der Gedanken, so wie Melodie das Kleid der Harmonie. Man kann in dieser Rücksicht die Harmonie eine Logik der Musik nennen, weil sie gegen Melodie ungefähr in eben dem Verhältniss steht, als in der Sprache die Logik gegen den Ausdruck . . . So wie nun richtig denken billig vorher gehen muss, ehe die Erlernung des richtigen Ausdrucks des Gedachten möglich wird, so hat auch wirklich die Erfahrung gelehrt, dass keine reine, richtige und fliessende Melodie, ohne vorhergegangene Kenntniss der Harmonie, möglich ist. Alle geschickte Compositionslehrer, deren aber freylich nur sehr wenige sind, haben dieses gefühlt, und ihren Schülern aus Erfahrung den Rath gegeben, sich nicht eher an den melodischen Ausdruck musikalischer Gedanken zu wagen, bis sie erst durch Kenntniss der Harmonie ihr Gefühl für Wahrheit und Richtigkeit derselben hinlänglich geschärft haben. Indessen müssen beyde unzertrennlich mit einander verbunden seyn; sie klären sich einander wechselsweise auf, und wenn niemand im Stande ist, Vorschriften zur Verfertigung einer guten an einander hängenden Melodie zu geben, ohne sie aus der Natur der Harmonie zu holen, eben so wenig als ein Sprachlehrer Vorschriften zu einem guten und richtigen Ausdrucke geben kann, wenn er sie nicht aus der Kunst richtig zu denken hernimmt; so kann auf der andern Seite auch keine harmonische Fortschreitung gut seyn, wenn sie nicht zugleich melodisch ist. Trockene Harmonie ohne melodische Verbindung gleicht einer Logik, welcher es an Sprachausdrücken fehlt.

2. Rhetoric and the Concept of Musical Form in the Eighteenth Century

At note 1: So nennen einige Tonlehrer diejenige zur Setzkunst gehörige Wissenschaft, nach welcher einzelne melodische Theile nach einem bestimmten Zwecke zu einem Ganzen verbunden werden. Durch die Grammatik wird der materielle Theil der Kunstausdrücke berichtiget: die Rhetorik hingegen bestimmt die Regeln, nach welchen sie bey einem Kunstwerke dem auszuführenden Zwecke gemäss zusammengesetzt werden müssen. Obgleich viele Materialien zu einer musikalischen Rhetorik in den Schriften über die Tonkunst, und in solchen, die den schönen Künsten überhaupt gewidmet sind, hier und da zerstreuet liegen, so hat es dennoch dem menschlichen Geiste noch nicht glücken wollen, sie in eine wissenschaftliche Ordnung zu bringen, und die dabey noch befindlichen Lücken auszufüllen. Der Tonsetzer muss daher einstweilen diese Bruchstücke zu sammeln, und den Mangel ihres Zusammenhanges durch feines Kunstgefühl zu ersetzen suchen.

At note 6: Mein Fürst war mit allen meinen Arbeiten zufrieden, ich erhielt Beifall, ich konnte als Chef eines Orchesters Versuche machen, beobachten, was den Eindruck hervorbringt und was ihn schwächt, also verbessern, zusetzen, wegschneiden, wagen; ich war von der Welt abgesondert, niemand in meiner Nähe konnte mich an mir selbst irremachen und quälen, und so musste ich original werden.

At note 8: eines der allgemeinern Wörter, deren man sich bedient, die Wirkung zu bezeichnen, welche ein Tonstück bey seiner Ausführung auf unsere Seele macht.

At note 9: Durch dieses Wort giebt man oft im Allgemeinen zu erkennen, dass die Ausführung oder das Anhören eines Tonstückes entweder eine gewisse Wirkung auf uns hervorgebracht, oder einen gewissen Nachklang dieser Wirkung in uns zurückgelassen habe.

At note 11: Es war gewiss einer der schwersten Aufgaben, ohne untergelegten Text, aus freier Phantasie, sieben Adagios aufeinanderfolgen zu lassen, die den Zuhörer nicht ermüden und in ihm alle Empfindungen wecken sollten, welche im Sinne eines jeden von dem sterbenden Erlöser ausgesprochenen Wortes lagen.

At note 12: es war mir daran gelegen, das Publikum durch etwas Neues zu überraschen.

At note 16: Redekunst und Dichtkunst sind mit der Tonkunst zu genau verwandt, als dass einer, der die Musik ernstlich studiren will, damit unbekannt bleiben sollte Sie arbeiten sämmtlich zu einem gemeinschaftlichen Endzweck, unserer Empfindungen sich zu bemeistern, und unsern Leidenschaften eine bestimmte Richtung zu geben.

At note 19: Nach dem allgemeinen Begriffe von den schönen Künsten, der in diesem ganzen Werk überall zum Grunde gelegt worden ist, sollen sie durch ihre Werke auf die Gemüther der Menschen dauernde und zur Erhöhung der Seelenkräfte Eindrücke machen. Diese Bestimmung scheinet die Beredsamkeit in dem weitesten Umfang erfüllen zu können. Sie macht vielleicht nicht so tief in die Seele dringende, noch so lebhafte Eindrüke, wie die Künste, die eigentlich die Reizung der äussern

Sinnen zum unmittelbaren Zweck haben; dafür aber kann sie alle nur mögliche Arten klarer Vorstellungen erwecken, die ganz ausser dem Gebiete jener reizendern Künste sind. Also verdient diese Kunst auch vorzüglich, in ihrer wahren Natur, in ihren Ursachen und Würkungen, in ihrer mannigfaltigen Anwendung und in den verschiedenen äusserlichen Veränderungen, die sie erlitten hat, mit Aufmerksamkeit betrachtet zu werden.

At note 23: Da es so verschiedene Arten der aesthetischen Ausführungen gibt, prosaische und poetische, theatralische, epische u.s.w. so ist nicht zu leugnen, dass nicht diese Gesetze, in den besondern Anwendungen, verschiedene Zusätze und Einschrenkungen bekommen sollten. Allein diese Untersuchungen gehören, in die Redekunst und Dichtkunst.

At note 31: Die Musik allein aber ist unbeseelet, und unverständlich, wenn sie nicht an Worte hält, die gleichsam für sie reden müssen; damit man wisse, was sie haben will.

At note 33: Le musicien composera chacun de ces trois morceaux en particulier, comme s'il travailloit à un grand air où une ou plusieurs voix chercheroient à exprimer des affections plus ou moins vives: il remplacera ces voix par le premier violon, ou par d'autres instrumens aisés à distinguer; de temps en temps il cherchera à imiter les accens de la voix humaine par des instruments susceptibles d'inflexions douces ou pathétiques.

At note 37: après tout, si on ne parle pas aussi distinctement avec un instrument qu'avec la bouche, et si les sons ne peignent pas aussi nettement la pensée que le discours, encore disent-ils quelque chose.

At note 39: Nun ist die Musik nichts anders als eine künstliche Sprache, wodurch man seine musikalischen Gedanken dem Zuhörer bekannt machen soll.

At note 47: durch Instrumente etwas, so viel als möglich ist, auszudrücken, wozu man sonst viel bequemer die Singstimme und Worte brauchet.

At note 52: Vernehme ich in der Kirche ein[e] feierliche Symphonie, so überfällt mich ein andächtiger Schauder; arbeitet ein starcker Instrumenten-Chor in die Wette, so bringt mir solches eine hohe Verwunderung zu Wege; fängt das Orgelwerck an zu brausen und zu donnern, so entstehet eine göttliche Furcht in mir; schliesst sich denn alles mit einem freudigen Hallelujah, so hüpfft mir das Hertz im Leibe; wenn ich auch gleich weder die Bedeutung dieses Worts wissen, noch sonst ein anders, der Entfernung oder andrer Ursachen halber verstehen sollte: ja, wenn auch gar keine Worte dabey wären, bloss durch Zuthun der Instrumente und reden-den Klänge.

At note 53: J'ai nommé la Parole la première, parce qu'elle est en possession du premier rang; & que les hommes y font ordinairement le plus d'attention. Cependant les Tons de la voix et les Gestes, ont sur elle plusieurs avantages: ils sont d'un usage plus naturel; nous y avons recours quand les mots nous manquent; plus étendu: c'est un Interpréte universel qui nous suit jusqu'aux extrémités du monde, qui nous rend intelligibles aux Nations les plus barbares, & même aux animaux. Enfin ils sont consacrés d'une manière spéciale au sentiment. La parole nous instruit, nous convainc, c'est l'organe de la raison: mais le Ton et le Geste sont ceux du coeur: ils nous émeuvent, nous gagnent, nous persuadent. La Parole n'exprime la passion que par le moyen des idées auxquelles les sentimens sont liés, & comme par réflexion. Le Ton et le Geste arrivent au coeur directement et sans aucun détour.

At note 54: La mélodie, en imitant les inflexions de la voix, exprime les plaintes, les cris de douleur ou de joie, les menaces, les gémissements; tous les signes vocaux des passions sont de son ressort. Elle imite les accents des langues, et les tours affectés dans chaque idiome à certains mouvements de l'âme: elle n'imite pas seulement, elle parle; et son langage inarticulé, mais vif, ardent, passionné, a cent fois plus d'énergie que la parole même.

At note 55: eine allgemeine Sprache der Empfindungen . . . , deren Umfang eben so gross ist und seyn kann, als der Umfang einer ausgebildeten Ideen-Sprache. So wie nun in der Ideensprache Reichtum an Ausdrücken für alle mögliche Gedanken mit ihren Beziehungen, Richtigkeit und Ordnung in der Verbindung dieser Ausdrücke, und die Möglichkeit, die sämmtlichen Ausdrücke nach allen den verschiedenen Zwecken und Absichten, die ein Redender damit verbinden kann, zu biegen und zu gebrauchen, Merkmale ihrer höchsten Vollkommenheit sind; so müssen auch in der Tonsprache 1) Reichtum an Combinationen der Töne, 2) Richtigkeit und Ordnung in den Verbindungen derselben, und 3) gewisser Endzweck, die drey Hauptmerkmale einer wahren, guten und ächten Musik seyn.

At note 58: [Man saget] oft von Tonstücken, dass sie im Satz rein sind, wenn darinnen nichts vorkommt, was dem Gehör anstössig oder den Regeln der Harmonie zuwider wäre, obgleich in solchen Stücken oft gar kein Gesang noch Geist ist. Nach dieser Bedeutung ist der Satz nichts anders, als was die Grammatik bey der Sprache ist. Ein Mensch kann grammatisch rein und richtig sprechen, und doch nichts sagen, was unsrer Aufmerksamkeit würdig sey.

At note 61: So schätzbar mathematische, arithmetische und systematische Kenntnisse an sich selbst sind, so wäre doch zu wünschen, dass man weniger Geschrey damit erhübe, und nicht so viel davon der Musik, zu ihrer vermeynten Aufklärung, aufdringen wollte. Denn die Töne sich als Grössen denken; ihre Verhältnisse in Linien und Zahlen darstellen; die Intervalle, wie Zwirnsfaden, in einen Knäuel zusammenwickeln, ist doch noch lange das nicht, was zur Hervobringung einer guten Melodie und reinen Harmonie erfordert wird. Besser wäre es, den rhetorischen oder ästhetischen Theil der Musik mehr und fleissiger zu bearbeiten, so wie es von geschickten Männern mit dem grammatischen geschehen ist.

At note 64: [un] ouverage d'autant plus nécessaire que jusqu'à présent on a presque écrit uniquement sur la méchanique de cet art, c'est-à-dire sur sa partie matérielle, on n'a presque rien dit de celle qu'on peut appeler *intellectuelle* et qui regarde le goût et l'expression. Il me semble qu'on pourroit répandre beaucoup de lumières sur ce sujet, en rapprochant la musique de la peinture et de l'éloquence, surtout de l'éloquence poëtique.

At note 67: Bey der Zusammensetzung musikalischer Ausdrücke zu einem an einander hängenden Ganzen, bemerkt man vorzüglich zweyerley: erstlich die Verbindung einzelner Töne und Accorde zu einzelnen Sätzen, und zweytens die Verbindung mehrerer Sätze nach einander . . . Die Vorschriften zur Verbindung einzelner Töne und Accorde zu einzelnen Sätzen, sind in der musikalischen Grammatik enthalten, so wie die Vorschriften zur Verbindung mehrerer einzelner Sätze in der musikalischen Rhetorik.

At note 69: Le chant d'une Piéce n'est pas composé sans ordre & sans raison; il est formé de plusieurs morceaux qui ont chacun leur sens complet; & une Piéce de Musique ressemble à peu prés à un Piéce d'Eloquence, ou plûtôt c'est la Piéce d'Eloquence qui ressemble à la Piéce de Musique: car l'harmonie, le nombre, la mesure, & les autres choses semblables qu'un habile Orateur observe en la composition de ses Ouvrages, appartiennent bien plus naturellement à la Musique qu'à la Réthorique. Quoi qu'il en soit, tout ainsi qu'une piece d'Eloquence a son tout, qui est le plus souvent composé de plusieurs parties; Que chaque partie est composée de périodes, qui ont chacune un sens complet; Que ses périodes sont composées de membres, les membres de mots, & les mots de lettres; De même le chant d'une Piéce de Musique a son tout, qui est toûjours composé de plusieurs reprises. Chaque reprise est composée de cadences, qui ont chacune leur sens complet, & qui sont les périodes du chant. Les cadences sont souvent composées de membres; les membres de mesures, & les mesures de notes. Ainsi, les notes répondent aux lettres, les mesures aux mots, les cadences aux périodes, les reprises aux parties, & le tout au tout. Mais ces divisions qui sont dans le chant, ne sont pas apperçûës par tous ceux qui entendent chanter, ou joüer de quelque Instrument: Il faut être du Métier pour les sentir; excepté quelques-unes qui sont si grossiéres, que tout le monde les comprend; cependant elles se marquent dans la tablature, par les barres qui séparent les mésures, & par quelques autres caracteres dont je parlerai en leur lieu.

At note 70: Jeder Antrag, er geschehe mündlich oder schrifftlich, bestehet . . . in gewissen Wort-Sätzen, oder Periodis; ein jeder solcher Satz aber wiederum in kleinern Einschnitten bis an den Abschnitt eines Puncts. Aus sothanen Sätzen erwächst ein gantzer Zusammensatz oder Paragraphus, und aus verschiedenen solchen Absätzen wird endlich ein Haupt-Stück oder Capitel.

At note 71: ein kurtzgefasster Spruch, der eine völlige Meinung oder einen gantzen Wort-Verstand in sich begreifft. Was nun dieses nicht thut, sondern weniger hält, das ist kein Periodus, kein Satz; und was mehr leistet, ist ein Paragraphus, Ab- oder Zusammensatz, der aus verschiedenen Periodis bestehen kann, und von Rechtswegen soll.

At note 73: Onde la Cadenza è di tanto valore nella Musica, quanto il Punto nella Oratione . . . Et debbono terminare insieme il Punto della oratione, & la Cadenza.

At note 74: Die Instrumental-Melodie [ist] darin hauptsächlich von Singe-Sachen unterschieden, dass jene, ohne Beihülffe der Worte und Stimmen, eben so viel zu sagen trachtet, als diese mit den Worten thun.

At note 75: Die Namen, welche man den grössern und kleinern Gliedern einer Melodie beylegt, sind bis itzt noch etwas unbestimmt. Man spricht von Perioden, Abschnitten, Einschnitten, Rhythmen, Cäsuren etc. so, dass dasselbe Wort bisweilen zweyerley, und zwey verschiedene Wörter bisweilen einerley, Sinn haben.

At note 76: Jedermann siehet auf den ersten Blick, dass der rührendste Gesang aller Kraft und alles Ausdrucks gänzlich würde beraubet werden, wenn ein Ton nach dem andern ohne bestimmte Regel der Geschwindigkeit, ohne Accente und ohne Ruhepunkte, obgleich in der genauesten Reinigkeit der Töne vorgetragen würde. Schon die gemeine Rede würde zum Theil unverständlich und völlig unangenehm werden, wenn man nicht in dem Vortrag ein schickliches Maass der Geschwindigkeit beobachtete, nicht durch die Accente, mit der Länge und Kürze der Sylben verbunden, die Wörter von einander absonderte, und endlich durch keine Ruhepunkte, die Sätze und Perioden unterschiedete. Durch einen solchen unbelebten Vortrag würde die schönste Rede nicht besser ins Gehör fallen, als das Buchstabiren der Kinder.

Demnach geben Bewegung, Takt und Rhytmus dem Gesange sein Leben und seine Kraft . . . Durch diese drey Dinge schicklich vereiniget, wird der Gesang zu einer verständlichen und reizenden Rede.

At note 77: Wie man in der Rede erst am Ende eines Satzes den Sinn desselben gefasst hat und dadurch nun mehr oder weniger befriediget ist, nachdem dieser Sinn eine mehr oder weniger vollständige Rede ausmacht; so ist es auch in der Musik. Ehe nicht in einer Folge von zusammenhangenden Tönen ein Ruhepunkt kommt, auf welchem das Gehör einigermaassen befriediget wird, und nun diese Töne auf einmal, als ein kleines Ganzes zusammen fasst, hat es auch keinen Sinn, und eilet um zu vernehmen, was eigentlich diese auf einander folgende Töne sagen wollen. Kommt aber nach einer nicht gar zu langen Folge zusammenhangender Töne ein merklicher Abfall, der dem Gehör eine kleine Ruhe verstattet und den Sinn des Satzes schliesst, so vereiniget das Ohr alle diese Töne in einen fasslichen Satz zusammen.

Dieser Abfall, oder Ruhepunkt, kann entweder durch eine völlige Cadenz, oder auch blos durch eine melodische Clausel mit einer beruhigenden Harmonie, ohne Schluss in dem Basse, bewürkt werden. Im ersten Fall hat man einen ganz vollständigen musicalischen Satz, der in dem Gesang das ist, was eine ganze Periode in der Rede, nach welcher man einen Punkt setzet; im andern Fall aber hat man einen zwar verständlichen Satz, nach welchem man aber nothwendig noch einen oder mehr andre erwartet, um den Sinn der Periode vollständig zu machen.

At note 78: Eine Folge solcher Abschnitte deren keiner, als der letzte in den Haupt-ton schliesst, macht ein einziges Tonstück aus.

At note 79: Denn 4, 8, 16, und wohl auch 32 Täcte sind diejenigen, welche unserer Natur dergestalt eingepflanzet, dass es uns schwer scheinet, eine andere Ordnung (mit Vergnügen) anzuhören.

At note 81: So nothwendig in der Sprache überhaupt, und also auch in den Pro-dukten derjenigen schönen Künste, die durch die Sprache ihre Absicht erreichen, nemlich in der Dichtkunst und Beredsamkeit gewisse mehr und weniger merkliche Ruhepuncte des Geistes sind, wenn der Gegenstand ihrer Darstellung verständlich werden soll, eben so nothwendig sind dergleichen Ruhepuncte des Geistes in der Melodie, wenn sie auf unsere Empfindungen würken soll. Eine Wahrheit an welcher wohl noch niemals gezweifelt worden ist, und die daher keines weitern Beweises bedarf.

Vermittelst dieser mehr und weniger merklichen Ruhepuncte des Geistes lassen sich die Producte dieser schönen Künste in grössere und kleinere Theile auflösen; durch die merklichsten derselben zerfällt z.B. die Rede in verschiedene Perioden, und durch die weniger merklichen zerfällt wiederum der Periode in einzelne Sätze und Redetheile; und eben so wie die Rede lässt sich vermittelst ähnlicher Ruhepuncte des Geistes die Melodie eines Tonstückes in Perioden, und diese wieder in einzelne Sätze und melodische Theile auflösen.

At note 86: Colle cadenze si formano i *periodi musicali,* come nel discorso co' punti e colle virgole. Colla cadenza perfetta si termina un' periodo come con un punto. Per tanto potrà chiamarsi *periodo musicale* la modulazione contenuta tra due cadenze . . .

In somma una composizione fatta precisamente secondo le regole fondamentali della Musica è un discorso talvolta elegante; ma che non commuove nè persuade; la Musica espressiva è un discorso eloquente, che trionfa degli animi degli Ascoltanti.

At note 87: Ueberhaupt muss das ganze musikalische Stück in gewisse Haupt-theile, und diese wieder in kleinere Nebentheile oder Glieder zerlegt werden kön-nen, wenn es anders eine gute Wirkung hervobringen soll. Das Ab- und Zunehmen der Harmonie gehöret noch hierher.

At note 88: wohlangebrachte Einschnitten, Ruhestellen, etc. . . . ; dass eine gute Abwechslung des Rauschenden und Singbaren, oder nach der Mahlerey zu reden, des Lichts und Schattens getroffen wird. Und dann, dass die Regeln der Redekunst auch hierbey wohl in Acht genommen werden.

At note 90: Die Kunst, gut zu periodiren, [ist] einer der schweresten Theile der Beredtsamkeit . . . Alles übrige kann durch natürliche Gaben, ohne hartnäkiges Studiren eher als dieses erhalten werden. Hiezu aber wird Arbeit, Fleiss, viel Ueberlegung und eine grosse Stärke in der Sprache erfodert. Es scheinet nicht möglich, hierüber einen methodischen Unterricht zu geben. Das Beste, was man zur Bildung der Redner in diesem Stücke thun könnte, wäre, ihnen eine nach dem verschiedenen Charakter des Inhalts wolgeordnete Sammlung der besten Perioden vorzulegen, und den Werth einer jeden durch gründliche Zergliederung an den Tag zu legen.

At note 93: Es gehören sonst zu einer Composition dreyerley: Inventio, (die Erfindung) Elaboratio, (die Ausarbeitung) Executio, (die Ausführung oder Aufführung) welches eine ziemliche nahe Verwandschafft mit der Oratorie oder Rhetorique (Rede-Kunst) an den Tag leget; Die beyden letzten Stücke können erlernet werden; zum ersten hat sich noch kein tüchtiger Maitre, wohl aber, mit permission zu sagen, diebische Schüler finden wollen.

At note 99: Vor etlichen Jahren hat ein grosser Dichter, als etwas Sonderbares, entdecken wollen, dass es mit der Music in diesem Stücke fast eben die Bewandniss habe, als mit der Rede-Kunst. Welch Wunder! Die Ton-Künstler mögen sich wohl schämen, dass sie hierin so saumselig gewesen sind: Denn obgleich hie und da einer, aus dem Licht der Natur, auf gesunde Gedancken gekommen seyn mag; so sind die guten Herren doch nur am Rande geblieben, und haben nicht bis auf den Kern durchdringen, vielweniger die Sache in eine gehörige Kunst-Form, weder öffentlich noch heimlich, bringen können.

Um nun diesem Mangel einiger maassen abzuhelffen, müssen wir uns die Mühe geben, die liebe Grammatic so wohl, als die schätzbare Rhetoric und Poesie, auf gewisse Weise zur Hand zu nehmen.

At note 100: Zur Probe solls nur fürs erste ein Menuetgen seyn: damit jedermann sehe, was ein solches kleines Ding im Leibe hat, wenns keine Misgeburt ist, und damit man von geringen auf wichtigere ein gesundes Urtheil fällen lerne.

At note 103: Was nun, zum ersten, die Disposition betrifft, so ist sie *eine artige Anordnung aller Theile und Umstände in der Melodie, oder in einem gantzen musicalischen Wercke,* fast auf die Art, wie man ein Gebäude einrichtet, und abzeichnet, einen Entwurff oder Abriss machet, einen Grund-Riss, um anzuzeigen, wo z.E. ein Saal, eine Stube, eine Kammer, und so weiter angeleget werden sollen. Unsre musicalische Disposition ist von der rhetorischen Einrichtung einer blossen Rede nur allein in dem Vorwurff, Gegenstande, oder Objecto unterschieden: Dannenhero hat sie eben diejenigen sechs Stücke zu beobachten, die einem Redner sonst vorgeschrieben werden, nemlich: den *Eingang, Bericht, Antrag,* die *Bekräfftigung, Widerlegung,* und den *Schluss,* sonst gennant: Exordium, Narratio, Propositio, Confirmatio, Confutatio, & Peroratio.

At note 105: Steine, Holz und Kalk machen noch kein Gebäude aus, wenn sie gleich an sich selbst noch so gut und auserlesen sind. Sie müssen auf eine gewisse Art aneinander gefüget, und verbunden werden, wenn ein Haus daraus werden soll.

At note 106: Es würde . . . bey aller Richtigkeit, offt sehr pedandtisch heraus kommen, wenn man sich gar zu ängstlich daran binden, und seine Arbeit allemal nach dieser Schnur abmessen wollte. Dennoch aber ist nicht zu läugnen, dass, bey fleissiger Untersuchung, sowohl guter Reden, als guter Melodien, sich diese Theile, oder einige davon, in geschickter Folge, allerdings darin antreffen lassen; ob gleich manchesmal die Verfasser ehe auf ihren Tod, als auf solchen Leit-Faden, gedacht haben mögen.

At note 107: Es ist nemlich die Meynung nicht, dass alles, was in diesem Muster steht, unausbleiblich in allen vollständigen Reden angebracht werden müsste; oder als wenn nichts mehr hinzugethan werden könnte, was hier nicht steht. Nein, ein Redner behält allemal die Freyheit, nach Gutachten etwas hinzuzusetzen, und wegzulassen, wie und wo es die Umstände seines Hauptsatzes und seiner Zuhörer erfordern.

At note 108: Wer sich also . . . der oberwehnten Methode, *auf gewisse, ungezwungene Art,* bedienen will, der entwerffe, etwa auf einem Bogen, sein völliges Vorhaben, reisse es auf das gröbste ab, und richte es ordentlich ein, ehe und bevor er zur Ausarbeitung schreitet . . . Die Erfindung will Feuer und Geist haben; die Einrichtung Ordnung und Maasse; die Ausarbeitung kalt Blut und Bedachtsamkeit.

At note 109: Ich weiss aber nicht ob der vortreffliche Marcello daselbst die erwähnte sechs Theile einer Rede anbringen wollen, indem es auch gar nicht nöthig ist, alles in allen Theilen eines Stückes anzubringen. Es ist vielmehr höchstwahrscheinlich, dass der unvergleichliche Verfasser besagter Arie, weder an exordium, narrationem, confutationem, confirmationem, noch an die Ordnung, wie besagte Theile nach einander folgen sollen, gedacht habe, wie er sie verfertiget. Die Sache scheinet auch daher gezwungen zu seyn, weil Herr Mattheson einen und denselben Satz zum Eingang, Erzehlung und Vortrag machet.

At note 110: Marcello hat freilich, bey der Verfertigung der im Kern aus ihm angeführten Aria, so wenig, als bey seinen andern Wercken, wohl schwerlich an die 6 Theile einer Rede gedacht, von welchen man doch gestehet, dass ich gar wahrscheinlich gezeiget habe, wie sie in der Melodie vorhanden seyn müssen. Das ist genug. Gewiegte Meister verfahren ordentlich, wenn sie gleich nicht daran gedencken. Man kanns im täglichen Schreiben und Lesen wahrnehmen, da niemand auf das Buchstabiren sinnet.

Aber es folget daher keinesweges, dass Lernende sothane Anzeige und ihre Erläuterung sogleich für verwerfflich ansehen mögen, und keinen Vortheil daraus ziehen können. Dahin gehet die vornehmste Absicht, wenn die erreichet wird, so ist es gut.

At note 111: Wider den Zwang in diesem Stücke ist der fünffte Absatz des siebenden Hauptstücks im Kern dermaassen ausdrücklich und eigentlich gerichtet, dass es gewisslich eine grosse Pedanterey seyn würde, wenn einer die angeführten Theile alle, und in eben der Ordnung, bey jeder Melodie ängstiglich suchen und anbringen wollte. Das ist gar die Meynung nicht. Wir sind weit davon entfernet . . .

Die Mittel und Wege der Ausführung und Anwendung sind in der Rhetorik lange so verschiedentlich und abwechselnd nicht anzutreffen, als in der Musik, wo man sie viel öffterer verändern kann, obgleich das Thema gewisser massen dasselbe zu bleiben scheinet. Eine Klangrede hat vor einer andern viele Freiheit voraus, und günstigere Umstände: daher bey einer Melodie der Eingang, die Erzehlung und der Vortrag gar gerne etwas ähnliches haben mögen, wenn sie nur durch die Tonarten, Erhöhung, Erniedrigung und andere dergleichen merckliche Abzeichen, (davon die gewöhnliche Redekunst nichts weiss,) von einander unterschieden sind.

At note 113: Aber, mit Erlaubnis, ich habe doch gleichwohl auch nicht (wie man mich ferner beschuldiget) einen und denselben Satz solchergestalt zum Eingange, zur Erzehlung, und zum Vortrage gebraucht, dass eine und dieselbe Sache einerley Art und Weise behalten hat. Denn erstlich sind die angefochtenen Sätze wie weich und hart unterschieden; zum andern geben ihnen die Versetzung und der Wiederschlag eine gantz fremde Gestalt. Hoch und tief ist nicht einerley. Das lässt sich nach einer gemeinen Rede, wo dergleichen Dinge keine Statt finden, nicht beurtheilen.

. . . Ich gestehe selbst, im Kern, dass die Erzehlung in unsrer Aria dem Eingange derselben fast gleichlautend sey; . . . er, der Eingang, ist im Ton, in den Worten, in der Ausführung, in den Werckzeugen und Stimmen von der Erzehlung, auf fünffache Art, unterschieden, und also gar nicht einer und derselbe Satz, gar nicht eine und dieselbe Sache. Aehnlich ist ja nicht einerley.

At note 115: Die Musik ist eine Klangrede, und sucht wie der Redner seine Zuhörer zu bewegen; Warum sollte man denn auch bey der Musik die Regeln der Redekunst nicht anbringen können? Es gehört aber Verstand und Witz darzu, dass keine Schulfüchserey und pedantisches Wesen herauskommt. Ein Kunststück der Redner ist dass sie die stärkesten Gründe zuerst; hernach in der Mitte die schwächern, und zu letzt wiederum bündige Schlüsse anbringen. Dieses kann auch einen guten Kunstgriff in der Composition abgeben. Vor allem muss ein glücklicher Componist erst alles wohl überlegen ehe er zum Werke schreitet, und so zu sagen sein Vorhaben erst auf einem Bogen Papier auf das gröbste abreis[s]en, und ordentlich einrichten, bevor er solches ausarbeitet. Es gehet hernach die Ausarbeitung viel besser von statten. Wer wohl disponirt hat halb elaborirt.

At note 116: Das siebende Capitel führet endlich eine der wichtigsten Materien aus, die man nur in der musicalischen Setz-Kunst zu untersuchen hat. Wie nöthig ist es nicht, in der Ausarbeitung musicalischer Stücke eben so behutsam und eigen zu seyn, als in der Rede-Kunst und Dicht-Kunst? Wenn die Ausführung des Haupt-Satzes von dem Anfange auf merckliche Art abweichet, dass man nicht mehr weiss, wovon die Rede ist, so entstehet bey den Zuhörern oder Lesern eine Ungewissheit der abzuhandelnden Sache, und man empfindet eine Verachtung gegen den Verfasser, wenn man eine so unordentliche Ausarbeitung vernimmt.

At note 117: Er fand die Grundsätze in diesem Werke zwar für ihn nicht mehr neu, dennoch gut.

At note 120: Keinem Themati zu Gefallen muss die Melodie in ihrem natürlichen Fortgange gehindert, noch mercklich unterbrochen werden.

At note 121: die Form . . . eines jeden Wercks, einer jeden Melodie.

At note 123: Schon hieraus folgt, dass die Melodie das Wesentliche jedes Tonstückes sey, und dass ihr die Harmonie, so wichtig auch die Vortheile sind, die sie gewährt, und so sehr auch durch dieselbe die Ausdrucksmittel der Kunst vermehrt werden, dennoch untergeordnet werden müsse.

At note 124: Eine Melodie bestehet . . . aus Sätzen, welche eine Reihe auf einander folgender Töne sind, die zusammen einen musicalischen Gedanken oder Verstand in sich enthalten. Diese können aus einen, zwey und mehr Tacten bestehen, oder auch nur einen Theil eines einzigen Tacts ausmachen, und kommen mit den Commaten in der Rede überein. Derjenige Satz, welcher den Hauptgedanken einer Melodie ausmachet, heisset der *Hauptsatz* (Thema, subjectum) . . .

Eine Melodie wird wieder in Abschnitte oder Perioden abgetheilt, welche wie die grössern Unterscheidungszeichen in der Sprache anzusehen, und wieder als kleinere Melodien für sich zu betrachten sind.

At note 126: C'est l'invention & la conduite du sujet, la disposition de chaque Partie, & l'ordonnance générale du tout.

. . . Cette idée du *Dessein* général d'un ouvrage, s'applique aussi en particulier à chaque morceau qui le compose. Ainsi l'on dessine un Air, un Duo, un Choeur, &c. Pour cela, après avoir imaginé son sujet, on le distribue, selon les règles d'une bonne Modulation, dans toutes les Parties où il doit être entendu, avec une telle proportion qu'il ne s'efface point de l'esprit des Auditeurs . . . C'est une faute de *Dessein* de laisser oublier son sujet; c'en est une plus grande de le poursuivre jusqu'à l'ennui.

At note 127: La Rhetorique enseigne comme il faut disposer le sujet pour le mettre en Musique.

At note 128: la manière de conduire l'harmonie, le chant, le mouvement & la modulation, de telle sorte que tout se rapporte à une idée commune & ne soit qu'un; car dans la musique dramatique & dans toute musique d'expression, on doit, ainsi que dans l'art oratoire & dans tous les autres beaux-arts, traiter un sujet, sans s'écarter des règles d'unité qui leur sont communes.

At note 129: Le Musicien, avant de mettre la main à la plume, doit avoir un *motif,* c'est-à-dire, une idée primitive & principale qui détermine le chant, l'harmonie, la modulation, le mouvement, le nombre & l'arrangement des parties, & généralement tout ce qu'il doit faire.

At note 130: un chant que l'on veut faire régner dans le morceau que l'on fait, & qu'on a soin de rappeler dans les parties, & dans les différentes modulations où l'on passe . . . Le grand art du Compositeur consiste à dessiner d'abord en grand, à bien établir son motif, & à le représenter de tems en tems à ses Auditeurs.

At note 131: In allen musikalischen Stücken ist ein Hauptsatz nöthig, woraus die ganze Folge desselben unumgänglich entstehen muss.

At note 132: Thema, Entwurf / wornach das ganze musikalische Stück verfertiget wird.

At note 134: Il primo oggetto nel comporre sempre deve esser una Melodià . . . Come per essempio comporre qualche Minuetto, Solfeggio, o Sonatina; tenendo in vista la legge del' sostegno del Tema, come nel discorso.

At note 135: Il *Motivo* poi non è altro che l'idea principale della Melodia, il Soggetto, il Tema, dirò così, del discorso Musicale, e su di cui tutta la Composizione aggirar si deve.

At note 136: Selon la doctrine de Zarlin et de tous les maitres, soit anciens, soit modernes, il faut savoir que, dans toute composition, *Il y a un sujet,* sans lequel la composition ne peut avoir lieu . . . Cela posé, la composition est l'art de traiter un sujet.

At note 137: Hauptsatz. *(Musik.)* Ist in einem Tonstück eine Periode, welche den Ausdruck und das ganze Wesen der Melodie in sich begreift, und nicht nur gleich anfangs vorkömmt, sondern durch das ganze Tonstück oft, in verschiedenen Tönen, und mit verschiedenen Veränderungen, wiederholt wird. Der Hauptsatz wird insgemein das Thema genennt; und Mattheson vergleicht ihn nicht ganz unrecht mit dem Text einer Predigt, der in wenig Worten das enthalten muss, was in der Abhandlung ausführlicher entwickelt wird.

Die Musik ist eigentlich die Sprache der Empfindung, deren Ausdruck allezeit kurz ist, weil die Empfindung an sich selbst etwas einfaches ist, das sich durch wenig Aeusserungen an den Tag leget. Desswegen kann ein sehr kurzer melodischer Satz von zwey, drey oder vier Takten eine Empfindung so bestimmt und richtig ausdrucken, dass der Zuhörer genau den Gemüthszustand der singenden Person daraus erkennt. Wenn also ein Tonstück nichts anders zur Absicht hätte, als eine Empfindung bestimmt an den Tag zu legen, so wäre ein solcher kurzer Satz, wenn er glücklich ausgedacht wäre, dazu hinlänglich. Aber dieses ist nicht die Absicht der Musik; sie soll dienen den Zuhörer eine Zeitlang in demselben Gemüthszustande zu unterhalten. Dieses kann durch blosse Wiederholung desselben Satzes, so fürtrefflich er sonst ist, nicht geschehen, weil die Wiederholung derselben Sache langweilig ist und die Aufmerksamkeit gleich zu Boden schlägt. Also musste man eine Art des Gesanges erfinden, in welchem ein und eben dieselbe Empfindung, mit gehöriger Abwechslung und in verschiedenen Modificationen, so oft konnte wiederholt werden, bis sie den gehörigen Eindruck gemacht haben würde.

Daher ist die Form der meisten in der heutigen Musik üblichen Tonstücke entstanden, der Concerte, der Symphonien, Arien, Duette, Trio, Fugen u.a. Sie kommen alle darin überein, dass in einem Haupttheile nur eine kurze, dem Ausdruck der Empfindung angemessene Periode, als der Hauptsatz zum Grund gelegt wird; dass dieser Hauptsatz durch kleinere Zwischengedanken, die sich zu ihm schicken, unterstützt, oder auch unterbrochen wird; dass der Hauptsatz mit diesen Zwischengedanken in verschiedenen Harmonien und Tonarten, und auch mit kleinen melodischen Veränderungen, die dem Hauptausdruck angemessen sind, so oft wiederholt wird, bis das Gemüth des Zuhörers hinlänglich von der Empfindung eingenommen ist.

At note 139: Unter der Form versteht man die Art und Weise, wie die Gedanken in einer ganzen Melodie oder Periode auf einander folgen.

At note 140: eine allgemeine Abhängigkeit der Theile von einander, vermittelst welcher alle, nur zu einer einzigen Wirkung, das ihrige beytragen. Die Kunst das Ganze zu verfertigen besteht in den Verbindungen der Haupt- Neben- und Verbindungsgedanken und in der Vereinigung der Bewegungen im Hauptgesange, in der Entgegenstellung der Nebenstimmen, welche den Hauptgesang gehörig unterstützen, die Ohren an sich zu ziehen und zu ergötzen. Es ist nicht genug, dass die Theile eines Tonstückes, jeder an sich betrachtet, ihre Anordnung, Richtigkeit und gehöriges Verhältniss haben; sie müssen noch überdiess alle mit einander zusammen stimmen, und ein harmonisches Ganzes ausmachen. Eine einzelne Partie kann Unrichtigkeiten, e.g. verbothene Octaven oder Quinten enthalten, und das Ganze kann doch wohl gut abgefasst seyn.

At note 141: Eine Melodie muss gewisse Abschnitte haben. Ergo wo keine Abschnitte wie bey einer Rede, Commata, Semicola, Puncta, etc. sind, und die Melodie in einem fortgehet; so werden die Sinnen und der Verstand verwirret, und verhindert zu begreiffen, was einer haben will; zumahl, wenn man weder Anfang, Mittel und Ende unterscheiden und keine Symetrie dabey wahrnehmen kann. Würde man nicht über einen Redner lachen, wenn er ohne Distinction in einem fort redete, ohne den vorhergehenden Verstand mit dem folgenden zu unterscheiden? weil die Hauptsache, wovon die Rede wäre, und der klare und deutliche Begriff ganz und gar wegfiele.

At note 143: Ja, man gehe nur diejenigen Stücke durch, die allgemeinen Beyfall erhalten haben; man wird gewiss finden, dass nicht die Verschiedenheit vieler Gedanken diesen Ruhm erworben haben, sondern vielmehr, die gute Anordnung etlicher melodischen Glieder, ihre Zerlegung, und rechte Anweisung ihrer Stellen.

At note 144: Thema. (Motif, Hauptsatz, konzentrirte Empfindung.) Ohne Thema würde Einheit in der Mannigfaltigkeit fehlen. Der Setzer hat so gut seine Handlung, als bildende und redende Kunst. Also—Herfürstechende Empfindung, beym Tonkünstler. Interesse des Helden, beym Mahler. Konzentrirte moralische Wahrheit, oder spekulativer Satz, beym Dichter. Nach dem Thema wird Tonwahl, Bewegung, Eintheilung, und Dauer geformt. . . . Jedes musikalische Stück ist Erweiterung, Verändrung, Kontrastirung des Thema. Thema muss also immer herfürstechend seyn, damit die Empfindung immer mittheilbar bleibe, damit ich den Setzer stets verstehe, und den Ausdruck ohne Verwirrung fasse.

At note 145: Le premier point d'une sonate, d'un duo, d'un trio ou d'un quatuor, peut renfermer des traits bien caractérisés; et après un repos à la dominante du ton . . . ces mêmes traits différemment amenés et variés dans leurs tours, dans leur mélodie et dans leur harmonie, ce seroit, pour ainsi dire, apporter les preuves des propositions qu'on a faites d'abord; ce seroit suivre la nature.

At note 147: Veränderungen sind eine Art musikalischer Rhetorik, wo der nämliche Sinn in mancherlei Wendungen vorkömmt, mit dem Unterschiede, dass die Gränzlinien viel genauer in der Musik, als in der Redekunst bestimmt werden . . . Diesem strengen Bezug aufs Thema, den man nie aus dem Gesichte verlieren darf, unbeschadet, öffnet sich doch auf der andern Seite eine Aussicht in das weiteste Feld, wenn von der Einkleidung die Rede ist.

At note 150: Der Meister ist eben auch immer beym Thema geblieben. Ein Prediger kann ja das Evangelium nicht immer wiederholen und vorlesen; sondern er muss es auslegen. Er macht eben Uebergänge oder transitiones &c. Er hat nebst dem Satz aufs allerwenigste noch einen Gegensatz.

At note 151: Wird nun nicht bald ein aus dem Hauptsatze des Stückes fliessender Gedanke kommen? In jedem Tonstück muss doch unstreitig so etwas seyn, was unter dem übrigen ein wenig hervorraget. Dieses etwas, es mag nun sogleich zum Anfange, in der ersten Sectionalzeile, oder in der zweyten vorkommen, nenne ich den Hauptsatz, der durch Wiederhohlungen, Versetzungen, Nachahmungen und Zergliederungen bearbeitet werden muss. Die daraus auf verschiedne Art entstehenden Passagen dienen dazu, die Einheit des Tonstückes mit zu erhalten. Wenn man den Hauptsatz, oder die daraus fliessenden Gedanken, nach einem gemachten vernünftigen Plan, mit einem neuen Nebengedanken abwechselt, und diesen ebenfals wie den vorhergehenden, in gehörigem Verhältnisse, bearbeitet: so entspringet aus dieser Verbindung des Hauptsatzes mit dem Nebensatze, und der sowohl aus diesem als jenen entspringenden Theile, die gewissermassen so viele neue Sätze in ihrer Art sind, die Mannigfaltigkeit eines Tonstückes.

At note 153: Ein jeder Tonkünstler, der für Instrumente etwas gründlich zu setzen verstehet, weiss, dass man einen gewissen Vortrag, oder ein Thema sich wähle, welches man bald im Anfange, hiernächst vorzüglich in der Vollführung des Stückes, und dann wiederum am Ende, oder gegen das Ende desselben hören lässt. Ausnahmen sind freylich; aber davon rede ich nicht. Ferner giebt es gewisse Nebenvorträge, oder Neben-Themata, die ohngefehr auf gleiche Weise ausgeführt, wenigstens nicht ganz aus der Acht gelassen werden, wenn sie einmahl vorgetragen sind. Hiebey rede ich nicht vom contrapunctischen Nebenvortrage, wovon sonst viel zu sagen wäre . . . sondern ich bleibe nur bey demjenigen stehen, was eine einzelne Singstimme zu bewerkstelligen hat.

At note 154: Auch eben also macht es der Musiker, der . . . bald seinen Satz, oder Thema beybringt; daselbe, damit es recht verstanden werde, ein- oder zweymal kürzlich wiederhollet: sohin . . . bis er endlich alles Gemeldete neuerdings zusamm[en] fasse: und oft auch, nachdem er sich durch anfänglich seinem Absehen auch widrig-scheinende Gänge und Läufe durchgeschlagen, nachdem er auch durch ausgesuchteste Tonklänge und Bewegungen alle zu seinem Absehen dienliche Affekte und Leidenschaften rege gemacht, letztlich wiederum durch seine Wege zu seinem Satz und Ziel in dem Grundtonklange selbst gelange.

At note 172: Denn dieser Styl ist die allerfreieste und ungebundenste Setz- Sing- und Spiel-Art, die man nur erdencken kann, da man bald auf diese bald auf jene Einfälle geräth, da man sich weder an Worte noch Melodie . . . bindet, . . . ohne förmlichen Haupt-Satz und Unterwurff, ohne Thema und Subject, das ausgeführet werde.

At note 173: Eine Melodie, die sich weder an einen Hauptsatz noch an einen bestimmten Rhythmus bindet, wird eine Fantasie oder Capriccio genennet.

At note 174: Ein Tonstück, bey welchem sich der Componist nicht an die bey den gewöhnlichen Tonstücken eingeführten Formen und Tonausweichungen bindet, sondern sich mehr der so eben in seiner Fantasie herrschenden Laune, als einem überdachten Plane überlässt.

At note 177: Ich setzte mich hin, fing an zu phantasieren, je nachdem mein Gemüt traurig oder fröhlich, ernst oder tändelnd gestimmt war. Hatte ich eine Idee erhascht, so ging mein ganzes Bestreben dahin, sie den Regeln der Kunst gemäss auszuführen und zu soutenieren . . . Und dies ist es, was so vielen unserer neuen Komponisten fehlt; sie reihen ein Stückchen an das andere, sie brechen ab, wenn sie kaum angefangen haben; aber es bleibt auch nichts im Herzen sitzen, wenn man es angehört hat.

At note 180: Die ganz freie Phantasie, die weder Thema noch Absicht hat, und bei welcher man Künstler zuweilen überrascht, wenn ihre Einbildungskraft den Zügeln des Verstandes entläuft.

At note 182: Ferner, wer würde wohl zugestehen, dass er über ein grosses Stück, z.B. über eine Sinfonie, nicht mehr sagen dürfe, als sich über eine freie Phantasie sagen lässt? Es ist noch keinem Kritiker eingefallen die letztere einer Kritik zu unterwerfen, die erstern aber werden strenge kritisirt, wenn gleich, leider, nur selten in Schriften.

At note 193: Die musikalische Rhetorik ist in sehr vielem Betracht von der Grammatik blos darin verschieden, dass sie das im Grossen lehrt, was jene nur im Kleinen lehrte.

At note 197: Allein, zu seiner Zeit, oder vielmehr in der Zeit, in welcher der vollkommene Capellmeister erschien, war die Musik noch nicht von der Beschaffenheit, dass sich eine zusammenhängende musikalische Rhetorik aus ihr hätte abstrahiren lassen. Es fehlte ihr nicht nur Feinheit und Geschmack, sondern auch vorzüglich derjenige Zusammenhang ihrer Theile, der sie theils durch die Entwickelung der Gendanken aus einander, theils durch die Einheit des Styls u.s.w. erst zu einer förmlichen Empfindungsrede machte. Diesen höchsten Grad ihrer Vollkommenheit erhielt sie erst nach seiner Zeit von einigen wenigen unserer ersten Tonkünstler.

At note 198: Ein Redner würde unnatürlich und zweckwidrig handeln, wenn er eine Rede halten, und dadurch Unterricht, Ueberzeugung und Rührung bewirken wollte, ohne vorher zu bestimmen, welches sein Hauptsatz, seine Nebensätze, seine Einwendungen, seine Widerlegung derselben, und seine Beweise seyn sollten . . .

Da Tonstücke von einigem Umfang nichts anders als solche Reden für die Empfindung sind, wodurch man die Zuhörer zu einem gewissen Mitgefühl, zu sympathetischen Regungen bewegen will, so haben die Regeln der Ordnung und Einrichtung der Gedanken mit der eigentlichen Rede gemein; und so wie dort ein Hauptsatz, unterstützende Nebensätze, Zergliederungen des Hauptsatzes, Widerlegungen, Zweifel, Beweise und Bekräftigungen statt finden, so müssen auch hier ähnliche Beförderungsmittel unserer Absichten im musikalischen Sinn statt finden. Diese Ordnung und Folge der einzelnen Theile, heisst die ästhetische Anordnung der Gedanken, und ein Tonstück, in welchem sie so angebracht ist, dass sich alle Gedanken gegenseitig aufs vortheilhafteste einander unterstützen und verstärken, ist gut angeordnet.

At note 199: Die Anordnung musikalischer Gedanken, und die Fortschreitung der durch sie ausgedrückten Empfindungen so dass sie unserm Herzen in einem gewissen Zusammenhange beygebracht werden, wie die in einer Rede enthaltenen, nach logischen Grundsätzen auf einander folgenden Ideen unserm Geiste, ist daher ein Hauptpunkt in der musikalischen Rhetorik und Aesthetik . . .

Hierauf gründet sich demnach die Nothwendigkeit, dass in einem Kunstwerke (1) eine Hauptempfindung, (2) ähnliche Nebenempfindungen, (3) zergliederte, das heisst, in einzelne Theile aufgelöste Empfindungen, (4) widersprechende und entgegengesetzte Empfindungen, etc. herrschen müssen, die denn, wenn sie in eine gehörige Folge gestellt werden, in der Sprache der Empfindungen das sind, was in der Sprache der Ideen, oder in der eigentlichen Beredsamkeit die bekannten, und von guten, ächten Rednern noch immer beybehaltenen, auf unsere Natur gegründeten Exordien, Propositionen, Widerlegungen, Bekräftigungen etc. sind.

At note 201: Die *Bekräftigung* eines Hauptsatzes ist eine gewisse Art von Wiederholung desselben, nachdem vorher Einwendungen und Zweifel widerlegt worden sind.

At note 202: Wenn man alles dieses etwa auf eine Sonate anwenden wollte, so würde ihre ästhetische Einrichtung ungefähr folgende werden:

1, Der Hauptsatz, das Thema.

2, Darauf hergeleitete Nebensätze.

3, Bekräftigende Gegensätze.

4, Darauf folgender Schluss zur Unterstützung des Hauptsatzes, und Beschluss des ersten Theils.

Da der erste Theil einer Sonate gemeiniglich viel kürtzer ist, als der zweyte, so findet im ersten Theile noch keine eigentl[iche] Ausarbeitung, noch keine Zergliederung u.s.f. statt, sondern er enthält gleichsam wie der Eingang einer Rede, nur eine vorläufige Darstellung und Erwähnung der Hauptabsicht und des Zweckes eines Tonstückes. Der zweyte Teil hingegen enthält:

1, Den Hauptsatz versetzt, oder in der Harmonie der Dominante

2, Zergliederungen des Hauptsatzes.

3, Dagegen mögliche Zweifel, nebst Wiederlegung und Auflösung derselben.

4, Abermalige Bekräftigungen dadurch, dass der Hauptsatz wiederum in einer veränderten Gestalt, etwa in einer mit der Haupttonart verwandten Nebentonart vorgetragen wird.

5, Conclusion, die, so wie der erste Teil in die Harmonie der Dominante gieng, nun in der angenommenen Hauptton zurückgeht, und das Tonstück auf diese Weise endigt.

At note 205: Form. Es ist in der Musik, so wie in den übrigen schönen Künsten, oft die Rede von der Form der Kunstwerke, und man verstehet unter der Form eines Tonstückes die Art und Weise, wie es vor die Seele des Zuhörers gebracht wird.

Die tägliche Erfahrung lehret zwar, dass sich die verschiedenen Gattungen der Tonstücke blos durch ihre Form unterscheiden; die Sinfonie hat eine andere Form, als das Concert, die Arie eine andere als das Lied; allein, wenn die Aesthetiker behaupten, dass dasjenige, was man Schönheit eines Tonstückes nennet, in der Form desselben enthalten sey, so muss es allerdings noch eine zufällige Form geben, in welcher das Schöne enthalten ist, und die sowohl vorhanden seyn, als mangeln kann, sonst müsste z.B. jedes Rondo, wenn es seiner gewöhnlichen Form entspricht, ohne weitere Bedingung den Charakter der Schönheit behaupten.

Wenn demnach von der Form der Kunstprodukte in derjenigen Hinsicht die Rede ist, in welcher ihr der Inhalt an Schönheit zugeeignet wird, so hat man darunter nicht diejenige äusserliche Form der Kunstwerke zu verstehen, wodurch sich die Gattungen derselben unterscheiden, sondern vielmehr die besondere Art, wie das Mannigfaltige zu Einheit verbunden ist, oder die besondere Art, wie der Tonsetzer die Momente des Wohlgefallens, die in seinem Ideal enthalten waren, in das Kunstwerk übergetragen hat.

At note 206: Zu den mechanischen Theile der Ausführung rechnet man gewöhnlich die Tonausweichung und die Form des Tonstücks; und diese wird grösstentheils durch jene bestimmt. Die Form hängt theils von der bestimmten Anzahl der Hauptperioden, theils von der Tonart, in welche dieser oder jener Periode hingeleitet wird, theils aber auch von dem Orte ab, wo dieser oder jener Haupttheil wiederholt wird.

At note 207: Wir haben bey der Ausführung auf zwey Stücke zu sehen, auf dasjenige, was den Geist oder den innern Character des Tonstücks dabey betrifft, und auf das Mechanische derselben.

At note 209: Ich komme zu der Form der Sätze eines Tonstücks. Es ist nicht zu leugnen, dass eines Theils die Form derselben etwas Zufälliges ist, welches eigentlich wenig oder gar keinen Einfluss auf den innern Charakter des Tonstücks hat, und andern Theils hat man auch eben keinen Grund wider die Form unserer Sätze, sowohl in den grössern als kleinern Tonstücken vieles einzuwenden. Und dieses ist vermutlich die Ursache, warum viele grosse Meister z.B. ihre Arien beynahe alle nach einer und eben derselben Form gearbeitet haben. Es ist aber auch eben so wenig zu leugnen, dass durch den steten Gebrauch einer und eben derselben Form oft vieles von der Schönheit eines Satzes verlohren gehen kann. Wenn man z.B. so viele Arien, nach einerley Form gearbeitet, gehört hat, so prägt sich endlich diese Form dem Gefühle so stark ein, dass man gemeiniglich schon bey der Anhörung des ersten Perioden derselben, mit Gewissheit bestimmen kann, wohin die Modulation geführt wird, und welchen Hauptgedanken man an diesem oder jenem Orte wieder zu hören bekommen wird; und dadurch muss nothwendig, wenn keine besondere Wendung des Tonsetzers die Form belebt, der Satz verliehren . . .

Allein wie muss man sich bey der Ausführung seiner Sätze in Ansehung der Form verhalten? Ist es besser alles nach der gewöhnlichen Form zu arbeiten, oder ist es besser, wenn man bey der Ausführung auf neue Formen bedacht ist? Im ersten Falle würde man dem Genie unnöthige Fesseln anlegen, und es zwingen, manche schöne Wendung, die es hervorbringt, unbenuzt zu lassen, oder durch die Form zu verderben; und im zweyten Falle möchte vielleicht zu viel Unsinn zum Vorschein kommen, wenn man ohne besondere Ursach zu haben, auf neue Formen bedacht seyn wollte; denn wie oft würde nicht der Fall eintreten, dass man über der Form das Wesentliche der Kunst aus den Augen setzen, und bey der gebildeten neuen Form mehr verliehren als gewinnen würde. Am besten ist es daher, man wählet einen vernünftigen Mittelweg. Bearbeitet man einen Satz, dessen Inhalt in der gewöhnlichen Form schon ästhetische Kraft genug besizt, oder findet man schöne Wendungen bey der Ausführung, die der gangbaren Form entsprechen, warum sollte man da auf eine Abänderung der gewöhnlichen Form bedacht seyn? Hat man aber einen Text zu bearbeiten, der eine ganz eigne Form und ungewöhnliche Wendung erfordert . . . oder findet man gleichsam von ohngefähr (und dieses kann auch bey blosen Instrumentalsätzen geschehen) eine schöne Wendung, welche eine Abänderung des Gewöhnlichen in der Form nöthig macht, so binde man sich nicht ängstlich an die bekannte Form, sondern man bilde sie so, wie es der Satz den man bearbeitet, erfordert, wenn man versichert ist, dass man eine wirkliche Vervollkommung des Satzes bewürken kann, und wenn dabey im Ganzen kein anderer zufälliger Uebelstand zum Vorschein kommt.

At note 210: Da aber der blosse Musikliebhaber der Gegenstand derselben ist, der nicht selbst musikalische Sätze nach den Regeln der Rhetorik erfinden und zusammensetzen, sondern nur wissen will, wie sie zusammengesetzt seyn müssen, wenn sie schon erfunden sind; so ist eine richtige Kenntiss von der Anordnung musikalischer Gedanken, fur ihn wichtiger, als die Kenntniss aller jener Mittel und Wege, welche man insgemein zur Erleichterung der Erfindung vorzuschreiben pflegt . . . Die gute Anordnung . . . wodurch jeder Theil an den schicklischsten Ort gestellt wird . . . lässt sich vollkommen bestimmen, und muss eine[m] Musikfreund, der Kenner seyn, und einen Theil seines Vergnügens aus dem Innern der Kunst erhalten will, nothwendig bekannt seyn.

At note 212: So wie nun in der Redekunst oder Poesie ungemein viel darauf ankommt, in welcher Ordnung diese Beweise und Ueberredungen, oder Widerlegungen aufeinander folgen; so ist es auch in der Musik von der äussersten Wichtigkeit, alles so anzuordnen, dass der Zuhörer stuffenweise und aufs natürlichste zu einer Empfindung hin, oder auf eben die Weise von einer andern abgeleitet werde. Daraus entsteht eine eigene Art von Anordnung musikalischer Gedanken, die ich die ästhetische Anordnung nennen würde, wenn es mir erlaubt wäre, einer Sache einen eigenen Namen zu geben, die bisher theils von wenigen gefühlt, theils aber auch nur in die Lehre von der Periodologie gerechnet wurde.

At note 214: Allerdings hat man die Regeln vom Genie abstrahiren müssen, und niemand wird behaupten, dass sie vor dem Genie hergegangen sind . . . Allein, wie waren diese ersten Aeusserungen des Genies beschaffen? Waren es nicht die unförmlichsten Missgeburten, und mussten nicht erst Hunderte solcher unförmlicher Missgeburten hervorgebracht werden, ehe man anfieng, zu bemerken, dass sie das noch nicht waren, was sie seyn sollten, dass die Absichten, um welcher willen man sie hervorbrachte, durch sie noch nicht erreicht werden konnten? Das Genie sey also immer den Vorschriften der Erfahrung vorhergegangen . . .; so ist es doch die Erfahrung allein, die die Laufbahn des Genies erleichtert, die es vor Fehlern bewahrt, und ihm unter so vielen Wegen, zu einer Absicht zu gelangen, unter so vielen Mitteln, einen Zweck zu erreichen, den einzigen wahren Weg, und die zweckmässigsten, angemessensten Mittel zeigt.

At note 215: Une sonate est un discours. Que pensierons-nous d'un homme qui, coupant son discours en deux, répéteroit deux fois chaque moitié? "J'ai été chez vous ce matin; oui, j'ai été chez vous ce matin, pour vous parler d'une affair, pour vous parler d'une affaire" . . . Je parle sur-tout des reprises longues qui forment la moitié d'un discours. Les reprises pouvoient être bonnes à la naissance de la musique, quand l'auditoire ne comprenoit tout au plus qu'à la seconde fois. Je sais qu'un discours est souvent divisé en deux parties; mais, sans doute, on ne les répète pas chacune deux fois.

At note 216: Il y aussi des discours qui sont divisé en plus de deux parties; c'est ce qu'il faut imitier.

3. Continuity and Change in Later Metaphors of Form

At note 4: Der Theil der Musikwissenschaft, welcher lehrt, wie man melodische Theile zu einem, dem bestimmten Zwecke entsprechenden Ganzen verbinden soll.

At note 5: die Lehre von der rhythmischen, logischen und ästhetischen Anordnung und Verbindung homophonischer oder polyphonischer Theile zu einem Ganzen.

At note 6: In der Musik wird das Wort [Rhetorik] daher im Grunde nur bildlich gebraucht, aber es ist ein stehender Begriff geworden. Unter Rhetorik der Musik versteht man diejenige Wissenschaft der Tonsetzkunst, nach welcher einzelne melodische Theile nach einem bestimmten Zwecke und Massstabe zu einem Ganzen verbunden werden. Man setzt sie der Grammatik entgegen, welche den eigentlich materiellen Theil, die Elementarsätze der Composition behandelt. Die Rhetorik bestimmt die Regeln der Aneinanderreihung derselben zu einem vollständigen, ausdrucksvollen (rednerischen) Ganzen. Indess greifen Grammatik und Rhetorik hier auf unzertrennliche Weise in einander.

At note 8: La Grammaire musicale . . . est l'art de subordonner les idées l'une à l'autre, et d'en former des Propositions ou Cadences.

. . . La Logique n'est que l'art d'arranger les Pensées, les Cadences dans un ordre avoué par le bon sens ou la droite raison. Elle est toute du ressort du jugement.

L'art oratoire consiste à disposer les Pensées de manière à produire la plus grande impression sur l'esprit et sur le coeur.

At note 9: L'art de composer un discours est celui d'enchaîner un certain nombre de Propositions, selon l'ordre grammatical, logique et oratoire; l'art de composer un Morceau de Musique n'est que celui d'enchaîner, sous les mêmes rapports, un certain nombre de Cadences ou Propositions musicales.

At note 10: A l'aspect de l'immense collection de chef-d'oeuvres en tout genre, produits par ces hommes immortels, peut-on, de bonne-foi, douter encore que la Musique n'ait acquis ce caractère prononcé de vérité, d'énergie et de charme qui fixe d'une manière irrévocable une langue quelconque, et une langue naturelle sur-tout? En est-il une plus abondante en locutions nobles, harmonieuses et touchantes? Les périodes d'Haydn, si éloquentes et si nombreuses, le cédent-elles en rien, dans leur idiôme, à celles de Bossuet et des autres grands orateurs? Osons le dire, tous les grand-hommes, dans l'art dramatique et dans l'art oratoire, ont, dans la langue céleste des sons, leurs véritables pendans. S'il en était autrement, tout le coeur et l'esprit humain n'auraient pas passé sous la plume de nos compositeurs; la Musique ne serait pas encore arrivée à son degré de maturité.

At note 13: Er macht es wie ein schlauer Redner, der, wenn er uns zu etwas überreden will, von einem allgemein als wahr anerkannten Satze ausgeht, den jeder einsieht, jeder begreifen muss, bald aber diesen Satz so geschickt zu wenden versteht, dass er uns zu allen überreden kann, wozu er nur will, und wärs zum Gegentheil des aufgestellten Satzes.

So geht Haydns Musik glatt dem Gehöre ein, weil wir wähnen, etwas leichtfassliches, schon Vernommenes zu vernehmen; allein bald finden wir, dass es nicht das wird, nicht das ist, was wir glaubten das es sey, das es werden sollte, wir hören etwas Neues und staunen über den Meister, der so schlau Unerhörtes uns unter dem Anstrich des Allbekannten zu bieten wusste.

At note 14: Una composizione musicale è un discorso che si fa coi suoni figurati in vece delle parole. Il *motivo* ne è la proposizione, l'assunto che s'imprende a provare. Alla stessa maniera de l'oratore, dopo d'aver proposto il suo tema, lo sviluppa, ne adduce le prove, ne stringe l'argomento, e riepilogando il già detto, lo conduce alla conclusione; allo stesso modo progredir deve il maestro di musica nel suo lavoro. Egli di tanto in tanto ritorna al *motivo* e lo fa risentire, affinchè l'ascoltatore ne sia ben bene penetrato. Se questo *motivo* è tale che rechi piacere all'orecchio, egli è ben verisimile che col tornare in campo ci rinovi, confermi ed accresca quel piacer primo. Ma il dare al tema un'aria di novità tutte le fiate che vien richiamato, e non contentarsi già, come fanno i mediocri ingegni, di ripeterlo servilmente col farlo passare da un tuono all'altro; ma rinvigorirlo, aspreggiarlo talvolta, variarlo, rivoltarlo con dottrina e con garbo, e sempre più abbellirlo, questo è il vero distintivo del genio. Ne apello a quanti udirono le sinfonie di *Haydn*.

At note 15: Nella sola musica instrumentale il maestro può essere Oratore; nella vocale, egli non fa, che tradurre in lingua musica il discorso del poeta, e quindi non può e non deve essere che traduttore e imitatore, o parafrasista.

At note 16: In seinen Sinfonien . . . ist es eine Versammlung gewandter Redner, die in würdiger Sprache vor einem gebildeten Publikum Beweise ihrer Kraft im Auffassen und Durchführen einer Idee geben.

At note 19: Das erste, und gewissermassen unterste Erfordernis, beim Verbinden von Tönen und der Bildung eines musikalischen Satzes, ist, dass er vor allem nicht übel, nicht gehörwidrig klinge . . . Es ist dies ungefähr eben so, wie es das erste und unterste Erfordernis der Rede- oder der Dichtkunst ist, Sprachfehler zu vermeiden. Dieser Theil der Tonsatzlehre, welcher blos das technisch oder grammatikalisch Richtige der Tonverbindungen, blos die Reinheit der Tonsprache beabsichtet, heisset eben darum Lehre vom reinen Satze, oder auch Grammatik der Tonsprache, der Tonsetzkunst; sie beschäftiget sich mit den Gesetzen, nach welchen Töne, gleichsam als musikalische Buchstaben oder Sprachlaute, sich zu Sylben, diese zu Worten, und Worte sich endlich zu einem musikalischen Sinne (*sensus*) gestalten . . .

Der Lehre von der Reinheit des Satzes folgt die vom künstlicheren Satze, von der künstlicheren oder verwickelteren Bearbeitung und Ausführung musikalischer Phrasen, von gleichsam rednerischer Zergliederung, vielseitiger Beleuchtung und Durchführung einzelner musikalischer Sätze und Ideen, gleichsam die musikalische Rhetorik, oder wenn man lieber will, *syntaxis ornata,* Gesangverbindungslehre, oder Gesangverflechtungslehre. Sie enthält die Lehre vom sogenannten doppelten Contrapunkt, von Fuge und Canon und was dahin einschlägt, so wie auch die von der Anlage und Gestaltung der Tonstücke im Ganzen.

At note 28: Ein Musikwerk entwickelt sich im kunstreichen Genius nach organischen Gesetzen, will nichts anderes, als werden, wachsen, sich entfalten, blühen.

At note 30: Wie bei der Pflanze Blüthe und Frucht schon im Keime shlummern, so ruht . . . die fernere Entwickelung eines Musiksatzes schon im Thema, und noch enger in dessen Motiven . . . Nach diesen Andeutungen versteht sich nun schon von selbst, dass ein Kunstwerk, um diesen Namen zu verdienen, stets freie geistige Schöpfung, ein Product inneren Dranges sein muss, nicht ein Erzeugniss absichtlicher Combination des Verstandes, oder "mechanische Leistung auferlegter Forderungen" sein darf. Sonst ist es höchstens ein bloss technisches Kunststück.

At note 33: Gibt nemlich die Erfindung den Grundgedanken eines Kunstwerks und dessen geistige Belebung, so kann das Werk erst dadurch Existenz gewinnen, dass in ihm die einzelnen Theile zu einem Ganzen geordnet und gefügt sind, und es in dieser Gestaltung den Grundgedanken vollständig und rein ausprägt, damit der beschauende Geist sich vollkommen befriedigt und durch die Erscheinung eines Schönen erfreut fühle. Auch das musikalische Kunstwerk soll eine Welt im Kleinen umfassen und ein organisches Gebilde ausmachen, in welchem alle Theile zu dem Ganzen stimmen und das Ganze in jedem Theile sich abspiegelt.

At note 35: Ein jedes Tonstück ist aber ebensogut wie ein anderes Kunstwerk ein inhaltsvoller und aus Bedingungen des inneren Lebens entsprungener *Organismus,* dessen Theile unter sich und zum Ganzen im Verhältniss einer *inneren Nothwendigkeit* stehen. *Wahrheit und Einheit des Gedankens, Folgerichtigkeit seiner Entwickelung und Anschaulichkeit des Ausdruckes und der Darstellung* sind ebenso endgültige Bedingungen für ein Tonstück wie für ein Bildwerk oder eine Dichtung.

At note 39: Mechanisch ist die Form, wenn sie durch äussre Einwirkung irgendeinen Stoffe bloss als zufällige Zutat, ohne Beziehung auf dessen Beschaffenheit erteilt wird . . . Die organische Form hingegen ist eingeboren, sie bildet von innen heraus und erreicht ihre Bestimmtheit zugleich mit der vollständigen Entwicklung des Keimes . . . Auch in der schönen Kunst, wie im Gebiete der Natur, der höchsten Künstlerin, sind alle echten Formen organisch, d.h. durch den Gehalt des Kunstwerkes bestimmt.

At note 40: Nur müssen wir vorher die Frage aufstellen: wodurch die Form eines Tonstücks eigentlich bestimmt werde, oder was überhaupt die Form eines Tonstücks sei? . . . Weil bei einem jeden Tonstück eine bestimmte Tonart . . . als Haupttonart festgesetzt wurde, woraus eigentlich das Stück ging, und weil die in einem Stücke vorhandenen Modulationen nach fremden Tonarten, sobald ein Stück gut sein sollte, immer eine gewisse Beziehung auf die bei demselben zum Grunde gelegte Haupttonart haben mussten: so wurde die mehrfach verschiedene Einrichtung der innerhalb eines Tonstückes vorhandenen Modulationen das Merkmal, an dem man erkennen soll, zu welcher Gattung von Tonstücken eigentlich nach festgesetzten Regeln der modulatorischen Einrichtung eine Komposition gehört . . . Durch die im Verlauf eines Tonstücks vorhandenen Modulationen wird die Form desselben festgesetzt, und durch die Bearbeitung der dabei zum Grunde gelegten Themata wird der Werth eines Stückes nach gewissen Graden bestimmt.

At note 42: Delà, la Melodie exige la théorie du rhythme; celle des points de repos ou cadences; l'art d'enchaîner et de développer des idées pour en faire un tout; la science des périodes et de leurs réunions entr'elles.

At note 43: Il est remarquable, comme le sentiment suit ici une loi, que l'esprit l'adopte: car, dans un discours, il faut une exposition dont les idées soient dévelopées dans une autre partie.

At note 45: . . . pour ne point contrarier l'exposition du morceau, qui doit toujours être franche et nette, sans quoi la seconde partie perd de son intérêt, parce qu'elle ne se lierait plus d'une manière évidente avec la première: l'exposition manquée, tout le reste est manqué, comme dans le discours, parce que l'attention de l'auditeur se distrait, se perd, ou n'agit que trop faiblement pour pouvoir apprécier le reste.

At note 46: La coupe est le *patron* de la Mélodie et d'un morceau de Musique en général; et comme un *cadre* peut être carré, rond ou triangulaire, de même la Mélodie peut avoir cette différence de *cadre*. L'étude de ces cadres est très-importante pour un compositeur, et cependant personne n'en a encore parlé dans l'art musical.

At note 64: Eine dritte Schwierigkeit endlich, liegt in der Empfänglichkeit des Publicums beym Anhören einer solchen verwickelten und kunstvollen Musik, da, zumal bey dem jetzt gewöhnlichen, reissend schnellen Vortrage, nur ein, durch viele Uebung und öftern Genuss grosser Kunstwerke gebildetes Ohr und aufgeklärter Kunstsinn dergleichen Schönheiten und Prachtwerke zu fassen und zu geniessen im Stande sind. Kommt nun noch die gegenwärtig herrschende Modulirwuth und Unstätigkeit hinzu, welche keinen Gedanken zur eigentlichen Ausführung kommen lässt, und wobey Ohr und Herz so oft in seiner Theilname verstört und weggerissen wird: so wäre es gar kein Wunder, wenn man solch ein Kunstwerk beym Anhören, wie das pariser Publicum, seinen eigenen Sprechern nach, bewundernswert, aber *ermüdend* fände.

At note 65: die sinnliche Darstellung der Idee, die der Künstler (mehr oder minder klar bewusst) in sich trägt . . . Daher muss auch jeder Theil der sinnlichen Gestalt eines Kunstwerkes aus der dem Künstler dabei inwohnenden Idee hervorgegangen, erkennbar und nachweislich sein.

At note 67: Aus dem Kern des Hauptsatzes hat sich ein Leben entfaltet, das zuerst leicht, lustig, lieblich idyllisch begann, dann sich energischer, kämpfend erhob, streitsüchtig bis zum Ingrimm entzündete, selbst seinen Grundgedanken bei der Rückkehr dazu mit kriegerischem Ungestüm durchbrannte.

4. *Rhetoric and the Autonomy of Instrumental Music*

At note 3: Tanz und Liedermusik ist eigentlich nicht die wahre Musik. Nur Abarten davon. Sonaten—Symphonien—Fugen—Variationen—das ist eigentliche Musik.

At note 7: Gedanken, musikalische, sind kleine Theile einer Melodie, die doch einen Verstand haben müssen. Man theilt sie in *Haupt- Neben-* und *Verbindungsgedan-*

ken . . . Die Gedanken sind das erste, was man nach festgesetzten Plan zu der Ausführung desselben niederschreibt. Man überlässt sich hier dem Feuer der Einbildungskraft, und bringt dann das vorgenommene Stück zu der Vollkommenheit, die es haben soll. Die Gedanken werden erhoben, wenn die vorstehenden und nachfolgenden weniger Lebhaftigkeit, Schönheit und Ausarbeitung haben. Diese Nebengedanken müssen das ihrige allemal beytragen, den Hauptgedanken zu erheben und geltend, zu machen. Es folgt hieraus nicht, dass die Nebengedanken darum müssten vernachlässiget werden. Der Componist muss nur den Hauptgedanken allemal so zu erheben wissen, dass er vorzüglich ins Gehör falle und den stärksten Eindruck auf das Ohr und die Seele der Zuhörer mache.

At note 8: Der Hauptgedanke ist das Vorzüglichste der Melodie; er muss deswegen in allen Perioden derselben wohl angebracht seyn, weil sich eben hieraus erkennen lässt, dass die Perioden zusammen gehören, und weil die Einheit der Melodie dadurch bestimmt wird.

At note 9: dass wir unter dem Worte Thema . . . einen in wenig Tonklängen bestehenden kleinen Musikspruch, oder durch etlich wenige Noten angezeigten Musikgedanken, wie man sagt, verstehen, wie man etwa den Inhalt oder Vortrag einer Kanzelrede mit einem oder anderen Worte zu geben pflegt, der hernach der immerwährende Gegenstand, stets vorkommende Setzstoff und Ziel, hier des musikalischen Werkes; wie dort jener der Rede sey.

At note 10: Es pflegt manchem seltsam und lächerlich aufzufallen, wenn die Musiker von den Gedanken in ihren Kompositionen reden; und oft mag es auch so geschehen, dass man wahrnimmt, sie haben mehr Gedanken in ihrer Musik als über dieselbe. Wer aber Sinn für die wunderbaren Affinitäten aller Künste und Wissenschaften hat, wird die Sache wenigstens nicht aus dem platten Gesichtspunkt der sogenannten Natürlichkeit betrachten, nach welcher die Musik nur die Sprache der Empfindung sein soll, und eine gewisse Tendenz aller reinen Instrumentalmusik zur Philosophie an sich nicht unmöglich finden. Muss die reine Instrumentalmusik sich nicht selbst einen Text erschaffen? und wird das Thema in ihr nicht so entwickelt, bestätigt, variiert und kontrastiert, wie der Gegenstand der Meditation in einer philosophischen Ideenreihe?

At note 16: Wenn man den Leuten nur begreiflich machen könnte, dass es mit der Sprache wie mit den mathematischen Formeln sei.—Sie machen eine Welt für sich aus.—Sie spielen nur mit sich selbst, drücken nichts als ihre wunderbare Natur aus, und eben darum sind sie so ausdrucksvoll—eben darum spiegelt sich in ihnen das seltsame Verhältnisspiel der Dinge.

At note 18: [Bach] zeigte: die reine Musik sey nicht blosse Hülle für die angewandte, oder von dieser abstrahirt . . . Sie . . . vermöchte sich zur *Poesie* zu erheben, die um desto reiner sey, je weniger sie durch Worte, (die immer Nebenbegriffe enthalten) in die Region des gemeinen Sinnes hinabgezogen würde.

At note 19: Das Vergnügen an der Musik haftet gar nicht nothwendig an der Bedeutung ihrer Melodieen oder Modulationen, welche oft unbestimmt ist . . . Wir betrachten . . . in den meisten Fällen die Töne der Musik gar nicht als Zeichen, sondern freuen uns an dem harmonischen Spiel ihrer Mannichfaltigkeit unmittelbar.

At note 20: Vorübergehend ist also jeder Augenblick dieser Kunst und muss es seyn: denn eben das kürzer und länger, stärker und schwächer, höher und tiefer, mehr und minder ist seine Bedeutung, sein Eindruck. Im Kommen und Fliehen, im Werden und Gewesenseyn liegt die Siegskraft des Tons und der Empfindung.

At note 21: An Gedanken interessiert uns entweder der Inhalt, die neue, frappante, richtige Funktion, oder ihre Entstehung, ihre Geschichte, ihre Verhältnisse, ihre mannichfaltige Stellung, ihre mannichfaltige Anwendung, ihr Nutzen, ihre verschiednen Formationen. So lässt sich ein sehr trivialer Gedanke sehr interessant bearbeiten . . . Hier ist die Methode, der Gang, der Prozess das Interesse und Angenehme . . . Das Neue interessiert weniger, weil man sieht, dass sich aus dem alten so viel machen lässt. Kurz, man verliert die Lust am Mannichfaltigen, je mehr man Sinn für die Unendlichkeit des einzelnen bekömmt. Man lernt das mit Einem Instrument machen, wozu andre hunderte nötig haben, und interessiert sich überhaupt *mehr für das Ausführen, als für das Erfinden.*

At note 24:

Preis, Ehr und Ruhm den Unsterblichen,
ersten Kindern der alten chaotischen Nacht!
Ewig erzeugt und zeugend, Geburt und Gebärer,
nimmer getrennt, Eins rufend das Andre hervor:
Preis dir, Eros, und dir Anteros Preis!

Ihr führt der Götter Gaben
zu den Menschen herab;
etc.

At note 25: Ich lege von solcher Stelle erfüllt das Buch bey Seite, gerathe wohl ans Clavier, fantasire, bleibe dann in bestimmten Bewegungen, und schreibe hernach, was so fest gehaftet hat, auf.

At note 27: La scène se passe à la campange.

Un orage affreux est supposé régner depuis assez long-tems pour que les habitans du village aient pu se rendre dans le temple de Dieu. Après le coup de tonnerre, exprimé par la timbale, on entend commencer la prière.

. . . A la cinquième et à la sixième mesure, une exclamation, qui semble partir du fond du coeur de quelques jeunes vierges, est peinte par la flûte et les hautbois. Elles ne disent que deux mots: *grand Dieu!*

At note 39: Die reine Vokalmusik sollte wohl ohne alle Begleitung der Instrumente sich in ihrer eignen Kraft bewegen, in ihrem eigentümlichen Elemente atmen: so wie die Instrumentalmusik ihren eignen Weg geht, und sich um keinen Text, um keine untergelegte Poesie kümmert, für sich selbst dichtet, und sich selber poetisch kommentiert. Beide Arten können rein und abgesondert für sich bestehn.

At note 40: Was wollen sie, die zaghaften und zweifelnden Vernünftler, die jedes der hundert und hundert Tonstücke in Worten erklärt verlangen, und sich nicht darin finden können, dass nicht jedes eine nennbare Bedeutung hat wie ein Gemälde? Streben sie die reichere Sprache nach der ärmern abzumessen, und in Worte aufzulösen, was Worte verachtet? Oder haben sie nie ohne Worte empfunden? Haben sie ihr hohles Herz nur mit Beschreibungen von Gefühlen ausgefüllt? Haben sie niemals im Innern wahrgenommen das stumme Singen, den vermummten Tanz der unsichtbaren Geister? Oder glauben sie nicht an die Märchen?

At note 48: Es gibt keinen einfacheren Gedanken, als den, welchen der Meister dem ganzen Allegro zum Grunde legte und mit Bewunderung wird man gewahr, wie er alle Nebengedanken, alle Zwischensätze durch rhythmischen Verhalt jenem einfachen Thema so anzureihen wusste, dass sie nur dazu dienten, den Charakter

des Ganzen, den jenes Thema nur andeuten konnte, immer mehr und mehr zu ent-
falten. Alle Sätze sind kurz, nur aus zwei, drei Takten bestehend, und noch dazu
verteilt im beständigen Wechsel der Saiteninstrumente und der Blasinstrumente.
Man sollte glauben, dass aus solchen Elementen nur etwas Zerstückeltes, schwer
zu Fassendes entstehen könnte: aber statt dessen ist es eben jene Einrichtung des
Ganzen, so wie auch die beständig aufeinander folgende Wiederholung der kurzen
Sätze und einzelner Akkorde, welche das Gemüt festhält in einer unnennbaren
Sehnsucht.

At note 52: Ein einfaches, aber fruchtbares, zu den verschiedensten kontrapunk-
tischen Wendungen, Abkürzungen etc. taugliches, singbares Thema liegt jedem
Satze zum Grunde, alle übrigen Nebenthemata und Figuren sind dem Hauptgedanken innig verwandt, so dass sich alles zur höchsten Einheit durch alle Instrumente
verschlingt und ordnet. So ist die Struktur des Ganzen.

At note 53: Die ersten vier Takte enthalten das Hauptthema, der siebente und achte
Takt im Violoncell aber enthält das Nebenthema, aus welchen beiden Sätzen, wenige
Nebenfiguren ausgenommen, die zwischen die Ausführung jener Hauptideen ge-
worfen sind, das ganze *Allegro* gewebt ist. Um so zweckmässiger war es, den im
ganzen Stück vorherrschenden Gedanken in vier Oktaven unisono vortragen zu lassen; er prägt sich dem Zuhörer fest und bestimmt ein, und dieser verliert ihn in den
wunderlichsten Krümmungen und Wendungen, wie einen silberhellen Strom, nicht
mehr aus dem Auge.

At note 54: Es liegt eine tiefsinnige Erkenntniss darin, dass man auch in
Tonwerken von "Gedanken" spricht, und wie in der Rede unterscheidet da das
geübte Urteil leicht echte Gedanken von blossen Redensarten. Ebenso erkennen
wir das vernünftig Abgeschlossene einer Tongruppe, indem wir sie einen "Satz"
nennen. Fühlen wir doch so genau, wie bei jeder logischen Periode, wo ihr Sinn zu
Ende ist, obgleich die Wahrheit beider ganz incommensurabel dasteht.

Index